FALLOUT

EDIE BAYLIS

Boldwood

For my dad – you'll always be my hero.

PROLOGUE

10 JULY 1995

Tom Bedworth pulled his leather jacket tighter, his face screwing up in irritation. Whatever had died in the aid of making this coat certainly hadn't lived anywhere but a tropical climate, because it was about as warm as a fucking ice cube.

He knew he should have had a service done on this motor before leaving, but there wasn't the time to mess about checking if car heaters worked before putting a wide berth between him and the likes of the Reynolds and the Stokers.

What was left of them, anyway.

Tom grinned. It looked like he had been given a clean slate and, therefore, he intended to use it.

Now the Stokers had offed John Maynard, and hearing nothing else to the contrary, it must mean they had no inkling that *he* had been involved in anything. Or that he even existed.

Oh, yes, John Maynard had done him the world of good.

Tom smiled. Thanks to Maynard's connections with the Reynold family, Tom had made a nice sum for the sale of his own kid many years ago – albeit getting ripped off by the paltry price Len Reynold had paid for the prize of owning his offspring, but that would soon be rectified.

Yeah, John Maynard had been extremely generous for taking the rap for everything else since. *Oh, Maynard, you didn't die in vain.*

The Stoker boys lifting Maynard could only mean they believed him to be the one who'd killed their little brother, Gary, and who'd helped Len Reynold face-plant into a tree. They probably even believed him to be the one behind the blackmailing of Gloria Reynold. That's if they even knew about that bit, which was doubtful, considering they were all thick as shit.

This was, of course, wonderful, so the only thing of any concern was to proceed with his new plan, but he couldn't push his luck – not until he was 100 per cent sure he wasn't under suspicion. However, the most important thing – Samantha Reynold, his daughter – was still intact and very much alive.

Tom glanced out of the window at the coming dawn, unsure of the time. It was early, that was for sure. Okay, so it hadn't been part of his plan to spend days sleeping in the car, but why waste dosh on one of the few flea-ridden bed and breakfast gaffs around here when he needed to save every penny in order to tide him over until his ship came in?

And that wouldn't be long now. Not long at all.

Now on to Linda Matthews...

Thanks to his expert detective work and a few chinwags in a handful of the local boozers, it hadn't taken long to discover where the old slapper lurked.

Even picturing Linda's face – the way she used to fawn over him and cling like a limpet, wound him up. Getting her in the family way thirty years ago hadn't been one of his better ideas, but even epic fails had their upsides. If he hadn't got her knocked up, then he wouldn't have got that initial payout, and neither would he have had the ability to capitalise on it now.

So, yeah, he'd put up with Linda again. For a short period of time...

Actually, she was Linda *Devlin* now. Hearing this had freaked Tom out somewhat. A husband on the scene meant a spanner in the works, but he needn't have fretted. Someone *had* been stupid enough to marry the woman, but had seen sense and, according to what he'd been told, the marriage had been short-lived, with the bloke disappearing yonks ago.

It also hadn't taken much more digging to discover Linda was exactly where he'd expected her to end up. In this bloody ghetto of a dump.

Tom glanced up at the concrete monstrosity in front of him.

He'd also been correct in surmising her dictator of a father had long since dropped off the twig. As had his holier-than-thou wife, but Linda was still breathing.

And that was good.

Linda didn't know it yet, but *she* was the ticket to get him ensconced within the Reynold fold. And that would mean he got his money.

Tom rummaged in his pocket for his lighter. Yeah, Linda would come in handy. He'd got it all planned.

Instead of continuing to blackmail Gloria Reynold and threatening to tell the whole city that she and her cheapskate husband had paid a pittance for the child they had the cheek to call their own, Linda would get Samantha on side and explain who she really was. Once Sam had recovered from the shock, she'd fall over herself to help out her *real* parents and then he'd get the payout he should have received in the first place.

Ramping up the pressure with that old bag, Gloria, could now be reassigned as backup if the plan for Linda didn't pan out. And there were absolutely zilch reasons why it wouldn't.

As for Linda – well, he'd promise her whatever she liked, but in reality, she'd get fuck all. He'd put her in the same orbit as her precious long-lost daughter, so what else could she possibly want?

Tom winced as a freight train thundered past, its endless caravan of wagons jarring the teeth remaining in his head.

This night just gone had been the last he'd spend in the motor. Tonight he'd be in *there*. He looked up at the third floor. Yep, tonight he'd make Linda's life a thousand times better, and because of that, she'd welcome him with open arms.

Once things were in the pipeline, he'd fuck her off and head back to the Aurora to see how much his club's profits had increased during his absence.

Tom's mouth twisted into a self-satisfied smile. He'd also got an extra way of increasing his income further. It had been in his plan anyway and, although she didn't realise it yet, Samantha would be taking on that part.

This unplanned 'holiday' had given him time to set up the means of crack production. Hanging around this neck of the woods offered the handy ability to dig up more people he knew from old – many who were happy to earn a few quid and ask no questions. Purely because either they were desperate for cash, or plain fucking stupid.

Tom reached into the passenger seat footwell for the sandwich he'd nicked last night from the Spar. He stared at the sorry-looking item within the plastic packet, wondering which half of the sandwich contained the alleged ham.

As the sarnie had rolled around the footwell for the best part of the night, he hoped he wouldn't get food poisoning, but having eaten worse things, he'd take the chance.

Besides, he'd need all his strength to deal with Linda.

He'd eat this, have a bit of his remaining crack and then pay the scabby old tart a long-overdue visit.

1

Gloria Reynold didn't want to venture to the shops, but what could she do? Being completely out of bread, she had no choice but to go out to buy some.

Len had always arranged deliveries of their food from the best butchers and greengrocers in Birmingham, but since his death, she couldn't face returning the calls about her next orders. It was too much of a painful reminder.

There were lots of things in their well-stocked freezer, but she'd barely touched a morsel since Len's death and that dreadful business of Samantha finding out the truth. But there was only so long she could go on like this. At the very least, she must force a sandwich down.

Gloria walked towards the small collection of shops Edgbaston offered, sure everyone was staring at her.

The truth about Sam's real parentage could already be out. It may have been spreading around the city like an out-of-control forest fire for days, yet she had no idea because she hadn't seen anyone since the night she'd told the truth, including her daughter. Days now with no word and it was breaking her heart clean in two.

Not only had she lost her husband forever, but it looked as if she'd lost her daughter too.

Gloria kept her eyes fixed ahead as she continued walking, if only to keep the rising urge to break down in tears at bay. She wished more than anything that she and Len had told Sam the truth from the start. If they'd told her from an early age, then she might not be in this position of having damaged her daughter's trust and wrecked their relationship.

When Samantha had arrived in her life, Gloria had been so bothered about what everyone would think if they knew she'd had to adopt, but what must everyone think of her now? And Judith and Mal Stoker must hate her more than most for allowing the rumour to continue circulating that it was *their* youngest whose parentage was in question, rather than Samantha.

How could she have sat on the truth? How could she have pretended she didn't know that rumour was about *her* whilst allowing the suspicion between Judith's sons to continue? She still didn't know whether Gary Stoker had even returned to his family.

Gloria almost tripped on the pavement, her haste to return to the safety of being behind closed doors growing. She was a coward. A pathetic, snivelling coward.

Feeling a rising panic racing through her ribcage, her breathing became laboured, the blue sky lowered and the pavement tipped at a strange angle.

She couldn't continue. She needed to get away from the gaping expanse of the outdoors where there were people.

Rapidly stopping, Gloria yelped, almost passing out from sheer fright as she smacked into someone. Her handbag dropped to the floor, the contents scattering across the pavement.

'I thought it was you...' Liam Taylor took in Gloria's grey, terrified face. 'Are you all right?' Steadying her with his arm, he gathered the contents of the handbag from the floor. 'Come and sit down. You look like you might pass out!'

Gloria stared at Liam, wide-eyed. 'No. I need to go home. I...'

Liam gently lowered Gloria onto a bench at the side of the road. 'Just sit down for a second and then I'll walk you back. I'll call Sam and she ca...'

'No!' Gloria cried. 'You mustn't.' The tears ran freely down her cheeks. 'Sam doesn't want anything to do with me any more. I haven't seen John either and I don't know what to do.'

'What are you talking about?' Liam gasped. He hadn't seen Sam or John for the last week either. The only word he'd had was days ago when Sam had called, explaining she was taking a bit of time off to get her head together and that she'd be in touch.

Liam frowned. As their last meeting hadn't exactly finished on good terms, he'd thought it best to give her space, but now he wished he'd bypassed that.

He looked at the worry on Gloria's face. 'I don't know what's happened, but you should tell me so I can help you sort it out.'

Gloria sagged with relief; the need to unburden herself from the crushing weight of her terrible decision and what it had caused was immense.

Liam had been close to Samantha for ten years. He was almost like a son-in-law. Even Len had believed he would soon be just that, so if anyone could get through to Sam and put this right, it was Liam.

Clutching his hand, Gloria began to speak.

* * *

Andrew Stoker repositioned his well-built frame in the driver's seat of his Rover SD1 and rolled his shoulders to ease the ever-building tension.

Through the twilight, he focused on the small terraced house halfway along the street, then stole a glance at his Rolex. Most of this lot around here would be well away in the local boozer by now and wouldn't bat an eyelid. Not that anyone would dare question him – or *any* of his brothers. But that might soon change if things were allowed to slide.

His eyes fixed on the front door of the target house.

And *she* was not helping matters...

Andrew's mouth flattened into a thin line as he ran his hand across his cleanly shaven jaw.

Thanks to Baker, he was well aware of what had been alleged. And that would be sorted. Right *now*.

He snorted in derision, the air from his nostrils creating a small, fogged patch on the side window of the car.

It was all very well his brother, Seb, insisting on paying loads of money to keep Detective Inspector Baker onside, but what was the bloody point if he wasn't present when the cop showed his face?

Of course, Baker had come to speak to Seb, like everybody did. But Seb wasn't there, so *he'd* dealt with it instead...

And it was a good bloody job! All that grief he'd got from Seb about overriding his decision and killing Phil Blunt? Seb's high horse stance had been pointless! Phil knew Seb had killed that geezer in the Aurora, so *regardless* of what Seb thought, offing Phil was the right thing to do. Phil might have been one of their own, but they couldn't risk moving him out of the country, even as a temporary measure, like Seb wanted.

Oh, Andrew had tried to reason with his brother – what happened if Phil opened his gob down the line? Or if someone tortured the info out of him? Where would that leave them?

But Seb wasn't having any of it and still wanted to let the man walk, so he'd been overridden. Simple as that.

Andrew sighed. This latest development proved he'd been right to take the initiative and get rid of the man. Just look how untrustworthy his bloody missus had turned out.

Thought she was clever by involving the Old Bill, did she?

Andrew's handsome face twisted into a scowl. Luckily, he'd been around when DI Baker had shown up to tell them Tonya Blunt was flapping her gums, otherwise they'd have been unaware.

Staring at his neat fingernails in the dim gloom of the streetlight, Andrew knew he had to act fast.

Seb had barely set foot in the Royal Peacock for a week, finding it preferable to bark orders at him and Neil down the blower, rather than be there in person to deal with the problems they still faced.

Well, no guesses where Seb was now... and why...

Andrew resented Sam Reynold more with every minute that passed. But one burning question persisted: was it down to her using what was between her legs to twist Seb in her favour, or was the reticence down to Seb himself?

After all, Seb had spent the last few days at Sam's side rather than with *them* and Andrew would not have the likes of her diluting their power as a firm. For God's sake, Seb had been against the woman at the start, but since she'd got her claws into him, his attitude had miraculously changed, which was concerning. *Really* concerning.

Sam may have helped on the night of Gary's murder, plus she hadn't attempted to deny her cousin John Maynard was behind all of the problems, but that didn't give her the right to expect *their* family to carry the can for one of them not being a blood relation, when that unpalatable accolade belonged to *her* all along.

Sure, it was a shock for her, but to be frank, he didn't give a fuck. It certainly didn't justify why their brother was lying in a freezer like a pork chop and their mother still believed there was a chance her youngest son would return home any day.

Neither did it warrant running the risk that soon, and *very* soon, their mother would involve the Old Bill by filing Gary as a missing person. If it became public Gary had been offed, then other things could be uncovered too. They may have succeeded in deflecting that so far, but it would not last forever. And neither should it.

As much as he'd like to, Andrew couldn't take back the terrible way he'd treated his youngest brother, but the least he could do was ensure Gary got a proper send-off. And that should not be delayed a moment longer.

Seeing a light in the front room of the terraced house flick on, Andrew zipped up his leather jacket and fired the engine of the SD1, the throaty roar loud in the otherwise quiet Yardley Road.

Well, it stops here, Andrew thought bitterly. Sick of playing second fiddle, he wasn't toeing the line any longer. Not like Neil.

Andrew and his brother Neil might be identical-looking and think along the same lines, but when push came to shove, his twin followed whatever Seb decided. But *he* wasn't following what Seb decided. Their father had chosen the wrong son to run the firm.

There would be no more pussyfooting around with the firm's reputation and standing. *No fucking way*. And he wasn't having cops digging around because of Phil Blunt's tart wife, either!

Pressing lightly on the accelerator, Andrew reversed along the street. Killing the engine, he flicked the headlights off, then tugged a pair of black leather gloves from his pocket. Pulling them onto his large hands, he stepped from his car and rapped on the door of the house.

'Evening, Tonya.' Andrew ensured his voice sounded as amiable as it perhaps might have done if this stupid cow hadn't opened her gob.

A flicker of hope shone in Tonya Blunt's eyes. 'Is this about Phil?'

'I understand he's gone AWOL,' Andrew said, his voice cleverly neutral as he watched Tonya shuffle nervously. He glanced over the top of her head into the living room. 'We've located him.'

Tonya sagged with relief. 'You've found him! Oh, thank God! Where is he?'

'He's fine, but your kids? Any idea where they are?' Andrew asked, his eyes glinting.

'What do you mean? My sister's got the kids at the moment. I've been too worried about Phil to cope,' Tonya flapped. 'Where is he? Can I...'

'Come with me.' Sensing Tonya's building worry, Andrew smiled reassuringly before gesturing for her to step out of the house. 'Don't worry, he's at the club with Seb.'

'At the club?' Tonya frowned. 'Why hasn't he come straight home? I've been so worried.'

After a quick glance up the street, silently gratified to find the coast clear, Andrew steered Tonya out of the house and led her towards his car, chivalrously opening the passenger door. Getting in the driver's side, he replaced his smirk with an understanding smile. 'Things have been getting on top of Phil.' He started the engine and pulled away from the kerb.

Tonya looked horrified. 'But why?'

'Who knows?' Driving as quickly as possible out of Yardley, Andrew glanced at Tonya. 'We'll give him extra work at the firm, it if will help.'

'That's really kind,' Tonya said, her eyes filling up. 'Money has been tight lately. I – I reported him as missing only yesterday. I probably shouldn't have... I was just so worried. I hope the police don't cause you problems. I might have said things... things that ma...'

'It's understandable you've been concerned,' Andrew said calmly, his hands gripping the wheel harder.

Suddenly noticing the view from the window wasn't what was expected, Tonya paused. 'Why are we heading towards Spaghetti Junction? This isn't the way to the club!'

'You're right, it isn't,' Andrew said, his voice now a snarl.

Tonya scrambled for the door handle. 'I want to get out! This isn't right!'

Andrew chuckled. 'You're spot on there, love. But speaking to the police isn't right either.'

* * *

From her seat at the two-seater table she'd squashed into the corner of the tiny kitchen, Linda Devlin opened her fourth can of Safeways own-brand cider and took a long swig. Using her elbow, she swiped the Lego scattered amidst cigarette ash overflowing from the ashtray across the scuffed blue Formica tabletop onto the floor.

'Tayquan!' she shrieked. 'Get your arse in here now and clear this up!'

Fucking kids. Leaving a bloody mess everywhere all the goddamn time. With difficulty, she dragged herself off the rickety chair as her youngest raced into the kitchen like a dervish.

'What's up, Ma?'

'What's up?' Linda yelled. 'This is what's up, you little shit!' She pointed to the Lego on the floor and then prodded her son in his bony chest with her chipped fingernail. 'How am I supposed to keep this place tidy when all you do is mess the bloody gaff up? You know I'm knackered and your tea will be ready in a minute.'

Tayquan's bottom lip quivered as he stared at the Lego car he'd painstakingly built, now in several pieces on the floor. 'Me dad bought me that,' he sniffed. 'And you've bust it!'

'Then you shouldn't have left it in the way, should you?' Linda snapped, refusing to allow the sadness on her son's little face to pull at her heartstrings. 'If it's bust, your dad can fucking well buy you another one!'

Not that there was much chance of that. She'd only seen the boy's father three times since the birth and each time he'd filched money off her.

Watching her son scrabble on the filthy kitchen floor to retrieve what could be salvaged of his treasured Lego, Linda moved to the grill to check the fish fingers to deflect from her steadily rising guilt.

'Call your sister and tell her that tea's ready. There ain't anything else after this, so if she don't come and get it, it'll go in the bin.'

Watching Tayquan abandon his Lego to get his sister, Linda sighed. All she wanted to do was go down the pub, but there was no chance of that for at least another hour until these two were in bed.

Reaching for her can of cider, she took another swig, then sparked up a cigarette, waiting the last couple of minutes for the fish fingers to finish. There were no chips left, so they'd have to make do with a fish finger sarnie.

Christ, she was too old for this shit. Forty-five and still lumbered with two kids under seven. At least the rest of her kids were making their way in the world. Or she hoped so, anyway. Reminding herself of that on a regular basis made her feel a bit better about her failure. *Sort of...*

Linda's face screwed up into a scowl. Once a fine-looking woman, any trace of that had long since departed, thanks to years of abusing just about any substance she could get her hands on.

Pulling two plates from the sink, stacked high with unwashed dishes, she sluiced some water over them, drying them with the edge of her baggy T-shirt.

As she turned, she spotted her two youngest sitting patiently at the table. Forcing herself to smile, she shoved fish fingers between what was left of the bread, then dumped the plates in front of them. 'There you go. Eat up and then it's bedtime.'

Linda watched her two youngest shovel food into their mouths and wished they'd hurry up so that she could go out. Then she could finally relax. Except she couldn't because the guilt would still be there.

Miserably, she stubbed her fag out in the sink. As much as she preferred to tell herself it didn't matter, in reality it *did*. The guilt wedged in the back of her mind haunted her every day.

Each time she'd got pregnant, she'd convince herself *this* was the time to make up for all the other children she'd failed, lost or screwed up. But it never worked. Every time, she plummeted into an endless pit of despair and the kids suffered. And it was all because of the first one. The one who had been taken from her. It had all gone downhill from there.

That day in 1965 was as crystal clear in Linda's mind as it always had been. As though thirty years meant *nothing*.

She could see it now – watching herself staring through the mottled glass of her bedroom window in her parents' house. She'd known the car belonging to the stranger downstairs had cost more than a few quid and remembered thinking she should be relieved and grateful the person was well off and able to provide for her baby, but she hadn't been. She'd just wanted the man to leave.

She'd concentrated on the small bundle that she'd placed in the centre of her bed, creating the smallest of dents on the pink bedspread, and her heart had felt like it might shatter. She'd tried, tried *really* hard not to get attached, but she'd failed.

Scooping the baby up, she'd held the child tightly against her chest, her tears falling onto the tiny little face. Kissing the top of her baby's head, fuzzy little tufts of dark hair tickling her nose, she strove to commit to memory the smell – that unique scent she'd heard people say babies had, which she'd never fully understood until that moment. She'd promised to memorise every single detail of her daughter's perfect little face, watching tiny starfish hands jerk out to grasp anything within reach.

And then her mother had entered the bedroom. She'd just *walked* in, like it had been a normal day. And that day had been indelibly etched into Linda's brain ever since.

She'd *told* her mother that she didn't want to go through with it. That she'd changed her mind and that she wanted the man downstairs to go away, but it had fallen on deaf ears. She'd had no choice but to watch as the carrycot was lifted from the bedroom floor, her baby placed inside, and along with a small bag with the few items of clothing the child possessed, her mother had taken everything, shutting the door behind her.

Linda didn't want to think about this. Every bloody day, it forced itself into her mind and she was sick of it. She could never make up for what had happened. She'd tried, but all it did was make things worse. Fluctuating between hating herself and not giving a shit achieved nothing. But it all came back to the same thing. She was a worthless, pointless woman who should have been sterilised at birth.

Linda suddenly froze, hearing banging on the front door. She edged out of the kitchen, praying it wasn't the guy about the rent again.

She knew she was behind, but she just hadn't got it to spare. Not if she wanted cider and fags.

Deciding it was sensible to ignore the caller, she was about to shut the kitchen door to muffle the noise when a voice shouted her name. A voice that, despite not having heard it for a *very* long time, she'd have recognised anywhere. It was the voice of the only man she'd ever loved – the person who had started her on the downward spiral of her life.

A mixed bag of fear, anger and exhilaration rushed up Linda's spine as she reached for the door handle. Could this really be happening? Could it be that Tom had finally come back for her, like he'd always promised?

2

Putting the phone down in his apartment in the Royal Peacock, Seb Stoker scowled. He'd already briefed his police contact, Baker, over what must go on the record about Gary, so why were they here?

He glanced at himself in the floor-length hallway mirror, straightened his tie and smoothed his hand over his slicked-back, almost black hair. Whatever the police wanted, they'd better not take long. He had too much to catch up with.

It had taken a lot of internal power to pull himself away from Sam, but she was right. They had to get back to the business in hand. It had been several days since he'd properly concentrated on anything other than exploring every inch of her body.

Okay, so he'd kept things ticking over via phone, as well as putting things in the pipeline about Gary's death, but the main reason for his absence wasn't due to putting things into place at the Orchid, like he'd told his brothers. Not really, unless the phone call Sam had made to that Liam bloke last week and some other Kevin geezer counted?

But Seb regretted not a second of it.

For a short period of time and probably for the first time he could remember since walking out of school, not bothering to return for his

O-Levels, Seb had felt as though his life didn't consist solely of a large roundabout turning endlessly around problems, grief and issues surrounding the family firm. And for that short amount of time, he'd experienced what it might be like to be almost *normal* – whatever that was?

But it made little difference because this was his life and this was how it would be. End of.

And he'd barely been back long enough to put on a fresh suit before something else had kicked off. Something to rapidly remind him who he was and what his job consisted of. *Like he could ever forget...*

Pulling the apartment door closed, Seb hurried down the stairs. He let himself through the adjoining door leading into the staff area and saw Andrew heading his way. 'I got the message... What's going on?'

Andrew gave his brother a long, cold look. 'If you'd been here yesterday when Baker arrived to give you an off-the-record heads-up, then you'd know an official visit was expected today. It's about Phil.'

'Phil?' Seb ignored Andrew's reference to his absence and made long strides down the corridor towards his office. *Yep, not back an hour and already shit's hitting the fan.*

If the Old Bill were here because of Phil, then Andrew would do well to remember that it had been *his* actions that had caused this in the first place. 'I'll handle them. Have they spoken to you yet?'

'Yep. Me and Neil said exactly what we agreed, should this happen.'

Seb nodded and jerked his head towards the door. 'Make yourself scarce and I'll get rid of them.'

Seb gave Andrew time to slip out of the corridor before fixing an easy-going smile in place and opening the door to his office. 'Good morning, gentlemen. Sorry to keep you waiting. I hope this won't take long?' He glanced at his watch. 'I'm a busy man.'

He turned to DI Baker, noting the slight nod of acknowledgement. He wouldn't be held up. Not if Baker was here. The man was paid enough to ensure the Peacock and everyone in it was kept out of the limelight and had just received his highest payout yet.

'Sorry to intrude, Mr Stoker.' The younger policeman extended his hand. 'I'm DS Drakeman.'

'DS Drakeman has recently joined our team, Mr Stoker,' DI Baker explained pointedly.

Seb shook the proffered hand. A new plod with something to prove. He guessed Baker was accompanying the man to ensure things ran smoothly. 'I would appreciate it if we could make this quick. Now, how can I be of assistance?'

DS Drakeman's slightly overweight frame moved from one leg to the other. 'It's rather awkward...' He glanced at his superior. 'There's been an allegation...'

Seb raised an eyebrow. 'An allegation?'

'Phillip Blunt is missing. His wife contacted us two days ago. She said you might know something about it?'

Seb frowned. *He knew it. That silly bint had filed Phil as a missing person.* 'You're obviously aware the man works for me, otherwise you wouldn't be here, but if he's gone AWOL, why would I know about that? If anyone knows, it's his bloody wife!' he laughed. Catching the slight shake of Baker's head, Seb changed tack. This new DS was clearly not au fait with their arrangement, and it was better staying that way if he was as much of a jobsworth as he acted.

Folding his arms, Seb stared at the DS. 'Joking aside, it was recently brought to my attention that Phil failed to show for a shift,' he lied, watching the man jot something down in his notebook. 'It's out of character because Phil has always been reliable.' He pulled on a concerned expression. 'I hope he isn't involved in something untoward. We run a kosher ship here at the Peacock and if he's mixed up in something, then I'd appreciate it if it...'

'Mr Blunt is still missing, Mr Stoker,' the DS interrupted. 'His wife also informed us that he was hurt quite badly a couple of weeks beforehand and now that he's disappeared...'

Unease slithered into Seb's brain. *What the fuck had this woman said?* 'I hope you're not insinuating any of that is to do with me?'

DI Baker glared at DS Drakeman, then smiled at Seb. 'Not at all.'

Not taking the hint, Drakeman continued, 'Mrs Blunt said her husband refused to say how he came to be injured, but she thinks it mi...'

'Might be connected with me?' Seb finished the sentence, his blood simmering. Bloody Andrew disobeying him by taking Phil out had never been the plan. He'd been all set on giving the wife a decent payout, but now she'd decided to turn the tables, the silly bitch would have a long wait.

Looking at the date in question of Phil's disappearance in DS Drakeman's notepad, Seb pulled his desk diary from the drawer. He flicked through the pages, then closed it with a flourish. 'If you're in need of my whereabouts on the night in question, I can confirm I was here until 2 a.m.,' he said, his voice frosty.

That wouldn't be refuted. His staff knew how to play the game. 'That can be substantiated by the many people working here or the customers. I can provide you with a list of who was present that night.' Cutting DI Baker a look, Seb strode towards his filing cabinet and opened the drawer.

'That won't be necessary,' DI Baker said hastily. 'I think you've helped more than enough with our inquiries.' He looked at DS Drakeman. 'Would you not say, Detective Sergeant?'

'Well, erm...'

'Mr Stoker's account matches those of his brothers, so I don't think we need to take up any more of his time.'

Seb scowled. Until this business with Gary was sorted, he needed the bastard on side, but if Baker wanted their arrangement to continue, he needed to have words with his underlings before a healthy percentage of his monthly payments were docked.

DI Baker smiled uncomfortably. 'Again, apologies for interrupting you.'

Seb nodded tersely at the Detective Inspector, his body thrumming with resentment for the hundredth time since Andrew had taken the impetus to go against his orders.

DI Baker ushered DS Drakeman from the office. 'We'll see ourselves out.'

As the door closed behind the two men, Seb exhaled through his teeth and poured himself a shot of whisky. Knocking it back in one, he wiped his hand across his mouth and straightened his tie once again.

Nope. It hadn't taken long to feel like the pleasure of the last few days had been nothing more than a hallucination.

Walking into the Violet Orchid, Sam Reynold returned the doorman's smile and mechanically acknowledged the greetings from staff as she made her way along the corridor.

Approaching her office, she overrode the reluctance her legs felt nearing the area where Gary had been murdered. She'd been uncomfortable here since, but had hoped her short absence would have removed the uneasiness. Unfortunately, it hadn't. Neither had it done anything to dilute the long list of problems she still faced. If anything, they were clamouring louder than ever before.

Unlocking her office door, she pushed it wide open, the confident movement hiding the flickering nervousness she must keep under wraps.

All that's over now, Sam reminded herself. Slipping off her jacket, she placed it neatly around the back of her desk chair.

Sitting down, she retrieved her diary from the drawer and stared at it blankly. With the removal of John Maynard, the threats and the worry of who had been causing problems to her father's firm, along with the Stokers' business, was no longer an issue, yet there were so many other things to sort out.

Her lips pursed resolutely. Like stopping referring to the Orchid and all other parts of the business as her father's. It was *hers* now.

That was something else to deal with. It was imperative she found out the truth about her real identity. That was something she'd never paid attention to before. Why would she? There had never been a reason to think she was anyone other than who she'd always been – *Samantha Reynold*. She hadn't thought about how it must feel not to know who she really was, but now she did.

And it was horrible.

Sam fished out the small mirror from her handbag and stared at her reflection. The heart-shaped face, the dark hair and brown eyes framed by long lashes were the same. *Everything* was the same.

Except *she* wasn't the same.

What she did know was that she shared no blood with the people she'd always believed to be her family. And until she discovered whose blood she *did* share, she wouldn't rest.

Placing the mirror back in her handbag, Sam pulled the diary back in front of her. Although Seb had been a great help in explaining how certain parts of businesses like theirs worked, the vast majority of the ins and outs of the casino and its subsidiaries was still a gaping hole in her knowledge.

But what she did know was that the attitude of some of the workers had to change...

The casino staff had been accommodating of her taking her father's place, but the other side of the business – the side her cousin, John Maynard, had run – was a different story. And there she faced an uphill battle.

But she'd had to start somewhere, so she'd picked Kevin Stanton, one of John's main men, to run that side in her absence. Whether she could trust him, she didn't know, but what choice did she have?

John had done his utmost to make his staff robotically loyal. Nothing wrong with that, had it not been that he'd been working against her, her father and the business all these years.

Sam rested her chin in her hands. How would she explain that to the workforce? How could she explain *anything* without letting the collection of men, trained in savage extortion, violence, drug dealing and other unsavoury facets of the business know what John had done and what had happened to him?

Even *she* wasn't sure. After leaving the lockup that day, she had no idea where John's body had been taken or how it had been disposed of.

Something else she would have to discuss with Seb.

And they really should have spent more time discussing things like that, rather than...

Sam's cheeks flushed with the memories of the past few days. While Sebastian Stoker had brought her to new heights, her mind was not on the myriad of things plaguing her. The million and one issues sat on her shoulders like a weighted rucksack which dragged her further into the quicksand the more she thought about what they entailed and what it all meant.

During the time Seb's mouth was on hers, his hands on her skin and his body possessing hers, she'd thought of nothing, apart from the avalanche of sensations and the mind-blowing crescendos that, without fail, he gave her every single time.

In those moments, she was removed from the torturous confusion, worry and the all-consuming anger over everything that had occurred. But she'd known by making that decision to give in to what her body had yearned for since the day she'd met Seb Stoker brought its own set of issues.

Seb was dangerous, violent and unpredictable – the very *opposite* of what she should want. But want him she did, with every fibre of her being. He excited her, fired her, set her alight. Everything about him made her feel alive, but now the line had been crossed, she didn't know what it meant.

The sudden tapping at her office door took any further thoughts from her mind. Clearing her throat, Sam called, 'Enter.'

3

'How are things going with Kevin?' Liam asked. 'I passed him in the corridor on the way to see you.'

'It's a bit early to say as yet,' Sam replied tersely. She'd thought the knock on the door might be Kevin Stanton. She was expecting him for their first proper meeting since she'd asked him to temporarily take over John's position. She certainly hadn't expected Liam. She hadn't *wanted* to see Liam.

Wearing a neutral expression, Liam stared at Sam. He knew things hadn't been left well between them, but he'd faithfully stuck by her side, waiting in the wings for a *decade*, sure his patience would eventually be rewarded. But how long could he skirt around what he'd learnt from Gloria? What Sam hadn't breathed a bloody word to him about? And also the other question. *Where the hell was John Maynard?*

He studied Sam intently, his annoyance growing. He was right – she wasn't going to say a single thing.

'I bumped into Gloria yesterday,' Liam said, unable to remain silent any longer. 'She's in a real state. Why haven't you told me about what happened?'

Sam's head jerked up. 'She... she told you ab...?'

'She told me everything. You know... that little thing about her and Len not being your real parents!'

Sam flinched. She didn't want to discuss this. Not with Liam. Not with *anyone*.

Liam rubbed his hand over his goatee beard. Gloria had also added that Seb Stoker was present when she'd told Sam the truth and he couldn't quite put into words how much it galled him that particular man knew of this before *he* did.

His face screwed up. He'd fallen in the pecking order – something which had to be rectified. 'You used to tell me everything! I thought at the very least we were supposed to be friends?'

'We were!' Sam cried. 'I mean, we *are*.' And yes, she used to tell Liam everything, but that was before... before, well, *everything* changed...

Guilt twinged. 'I haven't even got my head around it myself.'

Liam bit back his scowl. She'd discussed it with Stoker, though. Oh yes, she'd discussed it with *him*, the bastard. 'Gloria said no one, including her, knows who these people are th...'

'I really don't want to talk about it,' Sam said, fidgeting uncomfortably.

Liam tried his best to look sympathetic, but really he wanted to scream at her for sitting there like she was the only person in the fucking world. But he'd continue playing the game because he intended to turn this around. As much as it stuck in his throat, he wasn't chucking away what he'd worked for because Sam was stupid enough to let Stoker shove his dick in her.

The thought of her sleeping with that man made his skin crawl, but he wasn't stupid. He'd heard on the grapevine that Stoker had been absent from the Royal Peacock, which, funnily enough, coincided with Sam's break away from the Orchid, so it stood to reason she *was* involved with that psycho nutter, just as he'd suspected.

'Sam?' Liam said. 'Your silence tells me something's not right. Where's John? I know you were unhappy with him for reasons you won't divulge, but he's only looking out for you and the business. If you stopped letting that Stoker man cloud your judgement, then y...'

'This is nothing to do with Seb Stoker,' Sam barked, losing her resolve to remain calm.

Liam swallowed the accusations he longed to make. She'd been *far* too quick in jumping to Stoker's defence. She'd only kept the control of the Orchid and become reluctant to go to John for assistance after Stoker had wheedled his way into her head. *Why couldn't she see the man was playing her?*

She'd morphed into a hard-faced cow that, in all honesty, he no longer knew, let alone much liked. But more to the point, all of this scuppered his plans for a comfortable future as Sam's intended. And he'd bet his last quid it was all down to Sebastian Stoker, but he'd have to swallow it if he wanted his payout.

Sam took another deep breath. 'I don't know where John is.' *That was true, at least!*

Liam blinked. 'How can you not know where he is?'

Thinking on her feet, Sam folded her arms. 'He's disappeared. In all honesty, I think he's had a breakdown.' Not long ago, she'd have told Liam the truth. As in the *real* truth. But not any more. He was someone else she no longer trusted.

'John's not the type to have a breakdown!' Liam exclaimed.

'Are you saying I'm making it up?'

'No, but I...'

'I didn't say it was definite. I said that's what I *think*,' Sam replied. She was getting good at lying and thinking off the top of her head and wasn't sure if that was a good thing or not. 'I can give no other reason for his disappearance...' *Apart from that he's dead...*

She shrugged. 'Look, it's complicated. It came to pass that John wasn't acting in the firm's best interests. My personal opinion is that he's done a flit because he knew it was only a matter of time before we all found out.'

'This makes no sense!' Liam exclaimed. 'John bent over backwards to help you.'

'I really can't go into any more details. I'd be speculating,' Sam said quickly. 'And I need you to promise me that y...'

'You can't, or *won't*? You say this is your opinion, but is it? Is it *your* opinion or is it Se...' Liam stopped himself uttering Stoker's name. John wouldn't disappear. Neither would he have had some kind of breakdown. Stoker was behind this. Stoker had killed John. There was no alternative explanation. And Sam was covering it up?

He inwardly fumed. That bastard Sebastian Stoker was taking everything and Sam was allowing it, the stupid, stupid...

'As I was trying to say,' Sam repeated, well aware of what was going through Liam's head, 'I haven't mentioned a word of this to anyone yet. I need to work out what to say to the staff.'

Liam stared at Sam. She was either lying or really was stupid enough to believe the bullshit she'd been fed whilst Stoker screwed her. This could not be allowed to continue.

His skin tingled with unbridled fury. 'Why have you only just told me? Where have you been? And what the hell are you going to do about Gloria? You can't just ignore her, Sam. It's not acceptable.'

Sam felt like slapping Liam, but she had to keep it together. 'That's why I took time off. I needed a few days out to think.'

Yeah, I bet you did, Liam thought acidly. *No guesses who with...* 'And Gloria?'

Sam remained silent for a few moments to control both her anger and to work out what to say. Liam had done her *one* favour, though – he'd underlined that she really *did* need a second in command.

She was grateful when her desk phone rang, its shrill tone punctuating the heavy silence.

Liam watched Sam pick up the receiver. Although he couldn't hear what was said, he *could* hear that gruff voice – the instantly recognisable one that sounded like the owner was gargling with barbed wire.

And judging by the look on Sam's face, whatever Seb Stoker was saying, it wasn't anything she wanted to hear.

Liam silently gestured that he'd leave Sam to it. He'd just had a good idea. A *really* good idea, and if it played out the way he wanted, it would kill two birds with one stone. And then he'd wait patiently until Sam saw sense. This time she'd run into his arms for good and he'd be sorted.

If, on the other hand, it blew up in his face, then he would lose everything he'd worked so hard to achieve over the last ten years. But if he didn't elbow Stoker out of the equation and out of Sam's life, then he was screwed anyway. The way things were heading, he had little to lose.

* * *

Tom reached over Linda and grabbed another can of lager from the bedside table.

Belching loudly, his eyes locked on Linda. How he'd kept the shock off his face when she'd opened the door last night, he hadn't a clue.

Helping himself to Linda's tobacco, Tom rolled a cigarette on his naked thigh, uncomfortably aware her eyes were resting on his now flaccid cock.

Forget the roll-up, he needed a ton of crack to continue screwing Linda for the foreseeable. But he shouldn't have smoked that rock last night... He'd wasted time when he could have been in here getting on with things.

He stole a glance at Linda's weathered face. In the cold light of day, she looked worse than she did last night, if that were at all possible? She was younger than him, yet looked nigh on twenty years older.

And he hadn't counted on there being two bastard kids here either. 'How many kids did you say you'd got?'

'I didn't,' Linda said. 'But eight in total.'

'Fucking hell!' Tom exclaimed. 'You don't mess about, do you?' Whatever else Linda had spent the last thirty years doing, the vast majority of it wasn't spent looking after her looks, but on her back – a stark contrast to the frigid virgin he'd broken in. 'Who do they all belong to?'

Linda shrugged and reached for her can of cider. 'No one you'd know.' She wasn't sure she knew about most of them either. Not for sure, anyway. Besides, it wasn't as if it mattered.

She inhaled slowly, the question she'd wanted to ask since the moment she'd opened the door still burning on her lips. 'Why are you here, Tom? I didn't ever expect to see you again.'

She watched Tom mull over her question. He'd retained a good percentage of that cheeky charm she'd been so besotted with as a teenager. But where had it got her, apart from a fast-track to a life down the toilet?

Seeing him again brought back his abandonment. Not that she'd ever forgotten. She'd just coped by drowning it out over the last three decades. But now – now it was just as fresh and painful as it had always been.

Whilst wondering what the hell to say, Tom watched Linda light a cigarette and balance the ashtray on the duvet. Judging by the trembling of her bottom lip, he'd better hurry up and say *something*. Something believable that would get his feet back under the table. Shit deal or not, he was relying on her.

He might have spent half the night screwing her, but there was more work to do than he'd thought. Jesus, why did women overcomplicate things?

Forcing the preferable image of the nubile young body of Tina, who he'd left at his club, out of his mind – a massive contrast to this wrinkled scabby tart – Tom grabbed Linda's hand. 'Babe, I know I let you down. I was young, stupid and scared.' He pulled his face into a practised contrite look. 'Your dad's threats terrified me,' he lied. 'I thought it best to get out of your life.'

'Threats?' A lone tear rolled down Linda's cheek. 'He gave you money and you took it. I heard everything. You never once asked about me. Or our baby. I...'

'Your dad said I'd ruin your life. He said our kid would have a good life. A *better* life. I thought I was doing the right thing. I was a prat.'

'But I loved you!' Linda wailed, throwing herself to the edge of the bed. 'You said we were meant to be together and that we'd get married. Then you disappeared. My life's been shite because of you, Tom Bedworth. Absolute shite!'

Tom watched Linda's shoulders heave in between her sobs. Christ, he must have been desperate for a shag if he'd said all that? And from what he recalled, the one time she'd opened her legs had been shit.

His nose wrinkled. Judging by what he'd just experienced, she hadn't improved much since either.

'That's why I'm here now. To make it up to you.' Tom's hand stroked Linda's back. 'I thought I might stay with you for a while and get to know each other again? I'm doing well now, Lin.'

'Oh, that's okay then, isn't it?' Linda lurched to her feet and staggered across the room. Why had she been so stupid to let this man back into her bed? 'As long as *you're* doing okay...'

Feeling exposed, she yanked her dressing gown on. *Wait!* Was Tom saying he wanted her back after all this time? Despite everything, it was what she'd always wanted.

'Lin, listen *please*, babe,' Tom whined. Getting up, he wrapped his arms around Linda's waist from behind and rested his chin on her shoulder, careful to miss the dried egg stuck to the filthy pink fur of her robe. 'I haven't been back in Brum long – only a few months. But I've got my own casino up the Hagley Road now and everything!' he said proudly.

His hand slipped inside Linda's dressing gown and played with one of her breasts. Feeling her nipple harden on cue, Tom smiled to himself. *She still wanted him like crazy. She'd be putty in his hands.*

Hopelessly fighting against the powerful desire Tom had always sparked in her, Linda groaned with pleasure. 'But why now, Tom? Why now?'

Tom grinned, his lips against Linda's hair. He bypassed the stench of ingrained chips and instead concentrated on getting his hands on that lovely money from the Violet Orchid. The thought of that was the only thing in this room that could possibly make him hard.

Pushing his erection against her buttocks, Tom continued kneading her breasts. 'Oh, Linda, look what you've done to me again.' He gasped for good measure. 'God, I've missed you, girl.'

'But what about our daughter?' Linda breathed, leaning over the bed in anticipation.

Tom paused. Was this a good time to drop the bombshell? It might save having to screw her again. 'That's the other reason I'm here. I've found out where our daughter is.'

'What?' Linda shrieked, spinning around. 'Oh, my God, Tom! Really? My baby girl? Where is she? Have you met her?'

Tom inwardly congratulated himself on his timing. *Bingo.* 'I've seen her, yes, but she doesn't know who I am.' He smiled sweetly. 'I thought it only fair not to introduce myself... That's partly why I've been desperately trying to find you these past few weeks.'

'Oh, Tom!' Linda wailed, now crying freely. She'd never thought this day would come. Giving up her firstborn had haunted her every single day. Maybe now she could put things right? Maybe at last she could be a proper mother to all of her children? 'Where is she? I want to go and see her.'

'We can't just turn up,' Tom said hastily. 'She might not even know she's adopted. And that's another thing... It should be *you* she meets, not me. Meeting both of us at the same time could overwhelm her.' He smiled sadly. 'She might even resent us for being together, being as we didn't keep her. We don't want her to think that, so it's better if I stay out of the way.'

Linda's heart crashed in her chest. So, Tom was back for good? To be here – with *her*? The two things she'd always wanted. Tom and her firstborn were within her grasp. 'What does she look like? Please tell me!'

'She's beautiful. Just like you...' Grimacing, Tom moved over to the other side of the room, glad to be away from Linda's close proximity. He fished a newspaper cutting he'd saved for this very purpose out of his pocket – the photo of Samantha Reynold taken at the Orchid before he'd made the unfortunate mistake of killing her pretend father. 'This is her.'

Linda snatched the crumpled newspaper from Tom's hand, her eyes widening. 'Oh, my God!' she cried, entranced. 'She's stunning!'

Tom smiled smugly, until Linda suddenly began sobbing and hyperventilating.

He stood aghast, panic rising. What the fuck was going on? Was she having a heart attack?

Oh, that would by typical. She drops dead just at the exact time she was finally of use.

'I'll call an ambulance,' he muttered, edging away. *Or should he leg it?*

'No!' Linda panted, her nails digging painfully into the skin of Tom's arm. 'I – I'm okay. I just need to lie down.'

4

'Not that you've asked, but in case you're wondering, the Old Bill have gone.' Seb threw his suit jacket onto the back of the chair in his office.

'Forget about them. They can't prove fuck all. I'm more bothered that it's been almost a fucking week you've been off radar, leaving us to deal with everything,' Andrew barked.

Seb wasn't in the mood to put up with his brother playing his face. 'And there was me thinking you'd jump at the chance for more responsibility. Isn't that what you've always wanted?'

Andrew glanced at Neil; identical irritation reflected in his twin's eyes. 'Responsibility for our club and the family firm, sure, but not because you buggered off to bat for the other side with our bloody rivals!' he spat. 'Jesus, Seb. You run *this* firm, not Samantha Reynold's. For fuck's sake, what were you thinking?'

Seb's eyes narrowed. 'How many more times? Yes, I've been helping Sam out, but I've also been putting things into place for us too.'

'We still have our own club and firm to run,' Andrew continued. 'You can't just swan off!'

Seb sat forward, his jaw clenched. 'I'm here, aren't I? If you two can't fucking cope running the basics for a couple of days, then that speaks volumes!'

'In case you'd forgotten, our brother is still lying in a chest freezer at the lockup. I've had Mum on the phone asking why we haven't located him yet and Dad's been in twice,' Andrew said, anger flooding to the fore. 'When are we dealing with it?' Pacing around, he raked his fingers through his thick dark hair. 'Jesus Christ. What's the matter with you? We can't keep it from them any longer. It's been ages already. Or is this just to protect your new shag?'

'You fucking *what*?' Seb glowered. Sam was certainly more than a mere shag. A *hell* of a lot more, but Andrew was right on one thing: their parents had to be informed of Gary's death. And they would be. Now Maynard had been dealt with and there had been no further trouble, it was time to break the news, but he couldn't say he was looking forward to it.

It was obvious Maynard, and Maynard alone, was behind everything. Despite things not adding up with his whereabouts the night Gary was murdered, he *must* have been the one to do it. But the whole city could not be allowed to know that a ponce such as Maynard had offed one of the Stokers. 'What I've put in place is a feasible way of putting Gary to rest without what happened becoming public knowledge.'

'It's not right these rumours haven't been put straight yet,' Andrew barked. 'Why the fuck should Sam Reynold be more important than our own mother's reputation?'

Seb scowled. 'When did I say that?'

'We all heard what Maynard said. Sam Reynold being an illegitimate bastard, belonging to God only knows who, isn't *our* problem. She should be taking the flak, so why haven't you quashed the bullshit about our family?' Andrew raged.

The expression on Seb's face only made Andrew's rage burn brighter. 'So?' he continued. 'When are we telling our parents? I need an answer.'

Seb sighed. 'We'll tell them tomorrow. We just need to decide how to word it.' Breaking his mother's heart and risking putting his father back in hospital was not something he relished. He would also have to warn Sam that the truth would be out about her family.

Neil watched the exchange with building interest. He too had been surprised when Seb had called, telling them he'd be absent for a while. No one had expected him to all but jump ship, leaving them in the thick of it.

He felt he should add something to this conversation. 'You said you sorted things with the cops and the coroner?'

Seb nodded. 'Atkins has issued a death certificate and I'd already briefed Baker to ensure no cops sniff around.' *And those things had cost a bloody fortune!*

'But what exactly do we tell our folks?' Neil asked, looking worriedly between his two brothers.

'Dad's not stupid. We tell them what's happened, but we leave out the bit about Maynard getting the last word, okay?' Seb's eyes narrowed. 'We tell him that *we* finished it, not that Maynard did it his bloody self. It's the only thing that will soften the blow. If anything can...' He sat down heavily. 'The crem's booked, too. Mum won't like that, but it's the only way to ensure nothing comes back on us down the line.' Folding his arms across his chest, he glared at Andrew. 'Coming back to the cops, have you any suggestions what we're going to do about Phil Blunt's missus taking it upon herself to point the finger in our direction, considering *you* caused the problem...?'

Andrew remained silent – his expression nonplussed. Seb could have all the digs he wanted and, sure, whatever suggestions anyone wanted to make was fine by him, but *he* was one step ahead. He'd already dealt with that and the same would apply to Samantha-bloody-Reynold if she didn't fuck off out of his business.

Seb was just not on the ball enough any more.

Andrew had already lost one brother and he was not losing

another. He would do everything he could to ensure the family, as well as the firm, remained in good working order.

* * *

Kevin Stanton tried his best to exhibit patience in front of the new boss. Even though he hadn't expected to be asked to keep an eye on things in Sam's absence, he'd done what she'd asked, but he couldn't say he was happy. Truth was, he'd been downright livid this girl had stepped into her father's shoes, rather than John Maynard, like everyone presumed would happen.

Like Maynard had *said* would happen.

But it hadn't happened. Maynard taking the reins hadn't materialised and now the man was nowhere to be seen.

Having a woman at the helm didn't bode well. Especially one as green around the gills as this silly bird. He frowned. All he and his men wanted to know, *needed* to know, was when Maynard was due back.

'Thanks for holding the fort.' Sam broke the awkward silence.

'No problem.' *Except it was a problem.* A frown creased Kevin's face. 'What's going on, Miss Reynold?'

Sam tapped her pen on the desk, knowing she had to offer some kind of explanation. 'I don't know where to start...'

Kevin didn't bother smiling when Sam looked at him. 'Try with where John is,' he said bluntly.

Sam overrode the intimidating look in the man's steely eyes. She would not have him or *anyone* make her feel uncomfortable. This was *her* firm now and was about time people accepted that. 'John isn't here,' she finally answered, her voice steady.

'I know that,' Kevin said. 'But it would be useful to know what the situation is.'

Sam stared at the hole punch on her desk, wishing it contained wisdom, answers and advice. It stood to reason John's whereabouts would be questioned. The man had been involved at the firm's epicentre for so long the business could easily have been mistaken for his.

Sam's lips twitched. And it almost *would* have been if he'd got his way, the lying, sneaky, two-faced...

Her mind scrambled for answers. She really *did* need a trusted member of the firm who knew the ins and outs and who she could rely on.

But who was there that *she* could trust?

Whoever she handed that job to, she would have to level with them about *everything*. And that was a massive gamble.

'Miss Reynold?' Kevin jolted Sam from her thoughts. 'You haven't told me when John's returning?'

'John's taken a few days off due to a personal matter. I'll call a meeting tomorrow to let everyone know.' Sam's fake confidence sounded impressive, even to her own ears.

She hadn't planned on calling a meeting at all, but she should have. There were a lot of things she *should* have done, other than bury her head in the sand. And it stopped *here*.

Knitting her fingers together, Sam returned her gaze to Kevin. 'I'd appreciate if you could continue doing what you've been doing in John's absence for the time being. Just until I can catch up with things here.'

She forced herself to smile, hoping her lies were as convincing. 'In the interim, feel free to come to me with anything you would usually speak to John about. Despite popular opinion, I know how this firm is run.' *If she kept saying that, perhaps it would become a self-fulfilling prophecy?*

Kevin shifted his massive frame from one leg to the other. 'Okay, then, tell me what my team are expected to do over this week's planned coke drops.'

Sam nodded as though she understood. 'The same as what you would normally do. Nothing has changed.'

Kevin frowned. 'But John was in the process of moving several drops to Team C, rather than Team B. And what about the new supplier? We've been left not knowing what's been sorted and the first drops are due the day after tomorrow.'

Sam nodded again, her brass neck surprising her. 'Ah, that... of course. Leave it with me. I'll let everyone know how to play it during the meeting.' She smiled brightly. 'Thanks for bringing this up.'

Shit. Now what? She hadn't a bloody clue what Kevin was talking about. She knew nothing about the planned drops, let alone what John had arranged with suppliers. Why had he been moving suppliers in the first place? From the small part she understood, the supply chain worked well.

Kevin's mouth flattened. It looked like everything Maynard had said about this chick was right. Samantha Reynold was about as much cut out for this firm as a fucking doily!

5

Tom craned his neck to peer out of the dirty kitchen window down to the road below. There was no one about that he could see, thank God. He'd been convinced that nosy cow next door might have called the social about Linda's sobbing and screaming last night. Or worse, the police.

He scowled. Aside from not wanting to be involved, it would slow his plan up and that was the last bloody thing he wanted.

That skanky neighbour, Vera, or whatever her name was, had wanted to come in to calm Linda down. Apparently, these 'turns' happened every so often. The cheeky old slapper even had the front to ask who he was!

Well, he wasn't having that. Neither was he letting the woman stick her hooter in. But what was all this shit about Linda and panic attacks? An excuse for being a cunt, if he'd ever heard it!

Tom shrugged, supposing he should be thankful the stupid bitch hadn't had a heart attack.

He rubbed his hand over his unshaven face. *Trust things to go tits up.*

Walking over to the fridge, he yanked open the door and glared at the diminishing stock of lager. He'd send one of Linda's brats out to replenish that later. He didn't dare go outside himself. Not yet. Plus, he needed to keep an eye on Linda to make sure the daft cow didn't go loony again.

The crack he'd given her last night had quietened down her hysterics, but if she made a habit of this screaming and crying stuff, she'd be carted off and then he really would be scuppered. He shrugged dismissively. She'd be okay once she'd got a couple of cans of cider down her neck.

She'd better be, anyway, because he didn't have time for this. He had to touch base with Lee and Steve at the Aurora and see how the land lay so he could get on with making more money.

The deal he'd made with Luke Banner to cook crack was a good one. The cheap way the gear was cut meant, if he was clever, he'd outprice most of, if not *all* the other suppliers in the city. And that would coin it in, as well as granting him a huge percentage of the monopoly.

It was a sterling idea – yet another brilliant twist in his luck. But there were two glaring issues: his plan of getting an easy supply of base cocaine from the Orchid was off, for the time being at least, so he needed more hands on deck, scouting for good base. And secondly, there was another taster batch of crack due at the Aurora any day now...

It had possibly already arrived and he didn't want those tarts helping themselves. It wasn't for wasting on that bunch of addled whores.

Pulling a can of lager from the fridge, Tom cracked it open. Raising it to his mouth, he greedily slurped at the tepid liquid. Jesus, even the fridge was fucked.

After everything he'd been through, he more than needed another drink. Having also smoked his last rock of crack earlier, things were getting desperate, so the sooner Linda got her miserable arse out of bed, the better.

Tom wiped the back of his hand across his mouth. Sparking up another one of Linda's cigarettes, he sat at the table, ignoring the kid eyeing him warily from the doorway. *He could piss off as well.*

Dragging the overflowing ashtray towards him, Tom scowled once more. This was supposed to be straightforward, but Linda was wasting time.

Shit the bed! Why was she making such a fuss? The news about Samantha was supposed to cheer her up, not cause a meltdown. Yet all she'd done was wail about being a bad mother and that it was *his* fault she'd failed and let down all of her kids.

That wasn't *his* problem.

Admittedly, it had been difficult, not to mention irritating, putting up with Linda's howling self-pity. And worse, having to be nice to her, calm her down, telling her she wasn't a failure and that she could put things right, when all he wanted to do was laugh. But he'd played the part. And he'd played it well.

He'd even convinced that nosy Vera bitch that *he* was more than capable of looking after the kids, as well as making sure Linda was all right.

Tom slammed his now empty can down indignantly. His eyes tracked back to the kid, still staring at him from the kitchen doorway. By the state of these kids' mugs, Linda clearly hadn't been fussy with her last two choices of men. 'What the fuck are you looking at?'

The little boy blinked. 'I – I'm hungry. I ain't had anything to eat since yesterday. Where's me ma?'

'In bed,' Tom growled. Forcing himself to rise from the table, he opened a cupboard. Pulling out a half-eaten packet of biscuits, he chucked them in the direction of the child. 'Get those down your neck and fuck off. I'm busy.'

'Why is Ma in bed? I heard her crying.'

We can all hear her bloody crying, Tom thought irritably. And the sound grated at his head. 'She's fine.'

'She cries a lot.' Tayquan's big brown eyes saddened. 'Aunty Vera says it's cos Ma gets sad sometimes, but not because of us.'

Tom's mouth flattened. 'That's strange, because your mother told me that you and your sister have ruined her life!'

Tayquan's mouth widened into a perfectly formed 'O' and his eyes filled with tears. 'That's not true!'

'Yes, it is. Now fuck off, kid. Like I said, I'm busy.'

Sobbing, Tayquan ran from the kitchen as fast as his little legs would carry him.

'And leave your mother alone! She don't need your moaning. You've done enough as it is by being here!' Tom shouted to the child's retreating figure.

For fuck's sake. If Linda didn't pull herself together soon, he'd have to rethink the situation and *fast*. He wasn't being lumbered with two kids, as well as a useless mental tramp, and leaving his well thought-out plans to go to shite.

* * *

Sam stared at the newspaper in disbelief. Since Seb's phone call yesterday afternoon, she'd expected the truth to come out. She knew it would get around quickly, but she hadn't expected it emblazoned on the front page of the *Birmingham Mail*.

Nausea flickered. For it to be already printed, this story must have been previously supplied to the press.

She stared back at the paper. Seb wouldn't have given them this story, would he?

No, of course not.

Her head pounded. The glaring truth was, she no longer trusted *anyone* and that in itself was horrible.

Sam snatched up the ringing telephone. 'Yes?' Pausing, she listened, her anger intensifying. 'No comment.'

Slamming the receiver back onto the cradle, she immediately picked it back up and stabbed in the digits for the Orchid's reception.

'Do not put any more calls through, is that clear? Not one... Yes, that's correct. No more calls for the rest of the day.'

Replacing the receiver, Sam stared it. That was the fifth bloody call from journalists this afternoon.

No, she had no comment to make on the story...

No, she didn't want their help in locating her birth parents...

She put her head in her hands. Could this get any worse? She could hardly threaten the press with legal action. Not when the story was true. But how had they got those details?

Snatching up the receiver again, she dialled Seb's office at the Peacock, picking her nails as it rang out. Why wasn't he answering his goddamn phone?

He'd phoned yesterday, granted, but she'd expected... expected *what*?

Perspiration gathering, Sam scraped her hair away from her neck and twisted it into a loose ponytail.

What had she expected? Flowers? What? She didn't know. *Christ, she was being ridiculous!*

Ending the call, Sam got up and paced around. Everybody knew her personal business now. *Everybody.*

Her eyes tracked back to the article; the headlines screaming out their poisonous words.

They'd made it sound so tragic. So desperate...

This was bad. She'd planned to get her head around the business before broaching this bombshell in her personal life, but now she'd have to deal with the fallout from *this* as well.

Sam smoothed her clammy hands down the well-tailored fabric of her black pencil skirt. Inhaling deeply, she moved back to the telephone and dialled the number before she could change her mind.

Her heart skipped as it rang out. Almost tempted to prematurely end the call on the premise that no one was in, she was caught off guard when a familiar voice answered.

'Hello?'

Sam stopped herself from automatically addressing the woman down the other end of the line as 'Mum'. 'I need to speak to you about th...'

'Samantha!' Gloria exclaimed brightly. 'Oh, I'm so glad you've phoned. I've been worried sick. I wanted t...'

'I need to know who my real parents are,' Sam said, her voice clipped. She bit down on her bottom lip, hearing the pain resonating through the receiver at her bluntness. 'You said you didn't know, but this isn't the time to hide things to save my feelings. Or your own... You *must* know who these people are, so the least you can do is tell me...'

There was a long pause and Sam thought the call may have been cut off until Gloria suddenly continued.

'I – I'm not hiding anything from you, Samantha, darling. What I told you was the truth,' Gloria said, the crack in her voice evident.

The truth? Sam thought bitterly, realising her hand was shaking. 'You must know something?'

'I swear, darling, I'd tell you if I knew anything more. I've told you all that I know and I'm sorry tha...'

'Was there paperwork?' Sam asked, her heart pounding.

'P-paperwork?' Gloria stuttered. 'Yes, there must have been, but I never saw any. Like I said, your father dealt with it. I was so over the moon to finally have a child that I never questioned the details... Samantha, can we please meet up? I desperately want to put this right. I...'

'I can't. Not right now,' Sam said, her mind spinning. 'Look, I need to go.' Without further hesitation, she replaced the handset, ignoring the hurt she could imagine plastering her mother's face.

Her mother... Except she wasn't...

She'd go and see *Gloria* at some point, but not yet.

Sam's eyes darted around the office. So there was paperwork? Or it was *thought* there was paperwork. There *had* to be. Her father had been too much of a stickler for details not to insist on legalities. He would not have allowed any stone left unturned or entertained a single 'I' not to be dotted, or a 'T' not to be crossed.

And being as he didn't want her to discover the truth, where would the paperwork have been stashed? It wouldn't be at the house. With her inquisitive nature as a child, she could have stumbled across it.

A memory of rooting through cupboards and drawers in the run-up to Christmas for evidence of what Father Christmas might bring flashed into Sam's mind.

That was it! Her father must have concealed the paperwork concerning her adoption and, hopefully, the details of her real parents in this very office!

Now she just had to locate it.

6

'Stay with your mother,' Mal Stoker barked to Neil and Andrew as he ushered Seb out of the lounge and down the hallway.

Shutting the door of his study, he faced his eldest son. 'Now tell me all the details of what you did to Maynard,' Mal spat, his eyes shining with suppressed malice.

Seb winced at his father's pinched face, devastation beneath the rage. How he wished he hadn't had to break this news. 'We made sure Maynard suffered. His agony was dragged out for a full twenty-four hours before we finished him,' he growled, hating the lie contained within his statement.

He'd toyed with the prospect of telling his father the complete truth – that Maynard had topped himself and beaten them to it by a gnat's knacker, but it would only have made things worse.

One thousand times worse...

It would haunt his father until the day he died to know Gary hadn't been avenged by a Stoker's hand. This grated enough on Seb's mind, but he'd rather live with that than destroy his parents further.

'And the Reynold girl witnessed this, you say?' Mal muttered. 'The execution of her kin?'

'Once she knew what he'd done and what he was behind, she was all for it.'

'But then...' Mal pulled a newspaper out of the top drawer of his mahogany desk. 'She's *not* his kin, though, is she?' Shaking his head, he pointed to the headline. 'And to think you lot were so quick to take those fucking rumours to be about our Gary...'

Seb stared at the front page of the *Mail* in shock. 'What the...?'

'I've kept this hidden from your mother. She'd be even more devastated to discover Gloria Reynold knew those rumours were circulating about our family, well aware they concerned *hers*.' Mal's eyes narrowed. 'I presume *you* knew about this? When were you going to tell us?'

Seb nodded. 'It was next on my list. Maynard spilled his guts about it the night he left this world. I had to give you the news about Gary before we could think about ending any rumours still doing the rounds. That will be done now.' Picking up the newspaper, Seb scanned the article once again. 'I can't understand how the papers got wind of this. Apart from us, only Maynard and his father knew.'

Folding his arms, Mal scrutinised his son. 'Well, *somebody* did... Why leave *any* amount of time before telling us about Gary and putting the rumour mongers straight, Sebastian?'

Seb pursed his lips. *He'd been expecting that question.* 'Everything had to be done and dusted over the disposal of Maynard's body before I broke the news. I had to make sure nothing came back from that. I didn't want an already bad situation made worse.' *He needed to steer off this subject now.* 'Jesus, Dad. Will Mum be okay?'

Mal's top lip curled. 'One of her sons is dead. Killed by some prick because he was in the wrong place at the wrong time, you reckon? So, no, she won't be okay, but I will ensure she remains as good as she can be.' His voice faltered. 'I presume you'll issue a press release about Gary's death?'

Seb nodded. 'I was planning to state a short illness.'

Snatching the newspaper from Seb's hands, Mal shoved it back in the drawer. 'Your mother is my main and *only* priority at this given moment. For that reason and that reason *alone*, I won't waste my energy asking you what it is you're not telling me.' His eyes narrowed. 'Because I know there's something you're not levelling with me on.' He put his hand on Seb's shoulder. 'I hope you're not losing your priorities, son.'

Seb stiffened. 'Losing my priorities?'

'I'm well aware I asked you to help the Reynold girl out after her father's death, but I hope you haven't allowed your head to be turned. I hope you haven't put how Samantha feels about finding out she's a nobody before your family's honour and the firm's reputation?'

* * *

Sam's eyes burnt from scanning the contents of the never-ending pile of letters, papers and information.

Pushing her hair off her forehead, she stared at the mess strewn over her desk. She'd been through piles and piles, finding nothing pertaining to her, and she'd only just touched the surface.

She stared up at the ceiling in desperation. Surely there must be something somewhere?

Sam's head shot up at a sharp rapping on the door. Before she could even contemplate whether to ignore it, the door opened and her heart sank as Kevin Stanton walked into her office uninvited.

Sam watched Kevin's eyes linger knowingly on the copy of the *Birmingham Mail* amid the mountain of paperwork on her desk. His top lip twitched into the hint of a smirk and her embarrassment surged.

A slithering reminder pushed its barbed tendrils into her brain. Courtesy of the press, everyone would be talking about her even more now they had this additional ammunition. 'What can I help you with?' she asked tersely.

'Prior to today's meeting, I wanted to check if there was an update on Maynard?'

Sam cleared her throat. If she wanted respect from these men, she would have to level with them. *Partly, at least...* 'It's complicated... All I can say is John won't be returning to the Orchid.'

'Why?' Kevin's eyes narrowed. 'Where is he?'

'I really can't go into details at the moment,' Sam said quickly. 'I'll tell the staff he's having time off for personal reasons and although I know you realise there's more to it than that, and you'd be right, that's all I'm prepared to give you right now.'

Kevin scrutinised Sam. 'Me and my teams deserve proper answers, Miss Reynold, not this!'

Sam nodded stiffly. 'I would have brought this up with you before, especially considering I asked you to step into my cousin's shoes, but as you're probably aware, I've had unexpected matters of my own to deal with...' Her eyes moved to the newspaper at the edge of the desk.

Leaning back in the chair, she met Kevin's accusatory eyes. 'I realise I'm asking you to trust me and appreciate that will be difficult, as I get the distinct impression you have little faith in me. But I need you on side in order for this firm to work.'

She smiled faintly. 'I'll tell you more when I can, but I need your assurance this conversation will go no further.'

Holding Kevin's stare, Sam was surprised to see a flicker of admiration behind his hooded lids.

Giving Sam a quick nod, Kevin abruptly left the office.

Sam waited until the door had shut and Kevin's clumping footsteps had retreated down the corridor before she put her head in her hands. *She had to sort this out.*

Picking up another handful of paperwork from the desk, she sifted through the mound of pointless invoices, her mind churning over what to say in the meeting, when the office door was tapped again.

She slammed the paperwork down once more. 'Come in.'

A petite woman with short blonde hair peered timidly around the door. 'Sorry to bother you, Miss Reynold. We need a new rota for the gaming tables. We've been using last week's, but it's messing up all of th...'

'Hasn't Liam supplied you with that?' Sam snapped, immediately feeling guilty as the woman flinched.

'H-he said to check with you.'

'Okay,' Sam nodded. 'Give me an hour to sort it.' She waited until the woman pulled the door closed before stabbing Liam's extension into her phone. Why hadn't he dealt with this?

Whether she liked it or not, she couldn't remain close to people who did not believe in her or trust her ability. She needed people onside if she were to make a success of this. And that, she was determined to do.

Hearing Liam's extension ring out, Sam slammed the receiver down, only for it to immediately ring again. 'Liam? I... Oh!'

She paused, listening to what the voice said. 'Yes... yes, that's right. I'll discuss that, amongst other things, during the meeting. Yes, it's at three o'clock.'

Sam left the receiver off the hook and laid it on her desk, the drone of the dial tone reverberating in her head.

Another one asking about John. Were this lot having a laugh? Were they playing with her to wind her up or catch her out?

Because it was working...

Panic and frustration rose. She didn't know the answers to those questions and, to top it all, didn't even know who she was any more. She had to face the world with everyone knowing she was a phony.

Angrily swiping perspiration from her brow, Sam contemplated whether to try to get hold of Seb again.

Her mouth set determinedly. How could she be so selfish? Seb had his own things to deal with and his own firm to run, plus he was telling his parents one of their sons was dead.

Neither did she want to come over as sad and pathetic and begging for his help again. If she was to make a go of this, then she had to stand on her own two feet and fight her own battles.

Sam rested her head against the cool leather of the chair's headrest and closed her eyes, willing herself not to let the escalating panic gain a foothold.

No, she would deal with this herself. *All* of it.

And she had to hurry up and think of a way to do so before everything either collapsed around her or she imploded.

7

Leaving the bedroom, Tom looked back at Linda slumped in the bed and tried not to gag at the thick trail of snot running from her left nostril into her gaping mouth.

What a fucking state!

Another day of giving her the spiel she needed to hear. Telling her that fretting about things she couldn't change would only take her concentration away from reconnecting with her firstborn; it would also hinder cementing the rekindling of their long-overdue relationship... The past wasn't her fault. It was *no one's* fault. Life worked like that sometimes...

Blah, blah, blah...

Tom scowled. He'd thought Linda had begun to see sense after a few cans of cider. That was until she'd started crying again. Waving her arms around like a lunatic whilst whining about being useless and pointless...

He could have told her that for nothing, the thick bitch!

Stomping into the kitchen, he glared at the fridge. Where were those bloody kids? Nigh on an hour ago he'd sent them down the shop.

He was gagging for a beer. He'd even told them they could have a packet of crisps each, the ungrateful, lazy bastards.

It wasn't like he was paying, but that had been the last tenner in Linda's purse and he only hoped her giro came tomorrow, otherwise she'd be fucked. He wasn't dipping into his last few quid to buy her fucking brats food.

Glowering, Tom stared out of the window onto the street below and saw two men having a fight, surrounded by a handful of kids cheering them on.

Christ. How long did it take to buy two packs of lager, some crisps and a fucking paper? They'd best not have buggered off with the money and caught the bus into town, the cheeky little shits.

Moving into the poky lounge, Tom wrinkled his nose at the stench of stale fags and beer and cursed under his breath as his bare foot stepped on something hard.

Scowling, he snatched up the Lego and threw it into the bin, his irritation rising further as the remains of the plastic car bounced off the overflowing metal bin, landing back almost where he'd found it.

Refraining from stamping on it, only because it would hurt his foot further, Tom made a mental note to smash it into the stinking carpet once he got his boots back on. From now on, all toys were banned. However long he had to doss in this shithole, the one thing he wasn't doing was leaving here a fucking cripple.

Jaw clenched, he glanced at the telephone on the top of a cheap wooden unit full of VHS cassettes, books and a selection of empty fag packets. While no one else was about, he'd call the Aurora and ask Lee how things were going. It was important no one should forget *he* was in charge. He may not have been gone long, but he knew what people were like, especially money-grabbing tarts.

He'd also check to see if that sample of crack had arrived. Or, more importantly, if there'd been any more visits from the Stokers...

Poking in the numbers with a pudgy finger, it took a moment

before Tom realised the phone was silent. Frowning, he stared at the greasy orange handset.

It was fucking dead as a door nail, for God's sake.

Smacking the button to cut the call, he wiggled the cord. *Nope. Dead.* For fuck's sake! Did nothing work in this crummy dump?

Now he'd have to risk setting foot outside to use a bastard call box. That's if he could find one around here with a working phone that didn't choke him out with the stench of piss, or worse, had a resident tramp still in situ.

Tom yanked the phone line clean of the BT wall socket and chucked the whole thing on top of the overflowing bin. No point keeping the fucking thing.

Hearing two pairs of footsteps skitter up the hall, he stormed into the kitchen. 'What took you two so long?' Tom barked, scowling at Tayquan and his slightly older sister. 'Did you get my beer and stuff?'

'Yes,' Shondra squeaked, holding out a carrier bag full of lager cans. 'Mr Gopal quizzed us for yonks about who they were for.'

'Unusual for anyone to bother questioning folk around here,' Tom muttered, inspecting the contents of the bag, pleased to see the brats had bought exactly what he'd told them to.

'It was *me* who convinced him,' Tayquan said proudly. 'Mr Gopal knows me ma usually drinks cider, so I said they were for me dad.'

'What do you want, a fucking medal? You haven't got a dad! You've got your crisps, so leave the change on the table and don't tell me there ain't any,' Tom snapped. 'Then fuck off to your room.'

Glad to see the back of the kids, Tom tugged at the ring pull of his first can. He wouldn't bother asking Linda if she wanted one.

Plonking himself down at the table, he necked the lager and, wiping his hand across his mouth, pulled the late edition of the *Evening Mail* from the blue carrier bag. He glanced dismissively at the front page, before freezing as the words came into focus:

A Silver Lining for Casino Heiress After Family Heartbreak?

Days after the funeral of Len Reynold – owner of the Violet Orchid on Broad Street – his daughter has discovered there could be a silver lining under her cloud of grief, albeit a surprising one.

An anonymous source informed us that Samantha Reynold, 30, is NOT the biological child of Len Reynold and his wife, Gloria. The source also alleged money was exchanged for the child.

Considering Mr Reynold's well-respected position in the city, this will come as a shock to many. It must be stated that although we have not been able to corroborate the story, when contacted earlier today for a statement, Ms Reynold did not deny the allegations, suggesting our sources' claims are true. No other members of the family were available for comment.

Understandably, this revelation must have come as a shock to Samantha Reynold, but we suspect it also offers a glimmer of hope during the dark days following the passing of the man she believed to be her father.

Our source insists Ms Reynold does not know who her true parents are, so if anyone knows, or if YOU are lucky enough to have this beautiful young lady as your daughter, please get in touch with us here at the *Mail*.

All inquiries will be treated in the strictest confidence.

Tom's face broke into a wide smile, unable to quite believe his luck.

He'd been racking his brains as to how he could put Linda in touch with Samantha and convince her to believe they were her real parents. Now someone had saved him the bother.

But who else could have known about this, apart from Maynard? Did this mean he wasn't dead after all?

He shrugged. It didn't matter. Not at the moment, anyway. He'd find out soon enough whether Maynard was still breathing, but it didn't stop him moving forward with the plan, did it?

No, it bloody well didn't.

But he was damned if he'd go through the channels of the *Birm-*

ingham Mail. He'd send Linda straight to the organ grinder. From what she'd told him about the day the kid was collected, she had details no one else knew and therefore could prove *she* was the mother – unlike the hordes of wannabes who undoubtedly were already lining up to lay claim to the newly-appointed Orchid heiress.

All good things come to those who wait, Thomas, he thought, as he scrambled up from the rickety table.

Grabbing a fresh can of lager and the newspaper, he made his way towards the bedroom. It was time Linda stopped feeling sorry for herself.

* * *

Back in his office at the Peacock, Seb was still fuming. How could he not be? He'd never put anyone before his family or the firm and neither would he. But the fact his father had insinuated, or rather, *accused* him of doing exactly that stabbed in his brain like the poisoned tip of a scorching hot poker.

Knocking back the remains of the fourth large whisky since leaving his parents' house, Seb stared between his remaining brothers in turn.

'I think they took it quite well, considering,' Neil said, eyeing Seb's expression warily. 'I mean, we knew they would be upset, but given that, I still th...'

'Oh, yeah, well isn't that just fabulous,' Seb snapped, helping himself to another whisky. His father eyeing him with suspicion and his mother a hollow, blubbering wreck didn't constitute what he classed as 'going well'. Neither would he tell them what their father had said. *No way.*

His brothers thought along the very same lines, but they were wrong. They were fucking way off. *All of them.*

'Now everything's out in the open, we can bury our brother,' Andrew added, his green eyes boring into Seb. 'Giving Gary a dignified send-off should be the only important thing now.' He clasped his hands together, the action making a strange slapping sound in the tense quiet of the room. 'We can also resume full concentration on the business...'

'It's a cremation, Andrew, not a burial.' Seb's static expression did not alter, even though he wanted to headbutt Andrew. His brother was determined to rile him, but he wouldn't rise to it. *Not yet.*

'Turn of phrase,' Andrew said, silently gratified to garner a reaction from Seb, however small.

Neil stared at the article in the *Mail*, bemused. 'Who did this, then?'

'Who cares?' Andrew's steely gaze remained on Seb. 'It doesn't affect us.'

'Could Maynard have set it up? Beforehand, I mean?' Neil suggested.

'He could have.' Andrew helped himself to a whisky. 'But, like I said, it doesn't affect us.'

Seb got to his feet. He also wanted to know how the press got that story. He'd find out, but for now, there was one more thing to do before the night was out. He shrugged on his jacket. 'I want both of you here tomorrow, first knockings. We have a delivery to finalise.'

'Where are you going?'

Half out of the door, Seb glanced irritably over his shoulder. *More bloody questions.* 'Bed. I'm knackered.'

Andrew raised one eyebrow as the door closed behind his brother. *Yeah, but whose bed?*

* * *

Walking from the Peacock, Seb glanced behind him. He wouldn't put it past Andrew to follow, making sure he was going to his own apartment. Not that he should have to justify his movements.

Gritting his teeth, Seb upped his pace, realising that maybe he needed to justify it to *himself.*

Nearing Sam's apartment, he glanced at his watch. It was almost two in the morning and he probably *should* have gone straight to bed rather than come here, but needed to put some space between him and Andrew before he swung for the twat.

His father's stinging words still grated on the nerves running the length of Seb's spine, but he was doing nothing wrong. He'd never let his family down and he never would.

Throwing his cigarette butt on the pavement, he ground it into the tarmac with the heel of his black leather shoe. Resisting the urge to light up another, Seb glanced up at Sam's Symphony Court apartment, unable to deduce if the lights were on behind the tightly closed drapes.

Well, *he* knew why he was here. He wanted to make sure Sam was okay. She knew what he'd been due to discuss with his parents today and he'd heard the reticence in her voice, despite her attempts to cloak it.

Seb frowned. But it wasn't just that. The pull Sam Reynold had on him was too strong to ignore. And he knew it.

* * *

Sam knew she shouldn't still be sitting here. She stared at the empty bottle of wine in front of her. There was another nicely chilled bottle of white calling her name from the direction of the fridge, but it was the middle of the night, and she couldn't afford to be off the ball.

In a trance-like state, she stared at the documents spread over her coffee table and blinked, hoping she'd made an intelligent decision by reverting the supply chain back to its original format. There may have been a good reason why John had wanted to move things about, but she doubted it...

Besides, it was the only option to take. The supply chain had functioned perfectly well up until now, so theoretically, it still would.

She stared at the paperwork, knowing she wasn't really looking at it. Her eyes might be, but her brain wasn't. *That* was as far away from supply chains as possible.

This paperwork didn't contain what she really wanted. And *that* she was no closer to finding. Maybe it didn't even exist? And if it didn't, what would she do then?

Sam jumped – actually *jumped* – at a sudden noise. Fear trickled up her spine and she tensed, unsure whether she'd heard anything or whether it was down to pure exhaustion.

The noise sounded again. This time, Sam recognised it as the intercom. She hastened to the speaker and pressed the buzzer. 'Yes?'

'Sam?'

Seb's gravelly voice brought both relief and apprehension. She pressed the door release button, her nerves fluttering. The contradiction between throwing herself into his arms and not wanting to act like a desperate woman ricocheted in her head.

Less than thirty seconds later, Seb reached the apartment door and as he pushed it open, all Sam's plans of acting calm and collected went out of the window.

8

It was unusual for Tom to get up anywhere near this sort of time. In fact, it was *unheard* of, but faced with Linda beside him in the cramped double bed, coupled with what had to be put in place this morning, was enough of an incentive to shift his arse with the first rays of dawn.

And he needed to shift his arse because time waited for no man – especially at the moment, so the earlier he was up, about and getting on with it, the better.

His face cracked into a grin. After risking the call to Lee last night, he now had it set in stone that no one was on the lookout for him. Even better, word on the street was that Maynard had gone AWOL – which translated as 'dead'.

Even so, that didn't mean Tom wanted to be spotted hanging around the Orchid. Neither did he wish to wait two days for Royal Mail to deliver the bloody letter either. Okay, so it meant trekking from Northfield to the centre of the city, but he had to get this letter in front of Sam Reynold before anyone else followed suit.

Pulling on his jeans, Tom glared at Linda, snoring like a walrus. She was a useless bastard. So much for wanting to meet her long-lost daughter. Last night the stupid cow had freaked out when he'd showed her the *Evening Mail*, especially when he'd suggested she book an appointment with the girl and explain who she was.

It should have been job done.

But that wasn't acceptable to the craggy old boot, was it? No, because she'd gone mental again – saying she couldn't face it... What if she wasn't believed? Someone like *her* would never be admitted into a place like *that*... She needed time... She wasn't up to it...

Tom's face slid into a scowl. Well, fuck that. There wasn't time to piss about.

But he'd done well in his restraint. He'd swallowed the easy option of smothering Linda in her own bed for being a useless, selfish bitch and instead, much as it had grated on his wick, he'd blathered that he understood. He'd even comforted her for a few minutes. But only because he had a Plan B.

He'd half-expected Linda to let him down. She'd always been a disappointment, but it was fine. He'd play it her way. Or rather let her *think* he was playing it her way...

Shoving the letter in his pocket, Tom was halfway out the door when Linda stirred. 'Where are you going?'

Swinging around, Tom replaced his snarl with a pleasant expression, despite how much it hurt his face. 'Just popping out, bab. Thought I'd get some supplies in.'

A glimmer of panic formed in Linda's brain. 'You *are* coming back, aren't you? You won't disappear again? I couldn't st...'

'Don't be daft!' Tom cried. 'After I've found you again? I'm not stupid, Lin.' But he *was* desperate and, despite wishing he'd never stepped back into Linda's train-wrecked, shithole of a life, needs must. 'I won't be long, I promise. Now get yourself up and dressed.'

Linda watched Tom's retreating figure hurry down the dark hallway and the familiar sense of desolation washed over her once again.

* * *

Lying breathless and satiated, not for the first time that morning, Sam waited for her thundering heart to resume a normal rhythm.

Her gaze moved to the large expanse of glass in the bedroom of the beautiful apartment that her father had bought for her. With the curtains wide open, despite the early hour, the sun filled the large room with warmth and she could hear the buzz of movement from the Gas Basin below through the opened balcony doors.

But the problems seeped back into her mind like they always did.

Her usually smooth forehead creased. Even looking around her own home brought back the sharp reminder that her father was no more, along with the conflicting anger that the man she'd always held as her hero had hidden the truth.

'How are you feeling this morning?'

Seb's deep voice pulled Sam's thoughts back to the present. Although they'd touched on a few subjects last night, desire had over-taken and her all-consuming need for the man lying in her bed had won. *Again.*

This time, though, Sam resisted the magnetic pull of Seb's intensity. 'I'm okay.'

She might feel like a lovesick teenager with the unfamiliar effect Seb Stoker had on her, but she didn't have to *act* like it. 'I'm dreading how many more people will call the Orchid today, claiming to be my long-lost parents.'

She'd played down how often that had happened yesterday. According to reception, over twenty people had called within two hours. Sitting up in the bed, Sam's eyes remained fixed on the expensive floor-length curtains framing the balcony windows. 'I just can't work out how that paper got the story.'

'My brothers think it could have been something Maynard set up before he died. Perhaps a measure of security?' Seb wrapped a lock of Sam's glossy hair around his fingers, watching mesmerised as it unrav-elled and fell back in a loose wave against her left shoulder blade.

Shivering from Seb's light touch, Sam turned to him. 'And what do *you* think?' Half-propped on pillows, she stared at Seb's muscular arms, now behind his head, her eyes travelling down the defined ridges of his torso, feeling the familiar burn of desire reignite.

'I think you're beautiful, that's what I think.' A soft smile appeared on Seb's full lips. 'I'll put some feelers out and get to the bottom of it. For a start, I'll pay that reporter a visit and convince him to tell me who his sources are.'

Sam held Seb's gaze; his eyes had that hypnotic green intensity that she found cold, yet so exhilarating. 'No, don't. You've got your own things to concentrate on.' She didn't want Seb fighting her battles.

She glanced over at the bedside table, hearing the answer machine click on. As a familiar voice rang out after the beep, Sam swallowed down the lump in her throat.

'Hello, love,' Gloria said, her voice shaky. 'I guess you must be at work... I just wanted to see how you are... and... oh... I... I was hoping you'd call... I wondered if... whether you'd had a chance to think about when we can talk? Okay... well... Call me when you can... I love you...'

'When are you going to do that, Sam?' Seb asked. 'Biological or not, she's still your mother. You should at least hear her out.'

'I'm not sure I can face it yet.' Sam didn't look up. Seb's gaze boring into her was pressure enough. He was right, but it was too soon to face the reminder of betrayal. 'How did your parents take it finding out my mother, or should I say, *Gloria* – concealed the truth over those rumours about Gary?'

Seb's face hardened, his father's words replaying once more. 'Like you'd expect...'

Sam sighed sadly. 'They must hate me...'

'No, they don't,' Seb said, unwilling to tell Sam what his father had intimated. That would not be spoken of or even acknowledged.

Sam studied the fleeting glimpses of nameless emotions behind Seb's eyes. 'Has something happened that I need to know about? Don't protect me from the truth. I've had more than enough of that.'

Seb ran his hand slowly down the length of Sam's arm, her soft skin like velvet under his fingers. He'd find out who had gone to the press whether Sam liked it or not. Someone who knew the score had done that with the sole aim of hurting her. And for that they would pay.

The truth was, he *did* feel protective of her. This woman sparked something in him. Something *unknown*. 'You don't need to worry, Sam. Everything's in hand.'

'But I *want* to know. Warts and all! Look, if I'm going to be successful wi...' Sam frowned, the click of the answer machine interrupting once more.

'Sam? It's me. Are you in...? Just checking you're okay. I haven't had chance to catch up with you since that bloody article... I was going to pop round last night. Thought we could have a bottle of wine and a chat... Anyway... Give me a call or... I guess I'll see you later...'

'Who the fuck was that?' Seb frowned.

'Liam,' Sam said quickly. 'A friend.'

'A *friend*?' Seb raised an eyebrow. 'What kind of friend? A friend who "pops round"?'

Sam bristled. 'Like I said. A friend.' *Or he was...* 'From the Orchid,' she added.

'Ah, *that* Liam,' Seb said, inwardly irritated. He remembered exactly who that bloke was. He was that one with the goatee – the one he'd seen with Sam during that party for her thirtieth. *And he hadn't liked him then either.*

'Yes, *that* Liam. Not jealous, are you?'

'I don't do jealousy.' Reaching out, Seb closed his large hand around Sam's arm and, with a lopsided grin, playfully pulled her towards him.

'We've got things we need to discuss,' Sam protested weakly.

'I know that, Samantha.' Pulling Sam astride him, Seb raised an eyebrow. 'But I'd much prefer to stay where I am for the time being, if you don't mind?'

Feeling Seb more than ready for her again, Sam knew she was lost and any further protestations she made would be downright lies.

9

Having picked up a copy of today's *Mail* from a newsagent as he walked from Sam's apartment to the Peacock, Seb tucked the paper under his arm and loped up the steps to the back entrance of the casino.

Pushing the metal door open, he moved down the corridor toward his office in a much better mood than he'd been in last night.

Seb rubbed his hand over his chin, a sheepish grin sliding onto his face. That woman! There had never been *anyone* who had kept his interest like this, his needs piqued to distraction. Over a week now and yet he still couldn't get enough of her. The feel of her – the look in her eyes... *something*... kept him primed like never before.

But more disturbingly, he hadn't liked how he'd felt hearing that Liam bloke saying he'd 'pop round'. Did the man go to Sam's apartment a lot?

Whether he liked to admit it or not – and he didn't like admitting it – Seb didn't want anyone else taking up Sam's time. This was another first – being bothered about something like that. Yep, Sam Reynold had certainly done something to him. It wasn't just her looks and exquisite body that made his veins thrum with relentless desire – it was *her*. Everything about her inflamed him.

Entering his office, Seb nodded to his brothers, their impatient faces diluting his good mood. 'Okay, let's get started,' he said, slinging his suit jacket messily over the back of his chair. 'There's lots to do.'

'We're ready,' Andrew remarked. 'We've been waiting for you...'

Ignoring Andrew's comment, Seb sat down, putting the paper onto his desk.

'Anything of interest?' Neil nodded towards the newspaper.

'I haven't had chance to look.' Seb poured himself a coffee. But he *would* be looking. And he knew exactly what for. 'Right, this delivery tomorrow... Can one of you call Benny and check the finals?'

'Yeah, yeah, I'll do that, but is it wise to do this delivery?' Andrew asked.

Seb frowned. 'Why wouldn't we?'

'Ah!' Andrew waved his hand. 'Sorry. It's just that now you're so close to Sam Reynold and the Reynolds never liked dealing with the Irish, you might prefer not to upset her and bin off the whole idea of guns?'

Neil glanced at Andrew warily.

'What's your fucking issue, Andrew?' Seb spat, his eyes hard. 'We've been through this. Sam has nothing to do with our firm or who we deal with. How many more times?'

Andrew rolled his large shoulders and held Seb's glare. He crossed one ankle over his knee and folded his fingers together in his lap. 'I have an issue when things are being concealed.'

Seb fought to control his escalating temper. 'What the fuck am I supposed to be concealing? Christ, Andrew! What's the matter with you?'

'You said you were going to bed last night, but you went out instead,' Andrew continued, determined to get a rise. 'No guesses where to...'

Neil leant forward. 'Andrew... let's just concentrate on matters in hand. What about that Lee bloke? The one that fat old goat at the Aurora said had told her to keep Maynard occupied? You know, the night we went there.' He looked at Seb. 'Should we not follow up on it?'

'Bollocks to that!' Seb barked. 'Our business with that place is done. Maynard was the issue and he's no longer in the equation, so neither is the Aurora. I'm more interested in what *he's* angling at!' His glare moved to Andrew. 'If you've got something to say, then say it! You think you know all the ins and outs and can call the fucking shots.'

Andrew's eyes gleamed. 'Are you denying you went elsewhere last night?'

Standing up, Seb glowered. 'What exactly has it got to do with you whether I went out or not?'

Andrew shrugged. 'Nothing... unless the person you saw is detrimental to your concentration and therefore this firm. Then it has *everything* to do with me. If you aren't being truthful about that, what else are you keeping to yourself?'

A vein in Seb's temple throbbed. He wanted to lay Andrew out – give him a good kicking. 'It isn't me causing the firm problems. Remember Phil? Who was that down to?'

'I had to step in on that bec...'

'You had to do *nothing* other than follow instructions.' Seb paced around the desk. 'I'm not having this conversation! Neither will I discuss my personal business with you or anyone else. Only things concerning this *firm* are discussed. Get over yourself!'

Leaning into Andrew's face, he smiled slowly. 'Let's reiterate one simple thing here. *I'm* in charge of this firm, not you and not anyone else. My personal life is *mine*. Now sort this order, do the business and remember we have our brother's funeral in less than a week. Or have you forgotten?'

Andrew stiffened, his knuckles whitening as he gripped the chair. 'Don't use Gary to score points.'

'Let's go!' Swiftly getting to his feet, Neil grabbed Andrew's arm, giving him a look that spelled loud and clear to leave it. 'Andrew? Now!'

Shrugging Neil's hand away, Andrew got to his feet, giving Seb a long hard stare as he was shepherded from the office.

Seb thrummed with adrenaline and pent-up frustration. He sat back down in his chair as the office door closed behind his brothers.

God, he hated this.

Out of all of his brothers, Andrew had always been the hardest working – in lots of ways, the one most similar to himself, but lately he'd become different. Resentful. *Unpredictable.*

And it all centred around *him* – like Andrew hated him. Hated *everyone.*

Opening the paper, Seb flicked through the pages. He'd remember that reporter's name as soon as he saw it. And when he did, he'd be making it his business to pay the bloke a visit, *regardless* of what Sam thought.

* * *

Despite it being one of her favourite salads and a restaurant she loved, Sam picked at her food, absentmindedly pushing it around the plate.

It was a beautiful day; the sun shone down onto the table's parasol in the alfresco seating area of the canal-side restaurant. She'd come here to give herself a break from the confines of her office at the Orchid, yet she could not shift the weight sitting around her shoulders.

After the night she'd just spent with Seb, she should be in a much better mood, but the feeling that something nameless was about to happen constricted her every breath.

If she didn't get people like Kevin onside, regardless of what Seb had done to help her, then she was sunk. She couldn't rely on third parties, whoever they were, to do this for her.

And she couldn't deal with anything while sitting here.

Catching the waiter's attention, Sam gestured for the bill and picked up her handbag.

Before the waiter had even released his hand from the plate

holding the bill, Sam placed a twenty-pound note on the table. 'Many thanks. Keep the change,' she said, smiling stiffly.

Sam hurried out of Brindley Place and moved back along the next road, avoiding looking in the direction she used to take to the design company where she had, up until recently, worked. That was when her life was simpler; when there was everything to look forward to, when she'd known who she was...

Reaching the Orchid, Sam headed through the lobby, purposely keeping her eyes fixed ahead.

'Miss Reynold?'

Sam toyed with ignoring the receptionist and carrying on to the sanctuary of her office. She couldn't face knowing how many more people had called, pretending to be her parents. Neither did she want the undertone of sympathy when people spoke to her or to see the slight embarrassment when they looked at her.

Not one of her staff had said a word about the proverbial elephant in the room. *Not one.* Every single person must have seen the paper and discussed it in hushed voices during their breaks. *Speculating...*

'Miss Reynold?' the receptionist trilled once more.

Sam plastered on a smile. She wouldn't resort to rudeness. It wasn't *their* problem her life had taken such a ghastly turn. 'Yes, Elaine? What is it?' She furtively glanced around for anyone parent-shaped that could be lurking.

'I've put a letter on your desk. I didn't realise you hadn't been given it until I came on shift.'

'Thanks,' Sam muttered, continuing into the corridor.

Shutting her office door, she put her handbag onto a spare chair and slung her jacket on the coat stand. She reached for a bottle of mineral water from the small chiller, spying the white envelope on her desk.

Frowning, she peered closer. *No postmark?* It had been hand delivered? At least it wasn't another huge packet from the *Mail.*

Unscrewing the water bottle, Sam sat down and ripped open the envelope.

Strange, she thought, eyeing the messy fold of the lined piece of paper – the type found in a child's exercise book.

Unfolding the letter, Sam's heart lurched at the scruffy misspelt words.

Dear Sammatha,

I saw the paper. I think your my daughter.

My names Linda Matthews (Devlin). I had a baby girl on 15th June 1965.

My parent sold the baby against my wishes to a wellthy couple. I don't know who they was.

I know your name is different now but I called you Violet.

Most nights I'me in the Hen and Chicks in Northfield if you want to meet. I hope you will come.

Linda

Sam's heart thumped. The paper hadn't mentioned her original name that had been on the note accompanying her as a baby. The only living people who knew that were Gloria, Seb and herself, unless Gloria or Seb had told anyone?

The date of birth was wrong, though – by two days.

Sam frowned. Was it possible the day she'd been told was her birthday wasn't the day of her actual birth, but the day she'd been sold?

Perspiration formed. This meant this letter could be from her mother. Her *real* mother...

The trembling in her fingers travelled through her hands into her arms, then into her body. Her heart beat so heavily she was sure it must be audible elsewhere.

She reached for the bottle of water, her unsteady hand knocking it over, the water splashing over her desk. She yanked the piece of paper up as though it was gold and stared at it once more.

The Hen and Chicks? A pub? Why hadn't this woman just given an address or phone number?

Placing the letter on a dry part of the desk, Sam rested her chin in her hands. She'd wanted a name for the faceless people who had created her, but she hadn't wanted to *meet* them. Had she?

Her eyes tracked back to the letter.

...sold the baby against my wishes...

She'd been adamant she wouldn't want to meet the people who had sold her, but now she wasn't so sure. Should she meet this woman? This woman who could be her mother? *Linda Matthews?*

10

Linda did her best to smile at Vera as she reached across the sticky tabletop to grasp the pint of Strongbow.

She'd cadged her drink from a bloke called Minto who was always happy to buy drinks for anything with breasts. It was a good job because she was skint. There were another two days before giro day. She could have sworn she had a tenner in her purse before, but it was certainly not there now, and the fiver Tom had given her hadn't lasted long. A few double vodkas and that was it. *Gone.*

Linda's hand fumbled with what remained of her squashed fags. They'd never last either. All she wanted to do was get off her head so she didn't have to think. Thinking was bad. It hurt too much.

She had to stay off the crack. She'd promised herself she wouldn't take that stuff again. It had taken ages to get off it all those years ago and she doubted she'd have managed had it not been for Vera. But when Tom had handed her the pipe after telling her about her long-lost daughter, it had been too overpowering to resist. In fact, she'd almost *welcomed* it. Anything to divert from the pain. But the clawing depression following her high was a classic sign of a downer. She wouldn't go there again.

Relying on cider, weed and pills had been sufficient to block out her life enough to get by since, so she just had to ensure those continued to work.

Linda stared at the rapidly diminishing level in her pint glass. It was all very well Tom insisting she go for drinks with Vera, but he should have checked with her first. She wasn't up to it. There was too much stuff swirling in her head.

Linda gulped at her cider. At least Tom had backed off about going to see the girl. She had to get her head around it first. And even then...

Wiping her nose with the back of her sleeve, Vera watched Linda scouring the bar for more contenders to put their hand in their pocket and buy her a drink. *Some things never changed.*

If Linda was so desperate to get out of the house and have a break, then she'd have thought the woman would have said more than two words? They'd been here over an hour and hardly a sentence had been spoken.

She mentally totted up how many more drinks she could afford before her cash ran out. No doubt Linda expected her to stump up for *hers* now too, giving her the usual spiel of paying her back. Not that she ever would.

Linda had never been good at making money last. And judging by the state of her the last couple of days, things had hit the fan.

'What went on the other night, Lin?' Vera asked. 'I could hear you sobbing from miles away.'

Linda's head snapped up. 'Oh, just one of my panic attacks. You know I get them sometimes.'

'But not usually that bad!' Vera frowned. 'And that bloke. Where's he come from? It wasn't anything to do with him, was it? No offence, but he was a bit cagey. Fucking rude, to be honest. He all but said I was a nosy bitch for wanting to see if you were okay.'

Linda swirled the dregs of her cider around the glass, then fumbled with her cigarettes. Her bottom lip quivered. If only she could tell Vera about Samantha and about who Tom really was, then she might get some guidance. But Tom had told her to say nothing to anyone about Samantha. *Including Vera.*

'It was nothing to do with him,' she lied. 'Things just got on top of me about the kids... you know...' Her face crumpled and she choked back a sob. 'I'm such a fucking awful person, V. I've let all of my kids down. *All* of them.'

Vera frowned. When she'd seen Linda's new bloke again this morning in the stairwell, she'd asked how things were, but he hadn't mentioned Linda's meltdown was about the kids, he'd just roped her into dragging Linda out for a drink.

'Oh, Vera,' Linda slurred. 'Tom keeps telling me none of it's my fault. He's been great, but I should have done better.'

Vera grabbed Linda's grubby hand. 'You mustn't think like that. What this Tom bloke said is right. There was nothing you could have done over what life's handed you. You're not an awful person. You've let no one down.'

Not exactly true. How many of Linda's kids had she actually brought up herself? Not many. The state had taken that responsibility, but Linda had been dealt so many crap cards over the years, it was hardly surprising things had turned out that way.

'But it *is* true and now... now it's even worse,' Linda blurted, helping herself to Vera's pint. Tears burned the back of her eyes. She knew what people thought of her. What her *kids* thought of her. Even what the kids she *didn't* know probably thought of her.

Drink was all she was good for. It was the only thing to take the edge off everything. All that *continued* to take the edge off what a bad person she was.

Vera watched Linda slurping at her hard-earned pint. Now the woman was blatantly drinking *her* beer? *Great...*

'I don't want to talk about this any more,' Linda muttered.

'How about you tell me who this bloke is, then? I've never seen him before, but he's living at yours already?' Vera nodded at Linda's belly. 'Be careful you don't cop again, eh?'

Linda shook her head resolutely, her alcohol-red eyes attempting to focus on her lighter. 'That will not be happening,' Linda said hastily. 'Tom's someone I was with ages ago. I really like him and... erm... we've decided to give things another go.'

Vera stared at Linda sadly. When they'd first met back in 1966 at an all-night café in Digbeth, Vera had felt sorry for the young girl – an obvious runaway hoping to make a few quid on the street. She'd immediately liked the quiet, pretty girl, so taking her under her wing had seemed the right thing to do.

Being a brass herself, she'd helped Linda by showing her the ropes; the best places to pick up men and how to avoid the grasping clutches of pimps scouring the streets looking for girls exactly like her. But Linda had been on a path to self-destruction and there was only so much Vera had been able to do. She couldn't force the girl to insist the punters wore condoms. Neither could she stop her from shacking up with bad 'uns who promised her the world and then disappeared.

Linda had once said, whilst off her head, some bloke promising to marry her, getting her pregnant and then buggering off was what had triggered the slippery slope of her life. Now it was as if she was punishing herself in the pursuit of someone who loved her like no other.

Hold on a minute. That bloke had been called Tom... Vera tugged Linda's hand. 'This man in your flat. It's not that one you told me about? That bloke from years back?'

Linda almost choked. 'No, of course not!' *Shit.* She'd been stupid for saying all of this. Could she tell Vera? Tom would never know. No. She mustn't. She'd promised.

Vera eyed Linda suspiciously. 'So what kicked off all this about your mothering ability?'

Linda wrung her hands in her lap. Vera was suspicious. She'd have to say something feasible – just not everything. She had to tell someone about Samantha. She just *had* to. 'Tom was one of the few who knew about my daughter. Th-that's why he came. He had news about her...'

Vera stared at the hope on her friend's face. It was something she'd never seen in all the years she'd known her and it revealed a glimpse of the beautiful young woman Linda had once been. 'You mustn't put faith into that. You told me ages ago no one knew where that baby went.'

'You don't understand, V,' Linda cried. 'By fluke, Tom has discovered where my daughter is, so now I can put everything right at last.'

* * *

Sitting in his motor in the station car park, Seb glanced at the dashboard clock, determined not to let his increasing frustration get the better of him.

He had a decent view of the trains coming and going, as well as clear sight of disembarking passengers. The next train due in from New Street should be here in precisely six minutes.

It didn't mean Brian Sumner would be on that train, but he hadn't been on the last two and there were only three more likely to contain the man. That was providing he hadn't chosen tonight to chase a story or go for drinks after work. Reporters were well known for not keeping sociable hours.

Seb cracked his knuckles. He hoped Sumner had clocked off at a normal time because he didn't have the patience to sit here people-watching all bloody night.

Sparking up a cigarette, he sighed, bored rigid. Normally, a runner would do a job such as this, but considering the question he would be asking, it had to be him.

He flicked the radio on. Keeping one eye on the raised platform in the distance, he half-listened to the news on BRMB: 'The body found at Gravelly Hill yesterday morning has been formally identified as Tonya Blunt.'

Seb's ears pricked up, his senses on alert.

'Speaking to relatives, it is alleged the thirty-five-year-old from Yardley had recent personal issues which may have led to the suicide. No one else is being sought over this matter. Our thoughts go out to Tonya's family, including her two young children. Anyone experiencing suicidal thoughts, please call the Samaritans on...'

Switching the radio off, Seb frowned, guilt prodding at the back of his mind. If Andrew hadn't offloaded Tonya's husband, then those kids might at least still have a mother.

Before his burgeoning anger could fester further, he heard the distinct rumble of an approaching train and his eyes darted back to the platform.

Squinting into the twilight, Seb scanned the people as they disembarked and filed down the metal steps towards the car park. As they thinned out, he resigned himself to wait for the next train. *Then he saw him.*

Getting out of the car, he leant casually against the driver's door, and waited until the man had drawn level.

'Mr Sumner? Do you have a moment?' Seb's voice was pleasant as he stepped from the shadows.

Immediately recognising the man blocking his way, Brian's stomach leapt into his throat, all thoughts of his long-awaited dinner diminishing. 'Mr Stoker!' he gabbled. 'Are you waiting for a train?' *Stupid question.* The man was leaning against a car that must be his. Not many people had motors like *that* around here.

Seb smiled, his straight white teeth bright in the darkening evening. 'I just want a word, if you have the time?'

Brian's feet did a strange fidgety dance. He desperately wanted to say he was busy and would call from the office tomorrow, but he knew he couldn't. *Not to Sebastian Stoker.* Instead, his mouth spoke against his will. 'Yes, of course!'

'Hop in.' Seb motioned to the passenger seat and waited for Brian Sumner to hesitantly clamber in. Shutting the driver's door behind him, he settled into his seat. 'I have a question I hope you can help with, Brian,' he said. 'You don't mind me calling you Brian, do you?'

Brian shook his head a little too fast. 'No, that's fine.'

Seb placed his hands on the steering wheel, running a finger slowly along the stitching of the top-quality leather. 'It's about that story...'

'Story?' Brian blathered. 'I cover a lot of stories... I...'

'The one about Samantha Reynold...'

'Oh, yes, a strange business, that. No one would have suspected in a million years th...'

'Has anyone called in about her parents yet?' Seb asked, still pleasant. *Slowly, slowly.*

Brian felt himself relax. 'We've had bloody hordes of them! All tricksters after a quick buck and five minutes of fame. You know what it's like?' *No! Don't say that. He might think you're referring to him.* 'I meant th...'

'You don't believe any of them to be kosher?'

'I don't think so,' Brian continued. 'But I've couriered the responses we've received so far over to Ms Reynold. After all, she deserves to know who she really is, doesn't she?'

The gurgling laugh following Brian's comment incensed Seb more than he thought possible. His jaw tightened. *This bloke really was a cocksucker.* 'Can I ask where you got your information?' He faced Brian, his pose relaxed, his eyes anything but.

'Oh, come now, Mr Stoker! You know we can't give out the names of our sources. That would break confidentiality,' Brian chuckled, still far too relaxed for his own good.

'But what about Samantha Reynold? Does causing problems for her not bother you? What if the story is untrue?'

Brian felt a flutter of fear and looked at Seb Stoker again in the half-light. He still seemed pleasant and relaxed, so nothing to worry about. 'Oh, it's true, all right.'

'The source?' Seb was rapidly losing both his patience and his nice act. 'I want the source.' *This bloke was getting on his tits.*

'But I...'

Seb's eyes glinted. 'You haven't answered my question and I suggest that you do.' His cold expression cracked into a full smile as he patted Brian just that little bit too hard on the shoulder. 'Longbridge is a small suburb. It won't be difficult to locate your home... Perhaps your wife would be... shall we say... more accommodating?'

Looking into the harsh glare of Seb Stoker's eyes, the piercing green visible even in the gloom, Brian knew he had no choice. Marge would have a fit if this man turned up at the house. 'Leave my wife out of it. What I report on is nothing to do with her!'

Seb smiled pleasantly, enjoying the man's discomfort. It served the greasy hack right. Running personal stories might sell papers, but it was shit for the people behind the headlines. 'I'm not sure why you think I'm insinuating anything might happen to your lovely wife, Brian? All I meant was that Margaret might be more amenable to questioning than you.' *Oh, he'd done his homework: Brian Sumner, fifty-two, married to Margaret. Three children. Yeah, yeah – come on, Brian...*

Brian paled further. *Seb Stoker knew Marge's name?* Why had he been so stupid to think otherwise? The man was notorious – everyone knew that.

Suddenly, a light came on in his mind. *Wait a minute. He was being daft.* Seb Stoker knew about this from the off. This was a test. His trustworthiness was being tested. *Thank God for that! Panic over.*

His smile returned. 'You had me worried there for a minute,' Brian laughed. 'There's no need to doubt me, Mr Stoker. Like I said, I keep my word.'

Seb stared at Brian unflinchingly. Was this bloke a sandwich short of a picnic?

Momentarily returning the smile, his face then morphed into a snarl as he moved at the speed of light. Grabbing Brian Sumner around the throat, Seb slammed him into the passenger side window. 'Don't take the piss,' he spat. 'You have precisely five seconds to tell me who gave you information about Sam Reynold.' With his free hand, he pulled his knife from his waistband and held it level with Brian's eyes.

With his cheek squashed against the glass and a crushed windpipe, it was difficult to move or speak, but Brian saw the glinting blade inches from his face as clear as day. His stomach fell from his throat down into his shoes, his bowels making a worrying gurgling sound.

An odd-sounding squeak escaped from his crushed voice box, which he hoped conveyed he'd talk. With relief, he felt the iron grip around his throat loosen slightly, but the vice-like grip remained in situ and the knife was definitely still there...

He closed his eyes in the hope that everything would go away, but it didn't. 'B-but you must know...' Brian spluttered. 'I thought tha...'

'Get. On. With. It...' Seb resumed the pressure on the man's neck.

'Y-your brother!' Brian squawked. 'It was your brother, Andrew. I – I thought... I mean, you knew, right?'

Seb faltered, but only for a split second. *Andrew? Andrew sold the story?*

Dropping his grip, Seb shoved the knife back in the holder under his jacket. 'That wasn't so hard now, was it? Just testing your resolve.' He smiled coldly. 'You fucking failed!'

Brian blinked, his hand rubbing the side of his head. 'But you're his brother! It's not like I said anything to anyone else. I wouldn't... I...'

'That's hardly the point. You still squealed. You're lucky it was to me and not anyone else.' Leaning across, Seb opened the passenger door and pushed Brian Sumner out onto the litter-strewn tarmac. 'There will be no more stories about Sam, understand? Now fuck off home!'

He couldn't have the likes of Brian Sumner or *anyone* knowing that he hadn't a clue Andrew had done that. That's if that was what had *really* happened. Undermined by his own *brother*? Well, he'd made his point. Sumner wouldn't be going down *that* road again.

Firing the engine, Seb screeched out of the car park before the shock underneath his black rage was noticed.

11

'Where's that bloke, Ma?' Tayquan asked. 'Has he moved out?'

Hacking up a ball of phlegm from the back of her throat after the usual morning coughing fit, Linda wiped her nose with the back of her hand and stared at her son accusingly. 'You'd like that, wouldn't you?' she snapped. 'Do you want me to be miserable all my life? Is that it?'

Watching Tayquan's face drop, a familiar wave of guilt washed over Linda. It wasn't Tayquan's fault Tom had bloody upped and left her for the second time.

And there she was, stupid enough to actually become optimistic for once in her godforsaken life that she could put things right, that things were on the up... She was back with her first and only love, her daughter was alive and well, and best of all, she now knew *where* she was. Yet, like yet another slap in the face, the glaring truth had hit her once again.

Opening the fridge, she stared at the forlorn, empty shelves. 'We haven't got any milk, or come to think of it, cereal, so grab yourself a packet of crisps.'

Tayquan frowned. Although more than secretly glad his mum's new boyfriend had lasted for less time than the usual ones, he was starving. 'I had crisps for breakfast yesterday, Ma. At school, they say that if you don't have a proper breakfast, it wi...'

'Then tell the school to provide your fucking breakfast themselves!' Linda snapped, despising herself even more.

And that was it, wasn't it? *Look at her.* A complete mess who couldn't even provide the two kids she had left with anything other than bloody crisps. All she did was bite their heads off. She was a hopeless, hateful, spiteful cow. It was no wonder Tom had run off into the sunset.

She must have been insane to think *anyone* would give her the time of day.

Pulling her dressing gown around her, Linda grabbed a can of cider from the otherwise bare fridge and slumped into the chair at the kitchen table, watching Tayquan root through the cupboard.

'I'm sorry for snapping at you. It's not been a good day,' Linda muttered, the sound of the can's ring pull loud in the otherwise quiet room. 'Where's Shondra?'

Tayquan shrugged. 'She went round a friend's place.'

'What? At 8.30 in the morning?' Linda cried, greedily slurping at the cider.

Tayquan didn't want to say that Shondra's mate's mum gave her breakfast every day, as well as a packed lunch to take to school. Even though his mum shouted at him half the time, he didn't want to upset her, and telling her that *would* upset her.

'Do you not like Tom?' Linda asked suddenly.

Tayquan shrugged his little shoulders noncommittally. 'He was okay,' he muttered. *No, he wasn't.* He hated him, but he couldn't say that either. 'I didn't like what he said about me and Shondra ruining your life, though.'

Linda was about to light her cigarette, her hand stopping halfway to her mouth. 'He said that?'

Tayquan nodded resolutely.

Linda's eyes narrowed as she slammed the lighter down, the noise making Tayquan drop his half-eaten crisps on the floor. 'You nasty boy!' she screamed. 'Tom wouldn't say something so wicked.'

'B-but he did! He sa...'

Getting to her feet, Linda pulled Tayquan away from the table by his arm. 'Get out of my sight!' she screeched. 'Don't ever lie to me again!'

Tayquan rushed from the room, trying desperately not to cry, leaving Linda to slump back down at the table.

Tom wouldn't have said that to the kids, would he? He'd said he was happy to take them on as his own. They'd be a *proper* family.

* * *

Seb walked along Corporation Street past Rackhams, returning nods to the greetings he received from people along the way.

This was like being back in the old days, he thought, mindful of the years he'd undertaken similar tasks during his steady rise to the guaranteed place as head of the Stoker firm.

These days, he or one of his brothers would just put in the bog-standard phone call to confirm the order once all the back-end work had been done by the runners. That would be the extent of the inner circle's involvement until the actual day of the deal.

The back-end work *had* been done for this job, but Seb needed a reason to not be stuck behind his desk at the Peacock. Sometimes it was nice to roll his sleeves up and not be the boss, but the *real* reason for this excursion was to put space between himself and Andrew.

Half the night he'd lain awake with what he'd learned from that hack reporter, and he didn't yet know how he would move forward with it.

Andrew couldn't have supplied that story to the press about Sam's parentage. Why would he?

Shoving his hands deeper into his pockets, Seb continued. Oh, sure, he knew there was no love lost between Andrew and Sam, but to do that? It was out of character. *Underhand.* Not how the Stokers worked.

In the same vein, Seb knew he could be asked why *he'd* been digging for that information in the first place. After all, the story about Sam's parents wasn't anything to do with him and it didn't affect the firm, so why had he given chase? Sam was nothing to do with them. But she was *everything* do with *him*...

Seb crossed the road, glancing at the distinctive signage of Oasis and figured he'd cut through the shop to Dale End.

Manoeuvring through the plentiful racks of studded leather jackets, hippy tops, PVC skirts and biker boots, Seb gritted his teeth as Dead Kennedys screeched through the tinny speakers at an ear-splitting level. Although he stood out like a sore thumb in his suit, groups of punks, bikers and goths nodded to him as he loped up and down the rabbit warren of stairs linking the different levels of the shop.

Finally exiting from one of the back doors, Seb pushed his way through the market and headed to the place he was after, his thoughts meandering. Aside from dealing with Andrew, what would he say about it to Sam? That he suspected his brother of splashing her personal business all over the city? The personal business that Andrew only knew because of what *he'd* recounted to his brothers as well as their parents?

Seb scowled. He couldn't tell Sam. She didn't need to know. It would upset her. And he didn't want to believe that Andrew had done it. It was better that way.

Firstly, though, he would deal with *this*. At least it was straightforward.

Reaching the shop, Seb ground his cigarette butt onto the pavement and looked up at the shabby façade – the perfect front for what went on in the background.

He pushed open the old wooden door of Bert's Fishing Tackle and walked in, the tinkling of the bell loud. The pungent smell of maggots and bait in trays on the counter assaulted his nostrils – one thing he hadn't missed by not coming here in person.

'Come through to the back, Mr Stoker,' Benny smiled, waiting as Seb followed into the backroom.

Seb scanned the multitude of boxes stacked on metal shelving around the perimeter of the stockroom. 'These mine?'

Benny nodded ingratiatingly. 'Yes. All of this here is yours.' He moved towards a row of metal racking at the back left and pulled out a large box.

Seb lifted the lid and peered at the selection of guns within. 'It looks a decent batch.' He then glanced around the rest of the jam-packed storeroom. 'Where's the rest?'

Benny nodded. 'The rest? This was all that was on order.'

Seb's brow furrowed. This man was talking bollocks. 'What the bloody hell are you going on about? The rest was confirmed yesterday.'

Perspiration beaded on the back of Benny's neck. 'I – I didn't receive a call yesterday...'

'Are you questioning me?' Seb snarled, his eyes narrowing. He distinctly remembered Andrew agreeing to put the call in to Benny. 'My clients are expecting their full shipment tomorrow. Untrustworthy is something I am not.'

'No, no you're not,' Benny blathered. 'Everyone knows how trustworthy you are. I... erm...'

'You've failed to deliver the goods we ordered, so don't expect your fucking commission, you prick!' Seb roared. 'But what are you going to do about making me look like a cunt?'

'I...'

'Fucking save it!' Seb glowered. 'I'm disappointed, Benny. *Very* disappointed. I need trusty suppliers, not dithering Boy Scouts!'

'B-but this is the first time anything like this has happened. We've had an arrangement for *years* and I've never let you down, Mr Stoker,' Benny garbled, his panic intensifying. 'I can assure you that I didn't receive a call yesterday from anyone. I...'

'Are you calling me a fucking liar?' Seb pinned the man to the stock room wall. 'I pay you handsomely to bring in the stock, yet you've fucked it up!'

Benny squirmed under the grip of Seb's crushing hand. 'I...'

'I'll send a van to pick this up tonight at ten. Make sure you're here to deal with it,' Seb instructed. 'I expect the rest tomorrow without fail. Is that clear?'

Sweat ran down Benny's back. He crumpled with relief as the grip around his neck loosened. 'I'm sorry about the mix-up. I was sure th...'

'I don't want excuses!' Seb snarled. 'Just sort it!' Turning on his heels, he yanked open the stock room door and passed through the shop.

'Fucking idiot,' he muttered as he sauntered back to the subway, stopping to buy a paper from one of the many kiosks imbedded in the subterranean walkway.

It was only as he put his hand in his pocket to grab some change that Seb recalled the dig Andrew had made about Sam's attitude towards the gun deals. Had Andrew purposefully not finalised the order to make him look incompetent?

12

The relentless sunshine burning into his eyelids forced Tom to open one eye. Faced with the searing of his retina, he shut it again just as quickly and began the job of unsticking his furry tongue from the roof of his mouth.

Which bastard had visited in the middle of the night and welded his gob then? He felt rougher than a bear's arse.

Summoning the courage to open both eyes, he bared his teeth in a grimace then blinked rapidly, hoping it would add moisture to his eyeballs.

He must have put away a shedload last night. Had he picked up some more gear? He hoped he had some left over because, by Christ, he needed some right now.

As the mildewed ceiling came into focus, Tom suddenly realised where he was and smiled at the arm belonging to Tina laying across his chest.

Yep, the Aurora. And by the looks of it, he'd had a good night.

The vague memory of smoking that crack sample, then telling Lee to place a large order, surfaced.

He grinned, then winced as his dry lips split. From what he recalled, that gear would do nicely.

None too gently shoving Tina's skinny arm off his chest, Tom raked his fingers through his hair, scowling as he caught a knot, pain stabbing in his thumping head.

His eyes ran appreciatively over the young, slim and naked body next to him and, despite feeling like he'd been dug up, a familiar throbbing began in his groin.

There must be a can of something lying around here. Once he'd wet his whistle, he'd give this bird another good seeing to.

He pushed himself up onto the thin, greying pillow and glanced around the bedroom, inwardly irritated with the mess. He'd told these tarts time and time again about keeping the rooms spick and span for the punters. Something else he'd have to drill into their thick heads again.

Spotting what looked like an unfinished can of Carling on the bedside table, Tom leant over to grab it, then froze.

Shit! His eyes darted to the clock. *Bollocks.* Ten o'clock in the bloody morning? Jesus Christ. Linda!

Clambering out of bed, immediately rendered incapable from the unbearable pounding in his skull, Tom clung onto the cheap metal bed frame. How could he have let this happen? After Linda had gone down the boozer with that addled old tramp, Vera, he'd grabbed the chance of coming over here. It was only supposed to be a quick catch up with Lee, followed by a sample of the crack and a decent shag. He wasn't supposed to crash out!

As the pounding in his head calmed to a manageable level, Tom scrabbled for his discarded clothes off the floor, his ragged breath rasping loudly as he dragged on his jeans and T-shirt.

Fuck, fuck, fuck!

He was supposed to get back before Linda had returned to see if Sam Reynold had arrived at the Hen and Chicks. Surely no one could resist the temptation of meeting their real mother? And he'd gone and missed it.

Spying a couple of tenners on the side that he presumed belonged to Tina, Tom shoved them into his jeans pocket, adding to what he'd helped himself to from the safe, then pushed his feet into his trainers. He had to get back pronto. Linda was so paranoid, she'd think he'd disappeared again and then he'd be back to square one.

Or worse – what if Sam *had* turned up and Linda had gone off with her?

He needed to get a move on topping Linda up with crack to keep her compliant. He'd heard from several sources she'd once been a heavy addict, therefore the urge would still be in her. It might be dormant, but it shouldn't take much and the couple of toots she'd had the other day should have kicked her off nicely.

Once an addict, *always* an addict. But by stupidly allowing himself to become complacent, he'd risked losing momentum. Linda might even start thinking for herself. That he could *not* allow.

Shrugging his jacket on, Tom felt like he might have a heart attack. He hadn't even had a fag yet, but there was no time.

'What you doing?'

Tom spun around to see Tina blearily staring at him, rubbing her tangled hair. 'I'm off. What do you think I'm doing?'

'But Tommy,' Tina whined. 'I thought you were back for good? Last night you said th...'

'Shut it!' Tom hissed. 'I ain't got time for your bleating.'

Tina petulantly folded her arms over her tiny but pert breasts. 'But you sa...'

'What the fuck has it got to do with you *what* I do, you silly tart?' Tom roared, finding the energy to jump onto the bed. Grabbing Tina's face, he yanked her towards him. 'I own this place and you work for *me*, remember?'

'Tom!' Tina screeched. 'You're hurting me!'

'I'll do more than that if you ever question me again, you stupid slag,' Tom spat. 'Now clear this fucking mess up, otherwise you'll find yourself out of a job!'

With that, he shoved Tina out of bed onto the floor. Rummaging through her discarded jeans, Tom helped himself to Tina's crack stash. This would see Linda through until he got his hands on more.

Leaving Tina sobbing on the filthy carpet, Tom stomped from the room and thundered down the rickety stairs, hoping his car was still in the car park. If that had been pinched, then he was even more screwed.

He had to get back and find out what had happened and could only hope he wasn't too late.

The door slammed against the wall as Seb burst into Neil and Andrew's shared office, along the corridor from his own. Storming over to the desk, he pulled the girl sitting astride Neil off his lap.

Neil's eyes jerked open in shock. 'What the...?'

'Get lost!' Seb growled at the woman, a speck of spittle landing on her cheek. Picking a red lacy thong up from the floor with his thumb and forefinger, he threw it into the girl's face. 'I haven't the first clue who you are, but get the hell out of my club.'

Yelping, the girl dashed from the room, her face the colour of a post box.

'For Christ's sake,' Neil moaned, shoving himself back into his trousers. 'Can't a man get any perks around here? What's the big deal?'

'Where's Andrew?' Seb's eyes were wide with fury. 'First the paper, then the balls-up with the order and now I return to find your office like a knocking shop? You call this helping run this firm, do you? I'm sick of this shit!'

'What's all the aggro?' Andrew burst into the office. 'I can hear you down the bleeding corridor!'

Seb swung around. 'I've just come back from Benny's. The rest of the order wasn't confirmed. Which one of you didn't bother to do that, then?' Moving forward, he poked Andrew in the chest. 'Because it was *one* of you.'

Grabbing Seb's wrist, Andrew twisted it and pulled it away. 'Now you wait a minute. Don't you co...'

'Being as you said you'd do it, I suspect it was *you!*' Seb jerked his wrist away from Andrew's grip. 'Neil's far too busy shagging to put the effort into ballsing anything up that matters!'

Andrew rolled his eyes. 'Wow! That's rich coming from the person who disappears with the rivals!'

Seb's green eyes glittered with rage. 'And that's your reason to sell a story to the paper, is it?'

'What?' A smirk slowly creased Andrew's face. 'Oh, hang on... I see... running to Little Miss Innocent's aid after that article? Did she cry whilst sucking your dick? Ask you to dig her out of the shit again? How very sweet...' Folding his arms, he perched on the edge of the desk. 'Ask yourself this... Why would I waste my time selling stories about a spoilt little tart?'

It was Andrew's laugh that broke Seb's resilience. 'You lying bastard! The reporter *told* me it was you!'

'And you believed him?' Andrew sneered. 'Jesus Christ! What has that bitch done to you? Addled your fucking head?'

Seeing red, Seb launched himself at Andrew, his fist driving into his brother's face.

Taken off guard, Andrew crashed into the desk, his right eyebrow splitting, gushing blood over a pile of invoices.

Seb jumped astride his brother, his hands closing around his throat. Seeing only black rage, he tightened his grip, pressing down harder on Andrew's windpipe.

Pinning his brother's arms with his knees, Seb could concentrate on nothing, apart from the feel of his thumbs digging into the hard outline of Andrew's windpipe. He'd had enough. Had enough of Andrew's digs; of Andrew slagging everything off. Andrew was screwing the firm up and he wasn't having it.

Andrew's eyes bulged, the tip of his tongue extending between his lips as he struggled under Seb's brute strength.

With an immense amount of effort, Neil dragged Seb off their brother. 'What the hell are you doing, man? Stop this madness! Just fucking stop it!'

Gagging, Andrew pulled himself up into a sitting position and glared from under his split eyebrow at Seb in a combination of shock and resentment.

Panting from exertion, Seb stared at Neil and then turned to Andrew. 'Whatever shit you're playing, it stops here, otherwise I will fucking kill you! And that's a promise!' With that, he turned on his heels and left the office, slamming the door so loudly that the glass panel shattered, scattering thick chunks of safety glass over the floor.

* * *

Tom remained casual as he entered the flat, despite the cloying smell of grease from the blackened remains of old oil in the chip pan making his stomach roil. 'Lin? You up yet?'

Walking into the poky lounge, he glanced around, not noticing Linda at first. Slumped on one of the old armchairs, she sat motionless, the remains of a burnt-down cigarette in her hand. His irritation flared, but at least she was still here.

He was desperate to shake her and demand she tell him what had happened last night. Had Samantha turned up? What had gone on? Instead, he overrode his repugnance and stroked her hair. 'Why are you sitting here like this?'

Linda stared at Tom blankly. 'I – I thought you'd gone...'

'Gone?' Tom exclaimed. *If only.* 'Why would I have gone?'

'You didn't come back last night,' Linda gibbered, her resolve not to cry betraying her, until her nose twitched. Her eyes narrowed suspiciously. 'I can smell perfume. Have you been with someone else?'

His fist clenching behind his back, Tom gritted his teeth, yet afforded a wounded smile to slither onto his face. 'Don't be daft. I'm with you now, ain't I?'

'Where have you been, then?' Linda pressed.

'If you must know, I went to check on my club. You know, the one I told you about... I did tell you before you went out with Vera. Don't you remember?'

Linda's brow furrowed. *Had he?* She'd had a few last night – even before she'd got as far as the pub, so he might have done... Relief that Tom was back overshadowed the prodding worry and she reminded herself the quickest way to drive a man away was to nag. *She should say nothing.* At least then he'd stay. She couldn't face losing him again.

Realising Linda had seen sense and was keeping her pathetic thoughts to herself, Tom ploughed on. 'Did you have a good night?'

Linda shrugged. 'It was okay...'

Tom smiled amiably. 'It looks like you've had a nice break. The colour's back in your cheeks and everything!' *No, it wasn't. He'd seen better looking corpses.* 'Did you see anyone?'

Linda shook her head. 'Only the usual people.'

Tom bit back his disappointment. 'What? No new faces?'

'Like who?' Linda stared at the burnt-out cigarette between her fingers and dropped it in the ashtray.

Tom stopped himself pushing further. Samantha hadn't turned up? *Damn.* Maybe she hadn't got the letter? A wave of dread wriggled through him. What if she had no interest in meeting Linda?

No, she would. He *knew* she would. All women were far too nosy for their own good. She'd go there at some point, but that meant Linda would have to keep going too, just in case.

He passed Linda a fresh can of cider and cracked a beer open for himself. Forget the dog – he needed the hair from a herd of fucking wildebeest to get rid of this hangover. 'Why don't you go out again tonight?'

Linda sighed. 'I should be here for the kids.'

Tom flapped his hand. 'Oh, don't worry about them. I'll keep an eye on them.' *Like hell he would!*

'But I haven't got any money until giro day,' Linda moaned.

'Yes, you have.' Tom's fingers brushed against the roll of notes stuffed into his back pocket. From the grand he'd helped himself to from last week's takings at the Aurora, half would go to Luke Banner for the crack order, the rest he'd keep for himself as a well-earned bonus. But Linda could have *this*... He fished the two crumpled up tenners courtesy of Tina from his pocket. 'There you go, love. That will buy a few drinks, eh?'

Linda brightened considerably. Tom really did love her. Maybe this would work, after all? 'If you're sure...'

'Course,' Tom grinned, resenting every second more than the last. 'And...' He fished Tina's crack supply from his pocket. 'This will cheer you up too!'

'Thanks.' Linda stared at the tempting rocks in the bag.

Tom smiled smugly. This had better be worth it. *All of it had better be worth it.*

13

The ring of the telephone disrupted Sam's thoughts. 'Sam Reynold,' she said, disappointment at hearing the receptionist's over-cheerful voice flashing through her. 'What? Another one? Okay... no, don't bother. I'll pick it up myself the next time I come through.'

Replacing the receiver, Sam stared at the phone. Another packet from the *Mail*? Her mouth tightened. She didn't want it. She hadn't even looked at half of the last lot, giving it up as pointless. A queue of people declaring undying love for their long-lost child, or asking for money...

She'd filed all of it away, most of it unopened, ignoring the nagging thought that there was a tiny chance one of them might be from her real parents. And if she didn't open them, she'd never know...

Her eyes tracked to her handbag. But now there *definitely* wasn't the need.

Reaching for the piece of paper she'd put safely in the zipped compartment, Sam took it out once more. She didn't need to look at those other letters because, deep down, she knew *this* one was real.

Unfolding it, she flattened it out on the desk and stared at the words once again.

Her mind made up, she placed it back in her handbag. She'd go to that pub tonight. If it came to nothing, then at least she would have tried. But if the woman proclaiming to be her mother was there and *was* the real deal, then she'd have the answers she so badly needed. She'd know where she really came from.

She glanced at the clock and tidied her desk in preparation for the meeting. She wasn't looking forward to this, but she could not stall on officially putting a second in command in place any longer. One which she truly hoped her instincts were correct on.

'Come in,' Sam called at the tap on her office door.

Smiling when Kevin entered her office, Sam unfolded the detailed map of the firm's territories and spread it over the desk. 'Can you confirm which of our areas have received deliveries this past week?'

She looked at Kevin's imposing frame as he leant over her desk; his presence was nowhere near as intimidating as it had been a few days ago.

After doing some unavoidable homework on the suppliers and the history of the firm's dealings, she'd made the decision to stick to the original plan, suspecting John's changes to the suppliers were yet another of his plans to impede the business. It may have been a blind gamble, but it had earnt her a smidgen of respect from the hard-nosed enforcers.

'Yeah, we've supplied all of these,' Kevin confirmed. 'Everything, apart from these two.' His chunky index finger stabbed the map. 'These ones were filched a while back.'

Sam stared at the thinning patch on the top of Kevin's square head as he leant over the map. 'Yes, I remember.' *Something else courtesy of John.*

Kevin straightened up from the desk. 'Well, miss, from what me and the boys can see, you're handing everything just fine.'

Reddening slightly, Sam was taken aback by how gratifying those words felt. *She was getting there. Slowly, perhaps, but getting there all the same.* 'Thank you,' she smiled. 'Call me Sam. And thanks for bringing me up to date.'

'No problem. Everything's running to plan.' Kevin shifted his lumbering frame towards the door.

'Good.' Sam nodded. 'Just before you go...' Folding her hands together, she placed them on the desk. 'How do you feel about taking over John Maynard's position? Permanently?'

Kevin blinked. 'Well, I...'

'I've appreciated your hard work and help. I know you're aware it hasn't been easy for me taking over my father's role, but I really think it would be a good move for the firm to have you by my side,' Sam said, hoping Kevin would accept. Apart from their unlikely but developing respect for each other, there were no other contenders.

A rare smile cracked Kevin's bulldog-like face. He extended his hand. 'I'd be glad to.'

'Wonderful!' Standing up, Sam shook Kevin's huge hand, inwardly breathing a sigh of relief. 'I'll let you give your staff the good news.'

A smile wandered onto her face at the absurdity of the situation. If somebody had told her a month ago that she would be discussing which pieces of the city were supplied with her firm's cocaine with a man who looked like a psychopath, she'd have laughed in their face.

Sam's amusement quickly evaporated. Now for the difficult part.

As well as Kevin's knowledge of the business making him the ideal choice for her second in command, Sam also knew he'd been close to John, so this could go one way or the other.

Her mind lurched from one possible scenario to the next. If it went the wrong way, it would have disastrous consequences. She had to pray she'd weighed everything up and her intuition would not let her down.

Sam took a deep breath. 'I need to level with you about what *really* happened to John and hope to hell I don't come to regret it...'

* * *

'I'll have to run this past Dad,' Andrew said, his fingers gingerly running over the butterfly stitches holding his eyebrow together.

Neil didn't want this conversation. Anything was better than discussing the earlier altercation between his brothers. Seb had turned on *him* once in the not so recent past, but this... this was different. Seb had almost killed Andrew. He'd been out of control. The whole equilibrium was skewed. He didn't like it but didn't know how he could stop it. Things had never been like this before. Not *ever*.

He casually turned over the proof for the order of service they'd just received from the printers, the photo of Gary emblazoned on the front – a glaring reminder prodding uncomfortably at the back of his brain. 'Are you talking about this?'

'No, not that, you muppet,' Andrew snapped, massaging the red-raw marks on his neck. 'You know *exactly* what I'm referring to. I can't let this continue. It's not good for business, let alone my fucking face!' His fingers moved back to the blackened flesh around his closed right eye.

'Try not to take it personally. Seb's under a lot of pressure and it sounds like Benny needs a slap. Don't involve Dad. The funeral is coming up and he doesn't need anything else to deal with.'

Leaning his elbows on his knees, Andrew knitted his fingers together, forming a cup for his chin. 'It's not just about Benny. It's a hell of a lot more than that and you know it!'

'Benny must have forgot what was said. The man's losing the plot,' Neil countered, not altogether sure why he was attempting to play things down.

'I don't think it's Benny who's losing the plot,' Andrew sighed. 'Seb's not concentrating. You can't say you haven't noticed. He's putting other things before the firm. He lied to us the other day about where he'd been and now this? You heard what he said. Accusing *me* of not finalising that order?' He folded his arms. 'Seb *always* deals with the gun orders, you know that.'

Neil nodded. That much was true. Seb *did* always deal with the gun orders. 'Yes, but didn't he ask one of us to finalise it yesterday? Didn't you say you'd do it?'

Andrew rolled his eyes. 'Oh, don't *you* start. No, I didn't.' He hadn't, had he? 'Seb would have done it, like he always does. Or rather, like he *should* have! No guesses why he forgot... and I can probably guess *exactly* where he was when he did...' He tapped his finger against his temple. 'Wherever he was, he wasn't looking after *our* firm, was he? Too busy dealing with someone else's. Or more to the point, someone else in *general*...'

'Right, but that doesn't mean th...'

'What, so you think it was *me*?' Andrew cried. 'That I'm the one so all over the place about some stupid woman to lie to my own family about where I've been and forget what I'm doing? I think not!'

Neil didn't like how this was going. 'It isn't good you and Seb being at each other's throats all the time. We've always run a tight ship here, but you're always on at Seb lately. You're constantly having digs. And there was that thing with Phil Blunt.'

Andrew scowled. 'That had to be done. The man was a liability. And so was his fucking wife...'

'Yes, but...' Neil stopped and stared at his brother, a horrible thought forming. 'You've heard she's carked it? Seb's mad about that too. Those kids... left without a mother.'

Andrew rubbed at his neck once more. 'Oh, my heart bleeds... Look, it was a frightener, that's all. She needed telling.'

Cold slithered up Neil's spine. '*You* killed her?'

'Have a word with yourself!' Andrew spat, getting up. 'All I did was make out we'd got her kids and if she didn't sort out what she'd said about us to the cops, then her kiddies would pay for it.' He shrugged. 'Not my problem she went off the deep end, is it?'

Neil felt sick. The nagging thought just wouldn't go away. Had Andrew offed Tonya Blunt? Made it look like suicide? Would he have really done that to a woman? That wasn't how they worked. *Christ, was Seb right about Andrew after all?*

'Look, I'm not trying to stir shit, but fuck me – whichever way you look at it, Seb isn't levelling with us about what he's doing. That's if he even knows! He's putting our firm – yes, *our* firm – in jeopardy and it's all because of that woman!'

Neil shook his head. 'Seb wouldn't do that... not Seb...'

'Did you not hear the rest of the shit he was spouting? About me bleating that fucking story to the papers!'

'Yeah, I know, but...'

'But what?' Andrew screamed. 'Are you telling me that you think it's feasible I'd run to the press over a silly manipulative woman? That bloody Sam Reynold might be under Seb's skin, but she ain't under mine! I don't like her, granted, or rather, I don't like how she's causing Seb to act, but you really think I'd do that?'

'No, of course I don't!' Neil cried. But *did* he? If Andrew wasn't being honest about what he'd done to Tonya Blunt, then...

No. Andrew was his brother and they thought too much alike. If *he* wouldn't do it, then neither would Andrew. 'Look, Seb's just frustrated and angry. He didn't mean it.'

'You want to bet?' Andrew scowled. 'For once in his life, Seb's out of his depth and it's sent him loo-lah.'

Neil laughed, despite his escalating worry. 'Seb's never been out of his depth. You're talking shit!'

'Am I?' Andrew spat. 'Think about it. Unless I'm very much mistaken, our brother's in love and it's fucked his head up.'

'But you won't really say anything to Dad about this, will you?' Neil asked, worry mounting.

Andrew grabbed his jacket. 'I'll say nothing this time, but any more of it and I'll have no choice. I won't let Seb balls the firm up so he can dip his wick. Neither will I be the scapegoat for his fuckups. Now, if you don't mind, I'm out of here. I need some space.'

Neil nodded and with growing despondency, watched his brother stalk from the office.

* * *

Shoving his hand into his pocket, Liam rummaged around for change. Seeing the phone box on the corner empty, he hastened his pace. He had to get this done before anyone else jumped in. Knowing his luck, a girl hellbent on having an hour-long row with a boyfriend would pip him to the post and he didn't want to be stuck waiting for ages.

Once he'd done this, he'd go and see Sam. He hadn't had chance to catch up with her, despite leaving messages. He needed to keep the pressure up and make her realise what she was doing.

Each time he'd gone to Sam's office lately, she was busy – more often than not with Kevin Stanton.

He glanced at the coins he'd pulled from his pocket, pleased to see he'd got plenty suitable for the phone.

Liam's brows knitted into a frown. From what he'd heard tonight, Sam had officially appointed Kevin as a new second in command, but he'd been secretly hoping Sam would perhaps approach *him* to do that job.

There was nothing involved with it that he couldn't learn. He'd had a good relationship with John, everyone knew that, so surely that meant he would get on well with that side of the business?

Though none of it changed the fact he needed to get Stoker out of the way.

Pulling open the phone box door, Liam stepped inside and picked up the receiver, ignoring the greasy handset against his ear. Holding the receiver against his neck, he took the piece of paper containing the scrawled number from his wallet and stabbed in the digits, waiting impatiently as the phone rang out.

'Hello?'

At last. Liam fumbled to insert a ten-pence piece. 'Hello? Brian?' Remembering himself, he lowered his voice and pinched the end of his nose. 'Brian?'

'Yes. Who is this?'

'Andrew Stoker.' Liam glanced over his shoulder at the empty street. 'I've got some more info about Samantha Reynold.'

'I won't be running any more articles about Samantha Reynold, Mr Stoker. Like I said to your brother, I don't want trouble and neither do I appreciate my wife being threatened.'

Liam's mind spun with this unexpected information. *How would a Stoker react to this rebuff?* 'You want to be careful what you say, Brian. Accusing us of threatening women,' he snarled, hoping that sounded convincing.

'Your family did not need to test my trustworthiness, but the threat was there all the same. There will be no more articles run by me.'

'Fuck you then!' Liam spat. Slamming the phone down, he stared at the receiver. *So Seb Stoker had threatened Sumner's wife?* Presuming it was Seb? Of course it was. Who else would be fighting Sam's corner?

He ran his tongue across his teeth. How could he make it look like Stoker was dishing the dirt on Sam if the paper wouldn't run further stories?

Although...

A smile spread over Liam's face at his forming idea. He hadn't much time to prepare, but that was okay. Some of the best actions were undertaken with minimal notice.

It was perfect. He'd give it a few hours, get the job done and then go and see Sam.

14

'And so that's about it.' Kevin's eyes met with every single man across the enforcement teams. 'John Maynard is not, for the foreseeable future, part of this firm.'

He watched the surprised and unconvinced responses of his men. He couldn't say he blamed them, given that Maynard had never been shy in spouting he had little confidence in Sam Reynold's ability to run the firm.

Kevin would admit he'd had little respect for Sam himself up until today, but he was canny enough to deduce when a whiff of a lie was being uttered, and there had been none.

The woman had taken a huge gamble with what she'd divulged and, for that alone, he took his hat off to her. She wasn't the mealy-mouthed girl he'd thought they'd been lumbered with. She'd signed off the execution of her own cousin, for God's sake, and that took some balls.

More importantly, he'd held the utmost respect for Len Reynold and so, from this moment on, he would back the man's daughter in every possible way.

His gaze moved back across the room. Changing this lot's mind might be more difficult, especially being unable to explain his change of heart.

'I just don't get it,' Craig said. 'Why would Maynard just disappear?'

Kevin shrugged his mountainous shoulders. 'A breakdown, by all accounts.' He didn't much care if he made the man out to be a loon. From what he'd learned, it wasn't far from the truth anyway. The details he was now party to underlined Maynard for the psychotic bastard he was. And that knowledge burned.

To discover Maynard wasn't in any shape or form who he believed him to be made Kevin feel foolish.

And he didn't like feeling foolish.

He folded his arms over his barrel chest. 'Boys, I'm in charge of this section and so, whatever your personal feelings are about Sam or about Maynard's absence, I want that put aside. I expect nothing but cooperation and full respect. Do I make myself clear?'

Seeing heads nod begrudgingly, Kevin dismissed his teams and flopped back into his chair.

* * *

Seb sat at the Peacock's empty bar. No customers were due for another hour, which allowed a drink away from the confines of his office without having to play to the crowd. He wasn't in the mood to be friendly. Or even civil. *Anything but.*

Losing his rag with Andrew the way he had was bad… very bad.

Seb gulped at his whisky, acutely aware of what might have happened to Andrew had Neil not been there earlier. *What the fuck was happening to them all?*

Along with losing his rag, this cockup with the shipment was playing heavily on his mind. If that order wasn't complete, it would be the very last one they'd get and to say he was irate about that was an understatement. A healthy percentage of the firm's takings stemmed from their longstanding relationship with the Irish and he did not, or rather *could* not, have that jeopardised.

If it wasn't sorted, Benny would be explaining to the Irish exactly *why*. And he'd be doing that from a fucking coffin.

Seb inhaled sharply in a bid to keep his temper under wraps. Who was he trying to kid? This wasn't Benny's fault, it was *Andrew's*. Despite Andrew's lame attempt to turn this back on him, it was Andrew who was supposed to put in the finals on that order, he was sure of it.

He gritted his teeth and finished his whisky. Why would Andrew want to screw things up for the firm? He didn't know, but it was becoming untenable.

Seb pushed himself off the bar stool and strutted through the casino, his mind scrambled. He entered the staff corridor, spotting Neil coming out of an office. 'Neil!'

As his brother turned around, Seb beckoned him over. 'Can you arrange a van to fetch the guns?' It wasn't like he could ask Andrew to do it. *Not now*. It was also no secret the man hadn't been seen since their earlier set-to.

Neil nodded sullenly. 'Sure. What time?'

'Ten. Take some of the boys, but I want you to oversee it.' Seb noticed Neil's distraction. 'Is everything all right?'

'Not really,' Neil muttered. 'You and Andrew... it's...'

'Yeah, I know,' Seb said. 'It will be sorted.' *Somehow*. 'Any other issues?'

Neil knew better than to push it. It would solve nothing. Telling Seb what Andrew had said would only make things ten times worse. 'Just got a lot on.'

'Haven't we all?' Seb walked towards his own office. He'd wanted to see Sam tonight, but with Andrew AWOL and Neil on the gun run, he'd have to remain on site.

Chucking his suit jacket over the chair, he rolled up his sleeves and dialled the Orchid's number.

'The Violet Orchid.'

'Miss Reynold, please,' Seb said, his voice gruff.

'Who's calling, please?'

'Sebastian Stoker.'

'One moment...'

The line went dead as the call was transferred. Seb waited, his fingers drumming impatiently on the table.

'I'm sorry,' the returning voice said. 'Miss Reynold is not available. Can I take a message?'

'No thank you.' Not available? It was only seven o'clock.

Hanging up, Seb then dialled Sam's apartment, waiting as it rang out for far too long. He slammed the receiver down, his blood pressure rising. If Sam wasn't at the Orchid or at her place, where the hell was she?

Having always been the one to pick up and put down women, this put Seb in unfamiliar and disconcerting territory. Now the boot felt as though it was on the other foot, and dare he say, it disturbed him.

* * *

From the back of the taxi, Sam fished her mirror from her handbag and scrutinised her reflection. *Had she overdone the makeup? Or not put on enough?*

She studied her brown and neutral eye shadow. Along with a small amount of eyeliner and a light coat of mascara, it wasn't too much, yet it set her dark eyes off perfectly. She hadn't gone overboard with foundation or blusher either. A layer of sheer red lip gloss completed the look. But now she wasn't so sure...

She glanced down at her black trousers. Should she have dressed up more? Not knowing what this pub was like made it difficult. If Linda Matthews was there, she didn't want the first impression to be that she hadn't made an effort.

A sheen of light sweat formed on Sam's face and she found herself opening the taxi's window.

'Going anywhere special, miss?' the taxi driver asked as he weaved through the traffic on the A38 through Selly Oak.

'Just meeting a friend.' Sam forced herself to meet the eyes of the driver in his rear-view mirror and her heart thumped painfully. Looking away, she busied herself with her handbag, not wishing to get into conversation.

Since making the decision to come tonight, she'd allowed herself to get more and more het up and her nerves were shot to pieces.

What if Linda wasn't there? What if it was another fake?

It couldn't be. The letter had mentioned Violet.

Sam fanned her face with her hand, the breeze from the open window doing nothing to calm the cloying heat within her.

She'd changed her mind countless times about whether to go or not and when an incoming call from Seb's direct line flashed up on the phone screen whilst waiting for the taxi, she'd almost answered it.

She'd wanted to answer the call. She really had. She'd wanted to hear Seb's voice and confide in him. She'd wanted to bin this whole idea off and remove all thoughts from her mind, but she couldn't. She had to do this. And if she was going through with it, she didn't need distractions. And that included Seb...

Besides, she hadn't told him about the letter, and he might try to put her off or insist on checking it out first.

'We're coming into Northfield now, love,' the taxi driver said loudly. 'Whereabouts are you going?'

Sam willed her racing nerves to steady. 'Erm, the Hen and Chicks.'

'The Hen and Chicks?'

'Yes, that's right.' Noticing the driver's eyebrows rise with surprise at her destination, Sam swallowed the urge to ask why this should be so strange. Instead, she stared out of the window.

Pulling up at a set of traffic lights, Sam recognised the shopping centre on the left, built from what looked like green corrugated iron. She'd noticed it many times on her way in or out of the city centre up the Bristol Road. She knew where she was, but when the car turned left down a hill and rows of Victorian houses flashed by, Sam was lost. She'd never strayed off the main road.

Turning left at the bottom of the hill, the taxi then took a right. Her heart crashed in her chest. 'Where is this pub?'

'Not far from the station. I take it you don't know the place?' The driver's eyes scanned Sam in the mirror with a hint of amusement.

Not trusting her voice to come out as anything more than a squeak, Sam remained silent, becoming more light-headed with every second that passed.

They turned down several more side streets. Even though it had been only a few minutes since turning off from the main road, this 'not far' seemed indeterminate. As they passed underneath the dual arches of a bridge, Sam focused on the graffiti scrawled onto the Victorian brickwork. That was a railway bridge. The driver had said this place was near the station, so they must be close. *It isn't too late to back out*, she thought, her clammy hands slipping on the leather of her purse.

Before she could contemplate whether to tell the driver to turn around and take her back to her apartment, they pulled into a car park – the looming building of an old pub rising in front of her.

'Here we are,' the taxi driver smiled. 'Have a good night.'

Overriding the impulse to cling to the inside of the door handle, Sam shoved a twenty-pound note into the man's hand. 'Thanks,' she mumbled, stepping out of the car straight into one of the many potholes.

As the taxi pulled away, Sam edged towards the double doors of the Hen and Chicks, the pungent smell of years of beer-drenched carpet already invading her nostrils.

She smoothed down her black trousers and stared up at the building in front of her. A massive place, the pub sat on a corner plot and spread out in a quadrangle. The large car park – a rarity in the inner city – had, as well as potholes and loose boulders, a handful of rotten, half-collapsed picnic tables, long since having seen better days.

Unsurprisingly, these were empty. Possibly because the view of the train line and a petrol station was far from idyllic.

She peered up at the burgundy pub sign with the 'Ansells' brewery sign above it, raucous laughter and the general buzz of chatter and music spilling from inside.

Taking a deep breath, Sam grabbed hold of the door, almost dislocating her arm opening it. Pulling harder, she found herself faced with a small lobby and a corridor running off to the toilets. There were also two doors either side and the sound of loud voices, mainly male, coming from both rooms.

Which bar should she try? It wasn't like she knew who she was looking for – not unless Linda Matthews bore an uncanny resemblance to herself.

Panic bubbled, the urge to turn back through the door to the car park growing.

She was here now, and go in she must.

Sam procrastinated, the garish flowery carpet making her feel seasick. *Which bar? Left or right?*

Her choice was decided when a man burst through the double doors and chivalrously held open the left-hand door. 'After you, love,' he grinned, exposing several missing teeth.

Nodding her thanks, Sam walked stiffly into the room, the fug of cigarette smoke stinging her eyes.

As the loud chatter and laughter dropped to a hushed whisper, leaving only a tinny rendition of 'American Woman' playing from the ancient jukebox, Sam self-consciously continued through the haze towards the large bar.

15

Cringing at the crunch of forcing the gear stick into fourth, Tom wished above everything that he'd forked out a few quid more for a motor.

The bloody clutch had gone floppy and the only way of getting the poxy thing to change up was to slam each gear in manually without using the pedal. Not only did that grate on his teeth, but it wouldn't be long before the whole gearbox gave out with this sort of abuse.

Now everything was panning out nicely, he could have afforded a better motor. *Bloody typical.* When would he learn that luck always saw him right?

Despite this, Tom grinned as he pulled up outside the house in Frankley. It was a top idea, placing the cookshop here. Anyone digging around would look nearer the centre of town, rather than a standard semi in a housing estate in this neck of the woods.

Getting out of the car, Tom walked up the neat pathway and knocked on the front door. Tapping his foot, he looked up as the door opened, surprised to see a teenage girl.

'Erm, hi. I'm looking for Luke Banner,' Tom said, glancing at the house next door. *Had he got the right place?*

'Dad!' the girl screeched over her shoulder.

Tom's eyes passed appreciatively over the girl. A decent looker with a nice body to boot. Running his tongue across his bottom lip, he wondered whether Luke had considered his daughter's future?

'All right, Tom?' Luke appeared, a half-eaten bacon sandwich in his hand. 'Come in.' Jerking his head, he retreated back up the hallway.

Tom glanced around the tidy kitchen: not a dirty cup left on the draining board, no overflowing stinking chip pan on the hob. 'Where's the wife?' he asked, his eyes moving back to the man's daughter.

'Disappeared with a Yardie.' Luke stared at the floor miserably, then looked at his daughter, who had tailed them into the room. 'Off you go upstairs, Debs. We need to talk business.'

The girl glared at her father. 'It's not like I don't know what you do. *Everybody* knows,' she snapped before flouncing off, purposely stamping on each step as she stormed upstairs.

Luke rolled his eyes. 'She's at that age where things embarrass her. Anyway, come out the back.'

Tom followed Luke, his mind whirring. If that snotty attitude was knocked out of the girl, she would be a prime candidate for his plans of upscaling the line-up at the Aurora.

He admired the large wooden shed at the end of the garden. 'It's bigger than it looked when I ordered it,' Tom said, impressed.

'Yeah, I appreciate you buying it, mate. It keeps this out of the house.' Luke fished a key from his pocket and undid the heavy-duty padlock on the door.

Inside, Tom stared at the various cabinets and drawers. A long workbench ran the length of one side, complete with scales and neatly stacked boxes. 'Many enquiries about orders?'

'A fair few, but I could always do with more... I got your order from Lee, so I take it you liked the sample?'

Tom considered the question. 'Yeah, it wasn't bad, but personally, I prefer mine a bit purer.' He may prefer freebase, but it was expensive.

Finding a cookshop using the riskier method of producing crack was difficult. The way Luke was doing it was easier *and* cheaper.

'I can remake your order, if you like?' Luke said. 'I've got someone else who'll take this batch.'

'I never said that,' Tom hastily interrupted. 'Look, I have a proposition for you...' He leant casually against a cabinet. 'You'll now be acting as my preferred supplier.'

'Regular orders from you, you mean?' Luke grinned. 'Yeah, that would be good.'

A sickly grin slid onto Tom's face. That was the *only* reason he'd earmarked Luke in the first place. The man was about as much of a dealer as Mother Theresa, but that was okay. He knew how to cook with baking soda and that was all that mattered.

Luke had always been an honest bloke – slaving his life away like a cunt on the shop floor at the Rover to pay for his family, but since he'd got laid off, well, folk were doing whatever they had to do, and it just so happened that once again Tom had been in the right place at the right time to offer the man the chance to make good money.

Of course, Luke had grabbed the offer with both hands. Who wouldn't? It was perfect. Now, not only did Tom have the ability to make crack, but someone on tap who was forever grateful.

Tom smiled carefully. 'What I mean is, from now on, you'll be supplying *only* me. No one else.'

'That's not how you said this would work,' Luke said uncomfortably. 'You said once I was up and running, then I could supply whoever I wanted. I'm getting more enquiries by the day. I'm not in the position where I can turn down orders. I need the money.'

A nerve fluttered in Tom's neck. 'I'm offering you the chance of an in with my firm.' *Not that it is a firm*, he thought acidly, but it would be soon, and this stage was the next step towards attaining that status. Then he'd be on the map for real.

'Look, mate. We know each other from way back, don't we? I know

I've been off the scene, but I'm back now and into big stuff,' Tom boasted, exhibiting the confidence that only resulted from a massive personal coke habit. 'I prefer to give old pals the option rather than offering the spoils to strangers. I know you had it hard, that's why I set you up with all of this in the first place.'

Luke shrugged sadly. 'That's why I'm doing this.' He glanced around his shed. 'I can't jeopardise the chance of paying back my debts.'

'You're not listening,' Tom spat. 'Like I said, you'll be my *only* supplier. You won't supply anyone else this side of fucking Queensway. Or in actuality, *anyone* else at all.' Swallowing his impatience, he resumed his smile. 'You'll get 30 per cent of the profits and we'll gain a monopoly on supplying the south of the city.'

He moved closer, his eyes narrowing. 'If you don't take my generous offer, then I'll tell the fucking council what you're doing at the back of one of their properties and see how they like that...' He smiled coldly as he leant back against the worktop. 'Just think... if that happened, how would you provide for your lovely daughter? Although, looking at her, I'd be happy to give her a job at the Aurora!'

And he'd be doing that for definite if this man was too stupid to gratefully accept what was on the table.

* * *

Linda stopped dancing on the seat when the bar fell silent, half-expecting Tom to have appeared, having changed his mind about her going out. A lot of the regulars weren't around when Tom had last lived in these parts and newcomers always caused a bit of a stir.

Judging by the way Tom acted around Shondra and Tayquan, spending the evening keeping an eye on the pair of them had probably already pushed him over the edge. But she didn't want to leave. She was having a much better time tonight and she'd managed to do so without giving in to the burning urge to pick up the crack pipe.

Linda glanced at Vera. Vera would kill her if she ever went back on the crack. Devil shit, she called it. And to start that old lark again when she should be more optimistic about life than ever before?

No. She mustn't. But she'd keep those rocks. Just in case...

Wobbling on unsteady legs, Linda grabbed Vera for support. She couldn't see Tom anywhere and, as the chatter resumed, she breathed a sigh of relief.

She was about to continue jigging along to the music when she saw the landlord pointing in her general direction. The miserable bastard didn't usually mind when she strutted her stuff. 'Is he pointing to us?' Linda hissed in Vera's ear.

'Nah, he's talking to that woman,' Vera said, swinging her ample hips to the music.

It was then Linda noticed the woman with dark hair staring straight at her. Her legs dissolved into jelly. *It was her. The woman from the paper.*

The cutting Tom had shown her, containing the only image she'd ever seen of her grown-up daughter, was indelibly etched in her mind. The woman at the bar was her. *It was Violet.*

Feeling the jelly-like sensation travel up from her legs into her body, Linda clutched Vera. 'Oh, my God!' she spluttered.

'What's the matter? I thought you liked this Joan Jett track?' Vera yelled over the music.

'I – I need to sit down.' Linda shakily clambered from the seat. Dropping heavily on the moth-eaten bench, she reached for her pint and gulped at the flat liquid. *The woman was walking this way...*

'Linda?' the woman asked. 'Linda Matthews?'

Linda found herself nodding eagerly. This was the moment she'd always dreamt of, yet she was as drunk as a skunk and hadn't a clue what to say.

* * *

Sam didn't know what she'd expected. She hadn't thought about how she would feel, being face to face with the woman who had given birth to her. It might have only been a short amount of time since discovering she wasn't who she'd always thought she was, but she'd still expected to feel *something*. A connection? A physical trait or characteristic that would hit her slap bang between the eyes, making it obvious Linda Matthews *was* her biological mother? But there was nothing...

Nothing, apart from disappointment. And for that alone, Sam felt guilty.

When she'd asked the landlord if he knew of a Linda Matthews, his smirk and the response, 'She's the one up on the seat on the left,' had thrown her off guard. Turning to see two drunk women – the one on the left with her skirt hitched high, gyrating her hips to the music – had made her cringe.

She'd contemplated turning on her heels. She hadn't, but listening to this woman and the language spilling from her mouth like a docker, Sam wondered whether she should have.

Sipping her vodka and Coke, avoiding the previous drinker's lipstick around the edge of the glass, Sam studied Linda Matthews as the woman waffled excitedly.

Her dark brown hair, liberally streaked with grey, was scraped back into a greasy ponytail with random tufts sticking out to drift aimlessly above her head; her eyes – the same colour as Sam's – were bloodshot and surrounded by grey-tinged, puffy bags which dragged her whole face down. Her tight, stained and unflattering clothes accentuated the slight belly that looked out of place on her otherwise stick-thin frame.

Sam castigated herself for forming an opinion on looks alone. She strived to be non-judgemental, but this... this wasn't what she'd imagined.

Involuntarily, an image of the woman who for thirty years she'd believed to be her mother flashed into her mind. Gloria always made an effort with her appearance and took the utmost care in everything she did. Even to the point of making shapes out of cucumber slices accompanying her packed lunch at primary school, cutting funny faces into toast at breakfast, or making clothes for dolls.

Would Linda Matthews have done that?

Doubtful. Linda looked like she'd comfortably spent her life in a boozer!

'I still can't believe you're here!' Linda grabbed Sam's hand. 'You're absolutely stunning. Ain't she, V? Ain't she gorgeous?'

Vera nodded, still shocked that the daughter Linda had given up all those years ago had walked into the Hen and Chicks. Not only had she done that, but she was that bird from the papers – the one who'd inherited that posh casino. She'd seen the article in the *Mail* last week, but she'd had no idea, absolutely no inkling it would turn out the woman belonged to Linda. *Who would have thought it?*

Sam gently eased her hand out of Linda's grasp, under the pretence of picking up her drink. There were so many things she wanted to ask, but she couldn't get a word in.

'Oh, my God! I just can't fucking believe it! Fancy you coming here!' Linda continued eagerly. 'You're so bloody similar-looking to me back in the day, it's untrue!'

Sam frowned, hoping she wouldn't end up looking or being *anything* like Linda. 'I wouldn't have known where to come had you not said in your letter.'

Linda glanced at Vera and then back to Sam. 'Letter? What letter?'

Sam's drink paused halfway to her mouth. 'The letter you sent me at the casino?'

Linda's brows furrowed, exaggerating the deep grooves in her forehead, as she watched Sam fish the lined paper from her handbag.

'This?' Sam held the letter up, unwilling to place it on the beer-soaked table.

Linda focused on the swimming words. She recognised that awful handwriting straight away. *It was Tom's.* Tom had written a letter pretending to be her? No wonder he'd wanted her to come down the pub.

A wide beam slid onto her face. Aw, Tom was so thoughtful. He knew she was petrified about meeting their daughter, so he'd arranged it himself. He really was a diamond.

She opened her mouth to say exactly that, then remembered what Tom had said about keeping out of it in case it caused problems. 'Oh, so I did. I completely forgot!'

'Forgot?' Sam exclaimed.

Linda flapped her hand, knocking her pint down her skirt. 'Oh, shit! Me fucking drink!' Staggering to her feet, she shook her skirt, splattering droplets of cider everywhere. 'I mean, I forgot I'd *posted* it. I wrote it after seeing that thing in the paper, but I was scared.' She smiled sheepishly. 'After a few drinks. I must have posted it.' *That sounded feasible, didn't it?* There was no way she wanted to freak out her beautiful daughter by bringing Tom into the equation. He was right. It would overwhelm her.

Sam smiled uncomfortably. 'Ah, I see...'

'Here, you do believe I'm your mother, don't you?' Linda said, her eyes wide with panic.

Vera stood up. 'I'll just get us some more drinks,' she said awkwardly and wandered over to the bar.

Sam turned back to Linda. 'In the letter you mentioned Violet?'

Linda nodded animatedly. 'Yes, your *real* name. I wrote that on a note with the clothes that went with you.' Her face dropped, the desolation of that day returning. 'I didn't have time to write anything else...'

Sam nodded, a smidgen of empathy forming for the woman in front of her at the raw pain still evident after thirty years. The note had indeed been in a bag of dirty baby clothes. 'But my birthday is the seventeenth of June,' she frowned. 'Your letter said the fifteenth.'

Linda shook her head. 'The seventeenth was the day you were *taken*. They must have given you that as your birthday, rather than your real one, which is definitely the fifteenth of June.' She smiled sadly. 'I'll never forget it.' She grasped Sam's hand again, her eyes filling with tears. 'I never wanted you to go, you know? I really didn't.'

Sam smiled, an unexpected burn of tears behind her eyes. *It was true, then?* Whether she liked it or not, this woman was her real mother. 'I believe you,' she found herself saying. *And she meant it.*

16

With the scent of fresh shampoo and a generous helping of aftershave, Liam smelt like he'd just stepped out of the shower. Probably because he had, but that wasn't unusual. He frequently got spruced up of an evening.

Having given himself the night off, he could think of nothing better than surprising Sam with an impromptu drinks invitation. An invitation that might be turned down, but regardless. His very presence at Sam's now afforded him an alibi to his whereabouts that he might need to rely on, on the off-chance things went off kilter.

Liam stared up at the apartment block, the buzzing in his fingertips now having calmed. Maybe Sam wasn't in? He shrugged. For once, it didn't matter. He'd achieved what he'd set out to do and doing such a thing had been strangely exhilarating. *Powerful.*

But he couldn't keep that bag in his flat until he got the chance to properly dispose of it. If it were to be found in his apartment, then it was evidence to link him to what he had done tonight. He needed to get rid of it quick smart and completely destroy it – burn it or something? But there just wasn't time.

Liam glanced in the direction of his car where the carrier bag sat safely in the boot. He'd risked bringing it back out with him as he needed to take it somewhere in the interim, where no one would think of looking.

His mouth curled into a smile as he turned on his heels and made his way back down the path of Sam's apartment block.

And he knew just where to leave the bag for safe keeping.

* * *

Getting the nod that the guns had been collected, safely deposited in one of their lockups in Erdington and that the rest of the order would be there tomorrow, Seb could breathe slightly easier.

Now Neil was back at the Peacock, Seb could do what he'd wanted to do all evening.

He was about to get out of the car, when a figure hurrying down the paved entrance path from Symphony Court made him freeze in his tracks.

Seb squinted through the darkness. *It was that Liam bloke.* Had the bastard just 'popped round' to see Sam again, like he apparently some-times did?

His teeth clenched and he fought against leaping from the car to pummel the man's head into the concrete pavement. Instead, he waited and watched Liam get into a car and drive away.

Getting out of his motor, Seb glanced over his shoulder before striding up the walkway to the closed security doors of the apartments. He pressed the buzzer for Sam's flat and glanced at his watch. *Almost eleven.* He'd already phoned the Orchid again, plus he'd called her apartment three or four more times since too and his stress level was steadily rising to fever pitch.

His finger stabbed the buzzer once again. 'Come on, Sam,' he muttered under his breath. 'I'm not here for a fucking laugh. If Liam's just come from yours, then you must be in.'

Sam wouldn't be absent from the Orchid *and* her home, so where the hell was she? Wouldn't she have told him if she'd planned to go out?

A horrible thought edged into Seb's brain. What if she was out with another man and Liam hadn't received an answer either? After all, he hadn't seen him *leaving* the apartment – just walking away.

His brow creased. Or what if Sam had been in there with Liam and purposefully ignored *him*?

Seb pressed the buzzer again, this time holding it down for longer, his frustration growing. The thought of Sam sleeping with another man snowballed, uncovering a strange rage that he had no right to feel.

Nothing was official. Neither of them had promised not to see other people. That subject hadn't even been discussed.

Seb dragged his hand across his mouth. No other woman he'd been involved with would have *dared* see anyone else. It had always been *him* who had walked away and moved on without a second thought.

Much to his growing shame, he silently admitted women had always been there for him as and when he'd wanted, but with her... with Sam...

Resorting to banging his fist on the shiny plate glass of the door, Seb then stood back and looked up at the towering building. 'Sam?' he roared.

He moved back to the intercom, his eyes feverishly scanning the other residents' buttons. Before he could stop himself, he began pressing them randomly. Someone would answer and they could damn well let him in.

'Yes?' a voice crackled.

'I need access,' Seb barked.

The intercom went dead and he waited for the door release buzzer to sound, granting him entry, but nothing happened.

'What the fuck?' Seb pushed against the tightly locked door. Was this a wind-up? *He was Seb Stoker and was never refused entry anywhere.*

Randomly stabbing the buttons again, he snarled at the impotence of the situation. 'I need access to this building,' he yelled with the next crackling of the intercom.

'I'll call the police if you don't go away,' the woman's voice threatened. 'You're trespassing. Now please leave.'

The intercom clicked off.

Seb punched the door, ignoring the pain reverberating through his knuckles. Leaning his forehead against the cold wall, he battled to regulate his breathing. He may have been Seb Stoker, but here it made no difference.

Having no other option, he turned on his heel and headed back to the Peacock, alone with his festering thoughts.

* * *

To Linda, the loud surroundings of the pub had vaporised, leaving her and Sam – her beautiful daughter – the only people in the room.

She was aware of the inquisitive looks people were giving her, but she didn't care. All that mattered was getting the chance to explain why she hadn't kept her firstborn. The chance she'd never thought she'd get.

She knew she'd barely stopped talking for the past two hours and, although her initial hysterical gabbling had calmed, the words still spewed from her mouth like verbal diarrhoea. Finally pausing for breath, she took another long swig of her cider.

Comfortably drunk she might be, but Linda hadn't forgotten what was important. So far, she'd steered the conversation away from questions about Tom. The last thing she wanted was for her daughter to feel she'd been left behind, like Tom said could happen. That wasn't the case. It had *never* been the case.

She'd also omitted as much as possible about the rest of her life. She was too ashamed. But she *had* learnt a little of Violet's life – or should she say, Sam's. And it was a lot better than what the girl would have got if she'd remained where she'd started...

Linda stared at her almost empty drink, humiliation burning. Sam had already bought several drinks and she wished she'd got money left to be able to buy one back.

Sam watched Linda, the question she wanted to ask rubbing like sandpaper against the back of her teeth. At odds with what she'd initially thought, as the evening progressed, she'd found it easier to sit with this stranger.

With the break in Linda's chatter, Sam snatched the opportunity. 'You said you had me when you were fifteen? That must have been difficult?' It meant the woman was only forty-five, but she looked substantially older.

Linda nodded. 'The day you were born was the worst, yet the best day of my life,' she said quietly. 'You see, whilst you were inside me, I knew you couldn't go anywhere, but once you were out, I – I knew it was only of matter of time and...'

'Who is my father?' Sam blurted before she could change her mind.

Linda's eyes shot up. She knew this question was inevitable, but how could she answer truthfully without messing up what she'd promised Tom? Or worse, alienating this girl? She stared at her now empty glass. 'I...'

At Linda's reticence, a horrible thought suddenly occurred to Sam. Fifteen was very young. Plus, she'd been forced to give up the baby...

Nausea rolled. Was it possible she was the product of something untoward? Paling, she inhaled sharply. 'Is it something you'd rather not discuss?'

'It was a very difficult time,' Linda said honestly, her eyes brimming with tears. 'I...'

'I'm sure you appreciate I want to know, but we can leave it for now, if you'd prefer?' Sam said, unsure whether she was deflecting for herself or for Linda.

Linda smiled gratefully. *She hadn't had to lie.* Once Sam had got to know her a bit more, she wouldn't be upset to discover that her parents had resumed their relationship. Then she could introduce her to Tom – her real father.

'I take it you're married now?' Sam changed the subject. 'Your letter said "Devlin"?'

Linda laughed callously. 'That was ages ago. He was a loser and fucked off, leaving me with a child and a bellyful of another.' She smiled wanly. 'Put it this way, I haven't had much luck where men are concerned...'

Sam scrabbled to take in that she had two siblings. That thought had stupidly never crossed her mind. Excitement fluttered. 'These children... where...?'

Linda's heart sank like a stone. There were some things she couldn't hide. 'Those two off Mickey Devlin would be...' She glanced towards the ceiling. 'About twenty-seven and twenty-eight by now.'

'*Would* be?'

Linda shrivelled with shame. 'I last saw Marina and Grant about four years ago. Maybe longer. They tracked me down, but, erm, things didn't go well and I haven't seen them since...'

She turned her drink around on the table awkwardly, aware that however much she wanted to hide it, she would have to admit the unsavoury truth about her failings as a mother and as a human being in general. She owed this girl as much of the truth as possible. She owed *all* of her kids that and a whole lot more besides.

If Sam walked out of her life afterwards, then Linda only had herself to blame. 'Th-the truth is, I don't know where most of my kids are. I've had eight, including you,' she muttered.

Sam failed to hide her shock. *Eight children? So, she had seven brothers or sisters?* Her pulse ramped up. She'd always wanted siblings. Could discovering Linda be good after all? 'Why have you lost touch with them?'

Linda wanted to hide in a large black hole. 'After losing you, I went off the rails. For years, I had a problem on and off with crack. There were lots of different men... I – I wasn't a good mother. I worked as a...'

Sam blanched. *Crack?* 'Are you still taking... erm...'

Linda shook her head hastily. 'God, no. I haven't touched the stuff in years. I don't intend to, either. Especially now.' *That small bit Tom had given her a few days ago didn't count, did it?*

An avalanche of questions invaded Sam's head. Crack wasn't good. And to have lost her children? But Linda had been honest enough to admit her failings, so surely that counted for something?

Surprising herself, she reached out and grabbed Linda's hand. 'You're clean now and trying your best, so that's what matters.' Sam decided she'd concentrate on the positives. 'Let me get more drinks and then you must tell me more about your other children,' she said, her eyes glittering.

Linda allowed the promise of more alcohol to appease her discomfort, but looking up at the drunken ruckus rapidly heading in their direction, her eyes widened.

Still completely enraptured, Sam reached for her handbag, realising too late there was trouble afoot. Seeing Linda's mouth gape in an unspoken warning, Sam's head shot towards the loud shouting. The sound of breaking glass around her rang in her ears and she could do nothing to prevent the fighting men slamming into her.

'It's really not that bad,' Sam protested as Linda pulled her along the pavement.

'At least let me clean it up,' Linda insisted, her arm gripping Sam's in a surprisingly strong hold. 'I may have been absent for thirty years, but I can do *this* for you.'

Concentrating on that lessened the horror that drunks had stuck a glass in her daughter's leg. She marched ahead stoically, anything to stop the tears of frustration flowing. 'I could fucking kill those bastards!' Linda spat, her eyes shining.

Sam bit back a smile. The shattered pint glass had only cut the surface of her skin. It could have been far worse. Her ribs hurt more than her leg. Slamming into the table from the full weight of the man falling on her was what bloody hurt, but she'd live.

Her head spun with the fresh air after the smoky, hot atmosphere in the pub. She really had drunk far too much. She glanced at Linda, seeing steely determination in her eyes and, with a jolt, recognised it as something she had seen in her own these past few weeks. Past crack addict Linda may be, but she deserved a chance, did she not? 'Is your place far?'

'No, we're here now,' Linda smiled.

Sam stared up at the ghastly 1960s buildings stretching into the distance. At five storeys high, there must have been hundreds of flats.

Moving into a dank, unlit stairwell, she groped for a railing, wincing as her ribs protested at climbing the concrete steps.

'I wouldn't grab that,' Linda said. 'Little bastards around here think it's funny to smear dog shit on the handrails.'

Quickly jerking her hand away, Sam hoped they would reach the flat soon. The smell of urine in the stairwell was stinging her eyes and, when a figure lumbered out of the shadows on one of the landings, she automatically jumped back.

'Fuck off!' Linda screamed in the staggering man's direction. 'Bloody junkies,' she muttered. 'Just ignore them.'

Sam edged around the unkempt man staring at her with unseeing, glazed eyes, drool hanging from his slack mouth, and was glad when, after two further sets of steps, they exited the stairwell onto a balconied walkway.

Rows of windows, some lit, some in darkness, stretched ahead, the concrete floor underneath her feet vibrating as a train thundered past not twenty yards away.

'Here we are,' Linda exclaimed, her heart sinking at Sam's face. She'd never been ashamed of where she lived before, but now she'd never felt more so. She'd almost forgotten this woman – her *daughter* – had been raised in what sounded like a palace in Edgbaston. She'd seen with her own eyes the Daimler that man had taken her child away in, so they'd probably even had servants, for Christ's sake.

Linda suddenly felt like crying. She'd been so relaxed and at home in the pub, she'd forgotten reality and now she was underlining how pathetic her life was. Sam was dripping in money and she'd brought her to this shithole? Sweat beaded as her shaking hands fumbled with the key. 'Y-you'll have to excuse the mess...'

With the smell of sweat and stale ashtrays cloying her nostrils, Sam shut the door behind Linda as she fumbled for the light switch, then followed down the short hallway, dimly illuminated by a bare forty-watt bulb hanging from a cobweb-covered fitting.

'Mind all the junk on the floor,' Linda mumbled as they moved into the kitchen, dark except for a yellowing strip light hanging precariously from under an orange wall cabinet.

Sam felt around, her fingers touching the grease-covered light switch. Pressing it, a fluorescent strip light flickered with a loud buzzing sound, the bright white light revealing the chaos in the kitchen.

Linda opened the fridge slightly so the contents, or lack of them, wouldn't be obvious and grabbed a couple of cans of cider. Using her elbows, she shoved dirty plates across the table to place the cans down. 'Sit down and I'll go and find some cotton wool to sort your leg out,' she said, her voice falsely bright.

'You don't need to,' Sam protested. Brushing a squashed chip off the chair, she looked around the room with a sinking heart as Linda scurried up the hallway.

Wallpaper peeled in strips from the damp ceiling, the standalone cooker was crusted with old, dried-on food and on what cupboards there were, most of the doors had dropped down on their hinges.

Sam's eyes moved to the ripped lino under her feet, covered with more old food, shoes and, Lego...

Lego?

'Found some!' Linda rushed back into the room, clutching a

handful of dusty cotton wool. 'Now, let's have a look at that cut.' She knelt down and rolled up Sam's trouser leg.

'Whose is the Lego?'

Linda froze. *Shit. The kids? Tom? Where was Tom?* She'd been so wrapped up, she'd forgotten Tom was here. How would she explain him to Sam? 'Oh, that's Tayquan's. He's always leaving it lying about.'

Sam blinked, inexplicably finding her eyes welling up.

'Yes, your brother,' Linda said. 'He's five. My erm, lodger, has been babysitting.'

'Ma?' Tayquan appeared at the kitchen doorway, rubbing his eyes. His eyes widened, seeing Sam at the kitchen table. 'Who's that?'

Sam stared at the little boy and held back the urge to rush over and hug him. 'Hi, Tayquan.'

'Go back to bed,' Linda said. 'It's late.'

'I – I can't sleep. Tom said we'd be taken away or murdered if we didn't go to sleep…'

Linda flapped her hand, diverting from the mention of Tom's name. *It was okay, Sam didn't know her father's name.* 'Ha ha! He's always joking around. Don't be silly, Tayquan. Now, go back to bed,' she said, softening her tone.

'But I ain't had no dinner,' Tayquan moaned. 'Tom went out and there's nothing in the fridge.'

Linda paled, sensing Sam's eyes burning into her. *Tom had gone out? Shit. What did that make her look like?* 'Forget about that,' she blustered. 'Come and say hello to your big sister.'

17

Linda watched Tom snoring, his mouth wide open. She had the urge to push it shut, but didn't want to wake him.

Gingerly reaching over his inert form, she grabbed a packet of cigarettes from the bedside table and sparked one up, wincing at the cracking sound of the lighter igniting. She wasn't sure why she was worrying. Tom Bedworth could sleep through a nuclear war.

Pulling her dressing gown over her baggy T-shirt, she exhaled long curls of smoke to collect in hazy clouds on the bedroom ceiling, a smile forming on her face. She couldn't remember the last time she'd really smiled. Yes, she smiled frequently, but they weren't *real* smiles. Not genuine ones. But this one was. And it felt nice.

Still trying to take in all that had happened last night, Linda went back over everything in case she'd dreamt any of it up, but she hadn't. It was real.

Despite the hangover clinging to the inside of her mouth and wrapping evilly around her intestines, Linda's memories had crystal clear clarity. Almost as if she'd been sober. She really *had* spent the evening with her daughter.

Her face split into a grin. They'd got on well. At least, she *thought* they had. Even with her gabbling and the humiliation of Sam's initial sight of her strutting her stuff on a tabletop...

Even with this bumpy start, Sam hadn't seemed fazed by her revelations of her past or even by the state of this dump. It was just a godsend Tom hadn't returned until after Sam had left.

Linda glanced back at Tom as he passed wind loudly.

It had been close, though. Sam's taxi hadn't been gone five minutes before Tom staggered through the door. She'd wanted to scream at him about where he'd been, rather than looking after the kids, before reminding herself he'd been sweet enough to contact Sam in the first place. She'd never have had the courage.

Linda's mouth pursed, outlining the deep grooves from decades of chugging forty fags a day.

She wasn't entirely sure why she hadn't told Tom that Sam had turned up at the pub. It might be wrong keeping the wonderful news to herself, but she wanted the warm glow of being reunited with her daughter to be her own happy secret, just for a short while longer.

She would tell Tom, she would. *Just not today...*

Tayquan better keep his gob shut. And the same went for Vera...

Hurrying out of the bedroom, Linda glanced over her shoulder. Satisfied Tom was still asleep, she padded along the hallway into the kitchen.

Seeing Tayquan rooting around in the cupboard, a wash of sadness shrouded her as she looked at her youngest child. Her kids put up with a lot, but now all that would change. Now Sam was back in her life, something had shifted. Now she could make it up to all of them. Now she'd finally be able to be a proper mother.

'I'll buy you some cereal today,' Linda said brightly, making the little boy jump at her unexpected entrance. 'No, I really will!' she exclaimed, seeing Tayquan's distrust. 'What do you fancy? Coco Pops? Or how about Rice Krispies?'

Tayquan beamed. 'Do you mean it?'

Linda nodded. 'Yes, I mean it!' She ruffled Tayquan's hair. 'As long as you promise me something...'

Tayquan frowned. 'Promise what?'

Bending down, Linda whispered into Tayquan's ear, 'Don't mention anything to Tom about that lady being here last night.'

Tayquan failed to hide his disappointment. 'I thought he'd gone? You said he'd gone.'

'Well, now he's back,' Linda snapped. 'Did you hear what I said about not mentioning that lady?'

'Yes, but why?'

Linda waved her hand. 'Just don't, okay?'

Tayquan nodded slowly. 'Okay... but I liked her. She was nice.' He frowned thoughtfully. 'If she's my sister, does that mean she's Shondra's sister too?'

Linda smiled. 'Yes, but don't say anything. There will be plenty of time to tell everyone, I promise.' At least, she hoped so. She hoped seeing Sam would be a regular thing.

'I knew you preferred Tayquan!' Shondra stomped into the kitchen, her bottom lip pouting.

Linda spun around. *Damn it.* 'Don't be silly, Shondra. It's nothing to do with that.'

'Yes, it is!' Shondra yelled, a tear sliding down her face. 'Tayquan has more toys than me too. I just heard you say not to tell me. I've always wanted a sister.'

Linda glanced up the hallway. 'Shh!' she hissed. 'You'll wake Tom!'

'But why didn't I get to meet her last night?' Shondra persisted.

'Because you were asleep and I wasn't!' Tayquan announced proudly. 'You should have got up like *I* did.'

'You could have woken me. You did it on purpose!' Shondra shoved her brother hard in the chest.

'Shondra!' Linda screeched. 'Pack that in right now!'

'No!' Shondra stamped her foot. 'It's not fair!'

'*And* I'm getting cereal...' Tayquan boasted, overjoyed to have one up on his sister.

'See? He gets stuff that I don't,' Shondra screamed. 'I hate you, Tayquan! You...'

'What the fuck is all this bloody noise?' Tom yelled, staggering into the kitchen, clutching his head. 'Can't a man get any bastard peace?'

Linda froze and stared at her two children, now still and silent.

'Can't you control them?' Tom spat to Linda, then swung to Tayquan, his lip curling in contempt. 'I expect this was *your* doing! Always fucking moaning! What's your problem?'

'N-nothing...' Tayquan stuttered, staring at the lino.

'No! Tell me! What were you arguing about?' Tom pressed, his eyes flicking to Linda. 'What's the matter with them?'

Linda shrugged dismissively, then gave Tayquan and Shondra warning glares. 'You know what they're like...'

'It's because Tayquan is selfish and wants to keep our sister to himself!' Shondra spat, jealousy coming to the fore. She stared at Tayquan with a gloating smirk.

Tom frowned. 'Your *sister*?'

'Shondra!' Linda hissed.

'Yeah, the woman who was here last night. Ma told Tayquan she's our sister, but didn't let *me* meet her,' Shondra continued.

Tom's eyes narrowed. Moving forward, he grabbed a handful of Tayquan's curls. 'Is this true, you little turd?'

'Don't you dare speak to him like that! Get off him!' Linda screamed, rushing forward.

Tom spun on his heels, fury pounding in his veins as strongly as his crack downer. He knew what Linda had done. She'd met up with Samantha Reynold, brought her back here and said sod all about it. She'd probably seen her the night before as well, the lying, conniving bitch. She'd wasted two whole days of his plan.

'You sly bitch!' he roared, backhanding Linda and sending her flying onto her back in the centre of the kitchen floor.

* * *

Sam scanned the sheet of monthly figures and nodded appreciatively. The roulette takings were definitely up. At least keeping Liam in charge of the gaming side of the business was paying dividends. 'This is looking good.'

Liam glowed with self-satisfaction. 'Glad you're pleased. Is everything okay?'

Sam looked up warily. 'Why wouldn't it be?'

Liam shrugged. 'No reason. It's just I popped over to see you last night, but you weren't in.'

'That's because I went out,' Sam said casually.

Liam waited for Sam to elaborate, but instead she busied herself rearranging her desk. Out with Stoker, was she? Was he worming his way further into her life so she wouldn't suspect him when he killed another member of her family?

Sam shuffled the loose paperwork. Not long ago, Liam would have been the first person she'd have told about Linda. But that was before the only things he said were either digs against Seb or against her choices over *everything*.

It hardly mattered that she couldn't say anything to anyone because she didn't know how *she* felt about any of it. The shift from the initial disappointment and, dare she say, embarrassment over Linda had slid into comfort. And she had an array of siblings? One of whom she'd now met!

The vision of Tayquan's dear little face flashed into Sam's mind.

But worry strummed along her spine. Linda's revelations about her previous addiction and the children were one thing, but something was still far from right in that woman's life. She'd *sensed* it.

But she was torn. She couldn't exactly ask what the problem was. She didn't know this woman from Adam. Neither could she deduce anything from one single meeting. But if there was something wrong, then didn't she have a duty to intervene?

But she didn't want to cause problems. She wanted to get to know Linda. And those children. She also wanted to find out about her real father.

Oh, God, it was all so difficult. So confusing.

'I take it you saw the announcement about Gary Stoker's death?' Liam watched Sam carefully. 'A short illness, it said in the paper. I guess you knew?'

'Why would I have known?' A sudden tapping on the door interrupted Sam's speeding thoughts. Twisting around, she drew in her breath as the pain in her ribs caught her unawares. 'Yes?'

The receptionist stuck her head around the office door. 'Sorry to interrupt. I just wanted to let you know that Mr Stoker called twice last night. He didn't leave a message, but he sounded agitated...'

Sam reddened, sensing Liam's eyes on her. 'Thanks, Elaine. I'll call him back at some point later.'

She already knew Seb had called her apartment again because she'd checked the last number redial after arriving back. Maybe she should confide in him about Linda?

Sam looked over to Liam. 'Is there something else?'

Shaking his head, Liam forced a smile before getting up. 'Fancy a drink later?'

'Not tonight. I've got plans.'

'Okay. Some other time?' Liam smiled again before leaving the office and shutting the door behind him, when really, he wanted to slap the taste out of Sam's mouth.

All these years, she'd played him for a fool. She'd let him believe his place was assured, yet now because of that psycho thug, he was getting bloody robbed.

Well, he wouldn't give up his hard work for nothing. Sam was *his* and, by proxy, the profits of this business were too. Seb Stoker would not get either.

Now he had just about enough time to nip out and make a quick but much-needed visit to someone.

18

'This,' Tom said, dumping a bag on the desk in his office at the Aurora, 'is to be put somewhere safe until I decide where it's going.'

He paused, his fingers clutching the handles of the Tesco carrier bag. Knowing he'd need a supply for his own consumption, as well as getting Linda's old habit back up to speed, he took a handful of individual bags from inside and shoved them into his jeans pocket. Satisfied he'd got enough for a few days, Tom flopped into his chair.

'Order me a new chair, will you?' he snapped, finally looking in Lee's direction.

'What sort of chair?' Lee took the carrier bag, placing it into the small safe at the back of the room.

'Anything is better than this,' Tom barked. 'An office chair. Leather or something. I'm not sitting on this poxy plastic thing any longer. It's bloody stupid.'

Lee nodded, wondering what had got Tom's goat. He'd been like a bear with one foot in a mantrap since he'd arrived, but it probably wasn't the best time to ask, nor to mention yesterday had the worst night's takings so far.

'I need more hands on deck. How is Steve getting on with that?'

Tom flexed the fingers on his right hand, still aching from belting that stupid cow. *What had Linda been thinking by slowing up his bloody plan?*

'Steve's built up a decent team. We've got a good collection of dealers lined up now. The main problem is trekking to Wolverhampton for the supply.'

Tom nodded. 'That won't be for long. Soon we'll have a supply of powder closer to home.' Every single minute relying on those Wolverhampton bastards for coke galled him. They charged over the odds. The greedy bastards knew that for him to be over the Black Country in the first place, rather than on his home turf, he was in a tight spot, but there was no way he could sniff around the main suppliers here. Mainly because the main suppliers were the Reynolds and the Stokers. But by the time Linda was finished, Sam would be in on *his* deal. Family was family, right?

His face slipped back into a grimace. Linda's two-faced whore attitude may have slowed that up, but it wouldn't be for ever. He'd heard the drivel spewing out of her mouth as she'd feebly attempted to explain her behaviour. Heard all that bollocks about how she'd only hidden telling him because she was getting her head around meeting their daughter. *Blah, blah, blah.*

Fucking crying as she lay on the floor like a tramp, clinging onto his ankle and gibbering her thanks for being so thoughtful to write to 'their' Sam... Well, fuck that! He wasn't bothered with that old clobber.

He didn't need Linda getting bloody sentimental. Who gave a shit? He just needed the stupid old witch to get things on track with the girl so he could get access to her goldmine of a business. *Then* he'd be fucking happy.

Christ, Linda was lucky she still had teeth left in that backstabbing gob of hers. He'd been tempted to smash his boot into her face to add to her split lip, but instead, he'd had the sense to disappear before he'd *really* lost his temper.

'You were saying?' Lee watched the expressions moving across Tom's face. Steve had only said the other day that he was sure Tom was round the twist. Lee had disagreed, but now he wasn't so sure. Tom's head looked like it may explode. 'About getting coke closer to home?'

'What? Oh, yeah, that's in hand.' With growing irritation, Tom knew he'd have to return to the flat and offer grovelling apologies to the wizened old hag. *For fuck's sake.*

Aware his teeth were audibly grinding, he dragged a somewhat calmer expression on to his face. At least Luke had made the sensible choice after being helped to see reason. 'We have a crack supplier now too, so if we have to continue with the Wolverhampton boys for the coke in the interim, then so be it.'

Lee's heavy-set eyebrows furrowed. Tom's excuses were wearing thin. Tom had *promised* him and Steve it would be worth their while to join him full time, so they'd taken the risk – not that they'd had much choice. What had been promised had better materialise, but the longer this went on, the less likely it was to happen.

The Aurora would go down the pan if something didn't change. He and Steve had only been talking about coming up with a Plan B the other day, should the need arise. He reckoned, between the pair of them, they had the nous to pull it off. From what he'd just heard coming out of Tom's mouth, it was time to do just *that.*

Deciding he'd run it past Steve later, Lee thought it wise to change the subject. 'Did you hear one of the Stokers died?'

'Yeah, I heard something,' Tom mumbled, quietly working out how long it had taken before that news had been publicly released. *Two weeks? Three? Silly fuckers. They'd managed to cover the truth, then?* 'An illness, wasn't it? I can't say I'm gutted.'

He pulled the newspaper in front of him, finding it almost impossible not to sneer.

Funeral of Gary Stoker

The funeral of Gary Stoker will be held on Wednesday 19th July at St Francis of Assisi, Bournville and Birmingham Crematorium for family only, followed by the wake – 2 p.m. at the Royal Peacock, Broad Street.

Flowers to be sent to Lamberts Funeral Directors.

Lee chuckled. 'I take it you're not going?'

Tom returned the laughter. How he'd love to stand among the other mourners, having the silent satisfaction of knowing he'd put one of those tossers in a fucking coffin, but he wouldn't. There were more important things to concentrate on.

* * *

'I knew there was something up when it took ages for you to answer,' Vera said. 'I only popped round to ask you how the rest of your night went after I went home.' She stared at Linda's bust lip. 'Presumably, not very well?'

Turning away, Linda arranged ornaments that didn't need rearranging. 'Oh, you know what I'm like with doors when I'm pissed,' she grinned, wincing as her lip split further.

'You expect me to believe that?' Vera glanced at Tayquan and Shondra. She didn't think she'd ever seen them so quiet. They usually raced around with the energy of Duracell batteries, but today the stuffing had leaked out of them. They looked terrified. Standing in front of Linda, she forced the woman to face her. 'Either Sam lamped you for giving her up, or...'

'That's out of order, V!' Linda gasped.

'*Or* it was that Tom bloke...' Vera continued, her eyes narrowing scornfully. 'At a wild guess, I'd say it was that bastard! He's a snotty one, he is.'

'It wasn't Tom!' Linda lied, glancing warily at Tayquan and Shondra. 'Like I said, I slipped and went headfirst into the door.' She forced another laugh from her dry throat. 'How embarrassing to do that in front of Sam. Hell knows what she thinks of me!'

Vera pulled Linda to one side. 'Stop the bullshit, Linda. I know it was Tom.'

'It's my own fault,' Linda gabbled. 'The bloody kids have got big gobs. They told Tom that Sam was here.'

'What the fuck has that got to do with him?' Vera yelled.

Linda's mind raced. 'Erm... he said I shouldn't say anything to anyone about Sam. He thinks people would use me for money,' she blathered. 'Then I stupidly blurted out I'd told you and...'

'What, so he thinks *I'd* hit on you for cash because of who your daughter is?' Vera's lips pursed. 'I've got a good mind to...'

'Please keep out of it, V. Don't spoil things for me. I love Tom. We're making a go of things and he's worried about the situation, that's all.' Linda smiled weakly. 'I was going to warn you not to mention anything about Sam, but it's a bit late now...'

Vera shook her head in disbelief. Linda blamed herself? She'd heard that excuse too many times over the years when it came to men like Tom. Would Linda ever see sense? 'So now what? Are you seeing Sam again?'

Linda's eyes, swollen from crying, brightened. 'I hope so. She said she'd be in touch and I gave her my phone number. I... I just hope she calls.' Her face fell. 'And I hope Tom comes back...'

Vera snorted in derision. Linda should be hoping he bloody well didn't.

'You won't say anything about this to anyone, will you?' Linda gestured to her bruised mouth. 'My life's going well for once. I've got everything I always wanted, and I don't want that ruined.'

Vera would have laughed if it wasn't so tragic. *Life was going well?* She held her hands up in defeat. 'Okay, if that's what you want. I'm not happy, though.'

'I know, I know,' Linda wheedled. 'But Tom won't do it again. It was a one-off.'

'Really...?' Vera scowled. She faced the silent children. 'Right, kiddos, what do you say to coming over to mine for half an hour so your ma can get herself washed and dressed in peace? The cartoons will be on in a minute, and I'll do you some nice cheese on toast? How does that sound?'

At the mention of food, both children returned from the dead. Their eyes lighting up, they jumped to their feet and scurried off to find their shoes.

'I'm telling you now, Linda. If that prick makes a habit of raising his hand to you, especially in front of the kids, I won't be keeping my gob shut, do you understand?' Vera warned.

Linda nodded. It was okay. Tom's outburst was warranted with what she'd kept from him. He wouldn't do it again. Especially once he'd met Sam and they were a proper family at last. At least then she could tell Vera the truth and it would make sense why he'd been so cross.

19

Gloria placed the mug of tea down on the coffee table next to Liam. 'You must excuse the state of me.' She self-consciously glanced down at her clothes. 'I wouldn't have usually answered the door, but I thought it might be Samantha...'

Liam had the good manners to look contrite. 'I shouldn't have descended unannounced.' He took a sip of the scalding hot liquid. 'I just wanted to make sure you were okay.'

Gloria sat forward, worry flooding her face. 'Has something happened?'

Liam placed his mug down. 'No. Well, not exactly... It's just...'

'Just what?' Gloria cried. 'Liam, you've always been a good boy. Len thought the world of you, as do I. If something is bothering you – something you think I should know, then you must tell me.' She swallowed dryly, barely able to form the words. 'Is... is it Samantha?'

Liam sighed loudly and nodded. 'Sam's not herself...'

Gloria looked down at her hands. 'This is all my fault. If only I'd told her... If only I'd...'

'It's not only that,' Liam interrupted. 'I mean, I know she's been upset, but it's more than that.'

'More?' Gloria frowned. 'What do you mean?'

Liam faltered. 'It's... erm... well, since she got involved with Sebastian Stoker, she's changed. I hate saying it, but it's like she's brainwashed and under control...'

'But Sebastian always seemed a very pleasant man. He helped Samantha after... after Len died. Without him, she'd have found taking over the club more difficult.'

'He's been doing a lot more than helping her run the firm.' Liam cleared his throat in mock embarrassment. 'They're, erm... they're...'

Gloria's eyes widened as Liam's words registered. 'You mean she and Sebastian are...'

'Sleeping together, yes.' The words burnt Liam's tongue. 'Sorry to be blunt, but it's the truth.' He hung his head. 'As you can imagine, it upsets me a great deal because I thought me and Sam... I thought we...'

'Oh, you poor boy!' Gloria patted Liam's knee. 'Are you sure about Samantha and Sebastian being involved?'

'Totally sure, but that isn't the sole reason I'm telling you. Obviously, I'm hurt, but I'm more worried than anything else. *Really* worried.' He saw a flash of unease behind Gloria's eyes. 'I believe Stoker is misleading Sam with purposefully bad advice.'

Gloria's mouth dropped open. 'Oh, Liam, Judith and Mal haven't brought their boys up to be like that. I cannot believe th...'

'Why does she keep disappearing and being cagey about everything, then?' Liam shook his head. 'It breaks my heart. I want to marry her, but she's obsessed with Stoker. She's turning into a horrible person, Gloria. For instance, like how she's treating you. She'd *never* ignore you like this if it wasn't for him.'

He could see it. There it was. The flicker of mistrust. 'You've got to remember that when all is said and done, the Stokers are the Reynolds' rivals and always have been. They also blame you and Sam for all this business with the rumours and Gary Stoker.'

'Oh, my God!' Gloria gasped. 'You mean you think Sebastian is using Samantha to get his own back on her? On me?'

Liam shrugged. 'I don't know. I have proof of nothing. Sam barely speaks to me. She won't even discuss it.' He silently congratulated himself at the sheen of tears in Gloria's eyes. 'All I know is that Sam's not usually like this.' He dropped his voice to a whisper, even though they were the only two in the large house. 'The Stokers are trained killers, Gloria. They're of a different ilk to Len and his kind.'

Gloria wrung her hands, finding it difficult to imagine that Sebastian could stage something so convoluted and underhand. To make Samantha pay for what she, herself, had made the mistake of doing was unthinkable.

'The thing is, I have no idea what I'm going to do about it. Or even what I *can* do about it.' Liam looked at Gloria, his face a mask of well-practised pain. 'I'd make Sam happy, you know I would. If she doesn't want me, then I have to accept that.' *No, I won't...* 'But I won't stand back and do nothing when some thug who doesn't know the meaning of love or anything good sets about destroying her and everything she holds dear.'

He paused, pretending to think. 'Perhaps you should go to the funeral yourself. At least you'd get a chance to talk to her.'

Sitting back in the chair, Liam reached for his mug, allowing his information to fester within Gloria's brain.

Once he'd given it a few minutes, he'd make his excuses to pop to the toilet and shove the carrier bag he'd left in the porch somewhere in one of the spare bedrooms. It would be safe here and then he'd have to get back to the Orchid.

* * *

Pushing open the door to the lobby to make her way down to Kevin's office, Sam was so consumed with the coming meeting, she almost walked past Seb.

'Seb?' she cried, heat rushing to her cheeks. 'What are you doing here?'

Seb leant against the patent top of the reception desk, his nonchalant demeanour masking his thoughts. 'I was passing, so I thought I'd pop in...'

Sam's stomach lurched with anticipation, before rapidly sinking. 'I'm afraid I'm on my way to a meeting.'

Without wanting to, her gaze roamed over Seb's frame, encased in one of the top-quality and meticulously tailored suits he prided himself on. Her eyes fell to his mouth, those full lips of his twitching into the hint of a smile. The urge to feel his mouth on hers grew into a rolling wave.

'I'm sure your meeting can wait for five minutes, can't it?' Seb's voice was smooth and clear, his eyes dancing with mischief.

It hadn't been difficult to reach the decision that acting like a jealous saddo as he had last night would not be repeated. The way he'd felt had jarred his senses. That sort of shit was not in his repertoire and would not become a habit. He refused to lower himself to question Sam about her whereabouts or who she was with. This visit to the Orchid today was to remind her that it was *him* that she wanted. No one else.

Talk of the devil...

Seb suddenly caught sight of the man himself entering the Orchid. Meeting Liam's eyes, Seb's cold gaze did not falter until Liam averted his stare to glance at Sam before heading off into the casino.

Seb's mouth curled with the ghost of a smile. *Yeah, that's right, Liam. She wants me...*

Sam tingled with anticipation. It was ridiculous for every nerve ending to jangle at the mere sight of Seb Stoker, but it happened regardless. She glanced at the receptionist, who was watching the exchange with intense curiosity. 'Can you let Mr Stanton know I'll be a few minutes late for our meeting, please?'

Turning back to Seb, she held his gaze. 'Follow me, Mr Stoker.'

Walking ahead, Sam confidently pushed through the doors to the corridor leading to her office, the burn of Seb's eyes melting her skin through her suit, the intoxicating chemistry crackling between them.

Sam's hand was on her office door when Seb pushed her against the wall with his body. Saying nothing, his mouth crashed onto hers. Gasping with desire, her arms wound around his neck, the intensity of his kiss almost flooring her.

'Mr Stanton, whoever he is, can wait,' Seb murmured into Sam's mouth.

Drunk with desire, Seb's words vibrated through her body, and Sam offered no resistance as he pushed open her office door, pulling her with him.

Shutting the door behind him, Seb smiled, his green eyes shining. 'Now... where were we?' With one swipe, he brushed the contents of Sam's desk to one side. Lifting her up like a doll, he sat her on the edge of the mahogany surface.

'Seb!' Sam cried giddily, unable to control the torrent of sensations sparking in her. She stared at his thick hair as he knelt in front of her and pushed her skirt around her thighs, his mouth moving lightly yet tantalisingly up her inner thigh.

She gasped with pleasure as Seb continued upwards, intense waves building rapidly. 'Seb...' she groaned, her fingers twisting in his hair.

Rising from his knees, Seb freed himself from his trousers, his mouth back on hers. Neither of them noticed the figure watching them through the glass panel of the door.

—————

20

'Craig and Stu are heading up this fourth team – Team D.' Kevin nodded towards the other two men present.

Sam smiled in acknowledgement, her mind far from the present conversation and still in her office with Seb Stoker. And every time she thought about that, electricity jolted through her body.

'So, what do you think?'

Sam's eyes darted to Kevin and then to the other pairs of eyes waiting for her response. 'Erm, sorry, could you repeat that last part?' she mumbled. *Come on, Sam, don't let yourself down.* Now these guys were on board, she mustn't push them back to thinking her incapable.

Kevin frowned. 'I was saying about the team I've set up to concentrate on the shared patches.'

Sam's attention focused. 'The patches we share with the Stokers? Is there a problem?'

Kevin rolled his huge shoulders. 'No, but as there was aggro not long ago, I feel a dedicated team policing those areas is the way forward.'

Sam leant over the map, her mind now fully centred. She looked at the marked groups, concern glimmering. 'Have there been further attempts to overtake any of our areas?' The thought that there might still be someone or another firm vying for their territories filled her with horror.

'Nothing more than we would usually get, with dickheads trying their luck,' Kevin explained.

Sam nodded. Telling Kevin the truth about John had been difficult, but it was the only way to enable him to function properly as her trusted second. And it had been worth that risk because he'd vowed what she'd said would go no further. She had to trust *someone* within her firm, otherwise everything would be impossible. And to give Kevin further credit, he'd gone out of his way to explain how other things worked in the business, too.

Sam glanced at the other men. Kevin had clearly stuck to his word and not informed anyone else of what he now knew, because these two didn't look too over-enamoured. 'I take it I'll expect a separate report on those areas in addition to the usual reports?'

Kevin nodded his oversized head. 'When will you have reports for Miss Reynold, Craig?'

'Every Monday,' Craig answered, unsmiling.

Sam felt strangely calm, despite the frosty atmosphere. She was no longer floundering alone.

'The last two drops went smoothly,' Kevin continued. 'The first drop went ahead last Friday after reverting back to the original schedule, as per your instructions.'

Sam smiled. 'And the vans and bikes are all running okay and legit?'

'Yep. I double checked through all the insurance and MOTs of all our vehicles myself only yesterday.'

Sam smiled. It had been something of a surprise to discover the firm's vans had specially strengthened panels and bullet proof glass. Up until the other day, she hadn't the faintest idea that most of the cocaine drops were done via motorbike either. 'And the next drop is due... when?' She flicked through the pages of her desk diary. 'Tonight?'

Stu cleared his throat. 'There is one due tonight, yes. That's being done by Team B and due to drop at...' Leaning across the desk, he pointed to another area on the map. 'The patch from the Hyatt down to Brindley Place.'

'Following the original routes?'

'All of the original routes are being followed, like you said,' Kevin said. 'The next one will go out this coming Wednesday, and that's to the Bearwood triangle patch, here...' He pointed to a section between Rotton Park, City Road and Waterloo Road.

'That all sounds good to me,' Sam smiled. There was so much to learn, so much to understand, but now she really was getting to grips with everything.

Kevin folded the map and placed it in his leather file. 'Last thing – how many representatives do you want attending the Stoker funeral?'

Sam blinked. *Shit. The funeral.* How could she have been so bloody thoughtless to forget that? After that rushed but immensely pleasurable interlude, both she and Seb had dashed off back to reality. There hadn't been time to mention any of the things she'd planned to – like *Linda*. Neither had she mentioned the funeral, but Seb was coming to her apartment tonight, so they'd talk properly then.

A smile drifted onto her face. She couldn't wait to see him again...

Sam cleared her throat. 'I'll be the sole representative,' she found herself saying. 'Gary Stoker didn't hold a major position, so a big turnout from our firm is unnecessary.' She winced at her words. They sounded so callous. So harsh. But they were true, all the same. It was how this worked.

* * *

'I said I was sorry, didn't I?' Tom repeated, the words sounding brittle through his clenched jaw. 'Why isn't that good enough for you?'

Willing himself to keep focused, his fingers twitched over the pocket where the crack he so desperately wanted to smoke sat.

He stared at Linda's split lip, hating her even more than he had before. Did she not realise that every minute he spent in this dump playing to her pathetic needs was another minute paying through the nose for overpriced coke? There was tons of it within the grasping hands of his daughter, and Linda wanted to take things slowly?

Tom continued glaring at her, wanting to ram the can of cider she clutched into her face. 'I asked you why my apology wasn't good enough?'

'It is!' Linda blathered. 'I know you didn't mean to hit me.'

That's what you think, Tom thought. In fact, he wished, along with the one measly backhander she'd received, he'd stamped on her face and continued doing so until she stopped twitching, the stupid bastard. 'Why leave Sam to do the running?'

Linda stared at her fingers, the nails bitten down to the quick. 'Sam said she'd call. I don't want to hassle her.'

The clicking sound as Linda picked at a jagged fingernail irritated Tom further. *Click, click, click – over and over and bloody over.* It was driving him mad. This whole situation was driving him mad. 'Are you telling me Sam won't want to see you again? Is that it?' *If Linda had fucked this up... If she'd put the girl off...*

'What did you do?' he ranted, pacing around the kitchen. 'There must be something to make you think you won't see her again? But then, it's not like you'd tell me, considering you weren't going to bother saying you'd even seen her!'

Linda stared at Tom, wide-eyed. 'Nothing! I didn't do nothing. We got on well. I explained why I didn't tell you.' Despite her promise not to break down, knowing it angered Tom when she cried, her eyes filled with tears. 'I told you I – I'm scared she might not want to take it any further.' *Like she doesn't want a mother like me...*

'Oh, well, that's okay then!' Tom snarled. He slammed his can of lager down, the vibration shaking fag butts from the ashtray. *Time for a different tactic.* 'Does it not cross your selfish mind that I want to see my daughter?' He pulled his hands through his unbrushed hair. 'If I'd have known you would shut me out and keep me away from her, then I wouldn't have come back.'

He grabbed the ashtray. 'And look at the state of this place. Who'd want to be here?' Launching the metal dish across the room; it rebounded off a wall cupboard, leaving a dent in the orange Formica. 'I thought we had something and that you still loved me. Christ, I've been so fucking stupid!'

Linda jumped to her feet, horrified. 'No, oh, no. That's not true. I *do* love you. I love you more than anything! I always have.'

As Linda clung to him, Tom stopped himself from shoving the rusty bread knife lying on the worktop into her jugular and instead continued convincingly pulling at his hair.

'Please listen,' Linda wailed, tears rolling down her face. 'It was you who said you wanted to keep out of it and that you didn't want to over-whelm our Sam with both of us. And I...'

'Now you're turning it round on *me*?' Tom screamed, impressed with his acting skills. 'Let's not forget she's not *our* Sam. She's *yours*. She's yours because you've made it that way. You're shutting me out and...'

'I haven't. I would never do that!' Linda's broken fingernails clawed at Tom's T-shirt.

'You *lied*.' Tom lowered his voice to a destitute whimper. 'Have you any idea how much that hurts? And over something so important as our daughter too? How could you, Linda?'

Linda's chest heaved, as sobs racked her body. It was true. She could see now that she'd lied for her own selfish needs and because of that, she risked losing Tom all over again. 'I'm sorry, I'm sorry,' she begged. 'I'll never do it again. *Please* let me make it better. What can I do to put it right? Don't give up on me. I couldn't bear it.'

Tom untangled himself from Linda and slumped in a kitchen chair.

Leaning on the table, he put his head in his hands, making sure his face was covered to hide the forming smile.

Linda timidly prodded Tom's arm. 'Sam said she'd call, so I'll make it right, I promise.'

Tom looked up. 'How can that happen when you haven't got a phone?'

'W-what?' Linda's head swung in the direction of where her phone used to be, noticing for the first time that all remained was a broken wall socket. 'I – I don't understand? I...'

'I chucked it out,' Tom spat. 'It was fucking dead and bust. A bit like everything else around here!'

Linda wrung her hands. 'I'll find a way. I'll think of something. Tell me what to do.'

Tom grinned. *Perfect.* Now Linda would fall over herself to do his bidding. *God, he was a clever one.* This was even better than letting things follow their natural course. All he had to do was word this carefully so Linda would line everything up in the best way possible.

* * *

Finally feeling coherent enough to hold a conversation, Liam hurried towards Kevin Stanton's office.

It was safe. Sam had left for the day a couple of hours ago and he knew this because he'd watched her. He'd wanted to scream at her, to smash his fist into her pretty face and make her list what Stoker had that he didn't, that had caused her to make a fool out of herself and act like a whore.

Oh, he'd seen her. He'd seen her at it with that greasy psycho in her office. Was it Stoker's violence that turned her on? Did she like how bastards like him fucked people over or killed them for less than the price of a bag of chips?

Because *he* could do that. He'd do whatever it took so Sam delivered what she'd promised all these years. And he'd already made a good start on that.

Sam was sleeping with the enemy. And it had to stop.

Okay, so balls were in play to screw Stoker and his oh-so-hot reputation up, but it obviously wasn't enough. Neither was it quick enough. And it needed to be quicker, otherwise it would be too late.

His veins pumped with adrenaline. The thought of losing everything was a bitch on his blood pressure, but at least he'd stopped shaking with rage enough to speak to Kevin.

Liam tapped on the door. Hearing a grunt, which he took to mean 'enter', he walked into the office. *The office that had once been John's.* 'Have you got a minute?' His heart sank on seeing two of Kevin's monkey-like enforcers present. 'In private...?'

Liam watched Kevin stare at him, as if trying to place him, then jerk his massive head in the direction of the monkeys. *Do this lot not speak using normal words*? he thought, hoping his impatience was hidden.

Kevin waited until the two large men lumbered from the room. 'Liam Taylor, isn't it?' he grunted.

'Yes, that's me.' Liam edged towards the desk. 'This is awkward... You probably know that I was on very good terms with John Maynard before he... disappeared. I know you also thought highly of him, so, under the circumstances, I think you're the one to speak to about this matter.'

Kevin nodded. He too had thought highly of Maynard, but that was *before*. He indicated for Liam to sit down.

Liam paused. 'I'm sure you're aware me and Sam go back years,' he continued. 'We've always been close and... let's just say I'm concerned.'

'Concerned about what?'

Liam lowered his voice. 'Sam. She's at risk.'

Kevin sat upright, clasping his meaty hands together. 'Go on...'

Liam took a deep breath. 'It's her recent involvement with Stoker that bothers me. That man hated John Maynard. Look, I don't believe

John disappeared – I think Stoker killed him. There was something funny going on the night of Len's wake. It all started from there.'

Kevin folded his arms, leant back in the chair and studied Liam carefully. Stoker hadn't killed Maynard. Sam had told him exactly what had happened. Besides, Maynard had deserved to die for what he'd done, so what was this guy's game? 'You'd better tell me what you think you know, Liam.'

21

Such was her need to see Seb, Sam all but skipped up the hallway to press the intercom. She knew it was crazy, but she didn't care. When she was with him, she felt like she could conquer the world.

She fidgeted, waiting as he made his way up to her apartment and smoothed her hair, hoping she hadn't overdone it. She glanced down at her purple halter dress. *Too much?* She didn't know, but they might be going out somewhere.

Before she could dwell further, Seb appeared at the door, his green eyes sparkling and a wide smile across his face – the very opposite of the face he revealed in public.

Sam loved seeing different facets of Sebastian Stoker – the playful side, the *happy* side. She liked to think these were sides no one else saw. Facets reserved just for her.

Pulling Sam into his arms, Seb kissed her, then grinned. 'I bought you this.'

Sam looked at the bottle of Château Lafite Rothschild in his hand. 'You don't drink wine.'

'No, but you do...'

'Are you trying to get me drunk, Mr Stoker?' Sam laughed, relishing that he'd already pulled her back into his arms.

Seb raised an eyebrow. 'Do I need to?'

'No, you don't.' Sam pushed herself up on tiptoe and kissed him. It was so tempting to throw all notion of talking out of the window and jump into bed, but that's all they'd done on the few snatched times together lately. Whether she liked it or not, they needed to talk.

It was when she took the bottle of expensive wine from Seb's hand that she noticed the bruising. 'What have you done?' She ran her finger over the vivid discoloration of his knuckles and the angry red scratches across the back of his hand.

Seb deflected by using his other hand to pull Sam back towards him. 'Something and nothing.'

'A fight with a cheese grater and a brick?'

'Something like that,' Seb laughed, having no intention of admitting last night's embarrassing action when he'd punched her door in frustration.

Sam walked over to the cabinet and unscrewed the whisky bottle. 'A drink for you?'

Seb watched Sam intently, savouring her every movement and mannerism. She looked ravishing – not that she didn't usually, but it was frustrating knowing he would soon have to leave. He'd love to leave Andrew and Neil to broker the gun deal, but there was no way he was chancing that the way things were. 'Just a small one,' he said, nodding at the whisky.

'We haven't had much time to talk, have we?' Sam handed Seb a crystal tumbler of whisky and set about opening the wine, leaving the path clear for him to speak first.

Seb walked across to the large lounge window and looked down on the canal below. The red Victorian brickwork walkways sparkled with hanging baskets full of brightly coloured flowers – a striking contrast to the Gas Basin he remembered before the regeneration project. The days when the stinking confines of the canal were surrounded by derelict factories, the only residents glue sniffers and squatters. *Not any more.*

Silence weighed heavy in the room and Seb toyed with telling Sam about the escalating issue between him and Andrew.

Why couldn't they just rely on their bodies to do the talking? It was easier that way. That way there were no awkward questions, no dreading of answers and no uncertainties. He didn't like uncertainty. 'What do you want to talk about?'

Sam fiddled with her wine glass, unsure where to start. 'If it's okay with you, I'll be attending Gary's funeral.' Why was this so awkward? It shouldn't be difficult.

Seb turned around. *Sam wanted to talk about the funeral?* She'd seemed poised to say something else. He waited, but she said nothing further. 'If that's what you want? I didn't expect you to personally attend.'

Sam floundered. 'I thought I should, what with...' Her voice trailed off. 'Will it be difficult? With your parents, I mean? You know... because my mo... *Gloria* hid the truth about those rumours?'

'Not at all. You'll be there to pay your respects,' Seb smiled. But it *did* concern him how Andrew or even his *father* might treat her. This shouldn't be an issue and the fact that it was rankled.

'Okay.' Sam felt deflated. The vibe of the evening wasn't what she'd hoped. 'Are you all right?'

'Yeah,' Seb shrugged. 'It's just difficult with Gary... you know...'

How could he tell her that as well as wanting to protect her from how his family might treat her, he also suspected Andrew of making him look incompetent and that his own brother could have been the one who went to the papers? He wasn't sure of any of it himself. Or more rightly, he didn't *want* to be sure. There had to be another explanation. Neither did he want to say his own father doubted him and blamed *her* for diluting his concentration.

If Sam knew this, she might walk away. The issues Gloria had caused within his family played on Sam's mind, he knew this, but he couldn't have her turn her back on him. She was the only good thing in his life. The only thing giving him something that was *real*.

Sam hesitated, but before she could stop herself, she blurted it out. 'I met my mother.'

Seb jolted in surprise. 'Your *mother*?'

Sam took a sip of a wine, as though her revelation was no big deal. Except it was. It was a really big deal and she had to tell him. She *wanted* to tell him. 'Yes, my real one. She wrote to me.'

'She knew where you lived?' Seb cried, aghast.

Sensing Seb's disbelief and annoyance, disappointment dripped through Sam. 'No, she wrote to me at the Orchid and gave me the name of a pub. So I went there.'

'Are you insane? You went to some random boozer? It could have been a fucking setup!' Seb paced around the room, his head swimming. 'Why didn't you tell me? I could have sussed her out and discovered if she was kosher. I *told* you I'd deal with the newspaper thing so you wouldn't keep getting this crap.'

Sam bristled. 'I already said I didn't want you dealing with anything for me over this. I didn't tell you because you'd have tried to stop me. It looks like I'd have been right.' For the first time in a long while, irritation surged. 'And, as it turns out, the woman *was* kosher. She *is* my mother.'

He wasn't supposed to react like this. She'd wanted Seb's support. She'd wanted to hear his opinion and help her decide what to do. Softening slightly, she reached for Seb's arm. 'Seriously, you don't need to worry. I know what I'm doing. Forget I said anything.'

Seb spun on his heels. 'No! I want to know exactly what happened. Which pub was it?' *Sam couldn't put herself at risk.*

'The Hen and Chicks – not that it matters!' Sam cried in exasperation. 'Christ, Seb, what's the problem? It's just a bloody pub in Northfield.'

Striding over, Seb grabbed Sam by the shoulders. 'It matters to m...' He stopped, seeing her wince, her hand moving to her ribs. His eyes narrowed. 'What happened at this Hen and Chicks, Sam? Because *something* did!'

Sam shrugged Seb's hands away. 'Oh, for God's sake! Nothing! Just some pissed-up blokes having a scrap and one fell on me, knocking me into a table! No big deal!'

Seb's face twisted into a snarl. 'No big deal? What fucking blokes? You can't be sure that wasn't the start of something aimed at you!' *Who the fuck had dared to hurt her?* He shoved his hand in his inside pocket and pulled out his Berretta. 'Take this. I've got plenty.'

'I don't want *that!*' Sam pushed Seb's hand away, like it was infected. 'I don't need a gun! And I don't need protecting either!' *She may be in this world now, but she wouldn't resort to violence.*

Seb shoved the gun back in his jacket. How could he keep this woman he loved – yes, *loved* – safe, if she wouldn't let him? Being independent and capable in business was one thing, but there were people, situations, that she wouldn't deal with – couldn't *physically* deal with, however much she wanted to think otherwise.

Fact.

Or was there another reason...?

He looked at Sam accusingly. 'I take it you went to this boozer on your own?'

Sam frowned. 'Yes, I went on my own. Why? What's that got to do with anything?'

Seb thrust his hands into his pockets in a bid to keep them still. Was Sam refusing his protection because someone *else* was supplying it? Digging his teeth into the inside of his cheek, he fought against breaking his oath not to let jealousy rear its ugly head, but distracted by his own thoughts, it pushed to the forefront.

'So, tell me, Sam, what's with Liam? Is *he* watching your back? Is that why he's always around here?' Rage twisted Seb's handsome face. 'Or is it Kevin Stanton – the bloke you almost bypassed me for this afternoon? Who the fuck is he, anyway?'

Sam's mouth gaped incredulously. 'What are you talking about?

Liam's hardly ever here and Kevin is taking John Maynard's place permanently.'

'So he'll be your right-hand man?' Seb barked, anger with himself rising. *Stop it, stop it!* 'Nice of you to let me know.'

'Why the hell should I let you know? You don't run my firm! What's the matter with you? You're being ridiculous!' Sam gasped, feeling the sudden urge to cry. There was no point telling Seb about Linda or trying to explain how she felt – he wasn't listening. No one was listening. 'How about *you* tell me something that *does* matter?' She turned to face him. 'Like what happened to John's body?'

Seb bit back his retort. One of the few people he didn't want to fight with was Sam, but her spoiling for a row was trying his unstable patience. He pulled his cigarettes from his pocket and lit one. *Calm down and realign yourself, Seb.* 'I told you. It's sorted.'

'Yes, I know you said that, but I want to know *how!*' Sam cried indignantly, resentment for the pressure of her embryonic experience in this world of Seb's exploding. 'You never told me and I need to know. Do I not have the right?'

Seb laughed, aiming to diffuse this escalating situation. 'That's what I'm here for. Let me deal with that sort of stuff. There's no need for you to worry about things like that.'

'What right do you have to tell me what I should worry about or not?' Sam scowled, knowing it was now *her* being pedantic.

Seb sighed. 'Okay, so you don't want my protection and refuse to protect yourself.'

'What the hell is that supposed to mean?' Sam yelped. Seb didn't want her at the Peacock, he didn't want her at his brother's funeral, and now he felt it was his right to dictate to her, question her whereabouts and who she was with. The final insult was he thought she had the brains of a pond skater.

'We're not arguing, are we, Samantha?' Seb said, his attempt at lightening the atmosphere failing miserably.

Finishing her wine, Sam slammed the glass down. 'I don't know *what* we're doing, but what I *do* know is that I'm not in the mood to go out tonight.'

Seb placed his unfinished whisky on the coffee table. 'That wasn't happening anyway because I've got somewhere else I need to be, unfortunately.'

Sam hid her hurt, unable to stop her mouth from continuing. 'I'll sit here then, shall I? Or perhaps I'll head out and see if I can get ripped off or murdered? Either that or maybe I'll go and see some of my "friends". You know, the ones you're so bothered about!'

Seb studied Sam silently for a moment before stalking towards the door. 'I'm trying to be here for you, Sam, so give me a call when you're feeling more reasonable.' Turning on his heel, he left the apartment, his jaw clenched.

Hearing Seb's footsteps thunder down the stairs, Sam leant against the wall and exhaled slowly. She hadn't wanted him to go. She'd wanted to talk to him and ask him what he thought about everything. Then they'd have gone out, had some drinks and spent the rest of the night in her bed.

Sam snatched up the bottle of wine, the memories of how much she'd been looking forward to the evening shattering into pieces around her.

This was as much her fault as his. She'd been equally as irrational. *What the hell was happening to her?*

22

Pulling the van into the layby where they'd arranged to meet, Neil glanced warily at Andrew. 'No grief tonight, okay?'

'I'm here for business,' Andrew said, the swelling of his blackened right eye accentuated by the shadows cast from the dim gloom of the lamppost. 'That's the main aim of everything I do. *Business*.' At least he had his priorities straight, unlike *some* people.

Neil nodded, placated. 'Seb will be glad to hear we've got the full shipment as promised.'

'Yeah,' Andrew muttered. Yet Seb hadn't even had the decency to broach yesterday's attack. He'd been half-choked, for fuck's sake, and what about his bust eye? And everyone, including *Neil*, was pretending it didn't matter?

It *did* matter. It mattered a lot. Their family was crumbling and all because Seb had given his heart to Sam Reynold instead? It wasn't good enough.

'I half-expected Benny to have his mug smashed up when I saw him.' Neil eyed Andrew curiously. 'I thought you'd perhaps reminded him how important the order was...'

'What are you going on about?' Andrew barked. He hated it when Neil talked in riddles. It rankled, putting on a united front with Seb for the benefit of the Irish. All he wanted to do was get this done and get out of here.

'I saw you last night...' Neil said carefully. 'I saw you coming in the back door of the Peacock.'

Andrew glanced at his watch dismissively. 'Oh, that? Just a scrap with some muppet in a pub. I wasn't in the mood for dickheads.'

'Which pub?'

'Can't remember. Why the fuck does it matter? Besides, it was just a bit of a friendly slap.'

'Lot of blood for a slap,' Neil pressed. 'Your shirt was covered. You can't go around publicly pasting people. It doesn't look good on the firm.'

'Yeah, and Seb wouldn't like that,' Andrew said bitterly. Seeing headlights pulling into the layby, he started the engine. 'Anyway, forget that. He's here. Time to rock and roll.'

Winding down his window, Neil frowned when Seb approached the passenger side. 'What's up? Don't tell me the deal's off?'

'Off?' Seb growled. 'Why the fuck would it be off? Just checking we're good to go.'

'We wouldn't be here waiting if it wasn't,' Andrew muttered.

'Get moving, then,' Seb barked. 'I'll tail you. I want this wrapped up quickly.'

As Seb stalked back towards his motor, Neil shut the window. 'I thought he'd be happy everything's here.'

Andrew scowled. 'Why? Haven't you yet realised he's never fucking happy?'

* * *

After personally depositing the huge amount of cash which had successfully changed hands in return for the arsenal of weapons into one of the many safes at the lockup, Seb floored it towards his next port of call.

Had tonight's deal not gone to plan, he'd have happily turned one of the Irish's newly acquired weapons on them.

He dragged viciously on his cigarette, glancing at the 30 mph speed limit. He was doing twice that, but he didn't care.

Wheel-spinning into the pub car park, Seb jumped from his car and pressed the button on his key fob, the double flash of the indicators lighting up the dark front of the pub with a vivid orange flash.

That Sam had been hurt by some lowlife in a boozer plagued him, prodding like a stubborn splinter. Arguing with her tonight bothered him. *Why couldn't she see he just wanted to look after her?*

Tugging his cuffs from under the sleeves of his suit jacket, he strode purposefully towards the front door, contempt for the people inside already at boiling point. One of these tossers had hurt Sam and he would be reminding whoever it was that was a mistake not to be repeated.

Being unable to tell Sam that she had become so entrenched in his thoughts was frustrating enough. The concept was new and the fear it might leave him open made itself known. It was difficult to put his feelings into words.

All this shit with his family... and acting like a jealous twat too? *Christ...*

Entering the small lobby, Seb picked the bar on the left to try first. Judging by the racket, it stood to reason the heavy-handed scrote was more than likely in that side.

He slammed into the room, the noise as the heavy wooden door crashed into the side of a fruit machine causing a sea of heads to turn in his direction. The raucous chatter dwindled to an uncomfortable silence as he continued across the room, knowing his face spelt out he wasn't there for a social drink.

A group of men sitting by the bar eyeing Seb drew his attention.

Walking over, he looked between each man in turn. 'Know anything about a dickhead who fell on a woman in here last night?'

The burliest of the group with one leg stretched out across an empty chair, looked up at Seb with the hint of a sneer. 'What sort of a question is that?'

Seb stared at the words 'Jim's Roofers' emblazoned on the man's grubby T-shirt. 'A relatively easy one, I would say, *Jim!*'

From his vantage point behind the bar, the landlord busied himself emptying the dishwasher. Jim might be unaware of who the big man in the suit was, but *he* wasn't. On any other day, he'd be chuffed to have a Stoker in his boozer, but not under the proviso of the gaff getting smashed up. 'Come on, fellas,' he said amiably. 'Let's have no grief, eh?'

Seb turned towards the bar. 'No trouble from me, mate. Just deducing which of your customers are devoid of manners.'

'What makes you think whatever you're talking about has anything to do with me?' Jim smiled, eyeing Seb with contempt.

Seb smiled back – a smile which displayed his straight white teeth whilst emphasising the coldness of his green eyes. 'I don't, but you seem the sort of prick to argue with their mates and end up hurting women, so I thought I'd start with you.'

'Or could it be this woman, whoever she is, was playing away and spouted some bollocks to hide her kinky bedroom antics that didn't include *you*?'

'Jim!' the man in the next chair hissed. 'Don't push your luck. That's…'

'I don't give a shit!' Jim spat. 'This is *our* fucking boozer, yet this guy comes in here playing his mouth and…'

'I don't care whether it was you or not,' Seb grinned savagely. 'But you'll do, regardless.' Effortlessly jumping onto a chair, Seb stepped off the seat onto Jim's outstretched leg. The man had no warning nor chance to move, and the noise as his shin broke in two places was surprisingly loud.

'Aaaargh!' Jim howled, his face a grimace of shock and raw agony.

'Listen, cunt...' Seb stepped over the man's writhing body, ignoring the white-faced horror of those around him, and yanked the man's head from the floor by the scruff of his grubby T-shirt. 'Any disrespect from you or *anyone* in this fucking dump or anything which results in hurting my woman pays for it. Got it?'

Slamming Jim's head onto the sticky carpet, he scanned the room. 'Did everyone understand that? Just to add – if she ever comes in here again, I expect her to leave at the end of the night in no way damaged.'

Casually wiping his hands down his trousers, Seb nodded to the landlord, then exited the pub the way he'd come in.

It took thirty seconds of stunned silence, short of Jim's howling, before anyone contemplated moving to look at the broken bones sticking through the skin of his shin.

Sighing, the landlord picked up the phone to dial for an ambulance, wondering what feasible excuse he would give to explain how *that* had occurred. He'd think of something. He usually did.

From her table opposite, Vera lit a cigarette, her fingers shaking. If Linda was here, she'd have known straight away that man was talking about her daughter. She'd have also realised that Sam was not only the owner of one of Birmingham's finest casinos, but was involved with the Stokers – one of the city's most notorious firms.

But there was a good side to this, and one Vera would use if push came to shove. That loser, Tom, had better watch his step, because if Sebastian Stoker ever found out Tom had whacked his future mother-in-law, then he was a dead man indeed.

* * *

Rushing to answer the intercom, Sam almost tripped in her haste. The bottle of wine she'd polished off hadn't helped. 'Seb? Is that you?' she said, pressing the door release button.

Leaning unsteadily against the wall, she stared at herself in the mirror. Licking her finger, she attempted to remove the black smudges of mascara her tears had left around her eyes, but it was no use and the subsequent tap of the door left no time to do anything else but open it.

'Sorry to just turn up, but I...' Liam frowned at Sam's dishevelled appearance. 'Are you okay?'

'Yeah, I'm fine,' Sam slurred, walking unsteadily back towards the lounge, leaving Liam to follow. *Not Seb, then?*

As Sam slumped on the sofa, Liam held up a bottle of white wine. 'I bought this, but you look like you've already had one.' His eyes moved from the empty bottle on the coffee table to the half-full tumbler of whisky. *Stoker?* 'I'm not interrupting anything, am I?'

Sam shook her head. 'No, you're not.' *Unfortunately.*

Liam opened the wine and poured two glasses, making sure Sam's was twice the size of his. Placing it in her hand, he sat down next to her. 'What's happened?' he asked gently. 'Come on, Sam, I can see you're pissed and upset.'

Putting his arm around her shoulders, he was bolstered to find she didn't pull away. Despite knowing that psycho had already been in her, he felt his groin twitch. His fingers gently caressed Sam's shoulder. 'I know things haven't been great between us recently, but I'm still here for you. Please tell me what's wrong?'

Taking a sip of her wine, Sam struggled to put the glass on the coffee table. She really shouldn't drink any more – she'd already had far too much. 'Everything's such a mess,' she said, refusing to allow her tears to fall.

Liam silenced the accusations dancing on the tip of his tongue. *Play it softly*, he reminded himself. *She's beginning to see the wood for the trees.*

He stroked Sam's hair, the growing tightness in his trousers becoming painful. He had to remain caring. That way, she'd give him something solid on Stoker, and soon Kevin Stanton would bring up the rear. That chat had been a good idea because Stanton was definitely on side and, from how it had been left, Liam was confident the man would now be even more against Stoker having any involvement with Sam. Hopefully, if he was correct in his assumptions, Sam would act on her new second in command's opinion.

He'd just quietly wait for that to unfurl. It shouldn't take long. Kevin didn't strike him as the sort to procrastinate over what was required to run things smoothly. Sam would kick Stoker out of her life and the business and then he'd be back in his rightful place.

'Can't you tell me what's happened to upset you so much?' Liam pressed.

The effects of the alcohol and the soothing, familiar arms around her almost made Sam tell Liam about her argument with Seb, about her worries for the firm, about Linda Matthews. But only *almost*.

Sitting up, she pulled away and reached for her wine. 'I'm okay, honestly. A long day, that's all.'

Liam bristled, the stinging rebuff only fuelling the need to release his aching erection. *She'd enjoyed him before, so why not now? Why should Stoker take everything?*

Keeping his mask of concern in place, he leant forward to cover the visible tenting of his trousers. 'Please tell me what's wrong?'

Placing his hand softly on Sam's face, his eyes strayed to her mouth. If only she'd give herself to him once again, then she'd realise he wouldn't give her the hassle Stoker did. Once his future and money were assured, he'd do anything she wanted. Everyone would be happy.

Sam moved to the edge of the seat. 'I'm fine,' she lied, suddenly feeling nauseous. 'I really should go to bed, but thanks for popping round.'

Hiding his annoyance, Liam got to his feet. Okay, so he hadn't hit the jackpot, but the way she'd just looked at him, she'd been considering it. Coupled with what would soon be coming her way about Stoker, all he had to do was keep up the nice act. 'As long as you're sure? I'll see you tomorrow.'

It was only on hearing the door shut as Liam left the apartment that Sam let out the breath she now realised she'd been holding.

She'd really thought Liam was going to make a move on her. That would have been awkward. The only man she wanted had stormed out of her flat earlier and was nowhere to be seen.

23

It was only by pure chance that Liam heard the conversation. He wouldn't normally come this way to his office, but the inconvenience of picking up the replacement suit had made him late.

Oh, he had plenty of suits, all very nice ones too, but the ruined one was his favourite. A *designer* one. He hadn't expected things to get quite so messy.

And he hated being late. He liked arriving before the croupiers came on shift to double check they all were properly turned out with impeccable uniforms. Not that one of them ever had been below par, but it was important. Something he'd always admired Len Reynold for – his attention to detail.

Still, being late offered an unexpected opportunity that he would otherwise have missed.

Seeing the men file out of their team room, he loitered in the corridor and flattened himself against the wall, waiting for them to disperse, hoping he could catch up with that runty one busy spouting what he'd stumbled upon last night. It was another nail in Stoker's coffin.

Spotting the man in question heading his way, Liam stepped

forward at the required moment. 'Can I have a word?' He gestured for the man to follow along the corridor. 'I happened to overhear what you just said in there.'

Seeing panic wash over the man's face, Liam leant closer. 'Look, I know most people know me and Miss Reynold are close, but do you not think you should tell her, rather than her finding out on the grapevine?'

The man shrugged. 'It's not my place, Mr Taylor. That comes from the enforcers. I'm just a runner. I report back and they pass on the necessary.'

A nerve twitched in Liam's neck. 'But I'm asking *you* to tell her. You know how her father felt about the Irish.' He smiled coldly. 'You say it's not your place, but will you still have a job if she hears *you* knew the Stokers were dealing with the Irish on her territory, yet you'd sat on it, saying nothing?'

The man blinked. 'But the enforcers wi...'

'Miss Reynold needs to know straight away, not tomorrow or during the next team fucking meeting,' Liam snarled. 'I'll be seeing her myself this afternoon, so let's hope she's been informed by then. For your sake...'

The man fidgeted uncomfortably. 'Okay, okay, I'll go and find her.'

Liam smiled. 'You do that.' In actual fact, he wasn't seeing Sam at all today. After last night, he felt it prudent to give her space – his absence would only make her realise she needed him. But this dickhead didn't need to know that. All the little runt had to do was help him regain his indispensable foothold. He turned to walk away and then stopped. 'Oh, and by the way, don't mention I was the one to tell you to speak up, otherwise that makes you look even more incompetent, doesn't it?'

* * *

Linda was convinced she was walking funny. Although she moved in the given direction, her legs felt stiff and unyielding, like they'd got callipers on.

Her eyes nervously darted around Broad Street as people brushed past, her paranoia growing, sure everyone was looking at her. She glanced down at her stained beige skirt. Putting this on, along with the yellowing blouse Tom had found at the back of the wardrobe, hadn't done anything to make her feel any more than she was. A selfish loser.

Her heart thumping relentlessly, Linda continued walking, the glaring brightness of the sun stabbing the backs of her eyes.

How Tom had convinced her that she looked respectable enough to do this she didn't know. She only had to look around to know that she didn't make the grade.

She sighed as a woman wearing a magenta skirt-suit tottered past, walking confidently in stilettos, making them look as effortless to walk in as flip-flops.

She'd seen that suit before. It was the latest one from Karen Millen. Not that she knew much about fashion. But she'd seen it in a magazine Vera had lent her the other week – *Cosmopolitan* – a posh, glossy thing containing adverts for sparkling watches and pictures of pouting perfect women. And magenta suits with a price tag more than a bleeding mortgage.

Sweat beaded on Linda's top lip. She dragged her hand over her mouth then stared aghast at the red smear on the back of her hand. *Shit*. She'd forgotten she had lipstick on. *Jesus Christ, she couldn't do this.* They'd never let her in. But she had to try. She must, because that was what Tom wanted.

Stopping, Linda stared at the building in front of her. She'd been hoping to miss it. That way she could return, saying she'd tried, but now it was too late.

But there was no missing *this*. Her eyes squinted against the sun.

The Violet Orchid.

Violet. *Her* Violet. How weird. It *must* have been fate.

Linda's eyes tracked to the shining double entrance doors at the top of a few steps.

The Reynolds had given her daughter a good life, so why was she here? Why was she getting involved in the successful life this girl had? A life that was way better than she could have offered.

Because Tom wanted her to, and she had to do what he wanted because she couldn't lose him again. *Not Tom.*

Linda felt sicker than ever as she placed her foot on the first step. Taking a deep breath, she continued to the entrance.

24

Sam found that continuing to half-heartedly search for the elusive paperwork her father must have concealed helped distract from the gaping hole inside her. The one which had split open since Seb had stormed from her apartment, allowing all the goodness and the spark of life steadily growing in intensity to drip out, drop by drop, emptying her of the nameless substance that made her tick.

She placed her hands on the desk and exhaled slowly. All night, she'd flipped between calling Seb to smooth things over and digging her heels in, her obstinate nature prodding silently from the other shoulder.

Despite his violent and brutal attitude to those who wronged him, he was the sort of man to fiercely look after those he cared about. Judging by his infuriating overprotectiveness and jealousy towards her, it was exhilarating to think she may have been coming close to being included under that banner.

And what about *her*? Seb might have thrown his weight around, questioned her promotion of Kevin, questioned where she'd been and who she was with, but *she'd* behaved equally ridiculously – like a spiky, sulky teenager.

Seb had helped her with the business when the shit had hit the fan, and okay, they'd slept together, but so what? She'd known sleeping with him might muddy the waters, but she could deal with that. What she couldn't deal with was feeling like *this*.

Sam's teeth dug into her lip. Seb was Seb – he'd promised nothing, so why was that not enough?

She stared at her fingernails, noticing the French polish would benefit from a trip to the beautician. Irritation with herself grew. She'd only gone and done what she should never have done.

She'd fallen in love with Seb Stoker.

Shaking her head, Sam sat up straight. She'd already allowed her concentration to slip enough, and she was better than that.

'Right!' she said out loud. 'Get on with it and stop being ridiculous!'

Moving back to the filing cabinet, she pulled out more paperwork, but hearing a commotion along the corridor, she slammed it down and rushed to the door.

Seeing members of one of the extortion teams surrounding another man, Sam marched up the corridor. 'What in God's name is going on?'

Everybody froze, including the man whose meaty hand was wrapped around the neck of another.

Receiving no response, Sam was about to let rip when Kevin crashed through the doors. 'I said to keep it out of... Oh!'

Sam folded her arms. 'Ah, Kevin. Would you like to tell me what's going on?'

Kevin jerked his head, signifying his men should leave. He could see that, despite Sam's calm voice, her eyes conveyed she would not be brushed aside.

Sam waited in silence whilst the disgruntled men filed out of the corridor. 'Please come to my office, Kevin.' She then stared at the man still frozen against the wall, his frightened eyes silently pleading for assistance. 'I have no idea who you are, but you can come with me as well.'

Kevin glared at the younger man. 'Cully is one of our runners.'

'The office, please.' Sam stalked away, leaving Kevin and Cully to follow.

Lowering herself into her chair, Sam indicated for the two men to sit down. 'I don't expect disputes in the corridor or, I should add, *anywhere* in my casino. In fact, I don't expect shit from people here at all! We work as one in this firm, so would you mind telling me what's going on?'

She wasn't in the mood for this today, but her rage was bringing her into her own. Finally, she felt completely capable of running this firm and it was about time everyone started understanding that – including Seb Stoker.

Kevin turned to Sam. 'I was planning to inform you about this, but Cully decided to take it upon himself.'

'And the rest?' She nodded her head at the door. 'What was their game?'

'My boys were reminding this moron that runners do the *running*, not the talking.' Kevin's top lip curled into a sneer. 'Enforcers don't appreciate those filching their way up the ladder. There's a hierarchy to be followed.'

Cully flinched. 'I – I wasn't trying t...'

'I'm not interested in excuses,' Sam sighed, losing patience. 'All I want to know is what I need to be informed of.'

Kevin cut Cully a death stare. 'Go on, then. Tell her!'

Cully quivered. 'I was doing my normal job, my normal thing...'

'Which is?' Sam asked, only to be disturbed by the sudden shrill ring of her phone. She snatched it up. 'Yes? What...? No! Tell them I'm busy!'

She slammed the receiver down. Now people were turning up off the street asking to speak to her? More fakes claiming to be her parents? *Would this never end?* She turned back to Cully. 'Carry on.'

'Part of my job is to top up the supplies of our dealers. I go between several patches per night depending what rota I'm on and...'

'Cut to the chase, dickhead!' Kevin snapped.

Sam swallowed a smile and nodded for him to continue.

'Well, I was at patch thirty-nine when...'

'Patch thirty-nine is the area spanning the territory between Bromsgrove Street and the Arcadian,' Kevin cut in.

Sam frowned. 'The Chinese quarter?'

Kevin nodded. 'Our half, yes.'

'There was a deal going down,' Cully said, his confidence growing.

Sam sighed. 'Another firm? I thought there was no sign of this?'

Kevin shook his head. 'It wasn't coke. It was guns.'

'Guns?'

'The Irish,' Cully added. 'They were dealing with the Stokers. I saw them myself. It was on our half too and... well, erm, being as you're with...'

'Pull your fucking head in,' Kevin growled. *This* was why he'd wanted to handle telling Sam himself. He'd known it would prove awkward. 'What Cully said is true. The Stokers were supplying the Irish and I know the Reynolds' take where guns are concerned.'

Sam raced to process the information, her brewing headache worsening. The Stokers had pulled an Irish gun deal on *her* half of the patch? On *any* part of the shared patch?

Cully smiled, proudly. 'When I returned, I said to the others that being as now you and the Stoker gaffer have a thing going, then you might have changed your mind about dealing with the Irish, but they sa...'

Kevin shook his head in disbelief, seeing Sam's eyes narrow. Cully really didn't know when to keep it buttoned.

'My stance on dealing with the Irish remains the same as whatever my father put in place,' Sam said frostily. '*Regardless* of what speculation there is about me and Sebastian Stoker...'

Seb was more than aware of her feelings about supplying the Irish. She'd made it clear on several occasions that would not happen on any patch the Reynolds had a say in – shared or otherwise.

Suddenly, his 'I have to be elsewhere' statement from last night filled Sam's mind. Now she knew exactly where he'd gone. Although, for a split second, this brought relief as it meant he hadn't been with someone else, it soon evolved into anger. *He'd bypassed her again? This was all she needed right now!*

Sam smiled tightly. 'Thank you for bringing this to my attention. Leave it with me.'

* * *

Ignoring the doorman's surprise, Sam stormed into the Peacock. If Seb Stoker wouldn't answer his bloody phone, then she'd stand in front of him.

Walking swiftly through the lobby, she headed straight for the staff corridor.

'Excuse me, Miss Reynold!' A male voice came from behind.

Ignoring the voice, Sam tugged at the gold door bar, her frustration rising to find it locked. She yanked at it, refusing to be stopped from telling Sebastian-bloody-Stoker what she thought of him overriding her by a mere door.

'Miss Reynold,' the voice repeated, this time more urgently.

Sam spun around, her chin jutting out defiantly. 'I need to speak to Sebastian Stoker.'

The door to the corridor flew open from inside. 'Samantha!' Andrew exclaimed, his mouth forming a cold smile. 'How nice to see you.'

'I need to speak to Seb. It's important.'

Andrew swallowed his resentment. Sam Reynold was demanding things again? The controlling little mare. What had happened this time? Perhaps she'd run out of face cream? Maybe Seb would disappear for another week helping her look for it? Getting a shag might snap him out of his shitty mood, but judging by the look on her face, he had no chance. 'Seb's busy, but I'm sure he'll make time for you,' he said, holding the door open. 'He usually does...'

Sam entered the corridor, aware of Andrew following behind. 'I won't take up much of his time,' she said, her tone clipped.

Andrew opened the door to Seb's office. 'You have a visitor.'

Seb nodded and waited for his brother to leave. No doubt he would get comments later, but for now, it didn't matter. That Sam had come to apologise lifted his frustration and hurt over her words last night. That was until he saw her face.

Sam stood against the door, her attraction to Seb still at an all-time high. That she'd allowed his handsome face to dupe her and go against what had been agreed was unthinkable, but she couldn't help it. 'You've been doing deals with the Irish,' she stated, her steady voice belying the inner tremble she always felt near him.

Folding his arms, Seb stood up. *He wanted to kiss her, not argue.* 'And there was me thinking you'd come to apologise.'

Sam moved closer. 'Don't patronise me. You went against what was agreed.'

Seb sighed. No doubt Andrew was in earshot and *loving* this. 'If you've come here to shout at me, then you won't get far.'

'I've *always* been against these kind of deals on my patches, yet you d...'

'*Your* patches?' Seb laughed, his green eyes flashing. 'I'll remind you they're *shared*. That means *mine*,' he prodded his chest with his finger and then pointed in Sam's face, 'as well as yours. That constitutes shared. And shared means exactly that!'

'Shared doesn't mean one side has monopoly over the other!' Sam countered.

Seb snorted. 'Len had the opinion over the Irish, not you.'

Sam's mouth gaped. 'You speak to me like I have no clue about anything, nor the right to my own opinion over my own business! Regardless of what you think, I seem to be doing okay without you!'

But she wasn't. She hadn't been able to think straight since they'd argued.

Seb's jaw clenched, the tell-tale nerve twitching in his neck. 'The whole world can't revolve around just you, Samantha. I've tried to be there for you and help you. I *want* to, but you don't want that. Apparently...'

'I wonder *why*!' Sam cried. But she did want him. *Badly*.

Seb rolled his eyes theatrically. 'Oh, here we go... back to little girl games?'

He caught Sam's wrist as she moved to strike him. 'You'll lose...'

Sam tugged against Seb's vice-like grip, her shame of almost resorting to violence intensifying.

Defeat cascaded over her. Seb was right. Despite becoming confident enough to call the shots at the Orchid, it was only because she'd relied on others knowing what they were doing. And how did she react to that? By becoming violent? Like him? *This wasn't who she was.*

Seb loosened his grip on Sam's wrist, his tone softening. 'Trusting people you're involved with in business is a requirement. Look, your firm relies mainly on cocaine to power your bank balance – mine relies on guns, so I need the Irish deals. You have to understand that personal dislikes do not equal cash.'

Sam dug her teeth into her bottom lip so hard she tasted blood. She didn't want to be a 'business requirement'. She wanted... wanted *him*.

She suddenly felt like she might shatter.

'You need to trust me,' Seb said, watching the conflicting emotions on Sam's face. 'I *need* you to trust me...' And he'd lied. He'd said the world didn't revolve around her, but *his* world was beginning to...

Sam's mind spun. It was when Seb gently tucked a lock of her hair behind her ear that broke her. 'But you don't seem to trust *me*. You need to let me get on with things myself. And... and...' Her breath caught in her throat, hating herself for what she knew she was about to say. It made her sound so needy, so pathetic. 'You don't want me at the funeral and I don't even know if y...'

'That's not the case.' Seb pulled Sam against his chest, all the stress melting with the feel of her body against his. The words he wanted to say jammed in his throat. He'd never had cause for a conversation like this and fear of losing what he'd got with her, whatever that was, pounded through him. 'I don't want to fight with you, Samantha,' he said, his voice low. It was all he could bring himself to utter, unable to say the words he wanted.

Sam's forehead pressed against the crisp cotton of Seb's shirt, the steady beat of his heart loud. 'Let's start again, shall we?'

* * *

Linda shut the front door of her flat with a mixture of relief and apprehension. Under the circumstances, she was glad Sam hadn't been available to see her, but how Tom would react when he learned she hadn't got anywhere worried her greatly.

She glanced into the bedroom as she moved down the hall. Her head was still pounding, the urge for crack strong. There was that rock in her bedside cabinet. She could smoke it now. No one would ever know...

It would give her the energy and the confidence to do what Tom wanted. She had to put things right after letting him down. He'd been her life from day one – even through all the years she'd spent without him. Now he was back she wouldn't lose him again. *Couldn't.*

Hearing scuffling from the kitchen, Linda frowned. 'Tom? Is that you?' Heading into the room, she stopped when she saw a man on his knees, pulling up a floorboard. 'Who the hell are you?' she screeched, her eyes fixed on the jagged cut of lino exposing the boards. *The fucker had used her bread knife?*

'This is Luke.' Tom appeared from the lounge. 'Luke's my new business partner.'

Linda eyed the nervous-looking stranger. *Hardly the business sort.* 'What sort of business?'

'I thought this was sorted?' Luke eyed Tom suspiciously.

'It is!' Tom shot Linda a look. 'Linda forgets things all the time. Just carry on with what you're doing, mate.' He slipped his arm around Linda's shoulders. 'Come into the lounge, babe, and tell me how you got on.'

Linda found herself steered down the hallway. The second Tom shut the door behind her, she knew questioning him had been a horrible mistake.

Tom slammed Linda against the wall by her shoulders, her head cracking against the brickwork. 'How dare you embarrass me like that, you stupid bitch,' he hissed.

Linda winced from the pain and the shower of saliva spraying in her face. 'Tom... I...'

Tom wrenched her face up at an angle. 'You crusty slag. I'm doing business and you made me look like a prize cunt!'

'I – I didn't mean to,' Linda gabbled, panic racing. *She'd upset him again. Why didn't she ever think?* 'I'm sorry. Listen, I... I went to the Orchid like you asked and...'

Tom dropped his hold and stepped back, forcing his ragged breathing to calm. 'And?'

Linda faltered. He'd hate her even more when he discovered she'd failed. 'Erm, Sam wasn't there...'

'Wasn't there?' Tom cried. 'What do you mean, wasn't there?'

Linda's mind scrabbled through possible scenarios. 'Well, she was there, but she was busy.'

Tom raked his fingers through his hair. *Was the stupid cow joking?* 'And she knew it was you?'

Linda swallowed. 'Not exactly. I...'

'You mean you didn't fucking tell anyone who you were?' Christ, he couldn't believe this. The stupid, pointless...

'I didn't know what to say. I gave my name – nothing more,' Linda wailed. 'I didn't know whether you wanted me to say that or not? I didn't know whether that would be wrong. I...'

'Oh, shut up!' Tom roared. 'I told you last night what we needed to do. It's fucking important!' He scraped his brain for reasoning. 'Do you really think Sam will want to know us as her parents if she thinks *this* is all we're capable of?'

He waved his arm around, pointing at things Linda hadn't ever noticed until Sam was here the other day. It was only then she'd realised what a dump she lived in. Like the curtains held up with drawing pins; the holes in the sofa with the stuffing spilling out; the dog shit stains on the carpet. *She didn't even have a dog...*

Linda's heart sank lower and her need for a smoke grew stronger.

She didn't want to use Sam, and what Tom had asked meant taking advantage. Normally, life dictated that she'd grasp at anything, but this was different. But if she didn't do what Tom asked, then he'd leave, she *knew* he would.

'If you do things properly, then you can show Sam you're finally making something of yourself. Isn't that what you want? After all this time...? After all your failures...?' Tom drew out the last sentence, knowing it would stab at Linda's heart more than anything else. *Apart from this...* 'If you don't want to do that for her, yourself and for us, then I really am wasting my time with you.'

Linda sank into the chair. She'd got it wrong. She was always getting things wrong. Tom didn't want her to strike up a solid relationship with Sam purely for the money. It was to enable them to be a family. She put her head in her hands. How could she have doubted him? What was wrong with her? 'What should I do now then?' she whispered.

Kneeling in front of Linda, Tom put an unwilling hand on her thigh. 'You should be happy to do anything so that we can be a family like we always should have been, so get yourself back there.'

Linda looked up in horror. 'What? Now? Oh, Tom, don't make me go back again today. Not with...'

'Have some of this.' Tom pulled his crack pipe from his inside pocket. From the plastic bag in his other pocket, he produced a large rock. 'This will make you feel better.' He smiled as Linda reached for the pipe. 'Have a smoke and then go and pay our daughter a visit.' He patted her arm. 'Once Luke's finished in the kitchen, I've got to go back out myself, so I'll leave you to it, okay?'

Kissing her on the forehead, Tom turned away to scrape his hand over his mouth, ridding himself of any trace of Linda.

Linda watched Tom leave the room, then stared at the rock in her hand. She'd really wanted to ask who that man was in her kitchen and what he was doing, but she hadn't dared.

25

Rush hour had been and gone, so it took surprisingly little time to get down the A38 to Longbridge. Seb clenched his jaw with building irritation.

It was Gary's funeral in two days. Having to put on a face for that was another thing, so anything to take his mind off it was a bonus. Being as he was on the road tonight, it wasn't too much of a detour to put in a quick courtesy call.

He had dealt with those muppets in the Hen and Chicks last night and it wasn't as if there would be any comeback from that fat fucker. Jim might be a dickhead, but he wasn't stupid enough to open his gob. Neither were any of those no-hopers in that boozer. They knew what would happen if they did. *Everyone* knew.

A smile slid across Seb's face, despite his bad mood. He hadn't lived his whole life like this to end up getting grief for snapping some fuck-wit's leg. People could not be allowed to overstep the line. But he needed to do *more*.

And that's why he was doing this now.

Turning right at the Rover, Seb clocked the road names as he continued towards Safeway. Spying the correct street, he turned off and drove up the hill, his eyes scouring the numbers on the fronts of neat 1950s semis. *There it is.*

Pulling on the handbrake, he jumped from the car and shook the creases from his suit. This wouldn't take long. All he wanted to do was tell Brian Sumner to quit sending Sam begging letters from people responding to his bloody article. She didn't need liars and money-grabbers writing to her all the damn time and if this prick was to be believed, it was all courtesy of Andrew. *That* was the other reason for this visit...

He couldn't bear this doubt and mistrust over his brother. He could not allow a situation to fester where he might lose control of his temper again, like the other day. Not with his family. His family meant everything.

He would check to see if Sumner wanted to stick to his original statement over the article's source or whether he'd prefer to change his mind. He'd give the prick one last chance to admit he'd named Andrew because he thought it would bring less hassle.

It was a nice try, but one thing was certain, and if it turned out the man had caused him to unnecessarily doubt his own brother, then he should be very worried. On the flip side, if Sumner refused to budge, then he'd force the fucker into the car, drag him to the Peacock and get him to say so in front of Andrew himself.

Then, and only then, if Andrew was behind the leak, brother or no brother, the shit would well and truly hit the fan.

Whatever happened, as from *now*, the paper would be leaving Sam alone. There would be nothing further printed, sent or even *hinted* about her or her family.

Seb grunted in agreement of his own decision. The least he could do was take some of the pressure from her.

Tapping the door of number fourteen, he stood back and looked at the garden gnomes placed around a manicured flower bed containing interspersed stones, the low wall inlaid with shells. He raised an eyebrow in amusement. *Gnomes?*

Spotting a neighbour peering suspiciously from two houses up, Seb nodded in acknowledgement before turning back to the door. *Was no one in?*

This time he rang the bell. Noticing the shut curtains, he prised open the gold letterbox and bent down to peer through, seeing packing boxes stacked in the hallway.

'If you're after Brian, you're too late.'

Seb swung around, finding the neighbour standing at the edge of the garden. 'Pardon?' he said, already disliking the suspicion plastered on this man's face.

'I said, you're too late.'

For God's sake. A shit-for-brains sticking his oar in. He contemplated whether to punch the nosy fucker in the face or knock the door again.

'Twenty years the Sumners have lived here and then, after that attack – whoosh! Gone! Just like that! It's very sad,' the man said, taking it upon himself to walk up the path towards Seb.

Seb paused, his finger hovering over the doorbell. *Attack?*

'Of course, you can't blame them,' the man wittered, reaching the bottom of the steps. 'I know how I'd feel if my wife was attacked in her own home! My missus is doing her nut with worry. It never used to be like that around here, you know? Very depressing, what the world is coming to.'

Seb faced the short, balding man. 'What happened?'

'Bri wouldn't go into details. All I know is that some bastard broke in and cut his wife's face up. Always a decent looker she was. Not any more…'

Seb's temples beat with a steady throb. 'You say the Sumners have gone?'

'Yep. Brian moved everything out straight away so the minute Marge gets discharged from hospital she can join him. She'll never have to set foot in this place again. No idea where they've moved to, mind.' He peered at Seb. 'Here, aren't you that bloke that runs that casino? I've seen you in the paper.'

'Yeah, probably,' Seb muttered. Elbowing past the man, he strode down the path to his car, his mind adrift with who would have scraped so low as to mess a woman's face up. Because it sure as hell hadn't been him.

* * *

Tom groaned as he released into Tina's mouth, the sensation long overdue. Sadly, abstinence was preferable when only Linda was on the menu.

Pushing the girl's head down further to eke out every last bit of pleasure, he ignored her muffled choking.

'How was that, Tommy?' Tina got up from her knees, her young voice anxious as she wiped the back of her hand across her mouth.

'Yeah, it was great babe,' Tom drawled, tucking himself into his trousers. 'Just what the doctor ordered.' Sparking up a cigarette, he leant against the flexible back of his new chair and eyed the shiny leather of the padded armrest. This looked the dog's. So what if it wasn't *real* leather. It looked all right to him. No more plastic crap. Things were on the up.

Hearing a tap at his office door, he glanced up. 'Make yourself scarce, sweetheart. I've got business to attend to.'

As Lee and Steve entered the office, Tom stared at Tina, wondering why she was still loitering. Remembering he'd forgotten her promised bonus, he reached into his pocket and pulled out a bag. 'There you go. Now scoot!'

'Cheers, Tommy!' Tina gathered her clothes from the floor and skittered naked from the room, clutching the bag of crack.

Lee watched Tina leave, his lips twitching with distaste. 'I don't want to speak out of turn, but being as we've an invested interest in making the Aurora work, we can't hand out rocks willy nilly.'

Tom sat forward, his eyes narrowing. 'We've just had a massive delivery. We can afford to do what the hell we like!'

Lee glanced at Steve before turning back to Tom. 'The thing is, mate, I'm not sure you've taken on board what's been happening. The takings are down in general, plus we're losing profit paying through the nose for the Black Country coke.'

'Through the nose?' Tom guffawed. 'I like your sense of humour. Through the nose... yeah, that's good.'

Steve shuffled from one foot to the other. *Tom wasn't listening.* 'Did you hear what Lee said, Tom? He said that the taki...'

'I heard what he fucking said!' Tom barked, his humour evaporating. 'I don't know what you're both flapping about. You're going on like a pair of birds, asking me the same things over and fucking over!'

He stubbed out his cigarette in the ashtray, immediately lighting up another. 'I told you yesterday that getting coke from Wolverhampton was only temporary and it *is*. We're now close to getting a supply nearer to home.' He formed a small gap with his thumb and forefinger. '*This* close, so quit panicking. It will all come good, you'll see.'

Lee sighed. He was sick of the same excuses, time and time again. 'But how? I don't know anything about any huge crack order. All we've got is in that bag you told me to put in the safe. Nothing else has arrived.'

'For fuck's sake!' Tom banged his fists on the table. 'I run this bastard place, not you!' Taking a breath, he collected himself. 'If you don't have faith in what I'm doing, then perh...'

'It's just that you're not around much,' Steve interrupted. 'From where we're sitting, it looks like nothing is changing. We're barely breaking even.'

Tom relaxed. 'Let me explain. The reason I haven't been around is because I've been busy lining up the goldmine which will soon be ours for the taking. The friend I'm staying with is helping move that along.' He smiled, showcasing the nicotine-stained enamel of his teeth. 'Crack is being produced for the Aurora and the Aurora *alone* – and that, my friends, is being stored at my friend's abode.'

Lee and Steve exchanged glances. 'You mean that bird you've shacked up with in Northfield?'

'I haven't shacked up with anyone!' Tom bellowed. 'I'm just staying there and you know why that is.'

'Yeah, but that's done now,' Lee pushed. 'Maynard's not here any more and the Stokers aren't sniffing around, so...'

'I'm staying there because of what I'm working on,' Tom interrupted. 'Trust me, fellas, it won't be long before we have more coke than the cookshop can keep up with. The markup on crack is immense.' He spread his arms wide. '*Huge*, I tell you!'

Seeing Lee and Steve still exchanging concerned glances, Tom continued. 'I'm storing the big orders there because it's too risky to keep here.'

Lee nodded. 'When will we get this properly priced supply of coke?'

Tom smiled. 'Soon, boys. Soon. We'll be rolling in it before you know it, so take a chill pill.' And if Linda had any sense, she would be at the Orchid right now doing exactly what he'd instructed.

* * *

Sam clambered from the taxi and shoved some money in the driver's hand. 'Wait here for five minutes. There's more than enough there to cover your waiting time. If I'm not back by then, you're free to go.'

She looked up at the blocks of flats and took a deep breath, bracing herself for the unsavoury trek through the revolting stairwells.

If she'd realised the person who'd come to the Orchid today was Linda, she'd have seen her, instead of saying she was busy. It had only been on returning from the Peacock that she had learned the visitor's name and, from the none too complimentary description the receptionist gave, it *had* to be Linda.

Guilt bloomed. Sam had said she'd call. It may have only been two days, but she should have made the effort to contact her again before now. The way Linda had almost begged her to stay in touch showed how eager, almost desperate, the woman was for it to happen.

She *had* planned to ring her, she really had. And, more to the point, she *wanted* to. It was just the whole thing was difficult to get her head around. And then there was all the confusion with Seb...

Taking the stairs as quickly as possible, Sam cleared the third stairwell, thankfully having not come across any junkies or dog shit, but she kept her hands well away from the metal handrails, just to be on the safe side.

Hurrying along the walkway of the third floor, Sam reached Linda's scuffed front door and knocked loudly.

Receiving no reply, she knocked again. She must have been almost five minutes already and she didn't want to get stuck, although she could just about remember how to get to the pub from here.

About to retrace her steps, the door opened slightly. Sam saw the small face of a young girl through the crack. 'Hello,' she said. 'Is your mum in?'

The girl couldn't be more than six or seven – extraordinarily pretty with dark hair, a rosebud mouth and wide brown eyes. Her heart lurched. *Was this her sister?* 'If your mum's not in, do you know where she is or when she'll be back?'

The young girl fidgeted, her small fingers gripping the edge of the chipped door.

'I'm, erm, a friend,' Sam continued. 'I think she came to see me today, so I wanted to make sure she's okay.'

Hearing movement from inside, Sam peered through the crack above the girl's head, but couldn't see anyone.

'Who is it?' came a voice.

Sam frowned. 'Tayquan? Is that you, sweetheart? It's Sam.'

The girl turned and hissed something that Sam could not catch.

'It's okay,' Sam heard Tayquan say. 'Mum won't mind.'

'Yes, but you know what w...'

Pushing his sister out of the way, Taquan opened the door wide.

'Hi again,' Sam said. 'How are you?'

Tayquan's small shoulders shrugged, and Sam would have to be blind not to spot the worry on both the children's faces. 'Is everything all right?'

Tayquan shuffled, his eyes fixed to the floor. 'It's Ma, she...'

'May I come in?' Deciding she had no choice, Sam pushed through the door, unwilling to wait any longer for an invitation. Shutting it behind her, she dropped to her haunches and looked at both children. 'Tell me where your mum is. I need to make sure she's all right.'

'She's in there,' Tayquan mumbled, pointing to the room on the right.

Sam rose to her full height and gently tapped the bedroom door. 'Linda? It's Sam.' Receiving no response, she glanced at the kids. 'You two go back into the lounge. I'll just check on your mum.'

Pushing open the bedroom door, Sam saw Linda lying on the bed. Her arm lay limply to one side, a can of cider in her hand. The double bed was unmade and there were men's clothes strewn around the carpet, mixed in with others clearly belonging to Linda.

Sam frowned as she moved into the room. Did her mother have a boyfriend?

Wait a minute... Aside from this, there was only one other room and that must be where the children slept, so where did the lodger sleep?

Up until this moment, she'd believed everything Linda had said, including her remorse over giving her up, but was she lying? Was the lodger more than a lodger?

If that was the case, why lie?

Sam stared at the once bright pink carpet, patches of it almost black with grime, and as well as clothes, plenty of empty cans of lager and cider littered the floor. She shook Linda by the shoulders, knocking fag butts over the duvet cover from the overflowing ashtray.

Linda jerked awake, her bloodshot eyes blinking rapidly. 'Fuck! How long have I been asleep? I'm supposed to be... Oh, shit! Sam? What are you doing here?'

'You came to the Orchid. I didn't realise it was you, otherwise I'd have...'

'You came all the way over here to see me?' Linda gasped, her voice thick with alcohol. Her eyes welled with unshed tears. *Was Tom here? If Tom was here...* He'd wanted her to go back to the Orchid, not to get pissed and crash out.

Sam frowned, suddenly noticing the object on the bedside table, which unless she was seriously mistaken was a crack pipe.

Her heart sank. *Had Linda lied about being clean too?* 'I thought you were off that?'

Linda focused on what Sam was staring at and panic bloomed. 'I am! Honestly!' Her mind scrambled for answers. 'I keep that to remind me of what I used to be.' *And she hadn't touched it. Those rocks Tom had given her were still unsmoked.*

Sam tried to smile. It was feasible, she supposed. Linda sounded genuine, so she'd give her the benefit of the doubt, but as Linda turned her face, she saw the split lip. 'What happened to your mouth?'

Linda laughed. 'Oh, I'm just clumsy.'

Sam wasn't sure she believed that. Something really was up with Linda's life, and it was time to find out what that was.

26

Liam poked his head around the door of Sam's office. 'Sorry to disturb you. Have you got a minute?' *Time to up the ante.*

Sam hesitated, then smiled. 'Sure. Come in.' Maybe she'd got the wrong end of the stick on Sunday when she'd been convinced Liam was about to make a move on her. After all, she'd been the worse for wear and it wasn't as though he'd made a fuss when she'd said she was going to bed. Besides, anything to deflect from her brain going over how things stood with Seb and how things would go with Linda on Friday night was appreciated. The concern that Linda had lied about everything, including about being off the drugs, still niggled.

She eyed Liam carefully. Could she confide in him? She could really do with someone else's opinion.

Liam plonked himself down in a chair opposite. 'How's your diary fixed for tomorrow morning? I want to run through more ideas for event nights. I was thinking along the line of themes, but I need an hour or so to explain everything I have in mind.'

The days when things had been heading in the correct direction and he'd seen Sam most lunchtimes and evenings were long gone. Now he had to book time with her? But that would soon change. He just wanted to see if she'd tell him – including what that runty little runner should have told her by now.

'I can't do tomorrow. What about Thursday?'

'Thursday?' Liam frowned. 'Nothing before that?'

Sam sighed. 'I've got Gary Stoker's wake to attend tomorrow, which I suspect will rule the whole day out.'

'Oh, is that tomorrow?' Liam exclaimed. *Like he didn't know.* It would hardly take all day, but clearly she'd planned to spend the rest of the time with the Stoker thug. He could only hope Gloria took heed of his advice and showed her face too. That should stir things up.

'Yes, it was in the paper. Did you not see it?'

'Can't say I did,' Liam lied. *Now for another seed...* 'Okay, Thursday it is. Hey, talking of papers, did you see that article about the reporter?'

Sam glanced up. 'Reporter? What reporter?'

'It was in the *Mail* the other day.' Liam pulled a newspaper from the pile on the desk. 'This is the one.' He flicked through the pages. 'Here it is.'

Frowning, Sam read the article.

SURPRISE RETIREMENT A GREAT LOSS FOR THE *MAIL*

After thirty years' dedicated service to the *Birmingham Mail*, Brian Sumner, one of our top reporters, has made the unexpected decision to retire with immediate effect.

During his long career, Brian, 58, has worked for various segments of our paper and has been instrumental in getting us some of the best and most popular stories.

Such a hard-working and dedicated reporter will be hard to replace and his energy and enthusiasm for the city's news will be greatly missed. All of us here at the *Mail* wish Brian and his wife the very best for the future.

Liam watched Sam closely. He'd leave it there for now. He'd give things a bit more time to naturally pan out and, if they didn't, he'd use his backup plan. Either way, this set the stage for what would undoubtedly be reported soon, if not already. 'It's good news for you. No more stories about your real parents,' he said brightly.

Sam eyed the article again. Liam was right. Now that reporter had retired, the stream of hopefuls queuing to get into her life should tail off.

'Have you sorted things out with Gloria yet?' Liam continued.

Sam stiffened. She didn't need reminding that was on her to-do list and something she really mustn't keep putting off. 'Not yet,' she said, briskly standing up. 'Anyway, I really must get on. I'll pop you into the diary for an hour on Thursday. Shall we say eleven?'

Liam got to his feet. He was being dismissed again, but it didn't matter. Soon Sam would be more than grateful for his unwavering support, and he'd happily pick up the pieces of her shattered heart.

* * *

Vera ruffled Tayquan's hair and handed him a fifty-pence piece. 'Go and get yourself some sweets. A nice selection of Pick'n'Mix.' She waited until the child had disappeared out of the front door before the smile dropped from her face. 'Where is he?' she hissed.

'Who?' Linda thought acting dumb was the best decision to take.

'Who do you bloody well think? George Bush?' Helping herself to a can of cider from the fridge, Vera sat at the kitchen table, waiting patiently for Linda to speak.

'Oh, you mean Tom?' Linda laughed just that little bit too loudly. 'He's out. Business stuff.' *And he hadn't come back. Again...*

Vera rolled her eyes. Business? Whatever business that jerk couldn't be much cop. 'Have you had any more grief?'

'No,' Linda lied. 'We're getting on great.'

Vera didn't believe a word. She'd known Linda for far too long and she'd always been a crap liar, but she wouldn't mention what had happened down the Hen and Chicks just yet. She'd save that revelation until it was useful to stop this muppet of a new boyfriend in his tracks if, or *when*, he laid another hand on her friend.

She studied Linda's unbrushed hair and washed-out pallor. 'You look as rough as badger shit. A hard one last night, was it? Where did you go, because it wasn't down the Chicks?'

Watching Vera drink cider, Linda fetched herself a can, swaying unsteadily as she did so. Her head was pounding and she felt dog rough. 'I had a few drinks,' she admitted. *More than a few... but at least she hadn't touched the crack...* 'Oh, and Sam came round...'

Vera's mood brightened considerably. 'That's great! What did she have to say?'

'Oh, you know, just chatting,' Linda said casually. The problem was, she couldn't remember much at all. However, she did have a fuzzy recollection of *one* thing...

Forcing her brain into gear, Linda chewed her split lip and panic loomed.

Seeing Linda's fast paling face, Vera frowned. 'What is it?'

'Sam's invited me to the Violet Orchid on Friday!' Linda blurted, still barely able to comprehend it.

'Wow!' Vera cried. 'Lucky you!'

'I can't go! What on earth would I wear?' Linda's panic hit an all-time high. 'I'd be a laughing stock!'

'Sam wouldn't invite you if she believed that,' Vera reasoned.

'Will you come?' Linda pleaded. 'I can't face going on my own and she's given me guest passes for two.' Shoving her hand in her jeans pocket, she retrieved two cards.

Taking the purple and gold edged card, Vera flattened out the creases.

Her heart lurched. She'd *love* to go to one of these fancy casinos. She'd tried once several years ago, but she'd barely reached the entrance steps before the doorman told her to sling her hook.

Vera's cheeks had burnt with shame. 'No brasses in this club, love. Not your sort, anyhow.'

She'd stumbled off into the night, refusing to let the man's words bother her, but they had. She'd carried on plying her wares at the back of Rackhams for the rest of the night and it was only when she'd returned home in the early hours of the morning that she had allowed her hot salty tears to fall.

She knew what she was, all right. It was no secret that escorts frequently accompanied blokes with wads of cash to places like that, but she hadn't been one of *those*. She wasn't a well-spoken, beautiful, classy escort.

Vera had been a cheap ten-quid street hooker. A skank. A tart. And she'd looked like one through and through.

Her chin set determinedly. She should have thanked that doorman really, because it was that incident that had broken the camel's back. That night was the last time she'd walked the streets, allowing men to possess her for a few quid. And she'd stuck to it ever since.

Linda clutched her friend's arm. 'You will come, won't you, V?'

Vera smiled. 'Yes, of course.' *This* time, she'd walk through the hallowed doors of a Broad Street casino with her head held high.

'But what will we wear?' Linda wailed.

Vera grinned. 'Let me worry about that.' She'd make sure they had decent clobber for once in their lives. And if she couldn't up the credit limit on her Kays catalogue account, then she'd damn well nick something.

* * *

Andrew waited for the kettle to boil and eyed the five mugs lined up on the kitchen worktop. Now he'd been promoted to chief tea maker? Making cups of tea like a good boy, whilst Seb and their parents solemnly gathered around Gary's coffin.

He stared at the sugar spoon. How easy would it be to stir poison into Seb's drink so he no longer had to be insulted watching their father's hard work go down the bog?

Andrew hadn't slaved his arse off, sitting in Seb's shadow and patiently doing his part all these years, to now stand by and allow his brother to chuck everything away because of a woman.

Growing up, he'd always treated Seb with reverence. As the eldest, Seb had their backs. There wasn't anything he wouldn't do for his brothers or his family. He shied away from nothing and dealt with everything. Seb had taught him all he knew and Andrew loved him fiercely. They'd thought so alike it was scary. Even more alike than his own twin.

But now Seb was ruining everything.

Picking up the kettle, Andrew poured boiling water into the mugs, imagining the sound of the water to be similar to how his respect for Seb now was – flowing out.

But when would it stop?

Andrew was so lost in thought, he didn't hear his mother enter the room.

'Are you going to tell me what happened to your face?' Judith asked.

Placing the kettle down, Andrew saw concern added to the ravage of grief on his mother's face.

Judith moved closer, her fingers tracing over the partly healed split of Andrew's eyebrow. 'Are you boys fighting again? I want you to be honest. I've had enough of secrets.'

Andrew pulled his mother into his arms, her small frame birdlike against his wide chest. The reference to secrets was down to Gloria Reynold. Gloria's silence over the circulating rumours had caused the rift between him and Gary which stabbed mercilessly and consistently in his brain. Now the Reynold daughter was causing a rift between him and Seb. And was he wrong for feeling the way he did?

No. Because the minute Seb had even contemplated bedding a member of the family that had wrecked his own, his respect and trust in his brother had disintegrated.

'Andrew.' Judith's face pressed against the cotton of her son's shirt. 'You haven't answered me.'

'There's nothing to worry about,' Andrew insisted. 'You know what we're like.'

Pulling away, Judith searched Andrew's eyes. 'I – I don't know what's happening to this family. I...'

'Where's the tea?' Neil sprang into the kitchen. Stopping in the doorway, his eyes darted to his brother. 'What's going on?'

'Nothing. We're just chatting.' Andrew cut Neil a look, then placed his arm around his mother's shoulders. 'Come on. Let's take these drinks in.' He leant close to Judith's ear. 'Everything's fine. I promise.'

But it wasn't. This discord was upsetting everyone, and he wasn't having it any longer. It was time to speak to his father.

27

Making short work of the tea Andrew begrudgingly handed him, Seb placed the mug on the coffee table. 'I'm sorry I can't stay longer.' Standing up, he kissed his mother on the cheek and nodded to his father.

He laid his hand on the coffin in the centre of the reception room and stared at Gary's brass plaque. 'I'll be here by eleven tomorrow.'

'You're leaving?' Judith exclaimed. 'I thought you might stay here tonight, like your brothers?'

Seb glanced at Neil and Andrew, standing either side of their father. If he wasn't mistaken, they were all eyeing him with a hint of disdain. 'I didn't realise that had been arranged. I can stay if you'd like?'

'It's fine, Sebastian,' Mal said, his face weary. 'Andrew and Neil are more than sufficient as a mark of respect, so carry on with whatever you need to do.'

Whatever you need to do? Seb swallowed any retort he might have uttered under normal circumstances and, after looking at the coffin once more, he let himself out of the front door.

That he had seen himself out had not gone unnoticed. His mother always saw him to the door, but not today. The atmosphere in the house was off. It would be easy to put that down to the strain of the funeral, but it wasn't just that. It was more than that. *Much more.*

Sure, there had been times, where his brothers and father were concerned, when he could cut the atmosphere with a knife. No more so than recently, but never in all his years had he felt that same thing from his mother. That unspoken distrust. Hurt. *Betrayal.*

Tonight he'd felt that and it chilled him to the bone.

Seb's temples throbbed. His beloved mother was a shadow of her former self. Always vivacious and full of life, she was proud of all of her boys, but since Gary had gone missing, a big part of her had faded. And since discovering his death, the faded part had completely died. No matter how much he believed he'd done what he'd done for the right reasons, the finger of blame of keeping Gary's death from them landed squarely on his shoulders. Not on him *and* his brothers, but him *alone.*

He also knew Andrew's injury, still fresh, would undoubtedly have been questioned. Although nothing had been said, it didn't take rocket science to guess they knew *he'd* inflicted it. That things had degenerated to such a level between them was something he felt very ashamed of.

Getting into his car, Seb slapped his hand on the steering wheel in frustration. He sparked up a cigarette, then reversed down the long gravel path to the road. He should go straight back to the Peacock, but tonight he would make an exception. Tonight he would do something he wanted. Something he *needed.*

Seb's mouth set determinedly as he turned his motor in the direction of Sam's apartment.

* * *

Steve calmed his nerves by grabbing a second Lion Bar, the crackle of the wrapper loud as he fumbled to rip it open with his thick fingers in the otherwise silent van.

'Do you have to do that?' Lee snapped.

'Just passing time,' Steve mumbled, his mouth full of chocolate. Lee's reasoning for what they were doing made sense, but he had a bad feeling about it. A *really* bad feeling.

Irritably brushing bits of chocolate off his jeans, his eyes flicked along the road, his stomach lurching with every headlight.

They should never have come on board with Tom. They should have known better. If they'd just stuck it out a bit longer in their usual work until trade picked up, things might have been okay. He glanced at Lee anxiously. 'Are you sure about this?'

Lee frowned. 'It's the only way. We've got to get this moving because *he* won't. Tom will spout the same old crap and, before he knows it, he'll have run out of brass.'

Steve nodded. *It was true.* 'I know, but...'

'How will we get paid if there's no working capital?' Lee snapped. 'The answer is, we *won't*. Like you, I've got bills and kids and can't afford to do this for fuck all, so it's up to us to sort it.' Seeing what could be a single headlight in the distance, his attention focused. He started the engine of the Transit. 'I think this is it.'

Steve's stomach catapulted into his throat. *Fuck.*

Lee gripped the wheel as the headlight came into focus, along with the unmistakable sound of a motorbike. 'It's the right time, so it must be them.'

As the motorbike approached, Steve gritted his teeth, the Lion Bar sitting heavily in the churning mess of his stomach.

Yanking the wheel to the right, Lee stamped on the accelerator and veered onto the road just as the motorbike cleared the back end of the Transit.

The deafening clang of metal splintered Steve's ears and the flash of a body hurtling past the windscreen made him duck down in his seat. Adrenaline pounding, he braced himself against the dashboard as Lee stamped the brakes.

Coming to an abrupt halt in the middle of the road, Lee killed the engine and pulled at the door. 'Come on. We've got to get this done quickly.' Scrambling from the driver's side, he raced to the motorbike lying on its side, petrol spewing from the cylinder head.

'What about the bloke?' Steve panted, seeing the rider lying in a twisted heap a few yards in front of the van. 'He doesn't look good.'

Lee crouched over the bike and tugged at the pannier facing away from the road. 'Forget him, we need to get these off,' he barked. 'Grab me something to free them, will you?' He turned to Steve. 'Come on! This thing's pissing petrol. We need to get these off and get out of here.'

With Steve frozen to the spot, Lee jumped up and ripped open the sliding door of the van himself. Grabbing an axe from a box of tools, he rushed back to the bike and started hacking at the chain securing the panniers, not caring if a spark caused the whole thing to blow. He didn't have time to worry about that.

Finally chopping through the chain, he pulled the pannier free of the bike's frame and stared despondently at the second pannier crushed into the tarmac, the whole weight of the bike on top of it. He pulled at the mangled handlebars, unable to shift the weight, the large bike's twisted front forks and bent wheel trapping it into its present position. 'Give us a hand!' he screamed.

Steve edged nearer the man on the floor. 'Look! He's groaning! We need to h...'

'Just fucking help me!' Lee screamed, panic outweighing his anger. With one eye on the spreading pool of fuel, he launched the pannier he'd removed into the back of the van.

'Someone's coming!' Steve gibbered.

Lee paused, hearing the quiet but distinctive noise of a car, then glanced back at the bike. *It was no use. They'd have to disappear.* He slammed the side panel of the van shut. 'Get in!' he roared. 'Now!'

As Steve clambered onto the seat, Lee spun the Transit around and floored it back in the direction they'd come. The overwhelming stench of petrol on his hands made his eyes water, blurring his vision. His heart pounded as they sped along the road. The quicker they put distance between them, the mangled bike and its equally mangled rider, the better.

It was only when they passed through the third set of traffic lights that Lee felt able to look at Steve. The man sat in a state of suspended animation, his eyes staring blankly out of the window. 'Thanks for your fucking help,' he spat. 'What were you doing back there?'

'We left him...' Steve muttered, his voice hoarse. 'We left that bloke on the road.'

'What would you suggest we do?' Lee barked.

'You weren't supposed to kill him!' Steve cried. 'You were just supposed to knock him off the fucking thing!'

'Bikes are dangerous,' Lee shrugged. 'Anyway, he's not dead. You heard him groaning. All we need to worry about is whether we've grabbed enough coke to help our cause.'

* * *

'I'm glad you finally told me the details,' Seb murmured, his finger tracing down Sam's cheek as she lay against his chest. 'I wouldn't have tried to stop you. I'm just looking out for you because I care about you.'

No matter how much Sam didn't want to think about it, what Liam had said about the newspaper grated at the back of her mind. 'Did you hear that reporter, the one who ran that story on me, is retiring?'

She watched Seb carefully, hating herself for running the risk of spoiling what was rapidly turning into a blissful evening with something that edged dangerously close to an accusation. 'His urge to retire so suddenly wasn't anything to do with you, was it?'

'I did go and see the bloke, yes, but I had nothing to do with his retirement.'

Sam frowned. 'What? After I said th...'

Seb sighed. 'I wanted to find out the source of his info. I wanted to stop you getting hassled.'

'Seb!' Sam cried indignantly.

Seb turned Sam onto her back. Leaning over, he silenced her with his mouth and then cupped her face with his hand. 'Stop trying to prove your independence! I *know* you're capable, okay? But I'd do anything for you, Samantha, so let me help occasionally!'

There. He'd said it. Or as close to saying 'it' as he could. Okay, so he'd omitted that he may have threatened the reporter, but he hadn't forced the man to retire, had he?

A burst of warmth radiated through Sam. She wanted this man more than she needed air itself. Despite Seb overriding what she'd asked, she couldn't help but melt at his words. He was trying to let her get on with things, like he'd promised. But there was one thing...

She rubbed her thumb across Seb's bottom lip. 'Who was the source?'

'God knows!' Seb said, deflecting by pulling Sam back over his chest. He couldn't say his own brother was his prime suspect. 'Forget about the reporter. Tell me about Linda. What's she like?'

Sam shivered as the deep rumble of Seb's voice reverberated against her cheek. She wanted to bury her face in his skin; his scent was intoxicating. Her fingers played with the dark hair on his muscled chest. 'I haven't quite worked that out.'

And that much was true. She propped herself up on her elbows. 'Linda's a bit rough around the edges.' That was an understatement, but she felt increasingly uncomfortable with the mixture of concern, embarrassment and disappointment she felt about the woman. If that's what it was?

Whatever it was, it didn't lessen the guilt. 'That makes me sound like a right snob, doesn't it?' she said, more as a statement than anything else. 'I'm not. Really I'm not, it's just...'

'Neither of us were born with silver spoons in our mouths, Sam,' Seb said. 'My parents worked their way up to their money, as did yours. And by *yours*, I mean Len and Gloria.'

Sam laid her head back against Seb's chest. 'I know what you meant. It's not that... I...'

'Then what?'

'Oh, I don't know,' Sam sighed. 'There's something... I don't know whether it's Linda or the situation.' Her fingers traced circles on Seb's chest. 'I just don't know what it is. I mean, she admitted she had a crack problem in the past and I know she's a big drinker. She's not what you would perhaps call... oh, I can't explain it!'

'Try.' Seb frowned, trying to keep his concentration on what Sam was saying rather than the feel of her fingers on his skin.

'It's lots of things and nothing at the same time. Just something's not right,' Sam muttered. 'The place she lives is an absolute shithole and there's young kids in there too.' She frowned. 'Maybe that's half of it? Kids shouldn't live in a dump like that. A boy and a girl... my brother and sister...'

A small smile tugged at the corners of her mouth before it fell. 'There's other children too, but she doesn't know where half of them are. Doesn't that seem odd? I think there's a boyfriend as well... and Linda had a bust lip the other day... Perhaps I expected something different? I don't know.'

'Not many things life throws are what we expect. Just because the place is a dump and she used to be on gear doesn't mean there's anything untoward going on. Life's hard for a lot of folks, Sam. Surely it's a good sign that she was honest with you about her past?'

Sam frowned. True – that's if Linda had been honest?

Seb ran his hand down the soft skin of Sam's slender back, desire throbbing in a persistent rhythm. 'When do I get to meet her?'

Sam stared at Seb curiously. 'You want to meet Linda? Why?'

'I'm intrigued,' Seb grinned.

'I've invited her to the Orchid on Friday, so you can meet her then if you want?'

'Maybe I will,' Seb whispered, his mouth searching for Sam's.

'Are you staying tonight?' Sam asked tentatively. She so wanted him to stay. Her stomach fluttered, realising she *never* wanted him to leave.

'Only if you promise not to entice and therefore delay me in the morning. I'll have to be off early to get ready for the funeral.'

'I promise I won't,' Sam whispered.

'Anyway, let's not talk about that.' Seb refused to think about funerals. After the unpleasant earlier episode at his parent's house and the nameless emotion clinging in the air surrounding his presence, coming to Sam's had definitely been the right call.

Being with her, talking like normal people, her opening up to him about her real mother was cathartic. And he didn't want to spoil how he felt right now by thinking about what lay ahead. Especially not when he'd got some proper time with this woman for once. This woman who he'd do *anything* for.

'And when I said not to entice me...' Lifting Sam on to him, Seb eased himself into her. 'I didn't mean not enticing me for the rest of *this* night...'

Moaning with pleasure, Sam moved slowly, wanting the love-making to last as long as possible.

'Ignore it,' Seb mumbled when the phone on the bedside table began ringing.

The ringing stopped, then started for a second time. Sam snatched up the receiver. 'Yes? Oh, hello, Kevin... What? When?'

Scrambling off Seb, she got up from the bed. 'Where is he...? Okay... I'm coming now.'

We'd both been about to until that bloody call ruined it, Seb thought, watching Sam put the phone down. 'What's the problem?'

Sam scrabbled for her clothes. 'One of my runners has been knocked off his bike. He's in a bad way. I've got to get to the hospital.'

'Bloody bikes,' Seb grumbled.

'You don't understand!' Sam slipped her trousers on, her fingers then fumbling with the buttons of her top. 'He was delivering coke. By the sounds of it, it was a jump. Kevin sent another runner to the scene the minute he heard. The police were already there, but he saw enough to clock one of the panniers had been taken.'

Seb sat up, suddenly alert. 'In that case, I'm coming with you,' he said, his face creasing with anger.

28

Tom turned over, the creak of the bed's rusty springs making him wince. He'd already had a hard time pretending to be asleep when Linda began pawing him earlier and he didn't want to wake her up.

Was it not bad enough sharing a bed with her in the first place, without *that*? He did his duty often enough to make her believe they had something, but he kept it to the bare minimum. Thankfully, he could top up his quota at the Aurora, otherwise he'd be pulling his hair out by now.

Downsides like Linda were worth putting up with now things were coming to fruition.

He swigged what was left of his beer, his face sliding into a grin in the darkness of the bedroom. He hadn't been planning to return tonight, but he was now glad he had. For once, he was pleased with what Linda had achieved.

After leaving her with that big rock the other night, he hadn't even been sure she'd have got as far as going back to the Orchid. He'd been convinced she'd have fucked herself up so much to manage jack shit, but he'd being wrong. She'd managed it with bells on.

Linda had gone back, got in there, seen Sam and, best of all, only gone and got herself an above-board invite to the Orchid on Friday night.

Tom smirked. Linda was over the moon about it. *So was he*. But he'd almost lost his rag when she'd told him Vera was accompanying her for moral support. As much as it grated, he needed to keep Linda sweet. She was the inroad to his fortune.

Thankfully, her services wouldn't be required for much longer. Once she become pally enough with Sam, their darling daughter would fall over herself to help her *real* parents. It wasn't as if she'd have a problem with them being in the supply game when she controlled half the city's drugs herself.

With Sam on board with his ventures, with her clout and standing, he'd shoot to great heights. Besides, she'd be so pleased to finally have a true 'family firm' it would make sense to hand it over to him. She probably wanted that more than anything anyway. What good were women in this game?

Throwing his empty can onto the carpet to join the others, Tom closed his eyes, finally feeling able to drift off, although this lasted for less than ten seconds before he was jolted alert by a banging on the front door.

Tom scrambled out of bed, feeling his way along the hallway as the frantic knocking continued. 'Who the bloody hell is that at this time?' he muttered.

As he opened the door, Steve and Lee pushed past into the flat. 'What the fuck are you doing?' Tom yelled.

'We need to store this with the crack you've got here.' Lee held up the motorbike pannier.

Shutting the door, Tom frowned. 'What is it?' He flicked the hallway light on, squinting as the bare bulb scorched his eyeballs. 'What's going on, lads? Why aren't you at the Aurora?'

'We've just saved you a shed load of money!' Lee grinned.

Tom led Steve and Lee into the kitchen and stared questioningly at the pannier. 'Well?'

Lee proudly placed the pannier on the table. 'We did a job on a coke delivery.'

Tom frowned. 'You did *what*?'

Grabbing a carving knife from the crusty wooden block on the side, Lee prised open the pannier, revealing several large tightly packaged blocks of cocaine. 'Ta-da!'

Tom's eyes widened as he lifted up two packages, revealing more underneath. 'Fucking hell! There must be eight or nine kilos here...'

'Let's just hope it was worth it,' Steve mumbled.

The tone of Steve's voice chipped at Tom's glittering elation. The man looked close to crying. With one package half-lifted from the pannier, unease wormed up his arm. 'What do you mean?'

'Take no notice.' Lee glared at Steve. 'Everything's fine.'

'We left that bloke on the fucking road, Lee!' Steve hissed.

'What bloke?' Tom's eyes darted between the two men. 'What fucking bloke?'

'Like I said, we jumped a delivery. Admittedly, the biker hit the deck harder than planned, but all that matters is we got the gear,' Lee casually explained.

Tom's eyebrows furrowed. 'You jumped a delivery? What delivery? Didn't I tell you I was sorting this?'

'No offence, Tom, but the Aurora is sliding. We're trying to keep you in business here. Keep us *all* in business.'

Tom wanted to be angry. In fact, he *was* angry. Did these bozos think him incompetent? But then, they'd just earnt him a shedload of easy money. Just think of how much crack Luke could cook with this.

Cutting a small slit in one of the packages, Tom licked his finger, stuck it into the opening and rubbed some of powder on his gums. Feeling his mouth deaden immediately, he beamed. 'This is top notch.'

'Good stuff, yes?' Lee's chest puffed with pride. He grinned at Steve, refusing to let the man's grim expression dampen his sense of achievement. *He'd saved both of their jobs, hadn't he?*

Suddenly, a horrible thought inched into Tom's brain. 'This wasn't from a Stoker patch, was it?'

Lee laughed. 'How stupid do you think I am? I know you don't want them on your tail.'

Tom's mouth relaxed back into a grin. *Then this must be...* 'You jumped a Reynold runner?'

Lee's wide smile said everything.

Laying the package of cocaine back in the pannier, Tom clapped his hands. If he wasn't so knackered, he'd jump for joy. *Oh, this was superb. He couldn't have done it better himself. Thank you, daughter.*

If they pulled this off a few more times, Sam would be itching to pass the hassle of running a firm with enemies over to her dear old father.

Lee grinned. 'It's definitely the way to go. That silly girl in charge doesn't have a clue. That firm's lost so much clout since old man Reynold pegged it.'

Something else Lady Luck had arranged, Tom thought with a smug grin. 'Come on, let's get this stashed. I'll deliver it to Luke tomorrow. Whilst you're here, take some of this crack back with you.'

Kneeling on the floor, he peeled at the edge of the lino. 'I take it things are in place to start dealing this out?'

Steve nodded numbly. 'Yes, all the dealers are on standby. It's just...'

'Just that we had to ditch the van,' Lee cut in, wanting to quieten Steve before his nagging conscience bleated out what they'd already agreed Tom need not know.

Lifting the floorboards, Tom shoved the pannier under an exposed joist. 'You mean there was damage to the van?'

Lee nodded. 'Sorry, mate. But better to get rid, rather than leave evidence.'

Tom retrieved a carrier bag of crack, then replaced the floorboard. Rolling the lino back over the wood, he ran his foot over the join. 'Normally I'd be pissed off at this being done without my say-so, but on this occasion, I'll let you off,' he grinned. 'And you did the right thing with the Transit. It's not like we can't afford to buy another one!'

And all of this at 100 per cent profit with no outlay. See? Luck was firing golden bullets, like it always did.

He handed Steve the bag of crack. 'There you go. That can be shifted now. Well done, lads.'

As Lee and Steve lumbered down the hallway, Linda slipped back into the bedroom just in time. With a pounding heart, she closed the door before anyone noticed.

* * *

Crammed into the small side room, Sam listened to the doctor. Her face remained calm, but perspiration gathered, her mind racing like a freight train.

The runner – Nigel Wallace – had died from massive internal bleeding just ten minutes ago. By the time someone called an ambulance and he'd reached hospital, there was nothing anyone could do.

She swallowed painfully and glanced at Kevin, his face a stone-like mask, evidence of his rage pulsing in the vein in his neck. With sinking dread, she knew exactly what this meant, but why and *who*?

'Again, I'm very sorry.' The doctor reached for the folder of medical notes.

'Thank you,' Sam said, her mouth working independently of her brain.

'I hate to add to your distress,' the doctor added. 'But when you're ready, the police wish to speak to you.'

Sam nodded, her pulse racing. Nigel was a member of her workforce and if it hadn't yet been discovered the remaining pannier was full of cocaine, it soon would be. She waited until the doctor's footsteps faded into the distance before speaking. 'Who do we have in the force on our payroll, Kevin?'

Kevin paced the room, his fingers running over stubble on his chin.

'No one with enough clout to shove this one under the carpet. Maynard ended the agreement last month with our main contact who could have swung it. He was in talks with another cop, but never put anything in place before he...'

'Fuck!' Sam should have had the foresight to double check everything John had altered or tried to alter.

'I'll kill the cunts who did this.' Kevin's bull-head jutted forward ferociously. 'This is a blatant jump and now we're lumbered with the aftermath. Wallace was a good lad.'

He stared at Sam in the silence of the room. 'Whatever shit has gone down tonight, these people are playing with fire, but we don't know what they're aiming for.' Kevin's thick eyebrows knitted harder. 'You need to be covered at all costs.' He glanced at Seb. 'On the occasions you're alone...'

Shoving his hand in the inside pocket of his leather jacket, Kevin pulled out a compact blade. 'Take this. Keep it on you at all times.'

Sam stared at the item in her hand. 'A flick knife? I don't want a...'

'Take it, Sam.' Seb stood up from his perch on the edge of the table. 'Kevin's right. Something's going down and you can't leave yourself open.' His eyes met with Kevin's, knowing the man was suspicious of his presence. If it were the other way around, he'd feel the same. He'd also admit taking an instant dislike to the guy because of his position in Sam's firm, but the bloke had his head screwed on. And that was important.

Seb watched Sam reluctantly put the knife in her handbag, a mixture of wrath and anxiety etched over her features. She was getting to grips with the business, but on this occasion, whether she liked it or not, she needed his help. 'Going back to people on the payroll, I have a contact. A high up one. I'll put a call in and get it sorted.'

Sam nodded, knowing she had to accept Seb's offer this time. 'What do we say to them?' she whispered, her head jerking in the direction of the corridor where the police waited.

Seb shrugged. 'Depends what they know, but act distressed and say you're not up to discussing anything tonight.' He nodded to Kevin. 'You know how to play the rest, I don't doubt.'

Kevin nodded grudgingly. 'I'll say we'll come to the station tomorrow to make a statement. Will that allow you enough time?'

'I'll make sure it does.' Seb placed his hand on Sam's shoulder, his fingers kneading the knotted muscles. 'Do what Kevin says, and I'll do the rest, okay? I'll let you know the upshot as soon as I can.'

29

Sam watched the dappled light filtering through the bedroom curtains to pattern the ceiling and inhaled deeply, hoping a lungful of Seb's scent would clear her crowded mind.

She'd hardly had a wink of sleep, her brain refusing to switch off from the never-ending roundabout of thoughts. No matter how much she wanted to prove her worth with running the Orchid and the firm, she'd have been sunk had it not been for Seb stepping in last night.

However, her gratitude did not dilute the nagging knowledge that she hadn't had a backup plan in place, and this caused doubts to resurface. These mixed in with guilt over that poor man who had lost his life doing his job for *her*.

Before last night, she hadn't even known the man's name, whereas her father had taken pride in knowing every single one of his employees and protected them all equally. He would be disappointed with what she'd allowed to happen and that she hadn't had the fore-sight to have a get-out clause.

She'd been complacent to believe John was the only possible contender to try something like this. Oh, sure, there had been no further attempts, but she'd readily accepted that was the end of it. And she shouldn't have.

The words Seb had said some time ago, 'Firms such as these have a habit of gathering enemies...' filtered back into her mind. They were proving all too accurate.

With the confusion over Linda and her tumultuous feelings about Seb, she'd allowed herself to take her eye off the ball and that needed to change. From now on, she'd cover all bases – including the parts she'd so far ignored. What had happened to Nigel Wallace would not happen to another member of her staff ever again.

Sam glanced at the clock. Now she had to make sure Seb did what *he* needed. He was burying his brother today and she would not be the cause of any more problems for him.

She turned to look at him, his face in sleep, peaceful. Her heart swelled. She'd fallen hard for the man. *So* hard. And she knew it.

Switching on the portable radio sitting on the bedside table, Sam placed her hand on Seb's chest. 'Come on! You've got to get going!'

As Seb's eyelids fluttered open, a sliver of green appeared. 'Do I have to?' he murmured, his voice heavy with sleep.

'It's almost ten.'

Seb rapidly sat up. 'Shit! I never sleep this late!'

And that's because of me too, Sam thought guiltily. It had been past 3 a.m. when he'd got back last night to tell her everything had been put in place, and a further hour of talking before they'd fallen asleep, exhausted. 'You've got plenty of time,' she insisted. 'The hearse is coming when? Eleven-thirty?'

Seb nodded. 'I said I'd be at my parents' by eleven. I've got to get showered, dressed and...'

'You'll be fine!' Sam repeated, watching the first trace of real sadness since the night his brother had died passing over Seb's face. She watched him pull on his trousers, wishing more than anything he didn't have to leave, until the morning news on the radio made her ears prick up.

'*The unprovoked attack happened around 11 p.m. on Saturday night. Margaret Sumner is still in hospital with severe but thankfully not life-threatening injuries after a man broke into the Longbridge home she shares with her husband, Brian. At this stage, it is not known whether the attacker was known to Mr and Mrs Sumner, but anyone with information or who witnessed anything, please call the police...*'

'Oh, my God! Sumner?' Sam gasped. 'That must be the wife of the reporter who ran that story about me. Jesus, I know that article brought me loads of hassle, but I wouldn't wish that on them. The poor woman. I hope she'll be all right.'

Seb kept his back to Sam under the guise of doing up his shirt. That way, she wouldn't see his face.

He'd told Andrew that Sumner had said he was the source of the article. He'd *told* him that. Could Andrew have attacked that woman in retaliation?

Seb's shirt clung to fresh sweat on his back. The neighbour said the woman's face had been cut to fucking ribbons. Andrew wouldn't stoop so low, surely?

Getting out of bed, Sam placed her hand on Seb's tense back. 'Are you okay? You seem on edge all of a sudden.'

Seb plastered on a smile. He had to get this notion about Andrew out of his mind. It couldn't be right, and thinking about it made things worse. 'I'm fine. Just stressed. I hate to rush off too, but I...'

'Seb, you didn't have to come back last night, but you did,' Sam said, reaching for his hand. 'And I appreciate that.'

Meeting Sam's eyes, Seb paused, about to utter that he'd do anything for her, because he loved her, but he swallowed it. 'Are you okay to deal with the police this morning?'

Sam nodded. 'Yes. I know what to say. Now, don't think about that any more,' she said, hiding her worry. 'You've got enough things to deal with.'

Getting out of bed, she pulled on her satin robe and wrapped her arms around Seb's waist. This felt so natural. So comfortable. So easy...

If only it was. 'I know the church and crem services are for family only and I'm not sure what time I'll get to the wake. It depends how long I'm in the police station. Whatever happens, I'll be thinking about you.' *Like I always do*, she thought. 'I'll be there as soon as I can.'

A fist crushed Seb's heart, strangling and pressing painfully, wishing Sam could be at his side all day. He traced his finger down her cheek. 'Sam... I...'

'Go!' Sam cried. 'Before we get side-tracked...'

Grinning despite himself, Seb shrugged his jacket on. 'Okay, okay. And don't worry about the cops.'

'You've already said that. And I'm not,' Sam lied.

Seb raised an eyebrow. 'Just saying. Right. I'll just go for a quick piss and then I'm out of here.'

* * *

Tom glared at the back of Vera, who he could see plain as day in his kitchen. Or rather, *Linda's* kitchen. If it had been *his* kitchen, there was no way it would look that shit. Or messy.

His teeth grated, the noise loud enough to make the kids look up from their magazines. Why he was even sitting here with these bastards, he didn't know. Blagging Linda they both felt too ill to go to school today didn't fool him. They were lying little shits and she was way too soft on them.

He jumped up from the sofa, purposely stamping on the face of Shondra's doll as he did so. He smiled nastily at the little girl's horror. 'You shouldn't have left it on the floor, should you?' he spat, loud enough for her to hear, but not so loud that Linda would.

He wished the kids would fuck off. They were in the bloody way, but being as he was so close to the off, he had to swallow it.

Pacing around a small patch of the lounge that wasn't cluttered with junk, Tom willed Vera to leave. Why couldn't she piss off to her own flat? How long could they discuss bloody clothes for?

He scowled, convinced Linda was doing it on purpose. Just because she'd achieved something by getting an invite to the Orchid, it didn't mean special bloody treatment. It certainly didn't give her the right to ask Vera as her guest.

Stomping into the kitchen, he glared at Vera. 'You still here?'

Vera returned Tom's sullen expression. 'Looks like it, doesn't it?'

Linda tried to catch Vera's attention. She didn't want anything winding Tom up. If he interrogated her again about her supposed visit to the Orchid the other night, she might end up blurting out she hadn't been at all, and that Sam had been here instead.

She peered around him, checking the kids were still out of range. They'd better keep their mouths shut too.

And then there was what she'd seen last night...

Linda's eyes tracked to the corner of the room. Now she knew what Tom was keeping under the floor. And in her flat too?

She'd tried to justify it because Tom hadn't been the one to organise it. It had been those other two who had stolen it from their daughter and *then* told Tom. But Tom had been laughing and she didn't know what to think about that. How could she face Sam, knowing her father had robbed from her?

Linda continued staring at the lino in the corner. She could see the jagged cut from here. Surely if she could see it, then so would everyone else. Or was it because she knew it was there, knew what was underneath and knew where it had come from...?

And knowing there was a shedload of crack only yards away was taking immense strength not to rip the lino up and help herself. But she couldn't. She had to keep a grip. She wouldn't end up in the same state she'd been in all those years ago. Not when she had the chance to put everything right.

'What are you staring at?' Vera peered in the direction of Linda's fixed gaze.

'Nothing.' Linda hastily averted her eyes. She'd wanted to tell Vera about what she'd witnessed last night and ask her if she should tell

Sam. But how could she tell Sam? It would ruin the chance of building a proper relationship with her daughter. Plus, she couldn't drop Tom in it like that. That would be wrong.

If Vera knew, she wouldn't be able to stop herself from questioning Tom. She'd accuse him of all sorts of dreadful things, like ripping off his own daughter.

'Not off down the Chicks?' Tom placed his can of lager on the open page of the magazine Vera and Linda were thumbing through. He didn't know why they were bothering looking for inspiration. They'd look like old slappers whatever crap they put on.

He needed them out of the bloody kitchen. He had to get a couple of kilos of that lovely base over to Luke to knock up another batch of cheapo crack. He'd have to remind him to wang extra baking powder in when he cooked this lot up. It was far too pure to waste on junkies without further cutting down.

'Do you fancy popping down the Chicks, Vera?' Linda asked. 'I haven't had a lunchtime drink for ages.' *Not at the pub, anyway*, she thought wryly. And if she could get some time away from Tom to think, that was one less thing to worry about.

Vera smiled. She hadn't planned to say anything about what happened at the pub the other night, but being as Tom was such a rude, irritating twat, she would – if only to enjoy the expression on his face. 'If you like,' she said, her lips curling into a smirk. 'I reckon you'll get treated differently in there from now on.'

Linda paled. 'Why?' She hadn't done something that she'd forgotten about, had she?

Tom sneered openly. 'Oh, for fuck's sake, Linda. What have you done now?'

'Contrary to what clever dick here thinks, you haven't done anything, bab!' Vera flapped her hand in Tom's direction. 'It's just you missed the surprise visitor the other night.'

Linda frowned. 'Who?'

'Sebastian Stoker...'

Linda's eyes widened. 'You mean that guy from that casino? The one who's in the papers all the bloody time?'

Vera nodded gleefully. 'The very one. You must have heard of the Stokers, Tom?'

Tom's nausea rose at an alarming level. *Heard of the Stokers?* Sebastian Stoker had been to the Hen and Chicks? *Shit. Fuck. Shit. Had he come looking after all?*

Linda rushed to place her hand on Tom's arm. 'Are you all right?'

Tom snatched his arm away and smiled weakly. 'Yes, I'm fine. Just a dodgy pint.' Picking up his can, he pretended to search for a sell-by date. 'Yeah, I've heard of the Stokers. Who hasn't?' He forced a grin even though it hurt his face.

Vera relished the expression Tom had done a crap job of concealing. If he was so shit-scared of the Stokers to begin with, wait until he'd heard the rest. Should she save that bit or add to his misery? Nah, fuck it. She'd add to his misery, the bastard. It would be rude not to.

'Stoker wasn't best pleased Sam got knocked over during that fight the other night.' Vera's eyes glinted.

Linda flushed. Tom wasn't pleased she'd told Vera about Sam, but at least Vera didn't know he was the father. 'But I still don't underst...'

'Don't you get it? Your daughter is with Seb-fucking-Stoker!'

Tom grasped the table as his legs went wibbly. He didn't want to, but he couldn't help it. *Fuck. This had to be a joke, right?*

Linda screamed with delight. 'Sam didn't mention a man in her life.' *Seb Stoker was a celebrity in this city!* 'Oh, he's ever so handsome! How long have they been an item?'

Vera shrugged. 'I don't know, but he *did* refer to her as his "woman" and said if she ever left there damaged again or if anyone upset her...' She lowered her voice. 'He snapped Jim Jones's shin in two. You should have seen it! I was almost next to them when it happened. Fucking blinding, it was!'

'Oh, my God!' Linda gasped. 'But it wasn't Jim who fell on Sam.'

'I know,' Vera laughed. 'But Jim thought it would be clever to be trappy, and let's just say, Seb didn't like it.'

Linda turned to Tom, a proud grin on her face. 'Did you hear that, babe? My daughter's only got one of the most notorious and famous men in Birmingham as her fella!'

'Yeah, I heard,' Tom muttered, amazed his tongue hadn't fallen down the back of his throat. *This couldn't be happening.*

'So yes,' Vera continued, loving the green tinge of Tom's skin. 'I think we can safely say Sam will be fine with Seb Stoker! He doesn't take kindly to blokes who hurt women, purposely or otherwise...'

Tom didn't bother even looking at Vera. He knew what she was digging at, the poisonous old witch. Something *else* Linda had been loose-lipped about, it seemed. He'd better lay off her for a while. But it wasn't just that which made him feel like he might have just screwed up.

Unable to help it, his eyes moved to the corner of the kitchen. The corner where he'd hidden that unexpected heist.

If Sam was screwing Seb Stoker, it was unlikely the man would take kindly to whoever had jumped one of her runners.

Sweat prickled along his back. *Christ.* They might even be sharing profits. The two firms had always shared certain territories, but if things had moved past that?

Fuck. Fuck. Fuck!

'Off you go then, girls,' Tom cried, his voice sounding like his balls were wrapped in barbed wire. Clearing his throat, he dragged a smile over his frozen face. 'You might as well make a day of it.' Pulling a wad of notes from his pocket, he peeled off three twenties and pressed them into Linda's hand. 'Have a good chat about the togs you're planning to wear on Friday without me cramping your style. I'll keep an eye on the kids.'

Linda threw her arms around Tom. 'Oh, thanks, love. That's fab, ain't it, V?'

Vera smiled smugly, not having any idea there was a hell of a lot more bothering Tom than giving Linda a clump. 'Yeah, really fab!'

Tom kept his smile fixed until the two women scurried from the kitchen, armed with their magazine and his money, before he dropped to his knees in the corner of the room.

The quicker he got rid of all traces of this coke, the better.

30

Rushing to answer the knocking on her apartment door, Sam frowned. She hadn't granted access via the intercom, so it must be one of the neighbours. Hearing Seb flush the toilet, she glanced over her shoulder, hoping her visitor wasn't that nosy woman from the flat above.

Pointlessly patting her hair, trying to look less dishevelled, Sam opened the door, her plastered-on smile immediately dropping.

'Miss Reynold? Miss Samantha Reynold?'

Sam stared at the two police officers in confusion. 'Yes?'

'I'm arresting you under the suspicion of possession or intent to supply Class A drugs at the Violet Orchid Casino.' The policemen pushed through the door into the flat, one gripping Sam's arm as he steered her back into the hallway. 'You do not have to say anyth...'

'Wait a minute!' Sam cried. 'What's this about? I...'

'You do not have to say anything, but it may harm your defence if you do not mention when questioned something you later rely on in court. Anything you say may be given in evidence.'

'This must be a mistake!' Sam yelped. 'I'm giving a statement at the police station this morning abo...'

'About the death of your staff member, Nigel Wallace? Things have changed. Large quantities of cocaine were found within the luggage on Mr Wallace's motorbike. That BMW R1100RT is registered to the Violet Orchid. Which *you* own...'

Sam tried to pull her wrist away as the other officer attempted to secure handcuffs. 'Wait! Th...'

'Explain down at the station, Miss Reynold.' The officer grabbed Sam's other wrist, securing it tightly.

'What the fuck is going on?' Seb roared, crashing up the hallway, his eyes wide with rage. Grabbing the policeman by the back of his jacket, Seb yanked him away from Sam and slammed him against the hallway wall.

'Seb!' Sam cried. 'You ca...'

'What are you fuckers doing here?' Seb snarled, his face inches from the policeman's face.

'Mr Stoker?' the other policeman sneered. 'I didn't expect to find you here.'

With one hand still pinning the policeman to the wall, Seb recognised the other officer to be the very same one who had accompanied DI Baker to the Peacock over that episode with Phil Blunt. 'What's that supposed to mean?'

A ghost of a smile appeared on DS Drakeman's face. 'Just saying it's surprising to find you in the personal accommodation of your well-known rival... Splitting cocaine profits between yourselves, are you?' He ran his eyes over Sam's satin robe, her lack of clothes underneath obvious. 'Unless you have a different kind of arrangement with the delectable Miss Reynold?'

'You rancid piece of fucking sh...'

'Mr Stoker, if you continue impeding us, then I'll have no choice but to arrest you for obstructing a police officer.' Drakeman reached for his radio.

Seb snatched the radio from Drakeman's hands and threw it to the floor. He ground his heel into it, splinters of plastic flying around the hallway.

Sam stared at the unfolding scene with horror as the second officer stepped forward towards Seb. 'You can't do this!' she screeched. 'He has his brother's funeral to go to. You came to arrest me, so get on with it!' She paused. 'There's obviously been some kind of mistake.'

'There will be no funeral for Mr Stoker today,' Drakeman beamed, pulling out another pair of handcuffs. 'Unless it's his own.'

Spitting with rage, Seb lurched forward, his forehead crashing down on the bridge of Drakeman's nose, knocking him out cold. The second policeman stormed forwards, only to receive a perfectly aimed right hook to his jaw.

Paralysed with shock, Sam stared at the unconscious bodies lying on her hallway carpet, then to Seb leaning against the wall with his arms outstretched, panting with exertion and rage. 'Seb, you need t...'

Seb's eyes burnt with fury. 'There's only one thing I need and that's to use your phone.' *He would kill Baker for this.*

* * *

'We can't leave without Sebastian,' Judith wailed, as tears streamed down her cheeks, mascara cascading in black rivulets onto her tired skin.

'We have to,' Neil said gently. 'We've waited as long as possible.'

He peered between the drawn curtains of the front room, seeing the hearse and pallbearers waiting patiently like they had been for the last forty minutes and a building crowd of onlookers standing on the pavement, speculating as to the hold-up.

'But it's not right!' Judith sobbed. 'Sebastian wouldn't miss his brother's funeral!' She wrung her hands, her anguish weighting the air. 'What if something's happened?'

Neil looked at Andrew in despair as his mother burst into a fresh round of sobs. What could he do to make any of this better? *Nothing.*

When their mother's legs buckled, both Andrew and Neil rushed forward to steady her, just as Mal walked back into the room, his face like thunder.

Andrew raised his eyebrows in his father's direction, receiving a slight shake of the head in return.

He glowered with rage. They'd all taken it in turns calling both the Peacock and Seb's apartment since he'd failed to arrive. There had been no answer and, judging by his father's expression, there still wasn't. Couldn't Seb even let Gary be put to rest without taking the limelight and causing additional anguish?

Mal held Judith in his arms. 'Love, we really must go. We can't wait any longer.' Hearing the pitiful sobs coming from his beloved wife only made the anger and disappointment over his eldest son's no-show spiral higher.

Aware of the knowing looks from Andrew's direction, Mal slipped on the mask reserved for the outside world and steered Judith and what was left of his family into the limousine behind the hearse.

* * *

DI Baker knew he was in deep water, but the only thing he could do now was damage limitation. Sweat soaked into his shirt underneath his jacket as he nodded to the men accompanying him. 'Get them out of here.'

He glared at DS Drakeman, now propped against the wall of Samantha Reynold's flat, holding a wad of kitchen roll to his nose, blood still trickling from his smashed face, then chucked a binbag between Drakeman and the other policeman, who looked equally disorientated. 'There's a couple of coats in there. Put them on over your uniforms and leave.'

Moving his unwilling legs in the direction of the lounge, Baker took a deep breath and raised his hands in submission. 'I really can't apologise enough, Mr Stoker. And to you, of course, Miss Reynold. None of this should have happened.'

Sitting on the sofa next to Sam, Seb scowled, his rage still at full throttle. He wanted to rip the grovelling smile from DI Baker's face with his bare hands. 'Shouldn't have happened? You're damn right it shouldn't have fucking happened!' He jumped to his feet. 'I pay you so things like this *don't* happen.' Moving stealthily towards the man, his mouth twisted. 'And I pay a *lot*.'

Baker backed against the wall, his stomach contents beginning to liquefy. 'I – I don't know how it happened. Drakeman said the instructions hadn't filtered through.'

'Bullshit! You assured me this was sorted. *Assured* me!' Feeling Sam's hand on his arm, Seb stopped.

'I know, I know,' Baker gibbered. 'It will be dealt with. I promise you that.'

'Yeah, like your promises are worth anything!' Seb spat. Seeing the beginning of bruising around Sam's small wrists, his temper sparked further. 'See this?' He grabbed Sam's arm and held it up. 'Your fucking clowns have hurt her!'

'Seb, just leave it,' Sam whispered.

'No! This fool makes a fortune from me and then lets me down!'

'It won't happen again.' DI Baker's eyes flickered over the marks on Sam's wrists, then in the direction of the hallway where shuffling and groaning signified his officers were leaving the apartment. *Those two shitheads were finished. Drakeman especially. The instructions hadn't reached them, my arse.*

He mentally resolved that when he got out of here, the first thing he would do was put in a transfer for Drakeman. He'd manufacture a sexual allegation from a WPC or something. Whatever happened, the man was gone from Steelhouse Lane nick and, if he could swing it, he would get him binned from the force completely. How dare the jumped-up prick make him look a prat.

Baker held his hands out. 'You'll get no further issues from Drakeman,' he said. 'And just to let you know, the evidence from last night has now been lost and destroyed...'

He plastered a smile onto his weary face, hoping it was enough to walk out of here with both legs still attached, as well as still holding the lucrative arrangement with Stoker. Damaged, no doubt, but still intact.

'You think that makes it okay?' Seb bellowed, still livid.

'Seb,' Sam hissed. 'He said he'd sorted it.'

DI Baker smiled weakly. 'You'll hear no more about this. Either of you. Of course, you no longer need to attend the station, Miss Reynold. I will file that I personally took your statement.'

Sam nodded. 'Thank you.'

'What are you thanking him for? The useless...'

'Do you realise what time it is, Seb?' Sam said quietly. 'I've been trying to tell you! It's nearly midday.'

Seb blinked. He'd been so in the zone, he hadn't realised. He swung around to Baker, his green eyes bright. 'Because of you, I've now missed my own brother's funeral,' he spat.

Sam kept her hand on Seb's forearm. 'Going late is better than not going at all. They'll understand.'

Almost hyperventilating, Seb glared at DI Baker. If looks could kill, Baker would be six feet under – like his brother would shortly be. Although that wasn't true because Gary was being incinerated and probably already had been by now.

And no, his parents wouldn't understand. They wouldn't understand or accept this under any circumstances. Especially *this* one.

'I'll put my shoes on,' he muttered. Giving Baker one last lingering look, he stalked away to the bedroom before he ripped every last piece of skin off the man.

Sam stared at the detective coldly. 'I suggest you see yourself out while you still can, DI Baker.'

31

Standing next to Judith, his arm around her shaking shoulders, Mal stiffened as the crematorium door opened. He wouldn't glance around. He didn't need to. He knew it was *him*.

His free hand clenched into a fist as he concentrated on the words the minister spoke for this final part in his youngest son's journey and fixed his eyes on the oak coffin lying on the dais, waiting for that dreaded moment when the curtains closed around it.

With footsteps approaching from behind, Mal kept facing the front, not turning when Seb stood next to Neil. *Sebastian should be flanking his mother,* he thought, his anger bright. And he would have been, had he bothered to get here on time.

For Christ's sake. Cremating the boy was hard enough without Seb making an already impossible day worse.

Seb had missed the *entire* church service and had only just made the cremation. He dug his teeth into his lip to stop from roaring at his son.

No one hanging around the church had remarked on Seb's absence, but they didn't have to. His lack of presence shone like a beacon. None of those people were witnessing the cremation – that was for family alone, but they would all be at the wake. And they'd all be wondering.

Just like he was...

Mal's jaw clenched harder. Sebastian had better have a good reason for this. And by that, he meant a *very* good reason. But whatever it was, it wouldn't be good enough. Nothing could excuse tardiness on a day like this.

As Judith clutched Mal's arm, a sob escaping from her throat, he tightened his hold of her, realising the curtains were slowly moving across the front of the coffin. His rage burnt brighter. He'd been so busy fuming over Sebastian, he hadn't been concentrating. Damn and blast the boy.

Goodbye, son, Mal thought, sadness finally overtaking his anger as the machinery taking the coffin below clanked behind the curtain.

Taking a deep breath, he turned to Judith. 'Let's go,' he said, quietly stepping away from the small row of chairs.

* * *

Tom was genuinely surprised he hadn't shunted into another motor from looking in the rear-view mirror for a possible tail, rather than at the road ahead.

It wasn't far to Luke's house, but his nerves were shattered. Every yard felt like twenty miles.

He frantically chewed the gum in his mouth. Faster and faster. Over and over. He'd be lumbered with jaw ache after this, but it gave him something to do other than grind his teeth, courtesy of the coke he'd snorted, along with the hideous knowledge the woman with his ticket out of here was in the sack with Seb Stoker.

That one he hadn't expected.

He dragged the back of his hand over his forehead, the sweat slick.

Pulling up at the lights to cross the Bristol Road, he slapped his hand on the indicator but hit the window wiper instead, the noise of the blades scraping across the dry screen making his teeth curl.

Chewing harder, blood pumped in Tom's head as he smacked the wiper lever. *Shut up. Shut up, for Christ's sake.*

Tom felt he might pass out when a horn blared from behind. *Shit! Was it them? The Stokers or the cops?* His eyes darted back to the rear-view mirror, droplets of sweat now dripping off the end of his nose.

Seeing the driver point and angrily mouth something, Tom faced forward again, his teeth gnashing harder. *Shit. The bloody lights had gone green.*

Crunching the gear stick into first, he bunny-hopped over the lights, sure he would die from stress.

Come on. Come on. Not far now...

He weaved his way through the housing estate in Frankley, his eyes moving back to the black holdall on the back seat. If he got collared with that, he was dead. But who would he prefer to collar him? The cops or the Stokers?

Tom's teeth worked harder, the chewing gum now reduced to a mere wisp of slime in his mouth.

If Sam was involved with Stoker, like Vera said, then she may not be as willing to hand him an opening to her firm. And if that man had a say in the *running* of her firm too, there was no way he'd allow Sam's business to be handed over to an unknown – even if that unknown was her own father.

Tom's face folded with further grotesque scenarios.

Once he and Sam had been properly introduced and picked up the necessary father/daughter relationship, would he have to do nasty things like go out for dinner with them? The prospect of sitting around a table with Seb Stoker made him feel sick.

Oh God, God, God. What if Stoker became his son-in-law and then he discovered what he'd done? Or found out that it had been *him* who'd killed his brother Gary...?

Tom's temples pulsed harder, his mind tripping out. It was only clipping the edge of a kerb as he turned into Luke's road that jolted him to his senses.

Calm down. You know nothing for definite, he thought. Winding himself into a frenzy was achieving nothing.

He pulled a cigarette from his top pocket and jammed it into his mouth. 'This is only on Vera's say-so,' Tom muttered, the sound of his own voice instead of the cacophony of screeching in his head strangely calming.

Knowing that withered old cow, she'd probably just made it up for effect. Trying to make herself look important. Women did weird shit like that, didn't they?

Fucking strange creatures, he thought, his panic stabilising.

As he yanked the handbrake on outside Luke's house, a lopsided grin formed on Tom's face. It would be easy enough to deduce what involvement Stoker did or didn't have in Sam's life and business because it would be the first thing to task Linda to find out on Friday when she visited the Orchid.

32

'Don't kick off,' Neil warned. 'Not today. Think of them.'

'I *am* thinking of them,' Andrew hissed. He'd watched his parents throughout. His mother's devastation held no bounds and his father had battled to control himself. But he'd also seen the look in his father's eyes when Seb had sloped in.

With what he'd already told his father, coupled with Seb's lateness, there would be words. *Plenty.* It was a case of *when.*

He glanced around the large, lavishly furnished function suite at the Peacock. It had been tastefully decorated to mark the sombreness of the occasion with drapes sympathetically hung to tone down the glitz of the room. It looked the part, but it wasn't right. *None* of this was right.

He watched the mourners mingle, offering the expected condolences to the family. He'd managed to gracefully accept the endless rounds of sympathy as expected, when all he wanted to do was rip Seb's head clean off his shoulders.

Still no one had referenced Seb's absence from the church, but the elephant in the room was clear. And that elephant consisted of the slim and attractive figure of Samantha Reynold.

Andrew's eyes narrowed, seeing her standing over the other side of the room in conversation. Adrenaline pounded in his already throbbing veins. He'd seen the way Seb's eyes searched the room the minute they'd arrived at the wake. And there were no guesses who he'd been looking for.

His eyes tracked back to his brother. Despite him also being in conversation, Seb's concentration was fixed on one person and one person alone. That's why he'd been late. It must be. Seb had missed Gary's service because he'd been with *her*.

How long would his father allow this to continue? Surely now he could see what he'd said last night must be acted on?

'Holy shit!' Neil hissed. 'What the fuck is *she* doing here?'

Andrew followed Neil's gaze, his anger compounding as he spotted Gloria Reynold loitering in the doorway. 'I don't believe this,' he spat. 'After allowing our family to cover for her lies, the woman has the audacity to show up here? Today? I don't think so, the cheeky bi...'

Neil grabbed Andrew's arm as he started towards Gloria. 'Leave it! Sam's going over. Let's see what she does first.'

* * *

'What are you doing here, Mum?' Sam whispered, steering Gloria towards the exit. Only after the words left her lips did she realise she'd automatically used the word 'mum'.

Leading her mother into the relative safety of the ladies' cloak-room, Sam shut the door, relieved to find the room empty.

She took in Gloria's pinched expression, her fingers clutching at the material of her jacket, and guilt bubbled. Seb was right. She should have sorted this out. When all was said and done, Gloria was still her mother. Maybe no longer by blood, but she'd always been there for her. But this wasn't the time or the place.

Realising Gloria hadn't uttered a word, Sam placed her hands on her shoulders. 'Why have you come here?'

'I had to!' Gloria said, her voice tiny. 'I had to see you and make sure you were all right.' Her hand moved to Sam's face, her eyes searching. 'Please tell me you're okay. I've been trying to call and you won't speak to me.'

Tears fell from her eyes, tracking down her gaunt cheeks. 'I know I hurt you, Samantha, and I'm so very sorry. It was the last thing I wanted. These last few weeks have been dreadful. I can't bear the thought of losing you.'

'I should have called,' Sam admitted. 'But you really shouldn't have come here today.'

'I know everyone despises me,' Gloria wailed. 'I've made such a mess of everything, but I wanted to apologise to Judith. I didn't mean to cause problems. It all just spiralled. I wanted to tell her. To tell you, but... but I couldn't. I didn't know how to. I'd promised Len. I...'

'Slow down,' Sam said quietly. 'You've got to calm down. You're shaking.'

Gloria sagged, her shoulders dropping. 'It was the only place I knew you'd be where you couldn't ignore me. When Liam suggested I should perhaps come today, I...'

'Liam?' Sam frowned.

'Yes, I bumped into him the other day and then he popped round to the house.' Gloria dabbed her eyes with a lace-edged handkerchief. 'He's worried about you. He thinks that Sebastian...'

'What has Liam been saying?' Sam stiffened, her tone guarded.

'I can tell by your voice I've made things worse,' Gloria wailed. 'I shouldn't have said anything. Now you won't tell me what's really going on.'

Sam blinked in confusion. What was really going on? What did she mean?

'I know Liam's hurt you've picked someone else over him,' Gloria continued. 'But he's such a good man, he's more worried about what's happening to you than himself.'

'I don't understand,' Sam replied. 'I'm not involved with Liam and never have been.'

'But if Sebastian is...'

Sam glanced up as the door opened and several women entered the cloakroom. 'We can't talk about this here,' she said. 'I'll get you a taxi. You must go home and I have to get back to the wake.'

'But...'

'I promise I'll come round soon and we'll talk then, okay? We'll sort everything out,' Sam insisted.

Nodding reluctantly, Gloria allowed herself to be led from the ladies' cloakroom and out of the foyer.

Putting her mother safely into one of the many waiting cabs, Sam watched it drive away before leaning against the wall.

Why hadn't Liam told her he'd been round to Gloria's? What was he doing?

Taking a deep breath, Sam walked back into the Peacock. She'd deal with this tomorrow. She hadn't even offered her condolences to Mal and Judith yet and that she must definitely do, however awkward it may prove.

* * *

Seb moved across the room towards his parents, feeling the frostiness before he was even near. Opening his arms, he hugged his mother, saddened but not altogether surprised to feel her tense under his embrace. 'I'm so sorry, Mum.'

'Oh, so you've finally come to explain yourself?' Mal hissed. It was taking all of his power not to knock his eldest son to the floor. 'Do you want to tell us what was so important to miss your own brother's funeral?'

Seb dragged his fingers through his unbrushed hair. 'I got held up. It couldn't be avoided.'

'Held up?' Mal spat, his voice rising.

'Mal, please! Not now,' Judith begged. It was bad enough that she'd spotted Gloria five minutes ago. It was a good job Mal hadn't seen her, as that would have set him off further. She'd have spoken to Gloria tonight, but Mal would never have allowed it.

She'd missed Gloria. She was the only person who really understood what this life was like. Although it had deeply hurt Judith that her friend had stalled in admitting the truth about who the rumours centred on, it wasn't Gloria's fault Gary was dead. But she understood why Gloria had faltered. She'd probably have done the same if it had been the other way around. The kids came first. Every mother knew that.

Judith glanced at Mal, his anger clear. She couldn't stand this bad feeling. She wouldn't lose another son. 'Mal, can we please not have any more cross words. Not today. There must be good reason for Sebastian's lateness, and he got here in the end.'

Ignoring his wife's pleas, Mal continued. He couldn't help it. He'd watched his son follow that woman around with his eyes and had seen a look on Seb's face that he'd never thought he'd see. He'd also seen how Samantha Reynold returned that look. It was obvious to anyone.

Andrew was right.

Mal looked Seb up and down, contempt he never thought he'd feel for his most capable son dripping from his pores. 'You haven't even got the decency to get properly dressed!'

Seb glanced uncomfortably at the suit he'd worn the day before. 'I know, I...'

'You smell of sex, Sebastian. *Sex!*' Mal barked. 'Have you no respect?'

'Malcolm!' Judith cried, her eyes glistening with tears. 'Please don't.'

'As I was leaving to get changed, the police tried to arrest me.' Seb's eyes narrowed. 'But it's sorted now.' *He'd kill that bastard Baker for this. Kill him!*

Mal's hands formed fists. 'And where was this, because you weren't at the Peacock or your apartment?'

Seb nodded. 'I was at Sam's. I...'

'And why were you there? As if I can't guess...'

Seb lowered his voice and leant closer. 'One of Sam's runners was jumped last night and the coke was nicked. Well, part of it, anyway. The runner died. I was sorting out with Baker to lose the evidence so that Sam wou...'

'You missed your own brother's funeral to sort out Samantha Reynold's problems?' Mal barked incredulously.

'Problems that could have turned into *ours*. I stepped in to control that.' Seb knew it might sound lame, but it was partly true. 'The info I gave that useless bastard Baker didn't filter down, but like I said, it's sorted. There will be no reprisals.'

Mal ran his tongue across his teeth, considering his next words carefully. 'Get out of my sight, Sebastian.'

Seb stared at his father for what seemed like an age before giving him a slight nod, then moving off into the crowd.

Mal watched his son walk away, feeling like he'd been punched in the stomach. There would have been no comeback on the Stoker firm for what had happened, so there had been no need for Sebastian to get involved. He'd *chosen* to.

His eyes moved back to Samantha Reynold. He'd never thought a situation such as this would ever arise. Regardless of Andrew's jealousy over his brother's position, Mal could no longer use that as an excuse. As much as he didn't want to acknowledge it, it seemed everything that had been said last night was true.

Sebastian's mind wasn't on the job and to learn that he'd refused to kill Maynard? His own *son* had refused to take revenge on the man who had killed his brother? And why?

Because he hadn't wanted to upset Samantha...

How could Sebastian let the family down like this? And all for that woman? It explained why there was so much bad feeling between his boys lately.

Mal's jaw clenched. The only saving grace was Andrew stepping up to do the deed, and if that hadn't happened...

He scowled. He may have asked Sebastian to step in and help Samantha after Len died, but not at the expense of the firm or his own bloody family.

The disappointment and rage were crushing. Sebastian had always been his prodigy. The son to keep the firm and family going once he'd stepped down.

Them against the world. With no exceptions.

But if that was no longer the case, then there was a very difficult decision to be made.

Mal watched Seb approach Samantha, his hand resting on the small of her back, her looking up at him with that smile...

This woman was now the problem.

It might not ever quash his overbearing disappointment, but before any decisions were set in stone, Mal would see if he could sort this out another way. A way that would be easier for everyone.

33

'Sling your fucking hook, kid,' Tom hissed, elbowing Tayquan in the side of the head. 'It's time you were at school.' Standing over the kitchen table, he poked the bowl of cereal. 'Where did you get those?'

Tayquan stared at his half-eaten bowl of Coco Pops. 'Me ma bought them.'

Tom's face screwed into a scowl. 'Why the fuck would she do that? Think you're posh or something? She'd best not have used any of my brass to buy that shit for you. You're spoiled enough as it is.'

Tayquan reached out to stop Tom snatching the bowl, but he was too late and could only watch miserably as the contents were emptied into a bin bag hooked over one of the broken kitchen cupboard handles.

'Oh, look – you've finished! Well, fancy that.' Tom jerked his head towards the door. 'School, then. Chop chop!'

With smug satisfaction, he waited until Tayquan silently moved out of the kitchen and left the flat. The girl had already gone, so now he'd go and give that horse-faced old slag a nudge.

'Linda!' Tom yelled up the hallway. 'Get yourself up!'

Linda shuffled out of the bedroom with bleary eyes and Tom bit back his urge to slap the taste out of her mouth. Going out and getting pissed on his money whilst he was left to sort everything out? The lazy bitch. 'Ah-ha! There you are!'

'What time is it?' Linda groaned. 'Where's the kids?'

'They're all sorted, fed and gone to school, I made sure of it,' Tom lied. 'Feeling a bit worse for wear, are we?' His mouth was smiling, but inside he wasn't. He yanked a can of cider from the fridge. 'Get that down your neck and get a grip. I need to talk to you.'

Linda paled. Tom hadn't changed his mind about her going to the Violet Orchid, had he? *Please, no.* She was so looking forward to it.

Tom gestured for Linda to sit at the kitchen table. 'Did you have a good time at the Chicks yesterday?'

Linda grinned. She still couldn't quite believe it. 'Blimey, you should have seen them! Everyone was queuing up to buy my drinks!'

Tom nodded, pretending he cared. He didn't. All he cared about was what it meant for *him.* 'You haven't mentioned anything to that old slapper about me being Samantha's father, have you?'

Linda shook her head. 'If you mean Vera, then no, I haven't. I said I wouldn't, but I don't understand why you don't want me to.'

Tom scowled. 'Because she's got a gob on her like the Mersey fucking tunnel, as have you when you're off your head, so I'm just checking.'

'Vera wouldn't say anything. She's my friend an...'

'Look,' Tom spat, banging his fist on the table. 'I said I didn't want you saying anything. I shouldn't have to give an explanation.'

Realising he wasn't sticking to his plan of being nice, Tom exchanged his snarl for a friendly grin. 'Sorry, babe. I'm just frustrated we have to keep where I figure in Sam's history under wraps.'

Linda smiled, relieved. 'I don't see why we need to, now. Surely it would make sense to tell her? You can get to know her then and y...'

'What have I told you about that?' Tom barked, before reining himself in yet again. 'Look, love, we need to let Sam get used to you first. It's only been a short amount of time and we don't want to overdo it. It's important to keep this to ourselves for a while longer.' *Or perhaps forever*. At the very least, until he had confirmation of where Stoker fitted into the equation.

Linda sighed. 'Okay. If that's what you think best.'

Pulling up the other chair, the metal legs scraping noisily against the lino, Tom sat opposite Linda and grasped her hands. 'Tomorrow night, I want you to find out exactly what Sam's involvement is with Stoker. Do you think you can do that?'

Linda frowned. 'Why are you so bothered? I saw your face last night when Vera told us. Have you had problems with him?'

'Problems? No, of course not!' Tom laughed loudly. 'I don't even know the man.'

'Then why do you want me to find out about him?'

Tom turned so that Linda wouldn't spot his snarl. 'I want to make sure his intentions towards our daughter are honourable. I've heard about that lot, and I won't have him ripping her off.'

Linda's eyes moved to the corner of the kitchen – the area where Sam's stolen coke had been stashed – and shook away her untoward thoughts. 'Okay. I'll find out what I can.'

Tom grinned. 'Right. Good. Now listen while I tell you exactly what I need to know. And don't go getting hammered and forgetting.'

* * *

Sam sipped her mineral water and looked around the empty casino. With the lights on full, the fruit machines switched off and the gaming tables devoid of customers, it looked a completely different place to how it would look in a few hours.

By tonight, the area would undertake a metamorphosis into a hive of activity; suited men, glamorous women, perfectly turned-out croupiers, clinking glasses, the clacking of gaming chips and chatter amongst the subtly-lit tables around the room. What a contrast.

Yet there was something eerily pleasant about this contrast. The only noise was the soft hum of a cleaner vacuuming the far end of the immense space.

Glancing at her Gucci watch, Sam rose from the table, placed her empty glass on the bar and slipped through the door to the corridor. As she rounded the corner, she saw Kevin leaning against the wall, waiting patiently.

'I'm not late, am I?' Sam smiled, slipping the key in the lock on her office door.

'No.' Kevin followed Sam inside the room. 'I'm early. I wanted to slip away before I got roped into refereeing "best ways" of dealing with what happened to Wallace.'

Sam placed her handbag on the floor and sat down. 'Has there been much unrest?'

'No more than expected.'

'It was remiss of me not to have pre-empted that. I should have put more thought into what John had or hadn't done in relation to the changes he was implementing.' Sam's eyes narrowed. 'What I will say, and I'll tell the staff myself later, is that I'll leave no stone unturned in finding who is behind this. I need to ensure this does not happen again.'

'By the way, the drop last night went to plan,' Kevin said. 'I must admit, I wondered whether it was risky going ahead under the circumstances.'

'I won't allow anyone to impede my business,' Sam said resolutely. 'I just won't. And you can rest assured people encroaching will wish they hadn't.' People needed to witness that she would not be pushed into a corner. Not for anyone.

Kevin nodded. He'd been so wrong about Sam Reynold. They all had. He'd witnessed her attitude hardening on a daily basis. Not many people would be big enough to admit they hadn't been as astute as they should have, but she had, and that gained her even more kudos. 'And you've heard nothing more from the cops?'

'Nope. And I won't either,' Sam said, hoping that was the case. 'Baker said he'd dealt with it, and it *has* been dealt with. Finally...'

Kevin eyed Sam inquisitively. 'As your second, I have to ask... can you trust him?'

'Who? Baker?'

'Stoker,' Kevin continued warily. 'No offence, but things seem to happen when Stoker is around. He put the call in to that contact of his in the force and then, lo and behold, the next day, the cops descend on *you*. It was *your* patch that got turned over, *your* runner that died, *your* neck on the chopping block for being tied into the source of supply. Who stands to gain if not Stoker?'

Sam nodded. 'I understand what you're saying, but I trust him.' With an inward jolt, she realised it was true. She could see how it may look from an outside perspective, but she *did* trust Seb.

Kevin sucked his bottom lip. 'This firm's already been burnt once. And the Stokers *are* our rivals...'

'The Stokers may be our rivals on many things, but not *everything*.' Sam smiled pointedly. 'Now, can we discuss the measures we're putting in place to safeguard territories?'

Kevin nodded. 'I've set up a sting for the drop that's going down tonight. We'll tail anyone who looks set to jump and interrogate them accordingly.'

Sam eyed Kevin knowingly. 'Good, but don't get carried away. We need to find out who's behind this.'

'Of course.' Kevin grinned mischievously. It would be a lot more than an interrogation by the time he'd finished with the bastards!

He thought for a moment, then made the decision to speak of what was playing on his mind. 'I also need to tell you what was said on Sunday.'

Sam looked up from her notebook.

'I had a visit from Liam Taylor.' Kevin watched Sam carefully, knowing Liam was a firm bet amongst the staff to be the one to marry Len's daughter. At least, he *had* been.

'Liam?' Sam frowned. First Gloria and now Kevin?

Kevin drummed his fingers on the table. 'He told me Stoker killed Maynard.'

Sam remained motionless. 'Liam said *that*?'

'Yeah, exactly.' Kevin nodded. 'He doesn't know what you told me. A couple of weeks ago, I'd have probably believed him, but that was then. And for the record, from what I saw of Stoker and how he dealt with the Wallace incident, I'm inclined to actually believe he's on your side.'

'You were testing me?' Sam asked. 'When you asked whether I trusted Seb?'

Kevin shook his head. 'Not really. Well, perhaps a bit. More for my own reasoning than anything else. Liam presumes because me and Maynard were like this,' he crossed his fingers, 'that I'd jump on board with his theory, but as you know – that was before...' He paused. 'My personal opinion is that Liam wants Stoker out of your life any way he can.'

Sam nodded, her surprise building to anger. 'Liam's hated Seb for some time now. What justification did he give for this accusation?'

Kevin shrugged. 'Reckoned he saw you with Stoker in here the night of your father's wake. He banged on about one of the other brothers too – said there was something funny going on and that Maynard was mentioned. That kind of stuff.'

Sam's anger burnt. 'And how did you respond?'

Kevin shrugged. 'I humoured him and let him speak. I knew it was bullshit, but let him think I was taking it on board and would deal with it accordingly.'

'Why have you waited all week before mentioning this to me?'

'I thought he might say something else, but he hasn't. I do know, though, that he's expecting me to make sure you see sense about Stoker.'

Sam nodded. 'Thanks for letting me know. And let me know as soon as you can about any info as a result of the drop.'

She waited until Kevin left her office before shoving her notebook back in the drawer and slamming it so hard the wall shook.

And to think only the other night she'd been tempted to confide in Liam, like old times. What had she been thinking?

She'd previously asked Liam how he knew she'd been here with Seb the night of the wake and he'd said the barman had told him, but that was a blatant lie. He'd seen her himself. Now he was trying to plant seeds of doubt with Kevin and suggesting Gloria go to a funeral where she would not be accepted? What was his game?

Sam stared at her hands, resenting that they were shaking. *Shaking with rage.*

Kevin's words also underlined that she and Seb would always be seen as rivals. Neither of them would be trusted within the other's camp and that didn't bode well for what was developing at a rate of knots between them. What *had* already developed.

Would things always be like this?

She snatched up her phone, her hand poised in mid-air, her fingers wrapped so tightly around the receiver that her knuckles whitened. *Wait a minute...* If Liam was in the corridor that night, then he might have also seen Gary's body.

Or...

Sam dropped the receiver back onto the handset with a clatter.

Fuck. Had Liam killed Gary Stoker in a crazy attempt to fit Seb up?

Sam shook her head, feeling sicker by the second.

No. Aside from his faults, Liam wasn't violent. He never had been, so it *couldn't* have been him.

Could it...?

34

Neil watched Andrew and Seb interact, surprised there was less vitriol after yesterday's funeral. Andrew seemed quieter than usual, and Neil couldn't help but feel that something was brewing.

He tried to keep focused on the discussion, but the plain truth of it was, he was worried. Worried that everything that mattered was falling apart.

He knew everyone saw him as the least business-minded of the family – the one more interested in skirt than the ins and outs of the firm. The one who'd bring in the strong arm when instructed, happy to take orders as long as no responsibility came with it.

Yeah, he was the playboy, the flirt, good with his fists. The one who left the running of the firm to people like his father. Or Seb. Or Andrew. And that was fine with him.

Neil knew he acted like he was only bothered about women, but his family mattered more to him than he'd realised. Gary's death had brought home just how much it all *really* mattered. It was the wake-up call.

Now the equilibrium had changed, he felt adrift – flailing in a sea where, at any moment, the current might turn and sweep him, his brothers and his parents away in different directions.

'We should get more scouts out to police our patches,' Seb said suddenly. 'At least for the time being.'

Andrew steepled his fingers under his chin. 'Whose benefit would that be for?'

Seb met Andrew's eyes. 'Whose benefit could it be for, apart from ours? Come on, Andrew, is this another dig?'

'Actually, I meant are we protecting our runners or looking for a *real* threat? Could this business you became "caught up" in be opportunistic?' Andrew had promised himself not to hurl any barbed digs, but by God, it was difficult.

'The unfortunate incident the other night may have been opportunistic, but we can't take chances either,' Seb said. Had his brother finally snapped out of whatever was bugging him? Both Andrew and Neil must be aware their father had all but chucked him out of Gary's wake. 'Look. I know things haven't been easy of late, but I want us to come through this together. I never want to reach the point where we drift apart.'

Andrew dug his nails into his palms. Seb's comment surprised him. He hadn't expected that, but he wasn't about to allow himself to think he'd been wrong about his brother. Words meant nothing and Seb should have thought about the family drifting apart before jumping ship, shouldn't he?

Okay, so what he'd told their father wasn't *entirely* true, but something had to be done before it was too late. And if that meant twisting the truth somewhat, then so be it. The cards had been dealt. It was just a matter of time to see if they would be acted upon. And if they were, then he would put this firm back to where it should be.

Neil looked from Seb to Andrew. *It was now or never.* He rested his hands on the table. 'I can't sit here any longer like this. You're doing my fucking head in, both of you.'

Andrew and Seb's heads swung around in unison. Neil never had much of an opinion. *Ever.*

Realising he'd got a stunned yet captive audience, Neil continued. He'd most likely pay for this, but he no longer cared. Either this was sorted out, or he might as well walk away from here. From *everyone.* He turned to Seb. 'Are you serious about Sam?'

'Like you have to ask that?' Andrew muttered.

'For fuck's sake, Andrew!' Neil spat. 'Either shut up or fuck off. I've had enough.'

'In answer to your question, Neil, yes, I'm serious about Sam,' Seb admitted. 'But contrary to what *he* thinks...' He jutted his chin in Andrew's direction. 'I don't allow how I feel about her to influence or cause issues with our firm.'

'Yeah, right!' Andrew griped.

Seb's fists clenched. He had no idea what Neil wanted to achieve by this, but it wasn't getting them anywhere.

Neil continued, unperturbed. 'How about you, Andrew? Did you kill Tonya Blunt?'

'*What?*' Seb yelled.

Andrew threw daggers at his twin. 'What the fuck is this, Neil? I already told you what happened.'

'Does someone want to tell *me* what's going on?' Seb raged, looking between his two brothers.

'I paid Tonya a visit a while back,' Andrew sighed. 'I told her if she didn't retract her statement to the Old Bill about her husband's disappearance being something to do with us, then her kids would pay for it.'

'You did *what?*' Seb roared.

'I didn't actually do anything, of course,' Andrew added. 'I don't hurt kids. Or women, come to mention it. I presume you know that! I was sorting out the problem. Something you should have done!'

'And did you screw up the gun order on purpose?' Neil continued, his eyes back on Andrew.

Andrew slammed his fist on the table. 'I didn't screw it up at all. Jesus Christ! What the hell is this? Are you siding with him now or what?'

'Siding with me?' Seb shouted back. 'Aren't we supposed to be on the same bloody side?'

'My point exactly,' Neil said, now on a roll. 'But you,' his thick finger pointed to Seb, 'don't trust Andrew. And you,' he glared at Andrew, 'don't trust Seb. That causes massive fucking problems!'

'How can Seb talk about sides when he's focused on the other one?' Andrew raged. 'Why do you think I'm sorting stuff out? Because he's not, that's why! He's too busy – with that tart!'

Seb jumped from his chair, his face red. 'Don't you dare call Sam a tart, you cunt! I warned you about that before wh...'

'When you almost choked him, you mean?' Neil also got to his feet. 'What sort of shit is that? I mean, what the fuck, Seb? Turning on your own brother? This distrust is ruining the whole family!'

Seb slowly sat back in his chair and stared at Andrew. 'I guess you're still adamant it wasn't you who gave the story to the papers about Sam? The reporter said it was, but oh, look – he's now retired.'

'And I suppose I attacked his wife too?' Andrew countered.

'Well? Did you?' Neil hissed. 'After all, you disappeared that night, then returned later covered in blood!'

Disbelief replaced Andrew's rage. 'I don't believe this! I told you that was from a pub fight.' He got to his feet and turned towards Seb. 'See what you've done?'

'Enough!' Neil bellowed. 'Even *I'm* doubting everyone! Seb, I'm doubting whether you're capable of running this firm any more and Andrew, I'm questioning whether you're so jealous you've lost all of your values. Can't either of you see what you're doing to each other? To *all* of us?'

Seb stared at Neil in astonishment, then snatched his jacket from the back of his chair. 'I'm leaving this here before I rip your fucking head clean off your neck, Neil.'

'Call yourself a fucking brother?' Andrew glared at Neil. 'You're as bad as him.'

He stormed from the room along with Seb, both walking in opposite directions along the corridor, leaving Neil to swipe his tumbler of whisky off the desk to smash on the floor.

Linda smiled as a fresh drink was deposited on the table in front of her. Yesterday, she'd thought all of her boats had come in when people fell over themselves to buy her drinks, but exactly the same was happening again tonight.

'See? Did I not say you'd be treated like a queen in here from now on?' Vera laughed, looking pointedly at her own almost empty pint glass. 'Unlike me...'

'Next time someone brings a drink over, I'll point out it's usual to buy *both* ladies a drink.' Linda grinned mischievously. 'After all, I'm sure Mr Stoker wouldn't take kindly to the lack of manners.'

'I can't wait to meet this man face to face. I wonder if he'll recognise me from in here?'

Linda shrugged, only half-listening. She might be joking about this, but the whole thing was freaking her out. She pulled the Violet Orchid VIP pass from her pocket and stared at it as if it were fashioned from gold.

What if she made a fool of herself? She and Vera may have spent the whole day yesterday poring over that magazine, but having decent clothes like that was a pipe dream. She couldn't stand being humiliated in front of her own daughter.

Seeing Linda's expression, Vera frowned. 'What's up, duck? Tom's not giving you a hard time about tomorrow, is he?'

'Oh, no, nothing like that,' Linda said, necking half of her fresh pint. Tom had been quite nice to her this morning – overly nice... and that was half the problem.

What had been put under her kitchen floor was still weighing on her mind like lead. Plus, she didn't know why Tom wanted her to discover the ins and outs of Sam's relationship with Seb Stoker either.

He even wanted her to find out if the man was involved in Sam's business. Why did he want to know that? What was the fascination?

Linda sparked up a cigarette. In the end, she'd had to accept his explanation of fatherly protectiveness, but she couldn't shake off the uneasy feeling.

'You're not still worrying about what to wear, are you?' Vera asked.

'Sort of,' Linda mumbled. *That was partly true.* If she told Vera about the rest of her misgivings, she'd feel a lot better, but she couldn't.

'Well, don't you worry!' Vera clapped her hands excitedly. 'All will be revealed tomorrow. I'll be round at lunchtime to give us time to get ready. But until then...' She jerked her head towards the bar and winked. 'Get yourself up there and get the next round in. Don't forget mine this time.'

35

'How many tables do you require, Miss Reynold?'

'Just the one. This will do nicely.' Sam pointed to the room plan, selecting a table near the corner of the room which would offer a degree of privacy. 'If you could reserve it from seven onwards tonight, please? Can you also set up an account for the table? For the bar and the gaming?'

It wasn't difficult to see Linda didn't have much money and the last thing Sam wanted to do was make the woman feel inferior. She chewed the inside of her cheek. Maybe inviting Linda to a casino had been thoughtless? She didn't want it to look as if she was flashing cash around.

Despite the trials of the last couple of days, Sam was looking forward to tonight. Since she'd taken over the running of the firm, she hadn't spent one single night in the casino itself, apart from hurrying through it to her office. Now her confidence was growing, it would be good to show her face and witness the Orchid from a consumer's point of view. It would also be nice to spend time with Linda and get to know her better, as well as putting her doubts to rest.

'What name shall I put on the reservation, Miss Reynold?' Elaine asked, tapping at her keyboard.

'Oh, erm, Lin... No, put it in my name. The table is for myself and two guests,' Sam said. That way, she could place money on the account and cause Linda no embarrassment. 'The guests have been issued VIP passes. Please inform me when they arrive and I'll come down.'

'No problem.'

Walking away, Sam knew Elaine was itching to ask who the guests were. And that was a good point... Who would she say Linda was? A friend? She could hardly say her mother... It was far too soon for that.

She frowned, unsure whether she'd ever feel like she could call Linda her mother.

Her nerves fluttered, wondering what Seb would make of Linda. That's if he was still coming?

It had been impossible not to sense the atmosphere at Gary's wake on Wednesday. She'd barely spoken to Seb, not privately, anyway. He'd seemed okay, but something had shifted, yet she had no idea what.

'I want you to do another one of your little jobs.' Tom tapped his ash into the ashtray – a nice crystal one he'd treated himself to. Leaning back in his chair, he waited for Lee or Steve to speak.

'I didn't realise you'd want us to do it again,' Steve finally said.

'Why not? If the opportunity is there, why not take it?' Tom grinned. 'Jumps mean no outlay.'

'I thought you'd sorted a supply? That jump we did was only to get things started,' Steve said, unease rising.

'There's no harm doing a couple more while we wait,' Tom reasoned. And after tonight, providing he got the correct answers from Linda's report on Stoker's involvement with the Orchid, it wouldn't be long.

He scanned the list of takings from the crack deals over the past three days and nodded appreciatively. 'I see this is going down a treat!'

'It's shifting like hot cakes,' Lee grinned. 'You were right – we're making a steal.'

Tom's teeth resembled mouldering gravestones in the yellowing light. 'Good, good,' he beamed. 'The next supply is being cooked as we speak – which brings me back to the original conversation...'

His beady eyes rested on Lee. 'As I was saying, there's no point looking a gift horse in the mouth. If I remember rightly, there's a drop due tonight at the Pershore Road patch.'

'You want us to do the same as last time?' Lee asked, getting the drift.

'You got it in one!'

Steve glanced from Lee to Tom. 'Now hang on a minute! We...'

'Never waste an opportunity!' Tom rose to his feet, slapping his arm around the shoulders of the bigger man. 'It's there for the taking.'

'No problem,' Lee said before Steve had a chance to balls up the next wedge of easy money coming their way. 'I take it the same cut will be on the table?'

'Of course.' Opening the drawer, Tom pulled out two rolls of notes. *Money always spoke louder than words.*

Removing the elastic band from the roll of tenners, he counted them slowly onto the desk. 'There's a grand there, which will be yours tonight if you do good.' His eyes sparkled. 'Not many people can claim such a good wage for, what, half an hour's work, can they?'

He ignored the dubious look on Steve's face. It didn't suit such a big man to have such a nervous disposition. If this one didn't get his act together soon, he'd lose his place. He had no time for weaklings.

'Take one of the bashed-up vans from the stock pool, then get rid if needs be.' Tom's face creased into a grin. 'But hopefully you won't be as clumsy this time, though, eh?'

* * *

'I was hoping to catch you,' Liam said, out of breath, having jogged along Broad Street.

'What is it, Liam? I'm on my way home.' Sam didn't want to speak to Liam, her head was still reeling from Kevin's revelation.

'Fancy some company?' Liam kept pace as Sam continued walking.

'I'm only getting changed and then I'm returning. I've got guests coming to the Orchid tonight,' Sam said, wondering why she was telling Liam this when all she wanted to do was ask him why he'd said those things to Kevin.

'What guests?' Liam asked. 'Is it Gloria? Have you decided to put things right between you?'

'Why did you go to see her, Liam?' Stopping, Sam turned to look at him. She would be seeing Gloria tomorrow, but she'd be damned if she was telling Liam that. She'd had enough of him – he was trying to manipulate her, she was sure of it.

Liam rested his hand on Sam's arm, his fingers stroking the material of her jacket. 'Just to see how she was.' He frowned. 'I didn't realise I wasn't allowed. I've always been close to your parents. We go back a long way.'

Yeah, and don't you love to keep saying that, Sam thought, moving her arm, wishing he'd stop with this touchy-feely attitude. It used to be comforting, now it made her feel sick. 'Gloria appeared at Gary Stoker's wake on Wednesday. She said *you* thought she should go. Why would you suggest that? You know it's awkward, with what the Stokers think.'

'And it's important to put what the Stokers think over your own mother, is it?' Liam cried. 'Jeez, Sam. I was thinking of Gloria, not the fucking Stokers!'

Sam's irritation snowballed. 'I'm surprised, as quite frankly, you seem obsessed with them.'

Liam's face screwed into a scowl. 'What the hell has happened to you? You used to be a nice person. Now you've turned into a hard-faced, uncaring bitch!'

Sam's cheeks flushed. 'How dare you sa...'

'You're throwing your life away and abandoning everyone who loves you because of that psycho! I'm worried about you.' *And I want what's mine. Stoker should have nothing.*

'I'm not abandoning anyone!' Sam cried. 'You speak like I've jilted you!'

'You didn't have any complaints the nights we spent together!'

'That was once or twice,' Sam hissed, glancing around the busy street. 'Plus, it was ages ago. We're just friends now. Christ, is this why you hate Seb so much? You're jealous? It's pathetic.'

She stared at him coldly. 'I'm sorry if I haven't done what you expected, despite making it clear I didn't want a relationship with you.'

Liam blocked Sam's path as she went to walk past. 'But you want a relationship with Stoker and will throw everything your father worked for down the drain? It's stupid, Sam!'

'Get out of my way,' Sam hissed. 'People are looking.'

'You should be used to that,' Liam spat. *Time to use the backup plan.* 'You have lover boy to thank for everyone knowing your bloody business in the first place. Stoker gave the press that story!'

'Oh, give it a rest, Liam. You're being absurd,' Sam sneered.

'Am I? The entertainment woman told me. You know – the one I speak to about the articles for gaming nights and functions?' Dropping his voice, Liam clutched Sam's arm. 'She was sat next to Brian Sumner when Stoker called. The man only retired because he was threatened by him.'

Sam wrenched her arm away. *No, Seb wouldn't have.*

Liam pressed on. 'Listen to me! Stoker threatened Brian's wife! And what do you know... the wife then gets her face cut up!' He could see Sam's brain whirring, no matter how hard she tried to hide it. 'And you wonder why I'm worried about you?'

'I'm not listening to this any longer,' Sam spluttered. Without waiting for a response, she stormed off up the road towards her apartment.

36

Seb waited for the black Jaguar to drive past before starting his engine. He'd been about to write off seeing his mother as a dead loss, but now his father had gone out, this was his window of opportunity.

He had just about enough time to check how she was before going to the Orchid as promised to meet Linda Matthews.

Pulling into the driveway of his parents' home, Seb's tyres crunched on the thick gravel. He jumped out of the car and loped up the steps to press the gold doorbell.

Come on, Mum, he thought, tapping his foot on the doorstep. He glanced over his shoulder for good measure, just to make sure his father hadn't had a change of heart about going for his usual Friday night beer.

'Hello, Sebastian,' Judith said, opening the door. 'Your father's not here.'

'I know,' Seb said. Walking into the hallway, he kissed his mother on the cheek. 'I waited until he left. I didn't want an argument.'

Judith moved into the lounge, leaving Seb to follow. He took in his mother's figure – tiny in comparison to him and somehow even smaller than two days ago. It was like she was shrinking in front of his very eyes.

He stood awkwardly, feeling for the second time like an outsider in the family home. 'I wanted to come round to firstly see how you are, and secondly to apologise about Wednesday.'

Judith sat down. 'You've already apologised, Sebastian. You do not need to do so again.'

Seb sat down in the armchair opposite. Leaning forward, he took his mother's hands. 'I think I do. I can assure you I wasn't late on purpose. I just wanted you to know that.'

Judith exhaled slowly. 'Your father didn't help matters.'

'I know, but I didn't want to cause further upset,' Seb said. 'I really am sorry, Mum. I'm just trying to do the right thing by everyone.'

Judith stared at her eldest son. 'What's going on, Sebastian? You boys are at each other's throats and your father, well, he isn't happy. And neither am I.'

Seb nodded. Since Neil's outburst yesterday, neither he nor Andrew had said two words to each other. 'I won't deny there's a problem, but we'll sort it out.' And they would. They *had* to.

That's why he'd been up all night. For the first time ever, Neil had a very good point. Seb didn't trust Andrew and he should do. He shouldn't for one minute have ever suspected Andrew of being responsible for any of the things he thought feasible. The question was, would Andrew ever come to the realisation that Seb wasn't selling the firm out, regardless of his resentment towards Sam?

'They can't see it, you know?' Judith said suddenly.

'Can't see what?'

'About Gary.' Judith blinked away her forming tears. 'They're angry, Sebastian.'

'Aren't we all?' Seb muttered.

'But you know, as do I, it isn't Gloria's fault Gary was killed. Neither is it Samantha's.' Judith dabbed at her eyes.

Seb swallowed. So this wasn't just about his lateness to the funeral?

'Your brothers blame themselves for believing those rumours. As does your father... not that he would ever admit it. The only way Andrew and Neil can justify how they treated our Gary is to blame someone else for what started all of this.' Judith sighed. 'Now, I have one thing to ask you, son. I already know the answer, but I want to hear it from you.'

'Go on,' Seb said slowly, worry prickling.

'Do you love her?'

Seb blinked. He hadn't expected that.

Judith smiled at Seb's confusion. 'Do you love Samantha?'

'I'm not jeopardising the firm, if that's what you mean,' Seb said calmly. 'I keep telling everyone that. Why does no one have faith in me?'

'I'm not questioning that, Sebastian. I'm asking if you love her?' Because Judith was not having loyalty-infused rules ruin any more lives. Neither would she be told who she could be friends with any more. It all had to stop.

* * *

In a foul temper after the run-in with Liam, Sam hadn't been in the mood to soak in the bath and had opted for a quick shower instead.

Liam's jealousy was untenable. God knows what else he'd said to Gloria. And then what he'd said to Kevin? And lying to her too?

Slipping on a pair of black stilettos, Sam zipped up the back of her red dress and inspected herself in the mirror, knowing she must shake herself out of this. She would not allow Liam's accusations to find a place in her brain. She just *wouldn't*.

She'd met a man she wanted to be with, she knew who her real mother was and had arranged to put things right with Gloria. Okay, so there were still many things left unanswered on all counts, but she was heading in the right direction.

She bit her bottom lip. Maybe Gloria and Linda could meet eventually?

Sam smiled. She was handling the running of the casino and firm well. There might have been bumps along the way – some of them bloody massive, but all in all, considering where she'd been only a few weeks ago, things weren't going too badly.

She would not allow Liam to poison anything. Not any more. As much as she'd hoped things wouldn't come to this, maybe it was time he moved on – not only from her, but from the Orchid full stop.

Enough. Time to concentrate on tonight.

Sam scrutinised herself in the mirror once again. She slipped a pair of diamond studs into her ears and fastened the beautiful solitaire necklace she'd been given for her thirtieth birthday around her neck. So many things had happened in the short time since then.

Hearing the buzz of the intercom, Sam glanced at her watch. *Seb, perhaps?*

She pressed the button. 'Yes?'

'Samantha? It's Mal Stoker. Can I speak with you, please?'

'Of course.' Sam pressed the door release, her heart thumping. *Why would Mal Stoker be here?*

Although she'd finally got a window to offer condolences to both Mal and Judith on Wednesday, she'd sensed a distinct coldness towards her. She'd expected things to be awkward, but maybe she should use this opportunity to clear the air?

Her mouth curled into a smile. If she had a future with Seb, and she thought she may have, then it was important to have a good relationship with his parents.

Perhaps Mal thought it was time to smooth things over too?

Hearing footsteps approaching, she opened the door before he knocked. 'Hello, Mal. Please come in.'

Shutting the door, she gestured to continue along the hallway to the lounge. 'Can I get you a drink? A whisky or a cup of...'

'No, thank you,' Mal said, his voice clipped. 'This won't take long.'

Sam faltered. 'Is something wrong? Is Seb...'

'Correct on both counts.' Mal stood stiffly in the open plan room, his back against the wall.

A wave of cold poured over Sam, fear of the unknown making her legs weak. A torrent of scenarios flashed through her mind, one after another. *Had Seb been attacked? Murdered?*

Steadying herself against the sofa, she searched Mal's face. 'What's happened?'

Mal studied Samantha. She certainly was a beauty and he could see why this woman was the one creature with the power to turn his son's head. What he was about to do went against the grain, but the line had to be drawn. He cleared his throat. 'As you know, things have been difficult for our family of late.'

Sam nodded. 'I know it can't have been easy for...'

'I had great respect for your father,' Mal cut in. 'When Len died, I felt it my responsibility to offer the hand of friendship to you, rather than rivalry, but that was not under the proviso that my decision ruined my family.'

Sam stood in shock. *Ruined their family?* 'I know Gloria not speaking out about my real parentage caused Judith and all of you hurt. It... it was a shock for me too an...'

Mal's expression remained unwavering. 'My wife is a shadow of her former self. The bad feeling between our boys those rumours caused has poisoned everything.' He clasped his hands together. 'I'll get straight to the point, Samantha. Because of your family, we've already lost one son and I will not stand by to lose another.'

Sam blinked. 'What do you...'

'Sebastian isn't thinking,' Mal interrupted. 'Having a relationship with you is absurd to say the least, but the damage it's causing is not something that I can allow under any circumstances.'

Heat rushed to Sam's face, her cheeks burning. Her shock made a response difficult to formulate.

'I cannot, nor will I, allow Sebastian to be negatively influenced by his wish to keep you happy.' Mal smiled thinly. 'I have nothing against you personally, my dear, but I'm here to tell you whatever is going on with my son must stop.'

Indignation overtook Sam's disbelief. 'What does Seb say about this?'

Mal shook his head. 'I'm expecting *you* to do the decent thing and call off this idiocy. You've caused unknown issues between my boys and when that affects business and loss of family honour, then that's the time when someone has to step in. And that someone is me.'

'Family honour?' Sam gasped. 'If this is because Seb was late for the funeral, then...'

'That and countless other things. Your cousin, for one,' Mal spat. 'What was given up for your sake there crossed the line alone.'

Sam frowned. 'What? I don't...'

'I'll leave this for you to rectify and presume further action from my side won't be needed.' Nodding curtly, Mal strode back along the hallway.

Sam blinked. *Was Mal threatening her?* She rushed up the hallway after his retreating figure, but the door had already slammed shut.

37

The relief Gloria felt to see Judith on her doorstep had been astronomical. That the woman had the decency to understand why she hadn't spoken up sooner meant a lot.

From what Judith had just told her as they'd sipped their tea, there were still many family issues, but she'd made the effort to come and put things right between them. With Samantha due to visit tomorrow, hopefully everything else would be sorted out too. It was time her life became liveable again.

Gloria looked at her empty cup. 'Can I get you another? It's so good to see you. Please don't rush off.'

Judith smiled. 'It's as much for my benefit as yours. Like I said, I've missed you and I'm happy to hang around here rather than knock around the house on my own.'

'I'm so glad. I'm just so sorry that I...'

'Please stop apologising,' Judith said. 'It might take the rest of them longer, but they'll get there in the end. They might have to, what with Sebastian and Samantha...'

'So it's true they're together?' Gloria exclaimed, Liam's words crashing back into her brain.

Judith nodded. 'And from what I can deduce, it's serious. I've never seen my son like this, let alone admit he loves a woman.' She sighed despondently. 'It's caused further ructions with Mal and the boys with... well, you know... Mal thinks Sebastian's putting Samantha before the family. Why do men have to be so ridiculous?'

Gloria listened carefully. Sebastian going against his father and brothers to be with Samantha didn't match Liam's version of events.

'Are you all right?' Judith reached for Gloria's arm.

'I don't want my family causing more problems for you,' Gloria said. She wouldn't repeat what Liam had insinuated about Sebastian. It hadn't sat right then and certainly didn't sit right now.

'Sebastian won't back down over something he wants. I know my son, and he wants Samantha.' Judith smiled. 'Personally, I'm happy about it, but getting off the subject, how are you coping without Len?'

The mere mention of Len's name made Gloria blanch. 'I've been plucking up the courage to sort his things out.' She smiled wanly. 'Seeing his stuff in the wardrobe every day only makes the grief constant.'

'Then there's no time like the present!' Judith stood up. 'I'll help you.'

Gloria could have burst into tears at this kindness. She'd never have been able to face this task on her own. Taking Judith's outstretched hand, she allowed herself to be pulled up from the armchair.

* * *

'Oh, my God. I can't believe we're doing this!' Linda babbled to Vera as they got out of the taxi. She shoved a twenty-pound note through the window into the driver's hand. 'Keep the change, love.'

Vera laughed. 'Hark at you!'

Linda grinned. She'd never been able to tell anyone to keep the change before, but thanks to the money Tom had insisted she take, tonight she could. It was so exciting.

And these clothes Vera had arrived with this morning were perfect. She'd never had such nice clobber. New shoes and everything. They must have cost a packet, but Vera refused to say how she'd got her hands on this new gear.

It didn't matter. Nothing mattered apart from this very moment. *And it was wonderful.*

Her face glowed with happiness. For the first time, Linda felt worth something; like a *real* person. She slipped her arm through Vera's and stared up at the illuminated frontage of the Violet Orchid, her other hand resting on her new velvet evening bag containing their hallowed VIP passes.

Her heart raced with excitement.

'Are you ready?' Vera asked, happy to see radiance on her friend's face, which was usually devoid of hope.

'As I'll ever be!' Taking a deep breath, Linda made her way up the entrance steps.

'Good evening, ladies.' The doorman opened the large glass door, his burly manner not unfriendly. He gestured in the direction of the casino reception desk and doffed his top hat. 'Sign in over there and have a good evening.'

Unable to wipe the huge grin from her face, Linda walked across the reception, feeling a thousand times better than the last time she'd set foot in here. This time, the thickly carpeted floor under her feet didn't feel like quicksand, it felt like walking on air.

'Wow, it's swish in here,' Vera exclaimed, looking around.

'Good evening.' The receptionist smiled, her false eyelashes defying gravity. 'Do you have your membership cards?'

'M-membership cards?' Linda's heart dropped. *Was that it, then? Would they have to leave?*

'She means the VIP passes,' Vera hissed.

'Oh! Hang on a tick!' Linda's fingers fumbled with her bag. In her panic, the contents spilt to the floor. 'Fuck!' she yelled.

As Linda dropped to her knees, Vera smiled apologetically at the receptionist. Bending down, she helped Linda scrape the contents of her handbag together. 'Calm down,' she whispered in Linda's ear. 'Stop panicking.'

Standing back up, Linda handed over the passes, her cheeks scarlet.

Taking the cards from Linda's trembling hand, the receptionist tapped on her keyboard, her pink-taloned fingernails making loud clicking sounds. Peering closer at the screen, she raised her eyebrows, then picked up the phone.

'Miss Reynold? Just to let you know your guests have arrived.' Replacing the phone, Elaine smiled. 'Miss Reynold will be down to greet you in just a moment.' Her talons pointed across the reception. 'If you'd like to leave your jackets at the cloakroom, it's just over there.'

'I'm not leaving my jacket anywhere, thank you,' Linda said. This jacket probably cost more than the rent the council paid on her flat.

Elaine nodded politely and busied herself with the keyboard, leaving Vera and Linda exchanging glances, standing awkwardly to the side of the desk.

Linda wrung her hands, beginning to feel she'd made a horrible mistake. 'Now what?' she whispered.

As Sam entered the reception, Vera broke into a smile. 'Now we'll be just fine.'

38

'I don't think this is a good idea,' Steve grumbled as they headed up the Pershore Road. 'You keep banging on about the Reynold bunch being hopeless since the old boy dropped off the twig, but they can't be so blind to not notice one of their runners was jumped last week.'

Lee snorted. 'Now Maynard's off the scene and with that bird in charge, they don't know their arse from their elbow.' He overtook a Maestro bumbling up the road, the engine of the old Transit screaming as he knocked it into second gear.

Steve cracked his knuckles – a habit he'd recently developed from nerves. 'I heard they got a tug when the runner ended up in hospital, but diddly squat since.' His eyebrows knitted, making one large furry line across his forehead. 'Now what does *that* tell you?'

Lee rolled his eyes. 'Erm, that they got a tug?'

'It tells you they know what they're doing! Why else would things be silent? It doesn't make sense. I also heard that bloke died...'

Lee sighed as he pulled into the layby he'd marked as perfect for a cut-off point. 'You worry too much,' he scoffed. Pulling the handbrake on, he faced Steve. 'Tom's getting twitchy with your lack of enthusiasm. You'll get binned off at this rate.'

Steve stared out of the window into the darkness beyond. Lee was hellbent on doing this, so he had no choice but to go along with it. But he wasn't happy about *any* of it.

'Look, mate,' Lee continued. 'It'll only be this one time, or worst-case scenario, once more after that. By then, Tom will have come up with the goods.'

Steve's mouth flattened. That he doubted. From what he'd seen, Tom's plans weren't coming to *anything*. And how long would it be before someone caught up with them?

'Look on the bright side,' Lee grinned, his eyes trained on the van's wing mirror. 'In an hour or so, we'll be a grand better off and that's not to be sniffed at.'

'If you say so,' Steve mumbled, thoroughly unconvinced.

* * *

'Any VIPs in tonight, Elaine?' Liam tried not to make it obvious he was attempting to read the list behind the reception desk, even though it was upside down. If he could just sneak a quick look...

He was beginning to wish he hadn't necked the remains of that bottle of rum kept in his desk for emergency purposes. But he'd required something to calm down the endless clamouring in his brain.

Sam may have flounced off earlier, but he knew her well enough to know he'd got inside her head. The stubborn splinter in the wound wouldn't hold much longer. Stoker was on the way out.

But who had Sam invited here tonight? She'd better not have reserved a table for that thug. Treating the firm's rival, *his* rival, to a night out in the very casino he should partly own by now would be the final insult.

'There's sixteen reservations for VIP tables tonight,' Elaine confirmed. 'Although one of those is for Miss Reynold.'

'Sam's booked a reservation?' Liam feigned surprise.

Elaine leant forward conspiringly. 'Her guests arrived a while ago.'

Her long eyelashes fluttered as if the weight was too much to bear. 'Not what I expected...'

'Meaning?'

'Well...' Elaine sniffed haughtily. 'Their clothes were okay, but they acted like they wouldn't have a clue how to use cutlery!' She lowered her voice further. 'And the language!'

Liam frowned. 'I wonder who they are?' It couldn't be any of Stoker's lot – they knew how to act, even if they were lower on the evolutionary scale than fleas.

'One of the women came in on Monday, but looked nowhere near as decent as she does tonight. I wouldn't have even recognised her until she opened her mouth.' Elaine's long fingernails flicked through the notebook on her desk. 'I thought she might be another one of those gold diggers, but she can't be if she's a guest here. Yes, here it is. Linda. Linda Matthews.'

Liam shrugged, acting nonchalant. 'Oh, well. I'd best go and see how things are going in there.'

He moved from the reception through the doors of the casino. It took all his strength not to break into a run.

Shouting up a double rum at the bar, the glass barely touched the marble surface before Liam downed it. Why would Sam entertain people with the manners of paving slabs and mouths like dockers?

This woman, this Linda whatever her name was, couldn't possibly be Sam's real mother, could she? Surely she would have told him?

Liam's eyes narrowed. Sam *would* have told him. Before Stoker robbed his place...

He walked around the perimeter of the room under the guise of ensuring everything was running as expected. Catching sight of Sam at a roulette table, Liam focused on the women closest to her.

He'd find an excuse to go and introduce himself later. Sam wouldn't be so rude as to snub him in public. In the meantime, he'd give the photographer a gentle nudge in the right direction. It might come in useful.

* * *

'This really is a top place, Sam,' Linda gushed, sipping her Bacardi and Coke. She didn't even like Bacardi, but it was more refined than a pint of cider. And tonight, she was going to be classy.

She glanced around, still taken aback by the opulence and glamour. *And her daughter owned it.* Even the bloody glasses were posh!

'You both look lovely,' Sam said, determined to have a nice evening, despite the bitter taste Mal's visit had left.

'What, this old thing?' Vera winked, glancing down at her dress. How she'd got past the Rackhams security guard was a miracle, but old habits died hard. And she was determined not to let herself or Linda down tonight. And she hadn't, because here she was – seated at a table in one of the finest, if not *the* finest, casinos in Birmingham. On a reserved table for VIPs, no less. With the *owner*.

It didn't get much better than that. To top it off, she'd won £150 on her first go at roulette. Yes, she was having a fine evening indeed.

'Would you like a tour?' Sam suggested. 'Or maybe a game of poker? As you know, there is an account open for you.'

Linda beamed. 'I'm just overwhelmed at the moment, babe.' She clutched Sam's hand. 'I'm happy just sitting here with you.'

'How are things at home?' Sam asked, the underlying notion that something was wrong in Linda's life never having left. Linda's lip had just about healed, and there were no other outward signs of damage, but that could be down to clever use of concealer, rather than lack of problems. 'Tayquan and Shondra? How are they?'

'They're fine. Everything's fine,' Linda said hastily. She didn't want to think about home right now. That's if she could even call it that. It didn't seem much like home since Tom had moved in, along with everything else he'd brought with him.

The vision of her kitchen and what had been concealed there burnt, along with Tom's instructions. Should she tell Sam about any of it? She'd decide later. For now, all she wanted was to spend time with her daughter in these wonderful surroundings. Pretending to be a normal person for once was nice.

'How about your lodger?' Sam pushed. 'He still about, is he?'

'Lodger?' Vera exclaimed. 'What fucking lodger? If you mean that piece of sh...' She was quickly silenced by the toe of Linda's shoe booting her shin.

Linda glared at Vera, who made her displeasure known by snorting loudly, and then smiled in embarrassment at Sam. 'Well, erm, he's...'

'Why didn't you just tell me you had a boyfriend?' Sam asked. 'You didn't need to make something up.'

'I...' Linda felt crushed. Now Sam thought she'd lied to her. Well, she had, but not because of... *Oh, trust Vera to drop her in it.*

Sam squeezed Linda's hand, then signalled a waiter. 'Never mind that now. Let's get some more drinks in.'

As the waiter deposited fresh drinks on the table, her eyes scanned the room. No sign of Seb yet. Her pulse skipped. Was he aware of his father's visit? How should she broach that? Should she say anything?

Sam's growing unease amplified. She'd had no idea there was so much bad feeling towards her within the Stoker camp. She knew Andrew didn't like her – he'd made that clear – but learning of the deep-seated resentment from the whole family had been a surprise.

And not a nice one, either.

This was about more than being late for Gary's funeral. What did they believe Seb had done for her that would go against them? She didn't want in any way, shape or form to be responsible for his family turning against him.

'Sam? That bloke's trying to get your attention,' Linda whispered, nodding at the photographer standing at the foot of their table.

Sam smiled. 'What can I do for you?'

'We don't see you in here very often, Miss Reynold. Can I get a photo?' The photographer gestured to Sam, Linda and Vera.

'Of course,' Sam said, patting down her hair.

'What? Me as well?' Linda squawked. 'Oh no, I don't thi...'

'Rubbish! Come on, Lin. We'll be in the paper!' Vera grinned, already getting into a pose.

As the flashbulb went off, Linda blinked, temporarily blinded. 'Jesus wept!'

'Thank you,' the photographer said, pulling out his notebook. 'And who are these lovely ladies, Miss Reynold?'

'Sorry I'm late!' Striding over, Seb bent to plant a kiss on Sam's cheek.

Linda almost swooned at the incredibly handsome and notorious Sebastian Stoker. She could still barely believe that she, Linda Matthews, was sitting in a casino with the likes of these people. People she saw in the paper all the time. And one of them was her own daughter...

'Ah, Mr Stoker,' the reporter grovelled. 'A photo with you too, if I may?'

Seb stood behind Sam in the centre of the seated women. He placed one hand on Linda's shoulder, the other on Vera's and smiled widely for the camera as the flashbulb went off for the second time.

'Thank you,' the photographer gushed. 'Now if I can just take your companions' details?'

Seb saw Sam's unsurety. Placing his hand on the photographer's arm, he steered him away. 'You've got your picture, mate, so just put "Sam Reynold and friends", yeah?'

'Thanks,' Sam mouthed as Seb returned to the table, leaving the photographer to scurry off.

'Now then,' Seb grinned. 'Are you going to introduce me?'

39

Leaning against the bar and continuing his close observation of the group around the roulette table, Liam finished another large rum and signalled for a refill.

Oh, wasn't this cosy? Stoker joining the ladies for a group photo.

The pulsing of the vein in Liam's temple increased. He couldn't stand this any more. Why hadn't any of his carefully laid plans come to fruition? Why had Sam not put together all of the glaring hints he'd laid out? What else could he do? He was running out of time.

Liam stuck his finger in his collar. It was too bloody hot in here. Too stuffy.

He nodded his thanks for the fresh drink and raised it to his lips, the effects of the spirits he'd consumed catching up with him. Misjudging his mouth, he slopped rum down the lapel of his suit jacket.

Spotting the photographer walking past, Liam placed his drink on the bar and grabbed the man's arm. 'Get a good shot?'

The photographer nodded. 'Yes. And with Seb Stoker too! That makes a top photo for tomorrow's paper!'

Liam scowled. *Yeah, because Stoker's so bloody important. Wait... A* smile slipped over his face. 'You do know that woman is Sam's mother, don't you?'

'What?' the photographer gasped. 'Which one?'

'The one on the left,' Liam grinned. 'Sam told me ages ago that she was inviting her here tonight.' He didn't know which one it was. It might not be either of them, but it would cause more shit. Especially after he pointed out to Sam, once this hit the news-stands, that Stoker was behind it. *Again*.

Sam had seen Stoker pull the reporter to one side after the photo, so who else could it be? It couldn't be *him*, being as Sam hadn't yet even fucking mentioned it.

'Are you sure?' the photographer questioned, glancing back over to the table.

'I know it's a bit shocking, but why do you think Stoker's here? Sam's introducing her lover to the mother,' Liam sneered, getting that extra dig in for good measure. 'Oh, and her name's Linda Matthews.'

The photographer scurried away, hardly able to believe he'd got such a scoop. Liam Taylor might be half-cut, but the man knew Sam Reynold better than anyone, so it must be true.

* * *

Andrew hated it when he was wrong. and hated even more that he'd fucked up. He very rarely fucked up, and okay, he didn't much like admitting even those infrequent occurrences, but this time he'd ballsed up big time. He had to do something about it.

Pulling up in a reserved space in the Peacock's underground car park, he got out of his car and slammed the door. He felt like ripping it off its hinges, because he had the creeping dread he was too late to put things right and retract the embellished version of events he'd given his father.

Andrew opened the door to the building and loped up the steps to his office, hoping Neil was busy chatting up the birds in the casino like usual, rather than waiting for him like a spider.

Neil was right. They *had* lost their adhesion as a family and Andrew knew it was partly, if not mainly down to *him*.

He entered the shared office, stopping in the doorway as he spotted Neil. He hadn't spoken a word to his twin since the outburst, but now was as good a time as ever. He couldn't fester in denial any longer.

Yes, he might have been envious of Seb being the head of the firm, but it was more than that. He'd blamed Sam for making them think bad things about Gary, but he'd *chosen* to believe the rumours. And then he'd blamed Seb for being involved with Sam.

Instead of facing his jealousy, he'd treated Gary like dirt and could never put that right. He'd dumped his bitterness onto everyone. Now even Neil had lost faith in him.

It was only listening to what Seb had said, and *properly* listening, as well as hearing the desperation in Neil's voice, pleading for all this to stop, that it had finally hit him.

And Andrew could barely believe he could have got things so badly wrong.

Christ. What had he done? He'd allowed his misplaced bitterness to ruin the family and destroy Seb's reputation. If he didn't put this right, he'd succeed in ruining the firm and their family for good. And there could be no turning back after that.

'Where have you been?' Neil asked as Andrew continued inside.

Andrew dropped into his chair and put his head in his hands. He took a deep breath. 'I went to see Dad, but he wasn't in. Where's Seb?'

Neil shrugged. 'He went out early doors – don't know where to, but he did say he wouldn't be back tonight.'

Andrew nodded. Maybe he wasn't too late, after all.

Neil quietly studied his twin's silence and his own fear gained pace. Andrew and Seb hadn't had another set-to, had they? One more serious than the last?

Even though he didn't want the answer, Neil had to ask. 'What have you done?'

Andrew held Neil's eyes. 'I've fucked up, bro. And fucked up big time.'

* * *

After being dropped at the edge of a housing estate backing onto the Pershore Road, Kevin made his way over the patch of wasteland adjoining the main road. If his bearings were correct, through this patch of trees the layby where that van waited should be visible.

It was a gamble, but if he was right and the van was waiting for their runner, then this was the only way to do it without risking losing another one of their boys to whatever jokers were behind the wheel.

Kevin pushed through the undergrowth, scowling as a bramble snagged his jeans. Ripping it away, thankful of his thick leather gloves, he pushed on, aided by the dim illumination of the streetlamps through the trees. He had to find somewhere offering decent visibility down the road, as well as being within range for the off, without unveiling his presence.

Stopping, knee-deep in nettles, he pulled up his sleeve and glanced at his watch. Almost 10 p.m. Stu and Craig had returned to base to tail the bike whilst he did the job from here. But he needed to get a move on.

Kevin pulled the sawn-off from the deep inside pocket of his jacket and double checked it was loaded before continuing through the undergrowth, ducking under low branches and twigs that at any moment promised to catch him unawares and have his bloody eye out.

He could think of a thousand other things he'd rather be doing on a Friday night than this, but whoever thought they could pull a fast one, killing one of his lads in the process, was clearly stupid enough to push their luck twice. Except *this* time they wouldn't get away with it.

Kevin's face morphed into a scowl as he moved through the trees.

Keeping a good eye on where he put his feet, he tramped through the litter. These areas behind laybys were notorious dumping grounds and used as bogs by countless truck drivers. He could do without a turd stuck to his boot.

Happy his chosen area was adequately concealed and free from filth, Kevin squatted down and rested his shotgun on his thigh to wait.

He had a clear view of the knackered Transit not twenty feet in front and the outline of a man's head in the passenger seat. *Two of them?*

Yep, they were waiting for his runner who, by his calculations, should be approaching any time now.

Gloria put the fourth suit in the box and resisted the urge to bury her nose in the soft material to experience the smallest hint of Len's scent. This was difficult enough as it was and she didn't need an excuse not to do what was needed, especially when Judith was being good enough to help her.

She frowned. If Samantha and Sebastian had embarked on a relationship with a future, then making sure these age-old rivalries between the two firms and the associated bad feeling from the rest of the Stokers were put to bed had to be dealt with.

She'd ask Samantha how she felt tomorrow and also tell her what Liam had said. If she felt as deeply about Sebastian as Judith believed Sebastian felt about her, then nothing should stand in their way.

Gloria smiled inwardly. To all intents and purposes, she was still Samantha's mother, therefore she'd do everything to ensure Sam and Sebastian had a real chance, despite the mountain of opposing odds. True love was rare, and it could not be allowed to slip away over misplaced or divided loyalties.

Gloria glanced at Judith. The Stokers could resent her for the rest of time if they had to, but *not* Samantha.

'I think that's it for this box.' Judith broke Gloria from her musings. 'I thought only women had tons of shoes.'

'Len did love his Italian brogues.' Gloria glanced back in her own box. 'I can fit one more thing in this one.'

Reaching into the wardrobe, she slipped another tailored suit from a coat hanger and, before she changed her mind, took one last look, then shut the lid of the box. Despite the uncomfortable task, this past hour had made the invisible weight around her shoulders less crushing.

Lifting the box from the bed, Gloria moved to the landing. 'I'm putting them in one of the spare rooms for now.' She looked over her shoulder at Judith, only the top of her head visible behind the box. 'You'll have to excuse the mess,' she said as they moved into the cluttered bedroom. 'Most of this stuff is Len's. *Was* Len's...' Gloria corrected herself.

Judith placed her hand on Gloria's shoulder. 'You don't have to get rid of anything, you know? There's no right or wrong way to do this and it's certainly not something you have to decide right now.'

Gloria nodded, blinking away the returning tears blurring her vision. She twisted the key in an old wardrobe door. 'There's only books in here, but these can all go.'

Getting down onto her knees, she began removing the pile of books in the wardrobe. 'Oh!' Frowning, she pulled out a bag. 'What's this?'

Sam tried her best to get into the swing of things, but it was difficult. She watched Linda's face light up as her number came up on the roulette and the croupier pushed a pile of gaming chips in her direction.

'Fucking hell!' Linda screeched. 'Look! I've won 200 quid!'

Seb squeezed Sam's waist as they stood behind the seated players. 'She seems to be enjoying herself.'

'She does, doesn't she?' Sam hoped her face conveyed the smile she was desperate to hold in place.

'Is everything all right?'

'Of course!' Sam replied, a little too sharply. How could it be all right? She'd thought things were coming together, but today had shown problems on levels she hadn't expected.

What exactly Mal Stoker's 'further action' might be if she didn't call things off with Seb demanded her attention. Would Mal and the other Stokers wage a war on her and the Orchid if she didn't comply?

She glanced at Seb, his strong features prominent in the light hanging over the roulette table. Why should she lose what she had with this man because his family didn't like it? She couldn't. She just *couldn't*.

Spotting Liam strutting through the casino, she stiffened. His earlier harsh words still stung. He had to go. His interference and obsession were way past detrimental. He was no longer a friend and probably never had been. *And that hurt.*

'Is he causing grief?' Seb's breath was hot against Sam's ear.

Seb's proximity had its usual effect on her. How could she give this man up? But was she being selfish? Would he lose his family and his hard-earned career because of her?

'Sam...' Seb took her hand and raised it to his lips. 'If that prick is bothering you, then...'

'No, it's fine,' Sam said, her heart fluttering as Seb pressed his lips against the back of her hand.

It was strange to think those very same hands that brought so much pleasure to her inflicted unrelenting damage to others. But she knew how this game worked. It was pointless pretending she wasn't part of it. But she wasn't a hard-faced, uncaring bitch, like Liam was adamant she'd become, she knew that. She could and *would* not allow herself to lose sight of who she was behind the decisions she had to make.

She found herself looking at the fading bruising and scratches to Seb's right hand. She traced her finger over them, then stopped.

She'd asked how he'd done this, but he'd been vague. She focused. When was it she'd noticed it?

It was the night they'd argued in her apartment. The night she'd told him about Linda, the night he'd interrogated her, the night he'd left...

That was Sunday.

Her mind scrolled through the snippets of information. That was also the day after that reporter's wife was attacked.

Sam scrambled for answers. Was she with Seb on Saturday? What time did the radio say the attack happened? About eleven, wasn't it?

That Saturday was the night she'd met Linda and she hadn't seen Seb...

Sam shook her head. What the hell was she doing? Why was she allowing Liam's words to bear any weight?

40

Linda reached for her Bacardi and slurped at it. She'd hoped Sam might come and sit, but she was still deep in conversation.

He was a fine bloke, that Seb Stoker. A right handsome devil and rich to boot. But Sam looked troubled.

Linda's happiness wavered. Was she embarrassing her daughter? The thought that she might be messing things up by the way she looked or spoke tunnelled into her brain and the familiar feeling of inferiority pushed to the surface.

'Come the fuck on, Lin!' Vera shouted, her voice loud. 'They're about to spin.'

Aware of heads turning at the language, Linda nudged Vera. Vera had caned the house vodka and was already two sheets to the wind. They'd promised each other they wouldn't get smashed. Not tonight. Tonight meant a lot and she wouldn't have anything spoil that.

'What?' Vera laughed. 'I'm happy! What's wrong with that?'

Linda forced a smile, shoved a pile of chips against number seventeen and then sat back to wait.

Tom's instructions wormed back into her mind. Maybe she should give roulette a break? She hadn't talked to Seb yet. There had been introductions, but that was about it and she wanted to know everything about the man with her daughter. And she wanted to get to know *him* – not to interrogate the guy, like Tom insisted on.

When the roulette wheel stopped, Linda realised she'd lost and took it as a sign to move on. Leaving Vera at the table, she picked up her bag and moved towards Sam and Seb.

'Have you had enough of roulette?' Sam smiled as Linda approached.

'I thought I'd come over and get to know your fella a bit better.' Linda looked up at Seb. 'I hope *you're* not the cause of why my daughter looks so troubled?'

She cringed the second the words left her mouth. What the hell was she doing speaking to Seb Stoker like that? She was still more than a little in awe of the man and she didn't want to insult him. She *certainly* didn't want to get on the wrong side of the bloke.

Fresh perspiration beaded at the back of Linda's neck. Had she overdone the Bacardi or were her nerves getting the better of her? 'Sorry, I didn't mean to s...'

Seb pulled Sam in front of him and looked her up and down and laughed amicably. 'Your daughter looks pretty damn fine to me!'

Linda beamed with pride. 'You're more than right there,' she gushed. Turning to Sam, she squeezed her arm. 'I'm so pleased you've got a good man. He's lovely, babe.'

'*More* than a good man, I'd say,' Vera grinned, joining the group. She wavered unsteadily as she nudged Sam. 'If I were a few years younger, I'd be fighting you for this one!'

Sam laughed and pushed Liam's accusations back to where they belonged. *Nowhere.*

'Just to let you know, I really like these two,' Seb whispered in Sam's ear, then gave Vera one of his showstopping smiles. 'I think any man would be lucky to have you on his arm, Vera. Not quite as lucky as I am to have Sam, but lucky, nonetheless.'

Vera nudged Linda. 'Oh, isn't he just perfect! I told you Sam would be fine with him.' She staggered forward. 'Like I said to Linda, any bloke who snaps someone's fucking leg in two and brings a whole boozer to silence with one glare will always see you right!'

Seeing Sam's stunned expression, Linda tugged Vera's sleeve. 'V, I don't thi...'

'Oh, my God, you should have seen him!' Vera continued. Folding her arms, she adopted a deep voice. 'No one damages my woman!' She slapped her hand against Seb's lapel. 'You can be my knight in shining fucking armour any day!'

Seb laughed off Vera's ghastly faux pas. 'I don't know about that, Vera!'

'Where did all this happen?' Sam asked, her voice robotic. *Vera was joking, right?*

'The Chicks! Where else?' Vera cackled. 'Linda only went and fucking missed it, the silly cow, but you've done her a right favour though, Seb, mate. Thanks to you, Lin gets treated like royalty there now. No one wants to get on the wrong side of Seb Stoker's future mother-in-law!'

'Vera!' Linda hissed, wanting to curl up with humiliation. Her eyes darted to Sam, whose stony face spoke volumes. Now Sam would think she was using her name and her boyfriend to gain kudos. Look how angry she was. Vera had ruined everything now. *Everything.*

Scarlet-faced, she grabbed Vera's arm, her fingernails digging into her friend's skin. 'We'll just pop to the ladies,' she muttered, pulling Vera with her.

Sam watched Linda and Vera weave their way through the crowd. She'd like to think Vera was joking, but knew deep down everything she'd said was true. Seb had attacked a man because of the fight she'd told him about.

She turned to him. 'Do you want to tell me what that was about?'

'Ah, she's just pissed,' Seb laughed.

'Just tell me. Did you attack a man in that pub I went to?' Sam pressed.

Seb's mirth evaporated. 'Okay, so what if I did? What did you expect? You think I'd allow someone to hurt you, Sam?' He snorted in derision. 'I think not.'

* * *

'Here it comes,' Lee said, his foot poised over the accelerator. 'Bang on time. They really are lambs to the slaughter, the silly fuckers!'

Steve's eyes remained trained on the left wing mirror, watching a single headlight of a motorbike approaching. 'He's going quite a lick.'

'It's a question of timing.' Lee frowned, calculating when to pull out.

'I think they've got a tail.' Steve peered harder into the mirror. 'I reckon we should bin this off. It's too risky.'

Lee revved the accelerator. 'Bin it off? It'll be fine. I told you – it's timing.' He watched a vehicle behind the bike pull out into the outside lane. 'That van's overtaking, so we'll have plenty of room.'

Shaking his head, Steve braced himself for the impact. As the single headlight came into position, Lee grasped the wheel, ready to swerve in front, when Steve glimpsed a movement out of the corner of his eye. His head swung in the direction of the passenger side window as a flash and a deafening bang exploded from nowhere. He didn't even have time to open his mouth to warn Lee before the glass of the window blew out.

Ears ringing, the first thing Lee did was stamp on the accelerator. He didn't know what had gone on, but what he *did* know was that the bike and van had shot past and a tow truck was making its way into the layby.

Fuck. It had all gone horribly wrong.

Stamping on the accelerator again, amid the stench of burning rubber, Lee realised with horror they weren't moving. 'What the fuck?'

he muttered, his eyes darting to the mirror as the tow truck pulled up behind them.

'Do something!' Lee yelped. Turning, he realised his mate wasn't going to help. His eyes locked onto the gelatinous mass of tissue scattered over the dashboard and Steve slumped forward in the seat, half of his head missing, the majority of his face blown off.

'Fuck!' Lee feverishly scrabbled for the door handle of the van. The kebab he'd had earlier felt it might exit via his nose any minute. There was no time. *No time.*

His eyes darted back to the wing mirror, seeing a man clamber out of the tow truck, a gun in his hand.

Shit! A setup!

His bulging eyes strained through the broken window into the dark layby. There were trees and stuff there. If he got out the driver's side, he'd be shot, so he'd have to climb out of the passenger side.

Hefting Steve's body forward, Lee used his foot to cram his mate further into the footwell. 'Sorry, buddy,' he mumbled, clambering over the inert form, making sure he averted his eyes from the missing part of Steve's skull.

He tugged at the stiff door handle. *Fucking shit, crap piece of junk.* 'Open, you bastard!' he screamed, terror engulfing him. He had to reach that undergrowth. If he did, there was a chance he could still get out of this.

When the door finally gave way, Lee tumbled from the van into more broken glass on the concrete, along with an old sock and a puddle of what he hoped was rainwater. It didn't matter. He was out.

Almost there. Just get into those bushes...

He scrambled to his feet, only to draw level with the two very obvious barrels of a shotgun.

* * *

'Get in the fucking van,' Kevin yelled, his shotgun trained between the man's eyes. This was the loser who had killed one of his runners? The bastard looked like he had the IQ of a pigeon.

Lee's mouth flapped up and down, his voice box paralysed with fear. *Shit. He was done for.*

His head jerked towards the two men running from the tow truck behind, their eyes glinting maniacally in the dim light, then his eyes darted back to the undergrowth. *Could he still make a run for it?*

Desolation swamped him. He'd never make it. They all had guns.

'I said get in the van,' Kevin hissed, his finger itching to pull the trigger. But he couldn't yet. They needed this guy to spill the beans as to who was behind these jumps. *This* bloke clearly wasn't the organ grinder.

Stu placed a meaty hand on Lee's shaking shoulder. 'Get a move on, fuckface. We ain't got all day.'

Behind Stu, Craig kept his pistol aimed on Lee's chest and Lee knew he didn't stand a cat's chance in hell of not complying with their demands.

Tom would go mental. These must be heavies from the Reynold firm, which meant he'd underestimated that bird. He'd ballsed up and now he was about to be tortured.

Against his will, he found his legs moving towards the van.

Kevin nodded to the van. 'There's another one in the front, but he's had it.'

'We'll get this one in the back and then load on the truck.'

Lee's eyes widened. 'You're putting me in the back of my own van?' he squawked. There was no way he could go in there. 'I can't! *Please*! I'm claustrophobic...'

'Shut it!' Kevin growled, glancing down the dual track at the rumble of traffic. 'Just get a bloody move on.'

Eyes wide, seeing the gaping black cavern of the back of the Transit, Lee jerked backwards. *If he could just get away...*

'What the fuck?' Stu yelled as Lee darted around the side of the van. He made to follow, but stopped, the screech of brakes drowning out the impact as the man ran into the path of a passing artic.

In slow motion, the group watched Lee disappear underneath the wheels of the lorry before it ground to a halt several yards further up the road.

'Bollocks!' Kevin muttered. 'Stash the guns and get this van on the back of the truck pronto!'

41

'I am not discussing this here, Sam,' Seb hissed.

'I cannot believe you took it upon yourself to go and smash someone up! And to do it in broad daylight in a pub?' Sam paced up and down the staff corridor. 'Do you not think things are difficult enough as it is? I don't know these women and I'm beginning to wish I hadn't bothered!'

Seb's eyes narrowed. 'Your real mum not good enough for you? Is that it?'

'You're missing the point!' Sam cried. 'You broke someone's legs! For me? What are you? An animal?'

'I'm someone who will not have anyone hurt you. You need to understand that.'

'Understand it?' Sam cried. 'Under-fucking-stand it?' She looked to the ceiling in despair, her stress levels spiralling out of control.

First Liam, the guilt over Gloria, worrying about Linda, Mal turning up and now this? Seb had promised he'd let her get on with things, yet he'd steamed in again? And he stood here trying to justify his actions? She couldn't take it. Not today. It was all too much.

'You stand there with this "I want to protect my woman" caveman bullshit? I thought I was getting better at seeing through shit, but obviously not,' Sam raged. 'You told me you'd sort the reporter out and I told you not to! You even admitted you went to see him and then suddenly he retires and his wife gets slashed up? That you, was it? I saw the state of your hand the next day!'

'What the hell?'

'Just tell the truth for once in your fucking life. *You* gave the paper that story about me, didn't you? Then you backtracked because it pissed me off and when those people pretending to be my parents kept turning up, you followed through with your threats to that reporter and attacked that poor woman!'

Seb grabbed Sam's arm. 'Are you crazy? Who the fuck said this? Who the fuck sa...'

'Get your hands off me!' Sam struggled not to hyperventilate. Her lungs were so tight, she felt like she might drown. 'I can't believe I've been sleeping with someone who would stoop so low. Jesus Christ.'

'Sam...'

'Stop. *Please!*' Sam pulled away from Seb's grip. 'How could you? Making me love you? And then doing this?'

'You love me?' A half-smile formed on Seb's lips, the warm glow of happiness burning deep in his chest despite the situation. He reached for Sam.

Sam batted Seb's hand away, the stress of the past few days enshrouding her. 'Don't! I should have listened. I...'

'Listened to who?' Seb's euphoria dissolved. 'This is that fucking Liam wanker, isn't it? Filling your head so he can get in your knickers? I'll kill him! I'll...'

'Don't you dare hurt anyone else!' Sam cried. 'I trusted you. *Trusted* you!' She willed away the threatening tears. *She wouldn't cry. She just wouldn't.* 'You can tell your father he doesn't need to worry about our "relationship" any more either, so his visit was pointless.'

'My father?' Seb froze as the door to the corridor burst open and Kevin Stanton rushed in.

'Not now, Kevin! I'm busy,' Sam snapped.

'We have a problem...'

Sam saw by Kevin's face that whatever the problem was, it wasn't something that would wait. 'In my office,' she barked, then turned to Seb. 'I can't talk about this any more.'

Seb stormed from the corridor, slamming the door behind him, whilst Sam shut the door to her office with a bang.

Only then did Linda drag Vera from the toilets, tears cascading down her face. She'd caused this trouble. The night was ruined and so, by the looks of it, was the budding relationship with her daughter.

* * *

Rushing back to the gaming room, Sam moved through the milling customers. 'Excuse me,' she said, edging past a group near where she'd last seen Linda and Vera.

She didn't want to abandon the women after inviting them here. She'd already been gone almost an hour, but now she certainly had no option but to call it a night.

Smiling tightly, she inched past the group, only to see neither Linda nor Vera. *Where were they?*

There was no sign of Seb either, but that was hardly surprising. She'd allowed the pressure of Liam's words, Mal's visit, Linda and Gloria to override her logic. She shouldn't have flown off the handle. She'd reacted in a way she would have done before her life had become embroiled with this business. Those two parts of her no longer fitted together.

She wanted to run after him and find him to explain. No, he shouldn't have bust that guy's leg on her account, but neither should she have lashed out. All of this week's events had snowballed and she'd taken it out on him.

And now *this* – another bloody jump, except the casualties were on the other side. *This was a fucking mess.*

Sam hurried back through the casino to the reception, shrugging her jacket on as she went. She couldn't spend any more time looking.

'Miss Reynold, you've had three calls whilst your phone was on divert. They were fr...'

'Leave a note on my desk, Elaine. I have to go out,' Sam said, her mind still reeling from what Kevin had told her. She couldn't say she was looking forward to sifting through the one remaining corpse's pockets before the body, the van and the tow truck were torched, but she had to. If there was even the remotest chance there was anything, no matter how small, giving the ID of the person behind this latest attempt to jump one of her runners, then she must do it. She would not let her staff or firm down again.

She was halfway out of the door before she stopped. 'Could you let my guests know I've been called away on urgent business?'

'Your guests left half an hour ago, Miss Reynold,' Elaine said. 'They seemed upset. Is everything all right?'

'Yes, yes, it's fine,' Sam lied, hurriedly moving through the door and down the steps, her mind racing. *Linda had left?* She'd call her tomorrow. She couldn't stop to find out what had happened now.

And Seb? She'd call him later. Or tomorrow. Regardless of everything, whatever he did, whatever she was – she needed him.

Sam scanned around for the dark blue Volvo Kevin said he'd use to take them to the warehouse. Broad Street was packed full of traffic and people out for their Friday night. Her eyes scoured the cars, black cabs and double-deckers inching their way along the road.

Come on, come on, she thought, moving to stand against the Orchid's wall, out of the way of the throngs of people.

Her eyes darted up and down the road, her mind turning over whether there would be any scraps of information left on that man's body.

'Sam?'

Swinging around, Sam found herself face to face with Liam – the *last* person she wanted to see.

Her blood pounded, a headache throbbing. She'd had enough. Had enough of all of it. 'Are you following me?'

Liam placed his hand against the wall to the left of Sam's shoulder. 'I was about to introduce myself to your guests, only you'd disappeared. That woman you were sitting with – that was your mother, wasn't it?'

Sam's mouth fell open. 'What has that got to do with you?' She glared at Liam's arm barring her way. 'Let me past. I've got things I need to do.'

'It *was* your mother, wasn't it? God, Sam, what are you thinking? You don't want everyone discovering someone like *that* is your flesh and blood.'

Sam received a strong blast of spirits on Liam's breath. Linda was her mother, and she would not apologise for that. Or justify it. She was sick of Liam's insinuations, comments and bloody meddling. This was the last straw.

She yanked his hand away from the wall. 'For God's sake, Liam, you're pissed. And – you're fired!'

The buzzing in Liam's ears which had started as quiet background noise now became all-consuming. *She was firing him? That could not happen. Not now. Not after all his hard work.* He grabbed Sam's arm.

'What do you think you're doing?' Sam yelped as she was pulled down the alley at the side of the Orchid. She found herself pressed against a dank wall, the drip of the overhead guttering soaking the bricks behind her. 'What's wrong with you? Wh...'

'You think I'll let you fire me? After everything I've done?' Liam glowered. He wanted to strangle the life out of her; punch her in the face, then fuck her senseless and remind her that she would be *his*.

'I've been the one holding things together,' he spat, his breathing laboured. 'I was there for you after Len died. I even helped you after you disappeared with that psycho – who, I might add, is nowhere to be seen. I saw you arguing earlier. Get bored of fucking you on desks, did he?'

'Get the hell off me!' Sam cried. Liam had been spying on her? Watching her with... oh, God...

Liam pinned Sam against the wall with his forearm, his free hand grasping her breasts. 'Come on, Sam. You like it with people who'll kill for you, don't you? You get off on that sort of shit, yeah? Well, I can do that.'

Sam remained paralysed with shock and terror. Wanting people to kill for her? What was he saying?

'All these years, I've patiently waited to gain my fucking place. I've done *everything* it said on the tin. I've put up with your trivial rubbish time and time again,' Liam ranted. 'You blow hot and cold, mince about with silly ideas, yet you get handed *this*?' His arm swiped across the side wall of the Orchid. 'You didn't even want this damn place, but I do. It should be me, Sam. *Me.*'

Sam listened in disbelief. *She had to get out of here.* 'Liam, you need to...'

'Need to what? Need my well-earned place in your life? Get my financial dues? You're telling me! Now you think you can fire me? What else do you need to show you Stoker is a wrong 'un? Don't you listen? You're supposed to listen. That was the point! Deals are being pulled on your patches. I even told you what Stoker did to that woman.'

Sam scrambled to decipher Liam's words. How did he know about the deals? And yes, he was the one who'd told her about all of the other things... and she knew for a fact that he'd lied to Kevin to get him to turn her against Seb.

Liam staggered forwards, pushing harder against Sam's body. 'You fucking owe me. I've endured years of bullshit to get my place, you selfish bitch!'

Spittle landed on Sam's cheek and she stared into Liam's bulging eyes, jerking her head away as his mouth lurched towards hers.

'You *will* kiss me!' Liam raged. 'You gagged for it in the past. I'd tell you how beautiful you were, that I loved you – whatever you wanted. I said all the right shit, when really all I had to do was fuck a few people up and that would have done it for you. Well, I can be just as mean as him – that bastard, Stoker. That's what you want, isn't it? Well, you should be careful what you wish for.'

He backhanded Sam across the face, her yelp of pain only making the relentless ache of his arousal unbearable. 'You spoilt cunt!' he spat. 'Time to pay up!'

Yanking Sam's skirt up around her waist, his fingers tore into her knickers. 'Now do what you should have done from the start. It's going to be me and you from now on.'

With her face throbbing and blood from where she'd hit the wall running down her chin, Sam's fear morphed into cold rage. Swallowing the mix of raw bile, along with the crushing hurt in her soul, she bit the inside of her cheek and closed her eyes as Liam plunged his fingers into her, a grunt escaping from his lips.

If she kneed him in the balls? No, he was too close.

Her eyes darted to her handbag at her feet, then to the mouth of the alley. There were hundreds of people just yards away and not one of them knew what was happening. But what did that matter? No one could see this.

'You see?' Liam panted. 'Stop playing games. All I want is my share of the money, yeah? Stoker will soon be finished, and you know me – we've been close for years and we can be again.'

Satisfied Sam had finally seen sense, Liam dropped his arm from across her neck and pulled his other hand from her knickers to fumble with the fly of his trousers. 'God, I'm so fucking horny I think this is stuck.'

Sam mentally calculated the distance between where she was and the alley mouth. *She'd never make it*. Cold acceptance flooded her. 'Let me take my heels off. I'll fall over otherwise,' she said, bending to pull the strap of her shoe away from her ankle.

She had a split second to do this and if she didn't get it right... but she *would* get it right. She *had* to.

Under the guise of fiddling with her shoes, Sam's hand dipped into her bag, thankful she hadn't zipped it up in her rush to leave the Orchid. Her fingers closed around the cold metal handle of the knife.

Jumping to her feet, she pressed the button of the blade and flicked the knife open, swiping it left to right across Liam's throat in one fluid movement.

Shock plastered Liam's face as he staggered backwards, his hands raising to the gaping slash across the front of his throat.

Sam watched with detachment as thick arterial blood pumped from Liam's neck down the front of his crisp white shirt. His one hand stretched towards her, his eyes wide. His mouth opened, but nothing came out, just blood bubbling from the deep wound.

She willed her breathing to remain stable and concentrated on the slow dripping of the gutter above as Liam collapsed first to his knees and then onto his front, the noise and general bustle from the busy street mere yards away fading to nothingness.

With Liam's wide staring eyes unable to fathom what had happened, Sam waited, her back stiff against the damp brickwork.

She watched the fingers on his right hand twitch and then still.

Was that it?

Sam glanced around the alley and then at the knife in her hand, the blade wet with blood.

Robotically, she dropped to her haunches and pulled a tissue from a small packet in her handbag and methodically cleaned the blade. Closing the knife, she put it, along with the bloodied tissue, in her handbag, then zipped up the bag.

So now what?

42

Seb crashing into the office wasn't what Andrew had been expecting. And hearing what had transpired between his brother and Sam hadn't been expected either.

It had hardly been the best time to hold his hands up, admit what he said to their father and offer his apologies. It was one thing admitting he'd taken his personal guilt over Gary out on Seb, but another thing completely to commit the cardinal sin and attempt to make Seb to lose his place within the firm.

But when Seb told them what Sam had hinted about their father, Andrew knew he had no choice. Seb had been about to go to see their father to demand answers, so it would only have been a matter of time.

As expected, Andrew's revelations hadn't gone down well, yet he was taken aback Seb hadn't gone for him. In fact, Seb had barely raged. It was *Neil* who was angrier.

Andrew continued staring at his hands. He felt bad enough about everything as it was. He'd really hoped he could retract what he'd said before anything came of it, but by the sounds of it, their father had already been to see Sam.

He finally raised his eyes to see Neil glaring at him with pure malevolence.

'I still can't get my head around this,' Neil spat. 'Lying to Dad about you being the one to take Maynard out is bad enough, but purposely making out it was because Seb *refused*? That's unbelievably shit – the lowest of the low.'

Andrew put his head in his hands. 'I know and I'm sorry. I let all this shit with what happened to Gary mess with my head. I was wrong. What else can I say? I'll tell Dad that I lied, and I'll step down. I deserve it. I'm fucking sorry, I really am.'

'I'm not even sure any of us can carry on,' Neil raged. 'How the fuck can we trust you?'

Andrew's guilt burnt harder. Neil was right. Again. He'd let everyone down.

Seb got up and walked over to the drinks cabinet to pour himself an extra-large whisky. He hadn't thought this night could get any worse. But it stopped here. 'Neil, you're doing exactly what you picked us both up on,' he sighed.

He sat heavily back in his chair. 'I was at fault too. I suspected Andrew of things I never should have. And, as you quite rightly pointed out, I turned on him with my fists. We've all been wrong.'

Neil frowned. 'Yeah, but that's not th...'

'We either do this together or not at all. We can't change what's happened.' Seb slammed his fist on the desk. He turned to Andrew. 'You won't step down and, regardless of what you've said to Dad, nor will I!'

'He'll sack me himself once he knows I lied to him to make myself look better,' Andrew murmured, cringing at just how pathetic his reasoning sounded out loud.

Seb necked his whisky. 'He can't because *I'm* in charge – legally and otherwise.'

'It *was* me who forgot to put the finals in on that order too. It wasn't purposeful, though. I did genuinely forget,' Andrew said. 'I should apologise to Sam. I'm going to do that now.'

Ignoring Neil's glare, Andrew left the office.

He would go to the Orchid, no matter how cringeworthy it would be. He'd just grab a stiff drink from his own office on the way out first.

* * *

Out of breath, Sam hobbled up the steps to one of the back entrances of the Peacock. It wasn't one used very often, and she was glad about that. She couldn't risk being seen like this by anyone.

Aside from returning to the Orchid, which was out of the question, the only other place reachable from the network of back alleys where she could remain unseen was here.

After going off at Seb earlier, Sam felt this was the last place she should come to. What if he turned his back on her?

No. He wouldn't. And by God, if ever she needed Seb, now was the time.

Glancing over her shoulder for the umpteenth time, she banged on the door.

Hearing nothing from inside, Sam wanted to cry.

Her mind flitted to Kevin. She'd made such a big deal of insisting she be present to check for any form of ID on that man's body and now he'd think she'd changed her mind. If only she could have got back out to the main road. But how could she walk out into the bustle of a Friday night on Broad Street looking like she suspected she did?

Her hand traced over the grazed flesh of her cheek and bile rose up her throat. She banged on the door again, the metal painful against her fist.

'Come on, *please*,' she whispered. She had no idea how long she'd stood in the alleyway staring at Liam's body. It could have been minutes or hours, but the sudden jolt of lucidity which had knocked her from the trance made her realise that if she didn't move, it was only a matter of time before someone wandered along to relieve themselves or for a quick fumble with their latest conquest. And if that happened, she'd be going to jail.

She stared at the metal of the door – its unyielding presence speaking volumes. One last knock and then she'd have to accept no one was answering.

She banged again, this time harder, and leant against the cold metal, exhausted, only to lurch forward as it opened.

'Sam! I was just about to come and find you to apol...' As the light from the corridor filtered over Sam's grazed face, the bruise marks around her neck and the tear across the front of her clothing became all too visible. Andrew pulled her inside, quickly shutting the door behind him. 'What the fuck has happened?'

Even the prospect of being faced with Andrew Stoker didn't dilute the gratitude that he'd pulled her away from... from what she'd done. The torrent of everything she'd held inside her for the past however long flooded over her like a burst dam.

Sam knew Andrew was talking. She could hear him, but she couldn't concentrate enough to decipher the words. The relief to have a brick wall separating her from where the body of the man – her one-time friend – lay dead was overwhelming.

'Whoa!' Andrew slipped his arm around Sam's waist as her balance wavered. 'It's okay,' he said. 'You're okay.' He walked her along the corridor to his office, her body moving in the fashion of an automaton.

Sam allowed herself to be steered into a room and felt herself being lowered into a chair, a glass of something being placed in her hand.

'Find Seb,' Andrew hissed, as Neil stared in horror at the unexpected visitor.

* * *

'You need to slow down,' Andrew said as Sam poured out the events in a stream. 'We'll sort it, okay?' If only he'd gone straight to the Orchid after speaking to Seb, he may have been able to stop this from happening.

'Are you listening?' he pressed, meeting Sam's unblinking eyes. Seb would go crazy when he saw the state of her.

Sam nodded robotically, her mind looping. She'd recounted what had happened – had dumped the whole lot out in one go, her voice surprisingly lucid and clear.

The only way she was keeping things together was by acting like the last hour had happened to someone else. Except she hadn't mentioned one part. *Not yet.*

Uttering that out loud would make things real and then there was no turning back. But she had to, otherwise it would all have been for nothing.

Seb crashed into the office, his face creased with worry. 'Jesus!' he exclaimed, knocking a pile of paperwork from the desk in his haste. Dropping to his knees, he scooped Sam into his arms. 'Who's done this to you?'

Their earlier exchange disappeared into the ether as he took in the marks on Sam's neck, the cuts to her face, the rip to her dress... His eyes narrowed. 'Who did it?' he hissed through clenched teeth, his eyes moving to his brothers. 'Has she said who's done this?' Seb cupped Sam's face in his hands as Andrew quickly recounted what Sam had said. 'I'll deal with it.'

'I'm sorry,' Sam whispered. 'I should have worked out Liam was behind this. I just couldn't believe it... I...'

'It's fine,' Seb said. *No, it wasn't.* It wasn't fine that bastard, Liam Taylor, had tried to frame him, but worse than that, had done *this*...

His eyes tracked back over Sam's beautiful face, the blood from the grazes and cuts congealed on her cheek and chin. Adrenaline pumped mercilessly in his veins. 'What else did that cunt do to you?' he said, his voice quiet, but the malice held within frightening. 'Did he...?'

The word almost choked him. It stuck in his throat, stuck to his tongue. It burnt the enamel from his teeth like acid. He had to know.

Either way, the wanker was a dead man. Seb finally forced out the words. 'Did he rape you?'

Half in the cabinet getting the guns together, Neil shuddered. He could hardly bear to hear Sam's answer. The moment Andrew led Sam Reynold in here, he knew there had to be retribution. They had to stand as one. Seb was right. The only way to move forward was together – and that included Seb's choice of woman. What right did anyone have to take away another's stab at happiness? *None.*

'Sam,' Seb pressed. 'I need to know.'

Sam jumped as though she hadn't heard the question. 'He tried to, but...'

Seb's eyes flashed green fire. He gave Neil and Andrew the expected signal, then took both of Sam's hands in his own. 'You know I'm going to kill him, don't you?'

Sam shook her head. 'No, you...'

'Do not ask me to let this one go. That bastard has betrayed you in the worst way. Betrayed all of us,' Seb said. 'For fuck's sake! You can't protect him for...'

'Seb!' Neil warned. 'She knows what needs to happen.'

'You don't understand.' Sam's voice was clear and calm. Raising her eyes, she held Seb's gaze. 'You don't need to kill Liam because I've already done it.'

Temporarily speechless, Seb looked to Andrew and then Neil.

'He's lying in the alley down the side of the Orchid,' Sam continued. 'And we need to get rid of him before anyone else finds him.'

43

'All bastard night,' Tom muttered, slamming his foot on the accelerator as he sped over the lights at Bell Hill. Even the crunch of his slowly dying clutch wasn't grating as much as this latest disaster.

Throwing his fag end out of the window, he scraped his jacket sleeve across his mouth.

He'd waited patiently at the Aurora the whole night for Steve and Lee to return. *The whole fucking night.*

At first, he'd been happy overseeing pissed-up gamblers losing their hard-earned wedge, but even that got boring, so he'd got his end away with Tina's sister. Stella wasn't quite as good in the sack as Tina, but she looked younger, so that made up for it. Plus, it kept his mind from clock-watching and waiting for those two goons.

Eventually, the concept of Lee and Steve having turned him over gained pace and he'd lost patience. He'd all but convinced himself the greedy cunts had run off with the coke and bypassed him to sell it themselves, when word had reached him about the accident on the Pershore Road.

At first, he'd thought it couldn't be anything to do with them, but then one of Steve's runners mentioned seeing their van in the layby.

And the other men. And the artic...

Tom blasted his horn at a woman crossing the road with a pushchair. *Did she want to fucking die?*

He opened the window further, desperate for air. He was suffocating to death from the inside out.

Now he'd passed the cordoned-off scene himself. He'd seen the meat wagon next to a tented area the other side of the road. It was true. Steve and Lee had been jumped. *His* fucking jump had been jumped! And no guesses who by...

Tom screeched to a halt outside the flats.

While Linda had been poncing about in that bloody casino, he'd had his money-maker bulldozed.

His bitch slag of a daughter had found out another jump was planned. Lee had said she hadn't the manpower to deal with that, so this meant Stoker must be involved and had sent his men to deal.

Concentration stinging his brain, Tom leapt from his car, slammed the door and steamed into the stairwell.

That ugly, useless slapper had better have followed his instructions. She'd best have oodles of info on exactly what Stoker's involvement was with Samantha's firm. If Stoker had foreseen a further jump on his latest shag's patches, then Tom's plan of getting free coke was utterly screwed.

His teeth grated. Now he'd lost at least one of his best men. But did they have the other? And was that one talking?

Sweat ran down Tom's back. If one of them had been interrogated, he might be in shit as high as his neck. Especially if it was Steve. He was the weak link.

'Get out of my fucking way!' Tom snarled, barging past a group of teenagers on the walkway.

He needed to know *exactly* what shit he was in. Whichever way he looked at it, his plan had to change. *Again...* He'd have to revert to getting on side with the stupid daughter, meaning everything fell back on Linda.

Shit the fucking bed. This was a disaster.

Fully primed to drag Linda from her stinking pit to dish the dirt, Tom raced into the flat, incensed to hear Vera's squawking voice.

Why the fuck was that old bitch here? Well, she could fuck right off, right bloody now.

Stopping halfway down the hallway, he held his breath.

They were arguing...

Dashing into the lounge, Tom grabbed both Tayquan and Shondra by their arms and dragged them from the seat. 'Don't make a fucking sound,' he hissed, his eyes wild. Shoving his hand in his pocket, he squashed a tenner in their hands. 'Fuck off out of here and don't come back for a few hours.'

Glancing at each other, the kids scurried from the room, leaving Tom pressed against the lounge wall to tune his ears into the conversation coming from the kitchen.

* * *

'I said I was sorry!' Vera shouted. 'For God's sake, Linda, you overreacted. There was no need to bloody well drag us out of there!'

Twice now she'd apologised. She'd even apologised last night. *At least, she thought she had.* She couldn't remember much. That bloody house vodka was like paint stripper. She hadn't meant to get so plastered, but she hadn't done anything so bad. Gorgeous Seb hadn't had a tantrum about what she'd said, had he? Just Linda.

She hadn't meant to ruin Linda's night. *Linda* had ruined it herself by making such a big deal. If she'd just laughed it off, there would be no issue.

Linda slurped at her can of cider. 'You don't get it, do you?' she raged. 'You think sorry cuts it? Thirty years I've waited for this, and you fuck it up? How could you, V?'

Tears burnt Linda's eyes. Groping for her cigarettes, she shoved one into her mouth, her shaking fingers fumbling with an empty lighter.

'For fuck's sake!' she screamed, launching the useless lighter across the kitchen.

'That Seb bloke didn't take affront at what I said.' Vera passed her lighter to Linda. 'You worry too much.'

Linda snatched the lighter and shakily lit her cigarette. 'But Sam wasn't all right! Can you not remember the argument we overheard from the staff bogs?'

Vera shrugged noncommittally. Everything after the roulette was a bit of a blur. 'I'm sure it wasn't that bad.'

Linda stubbed her unsmoked cigarette out, then lit another. 'Sam was really angry with Seb. And she was also embarrassed. About you...' Her voice faltered. 'About *me*...'

'She said that?'

'Not in as many words, but if you hadn't been so fucking pissed, you'd remember and know I'm right.' Hot tears flowed down Linda's cheeks. As well as hearing Sam accusing Seb of all sorts, she'd never forget hearing her daughter say she wished she'd never bothered meeting up with her...

Vera's teeth dug into her lip. 'It's just a misunderstanding.'

Linda's shaking hand reached for her cider. 'Tom will go berserk. He's expecting me to...'

'What the hell has this got to do with Tom?' Vera asked, her eyebrows furrowing.

Realising she'd spoken her thoughts out loud, Linda panicked, her mouth working independently of her brain. 'Tom stole Sam's coke.' Her eyes darted to the corner of the kitchen. 'He's been storing it over there – under the floor – along with the crack.'

Vera's eyes widened. 'You what? You're back on fucking crack after all the shit it caused you before? Oh, my God, you stupid bitch!' She stood up from the table. 'I'll kill him for this. Kill him!'

Linda grasped Vera's arm. 'No, I'm not back on the gear, I promise you. Tom thinks I've been taking it, but I haven't. He wanted me to do some digging about Stoker and find out if he was involved in Sam's business, but I couldn't. It... it felt wrong. I...'

'Did you tell Sam about the coke?' Vera eyed Linda curiously.

'Well, no... I didn't get chance...'

'You put that fucking waster in front of your own bloody daughter?' Vera sneered. 'Why the hell would you do that?'

Linda put her head in her hands and sobbed in earnest. She could explain it was because Tom was Sam's *father*, but she couldn't. *Or maybe she should?*

Vera grabbed Linda by the scruff of her T-shirt. 'You're bullshitting! You must be! There's no other reason why you'd protect Tom unless you're back on the fucking crack.' She glared at her friend, raw contempt in her eyes. 'And there was me feeling bad. Oh, fuck you, Linda.'

'No!' Linda cried. 'I'm not. It's just the...'

'Bollocks!' Vera raged. 'I won't listen to your excuses any more. You've put that devil shit and that wanker before your own daughter and the two little kids you've got left in your life.' She waved her arm in the direction of the hallway. 'You don't deserve *anyone* – let alone your kids!'

'Vera... I...' Linda tried to keep hold of Vera's arm, but she yanked it away and stormed up the hallway and out of the flat before Linda could get the rest of the words out.

She'd have told Vera the whole lot – *everything* – if she'd have stayed. This had gone too far, but Vera had left like everyone else did in the end.

Collapsing into a fresh round of sobs that racked her entire body, Linda didn't even notice Tom coming in.

44

Sam was glad of Seb's strong arms around her during the night. The enormity of what she'd done hit her in the small hours and she hadn't any tears left. Now she just felt hollow.

She had officially joined that special club. *She'd killed.*

Without Seb's unwavering logic and straightforward approach, she believed she'd have drowned. The hurt of falling for Liam's lies clawed at her more than killing someone she'd once classed as her best friend.

But Liam had been right about one thing: she'd changed into a heartless cold bitch. She'd become as violent as the rest. She'd become all that she'd promised she'd *never* be.

Seb replaced the handset of his phone and walked back across the lounge of his apartment towards Sam. He perched on the arm of his sofa. 'That was Andrew, confirming everything's sorted.'

Sam nodded numbly, Seb's fingers playing with her hair. That was it then. *Easy.* No trace of Liam; the alley devoid of clues; his body gone, never to be found... *the usual...*

This was hardly unusual in this new world of hers, except this time it was courtesy of *her*. And this thought made Sam both nauseous and chilled to the bone. Not just because she too had now killed, but because she felt nothing. She *should* feel something, shouldn't she? Shouldn't she be horrified? Disgusted? Repulsed?

She'd taken someone's life, yet she was sitting here like it was normal.

It wasn't normal. It wasn't normal at all.

But maybe it was. Now, anyway.

'He deserved it, Sam. I just wish you'd realise that.'

Seb's gravelly voice was low, calming. The voice Sam had grown so used to hearing. The voice belonging to the man she'd very nearly pushed away for good. *Not any more.*

'The first time is always the hardest,' he continued.

Sam took a deep breath. *Like that made it okay.* She hadn't wanted there to be a first time, let alone more. She got up from the sofa. 'I should go. I need to go to the Orchid and explain to Kevin why I didn't turn up last night. I also need to call Linda. I'm seeing Gloria later too. I'm not sure what I'll say if she asks me about Liam.'

Seb frowned. 'You'll say what you need to say. And are you sure it's a good idea going into the Orchid? Don't you... erm, need a bit of time?'

Sam's mouth set determinedly. 'It has to be business as usual. You should know that.' *Because she certainly did now...*

'Don't worry about Kevin. He's aware of what happened. He said to let you know there was no ID on that body.'

Sam sighed. 'You spoke to him? What about the trucks?'

'Disposed of,' Seb smiled.

'Thank you,' she whispered.

Seb pulled Sam into his arms. 'You don't need to thank me.' Especially not now he knew she loved him. She'd said it last night, loud and clear.

'What about your father?' Sam asked. 'I don't want to lose you, Seb, but I don't want you to lose your place either.'

'None of those things will happen, I can assure you.' Seb planted a kiss on Sam's lips, then watched her leave his apartment, a flash of hope for the future fixed in the base of his chest. He wouldn't lose her for anything or anybody.

* * *

Tom tore a page out of Shondra's English exercise book and slammed it on the table, his whole body shaking with rage. 'Pick up the fucking pen,' he snarled, twisting Linda's head round to face the blank sheet of lined paper.

'Please don't make me do this,' Linda whimpered, unable to see through her tears.

'Pick. Up. The. Fucking. Pen!' Tom repeated, each word hissed through his teeth stabbing holes in Linda's heart. 'Write exactly what I say.'

Linda's hand lurched towards the blue biro, the plastic end chewed and sharp. Her fingers shook so much she could barely hold it.

'Make it neat!' Tom's ire increased with every second the paper remained blank. *The stupid, stupid bitch.* He might have known this old crow would let him down. Now he had to pick up the bloody pieces.

His eyes bored into Linda's head, wishing the power of his hatred would kill her stone dead and save him the trouble, the two-faced, lying cunt of a whore.

He tightened his fingers on the back of her neck. The only thing stopping him from wringing the life from her was the pleasure of seeing her flinch. 'Come on!' he yelled. If she didn't hurry up and write this, he'd lose his temper and this letter would be out of the question. But his resolve was slipping.

Linda began writing, her tears dripping on the sticky tabletop. 'I wouldn't have done it, Tom. You must believe me. I only said all that because I was angry with Vera,' she gibbered, the paper scratchy under her trembling hand.

Tom switched off from Linda's plaintive bleating and continued dictating. Every word coming from her treacherous mouth, every lie, every false promise risked him blowing his stack before she'd finished. And he needed her to finish.

His eyes scanned the words, checking she'd written everything he'd said.

'It doesn't have to be like this,' Linda wailed, putting the pen down. 'I don't want to go, Tom. I love you.'

That was now a lie. After thirty years, she'd finally accepted Tom didn't love her and never had. Her heart was shattered, yet it was something she'd known deep down since the moment she'd seen him pocket his share of the money from the sale of their daughter with a smile on his face. It had just taken *far* too long to realise it.

'How will you ever get to know Sam if you send me away?' she pleaded. But Tom had never wanted to get to know their daughter. He'd just wanted to use Sam, like he'd used *her*. Now she'd say whatever to placate him. She needed just a bit more time to warn Sam, to tell Vera – to tell *anyone* who could stop him.

Linda forced herself to look up into the hate-filled eyes of the man she'd wasted her entire life dreaming of and clutched his arm. '*Please* don't make me leave. I wasn't going to say anything and nor will I,' she sobbed. 'I can't leave. What about Tayquan and Shondra?'

'Can't you read what you wrote? The brats are covered. Not that I give a fuck about them!' Tom smiled, yanking Linda up from the table by her hair.

'Tom, no!' Linda screamed, her scalp burning.

'Keep it down, you stupid cunt!' Tom smashed his fist into Linda's face. 'Haven't you caused enough problems?' *Everything was fucked because of her.* 'You tipped them off about my plan, didn't you?'

'What? No!' Linda mumbled through her smashed front teeth. She had to stop this. *Had to.* Heart crashing, she glanced towards the work surface. *A knife... Could she reach it?*

Unfortunately for Linda, Tom tracked where her eyes rested. Not that it would have made any difference. He'd already decided what was needed in return for her backstabbing ways. He'd just wanted the letter. *And now he'd got it.*

Dragging Linda from the table, blocking his ears to her pitiful yelping, Tom's teeth bared viciously. Smashing his fist into Linda's jaw once again, he followed her down as she crumpled to the floor and began laying into her in earnest.

45

'Come on, Lin!' Vera banged on the door for the third time. 'I don't want to fall out. We've been friends too long!'

She rolled her eyes skyward before noticing a woman peering through the yellowing net curtains two doors up. 'What the fuck are you looking at? Go and watch your husband on the *Jerry Springer Show*, you nosy bitch!'

Shaking her head with frustration, Vera rooted in the bottom of her PVC handbag. She had a key somewhere; Linda had given her a spare. That was years ago, mind, and the locks may have been changed since then.

Gratefully pulling the key from her bag, she shoved it into the lock, relieved to find it still fitted. 'Lin?' Vera called, walking into the hall.

Suddenly spotting the kids sitting at the kitchen table in silence, Vera smiled. 'Where is she? Has she told you to ignore me? Come on, kiddos, you know what adults are like. Always arguing.'

At the lack of response, Vera stomped into the kitchen. 'A joke's a joke, kids. Where's your ma?'

She'd come back here with the best of intentions. She shouldn't have said all that stuff earlier, but if Linda wanted to drag it out and play silly devils, then...

Wait...

'What's this?' Vera reached for the scruffy piece of paper the kids were staring at:

To V,

I can't do this any more. You were right. I'm a loser and back on the gear. I've ruined everything. It's time I moved on.

Please look after the kids. Tell Sam I'm sorry too.

Love

Lin

Cold washed over Vera as she looked at Shondra and then at Tayquan. Linda had done a bunk and left her kids? 'Have you read this?' She knew their reading wasn't up to much.

'Not all of it, but I know it's from Ma.' Shondra stared up at Vera with wide eyes. 'Is – is she dead?'

'Dead?' Vera cried. 'Nah, course not.'

Anger strummed in Vera's head. Linda had done it again. She'd put her crack addiction before her kids. Left them high and dry like she'd done so many bloody times before. And to think she'd believed Linda had meant it when she'd said she was putting everything right.

Panic surged. And to dump her with the two young 'uns? As much as Vera loved kids, her life wasn't destined for children, that's why she'd never had any. She could barely afford to keep going herself. Plus, she only had a bedsit, so where the hell was she supposed to put them?

Her face twisted in rage. *Damn Linda for this.*

Vera looked back at the worry etched on the children's faces. She couldn't let them go into care. She wouldn't have that. 'Where's Tom?'

Tayquan shrugged. 'Dunno. He wasn't here when we got back.'

Vera frowned, worry glimmering. 'Got back? Was he here before?'

'He turned up when you were rowing with Ma,' Shondra added,

her face crumpling. 'He gave us a tenner and told us to disappear for a bit. When we came back, they'd gone. Everyone's gone.'

'Don't worry,' Vera said calmly, although she felt anything but. 'Everything will be fine.' She placed her arms around the children's shoulders and pulled their small bodies against her.

Something wasn't right.

Her eyes tracked to the floor, noticing a shiny patch. One that had recently been scrubbed.

'Wait there,' Vera barked, racing up the hallway to Linda's bedroom. Linda's clothes were there, but all of that bastard's had gone.

Taking a deep breath, she shook her hands in a futile attempt to stop them trembling. Plastering on a smile, she returned to the kitchen and shoved the note in her bag. 'Right, kiddos! Get your shoes on.'

'W-where are we going?' Shondra asked.

Vera kept the smile across her face. 'We're going on a very exciting trip,' she grinned. 'We're getting the bus into town and I'm taking you to see that posh casino your sister owns.'

Sam would know what to do.

* * *

How Tom had refrained from chucking Linda off the third-floor walkway down to the street below rather than carting her down those fucking steps was a mystery. It would have been damn easier. His arms were aching, but, if he'd killed her, it would lead back to him. Things were screwed up enough as it was.

Thanks to Linda's big gob, he no longer had anyone he trusted enough to help offload a body and he couldn't have left her in the flat. Those bastard kids would have found her and there were too many traces of him in that poxy flea-ridden dump.

He glanced at the back seat as he sped towards the Aurora, his eyes falling on Linda's smashed and ruined face. Just looking at her made him feel sick. Most of that would heal. *Eventually*. Not the teeth, mind, but shit happens.

He groped in his pocket for another cigarette and lit it. Inhaling deeply, the smoke sat in his lungs, calming him as he waited for the lights to change.

At least he'd got out of that drug-addled hellhole before anyone saw him. He'd half-expected to see *someone* on his marathon drag-down, but then it was only lunchtime, and all the wasters would still be lying in their pits.

Even that interfering bitch, Vera, hadn't magically appeared out of the woodwork. But she would do. Women never left things long after arguing. They were too reliant on gossip to stay out of each other's lives, more's the pity.

Tom pulled hard on his cigarette. Then again, Vera's predictable behaviour of turning up like a bad smell was what he was counting on. She'd find the note and then, Bob's your uncle – she'd go batshit Linda had gone back to her old ways.

Oh, yes, Linda had told him how good Vera was with helping her get off the gear before, but had also let slip her friend would kill her if she ever touched that stuff again.

Despite his annoyance, Tom couldn't help but grin. Yeah, Linda 'I'm never touching crack again' Matthews.

Vera wouldn't believe that, especially after she found out that Linda had buggered off, leaving her kiddies high and dry – the one and only thing the slag had ever been good at. And being as the thick cow had been so stupid to bleat about having her own on-tap supply under her kitchen floor, he could almost see the cogs grinding in what was left of Vera's addled old brain.

But it wasn't all untruths, was it? Linda *had* just had a nice hefty whack of crack and she'd be receiving more every single hour whilst he kept her at the Aurora.

And no, it wasn't ideal carting her back to his club, but it was the only option available.

For God's sake. The ability to cook crack was now off and he dared not attempt another jump or even *supply* any patches. Not while Stoker had heavies ready to offload anyone in sight. Blackmailing Sam for the safe release of this scabby old bat was also off the cards. Linda's stupidity meant there wasn't enough of a relationship between them to matter.

No, he was fucked on that side of things, too.

Tom pulled into the Aurora's car park, relieved to be back, but resentful for having this unwanted baggage and failing in his mission.

Opening the back door of the car, he dragged Linda out by her feet, smiling as her head smacked on the concrete. She could do with some bloody sense knocked into her.

Whether he liked it or not, he'd have to stick to what was available. He looked up at the frontage of the Aurora. And that was *this*.

His experience was undoubtedly with getting sluts to make him money on their backs, so he'd just press on with that. Except *this* time, he'd fully concentrate on getting nice young flesh in.

He hefted Linda onto his shoulder. He'd keep this bitch dosed up and maybe even put her to work with punters who weren't fussy. Once a hooker, always a hooker, so she may as well pay her fucking way.

* * *

'You're sure you're okay?' Kevin questioned, his usual gruff countenance giving way to protectiveness and admiration. *Liam Taylor, the bastard.*

Sam stiffened at Kevin's fingers on her shoulder, then countered her reaction. She would not allow Liam's actions to define her. She would not let his betrayal and what he'd almost succeeded in doing last night make her behave like everyone was in the wrong.

What Liam *had* managed to do had violated her enough. She only wished she'd grabbed that knife and acted sooner. But she'd done what was needed and for that she would not allow guilt to eat away at her any longer.

She placed her hand over Kevin's and smiled. 'I'm fine, Kev. And thank you for helping to deal with... erm... last night. And for sorting the van and truck.'

She knew Kevin was part of the clean-up operation in that alley, but she wouldn't ask how it had been achieved. Things could only move forwards from now on. No turning back. This was her world now and she would give her all to that with no questions asked.

She sighed resolutely. 'It's a pity there were no clues on the body in the van.'

Kevin shrugged. 'There was nothing to find from the one on the road either – not that we could hang around long. I'm sorry that didn't go to plan.'

'You're the last person who needs to apologise,' Sam said, suddenly startled as her office door burst open. Her eyes widened as Vera lurched into the room with the children in tow, followed by an extremely flustered Elaine.

'I tried to stop her, Miss Reynold, but she barged her way down here,' Elaine gasped, her usually pristine face red with exertion.

'It's okay, Elaine. Come in,' Sam smiled, then gave Vera a look she'd understand. *Don't say a word just yet.*

Dismissing Elaine, Sam turned to Tayquan and Shondra. 'Hi, kids! Do you fancy a tour of the casino? Kevin here will show you around while I have a chat with Aunty V.'

Kevin jerked, taken aback. Children's tours weren't usually on his list of duties. He shot Sam a sideways look and hefted his large frame out of the seat. 'Come on, then,' he grunted.

Sam smiled in gratitude as the two children were led from her office, Kevin's sheer size making them look like ants in comparison.

'Linda's gone!' Vera cried, the second the door closed.

As Vera babbled out a run-down of the day's events, Sam's disappointment surged. *Linda had gone? She'd only just found her.* Sitting back,

Sam exhaled slowly. 'Linda said she'd once had a crack problem and I saw a crack pipe in her room. It's feasible she could have gone back to it.'

Vera shook her head. She'd held it together for the children's sake on the bus the whole way over here, but now her panic overwhelmed her. 'That's what I initially thought, but the more I think about it, the less I believe it. She'd waited her whole life to put things right with you and she wouldn't give that up. Nor those kids.'

Tears poured down her weathered face and she tried to conceal them with shaking fingers. 'Fuck, Sam. What am I going to do? I can't look after kids. I've got nowhere to put them.'

Sam poured a brandy and handed it to Vera. 'Let me see the note.'

Vera gratefully tipped the brandy into her mouth, then pulled the crumpled paper from her handbag. 'I'm sure th...'

'Let me read it,' Sam interrupted. She needed to think. She stared at the note. It was the same kind of paper as the one she'd received from Linda in the first place, but...

Putting the note down, Sam groped for her handbag and pulled out the letter she'd received all those weeks ago. Unfolding it, she stared at it, then at the note Vera had given her. 'You're sure this is Linda's writing?'

Wiping her hand across her nose, Vera pursed her lips indignantly. 'Of course I'm sure. I've known her donkey's years!'

Sam put the letter next to the note Vera had brought. 'Then the one I received was written by someone else...'

Vera compared the two notes. 'That's definitely not Lin's writing.' She pointed to Sam's letter. 'Linda can spell, for a fucking start.'

Sam's brain churned. 'Then who wrote this? Linda said *she* had.'

Vera's mouth flapped open as the penny dropped. 'It's him. That bastard. It must have been part of his plan.'

'Who? Who are you talking about?' Sam cried, utterly confused.

'Tom! The bastard Linda's shacked up with. He's been knocking her around and everything. She kept denying it, of course. The latest split lip she tried to pass off as falling into a door. She even said she'd done it in front of you.'

'She certainly did not!' Sam cried.

'I know! She admitted it was him in the end. A right wanker, he is. I told her I'd fucking drop him in it if he kept on. I told her he was no good! I *told* her.' Vera paced around, her hands clawing at her hair. 'He must have overheard us arguing this morning. Linda was telling me she wanted to tell you about the coke that was nicked. I thought it looked like the floor in the kitchen had been cleaned – that's what made me think... He must have killed her. Oh, my God.' She sank to her knees, sobbing uncontrollably.

Sam sat motionless. *Astounded.* Needles of dread pricked along her veins. 'Slow down! He can't have killed her.' *But there was another possibility...* What Vera had said, could it mean this boyfriend was linked to the jump on her patches? Was Linda part of it? 'Pull yourself together and tell me everything you know,' she said calmly.

46

Mal strode into the Peacock, his face relaxed but inside, he felt the opposite.

He'd gone against the doctor's strict instructions and spent the night caning the best part of a bottle of whisky to quieten the events of the past few weeks from going over and over in his head. It wasn't his usual style, but then neither was passing out and spending the night in his car. But it was all for nothing because the toss-up of what he would do, should his words not be acted upon, had been decided for him, courtesy of the morning edition of the *Mail*.

Judith would have his guts for garters for not coming home last night. He'd thought about not calling to let her know he was staying out, but even in his drunken state, he didn't want to be the cause of additional worry. Not that he could remember much of what she'd said, or more to the point, what he'd said, but either way, he doubted he was flavour of the month. Then again, he wouldn't win that prize when she heard what he was about to do, either.

And that's why he was here now.

Continuing through the foyer, he ignored greetings from the staff who had once been his and barged his way down the corridor towards the offices.

He didn't bother knocking on the door. Why should he? This was his office – the one he'd entrusted to Sebastian, but the boy had made his choice...

Entering the room, Mal found all three of his sons sitting around the table.

'Dad!' Andrew cried in surprise. He'd planned on having the dreaded conversation with his father as soon as this meeting was over, but it looked as though he'd been pipped to the post. Judging by his father's face, he already knew. Anxiety and dread churned. He'd never felt more ashamed.

Seb stared at his father, seeing a steely look of determination, as well as a clear hangover. 'What brings you here?' he asked coldly, bracing himself for the assault.

'*This* brings me here.' Mal threw the newspaper onto the desk, the photo of Seb, Sam, Linda and Vera emblazoned on the front page. 'I see you've made your choice, Sebastian?' His eyes sparked with disappointment and anger.

Andrew exchanged glances with Neil as Seb stood up from his chair.

Mal folded his arms across his chest. 'I've decided you're no longer in charge of this firm, Sebastian. Your loyalties are divided and the woman you have given it all up for has as few morals as her adopted mother!'

Seb's jaw clenched. 'You mean the "decision" is based on Sam not immediately ending our relationship when you took it upon yourself to go to her apartment and threaten her?'

Much to Mal's surprise, Andrew and Neil got their feet and stood on either side of Seb. It was Andrew who spoke.

'This firm is now legally Seb's and he's running it, not you. You wanted us to come together, and we have. It's taken a pile of shit – namely because of *me* – to bring us to that point, but we're here and we're standing together.' He held his father's astounded gaze. 'If Seb leaves, then we *all* do.'

Before his father could counter, Andrew continued. 'I was planning to come and see you to admit that what I said about Maynard was a lie... I was being a prick. The truth is that the twat topped himself before we could finish him. I know I did wrong by saying what I did and I'm truly sorry for that. It was nothing to do with anyone else.'

'Finally! Someone talking reason!' Judith appeared through the door and stood at Mal's side.

Everyone's eyes shot to Judith. None more so than Mal's. 'What are you doing here?' he spluttered.

Judith eyed her husband. 'I knew you'd come here to do something stupid the minute I saw the paper, so I waited outside until I saw you.'

'This is *not* stupid!' Mal blustered. 'If you knew anything about how the business worked, then...'

'I may not know much, Malcolm, but I *do* know you're my family. *All* of you. If Sebastian chooses to be with Samantha, then that's up to him, not you. I was speaking to Gloria and...'

'I told you to have nothing to do with that woman!' Mal barked.

Judith swung around to face Mal. 'And that's another thing! I'm not being told who I can or can't be friends with any longer. Neither should Sebastian be told who to love. There should *never* be unrest between us! It's this outpouring of bullshit testosterone that's killing everyone, not Gary's death. I won't put up with it any longer, do you hear me? And that goes for all of you!'

She looked at each of her sons in turn. 'Judging by what I heard when I arrived, I hope you've finally worked out what's important?' Judith would have smiled at the strong men shuffling awkwardly and looking at the floor like they were ten years old, had she not been so livid. 'And...' She turned her attention back to her husband. 'I love you dearly, but your attitude lately is infuriating. If you'd let me finish, I would have told you the rest.'

She was on a roll now and couldn't stop. 'Me and Gloria found something yesterday. She told me of her misgivings and what had been said about you, Sebastian.'

'Me?' Seb frowned.

Judith flapped her hand. 'I put two and two together. It's people like Liam Taylor you should be against, rather than each other.'

Mal rubbed his head; his hangover and Judith's scolding were painful. 'Liam Taylor?'

'He attacked Sam last night,' Neil said quietly, knowing even the mention of that man's name was boiling Seb's blood. 'He's been behind a lot of things. He pretty much admitted everything to Sam himself before...'

Judith blanched. 'Wait a minute! I didn't know about this. Last night, you say? And when you say attacked...' Her voice trailed off, the look on Sebastian's face answering her question. 'I take it you've...'

'Sam did,' Andrew cut in. 'She did it herself.'

'Fucking hell!' Mal muttered.

As the Stokers looked between each other, waiting for Mal to say something more, the ringing of the phone cut into the silence.

Seb snatched up the receiver. 'Yes?' His frown became deeper. 'Two minutes.' He slammed the phone down. 'Something's happened to Sam's mother. I need to go.'

Judith's hands flew to her mouth. 'To Gloria? Oh, my God!'

Seb shook his head as he shrugged his suit jacket on. 'Not Gloria. To Linda – her *real* mother.'

Mal glanced at the newspaper on the desk. *He'd got all of this very wrong, hadn't he?* 'You'd best get going.'

As Seb left the room, Mal put his arm around Judith. 'I'm sorry, love.'

Judith smiled up at her husband, hoping that he, as well as all of her sons, had turned a corner. She hoped so, anyway, because it was the only way any of them could continue.

* * *

Try as she might not to, Gloria's eyes moved back to the carrier bag sitting in the corner of the room like the proverbial unwanted guest. She didn't want it in here – didn't want it *anywhere* near her.

Not for the first time, terror convulsed through her in case the owner who'd stashed this bag in her spare room, under her very nose, returned for it. The person who she'd willingly let into her life and house and who she'd trusted implicitly. That she'd *believed* in and even relied upon.

The thought sickened her.

She shuddered. She'd been so surprised to find the blood-stained suit, she hadn't known what to think. Initially, she'd thought it must be one of Len's – a remnant from a 'problem' in the past.

She wasn't stupid – she knew the sort of stuff Len did – the sort of things Samantha was now undoubtedly dealing with, but Len had *never* brought his work or anything incriminating through the doors of their house. Their home was their sanctuary.

It was only when holding that jacket up yesterday, frowning at the dried blood splattered over the blue material, that it became obvious it was a lot smaller than one of Len's suits. Neither did he have such a distinctive blue suit.

And she knew this suit had been placed in the bag recently, because of the crumpled receipt for a sandwich in the bottom of the carrier, dated from just over a week ago.

There was only *one* person Gloria knew with a suit like this. And that person was the only person who had been in her house recently.

The suit was Liam's.

After Gloria had blurted out the conversation she'd last had with Liam – the day he must have stashed that dreadful bag in the wardrobe – it was Judith who had put two and two together.

What Liam had said about Sebastian only confirmed this. That conversation was the day *after* the attack on that woman that Liam was so desperate to make out Sebastian had been responsible for. The woman who was married to the reporter from the *Birmingham Mail* and the one who ran the story Liam said Sebastian purposefully leaked.

But Sebastian wasn't the only one who knew about Sam's parentage because Gloria had told Liam herself. *She'd* given him both the means and the ability to blame Sebastian in his pursuit to gain Samantha, or rather what Samantha now had.

Gloria put her head in her hands. She'd done it again, hadn't she? She'd caused these problems with her gross stupidity. This was why she'd ended up with nothing; with no one. Why she was doomed to rattle around this house on her own, with no one to care for. No reason to make her life worthwhile.

Liam was a danger – to Samantha – to *everybody*. She had to warn her.

Getting up from the chair, she snatched up the phone, before putting it down again.

Judith may have calmed her down last night, but Gloria had tried to ring Sam three, maybe four times after that. Perhaps even more. She'd tried her at the apartment and left messages at the Orchid, yet she'd not heard a word back. It was now a brand-new day and her nerves were shot to pieces. What if something had happened?

She shouldn't have sat on this all night. She should have located Samantha herself, but where to start?

The Orchid. She'd get a taxi and head over there now. She couldn't sit here any longer.

Rushing into the hall to fetch her shoes, Gloria jumped out of her skin with the shrill ring of the doorbell. *Had Sam come early?*

She raced to the door. 'Samantha! Thank God!' Gloria then froze, seeing that as well as Sam, there was Sebastian, a strange woman and two children.

'Hi.' Sam smiled thinly. 'Sorry I'm early...'

'Come in.' Gloria forced herself to smile at the strangers and tried to catch Sam's eye for a clue as to what was going on.

Vera stood in the large hallway, transfixed with open envy. 'Wow!

This is some posh drum you've got here. And this is where you grew up, Sam?' She ran her finger along the heavy drapes framing the large window. 'Velvet an' all. Nice!'

'Vera,' Seb said, taking her arm. 'Why don't you take the kids out to the garden?' He raised his eyebrows, giving Vera a look that she couldn't fail to understand and ushered her down the hallway towards the back of the house.

'Samantha,' Gloria cried. 'I don't know what's going on or who those other people are, but I need to talk to you about Liam. It's urgent. I've been trying to get hold of you. I...'

'I know about Liam,' Sam said, guiding Gloria gently towards the lounge.

Gloria had listened with both fear and amazement to what Sam and Seb recounted. She'd been even more horrified to learn of the attack on Sam. She could still barely get her head around it. To think she'd trusted Liam and been happy for him to have her treasured daughter's hand in marriage?

Her tear-filled eyes moved back to Samantha, sadness engulfing her at the betrayals she'd been forced to endure since taking over the reins of Len's business empire.

For the first time ever, she wished Len hadn't been involved with any of it. Sam had had her whole life set out for her before all this. She'd been happy and now she was lumbered with this... this nightmare? 'Oh, God, Samantha. I'm so sorry. I had no idea.' Dread washed over her. 'Liam's clearly deranged and obsessed, he won't leave you alone now and he'll...'

'Liam won't be doing anything, Mrs Reynold, I can assure you of that.' Seb's hand clasped Sam's.

Gloria looked from Seb to Sam. She'd seen that look and heard those words from Len before and knew exactly what they represented.

Sam read Gloria's thoughts. 'It wasn't Seb. It was me...'

'Y-you?' Gloria spluttered, searching Sam's face. 'You killed Liam?'

'I had no choice.'

Gloria nodded. It shouldn't be a surprise. It had been the same with Len. She'd never asked how many people Len had dispatched because it was better not knowing. But she believed in her husband enough to know that every single one would have been necessary. Despite them not being blood, it seemed Samantha had the same attitude. Regardless of the lies Liam had *almost* had her believe, it looked like Sebastian held the same morals as his own father too.

She was glad for that, if not for anything else. But that didn't explain what Sam had told her of Linda Matthews.

Tears welled in Gloria's eyes. Now she finally had a name for the woman who had given her Samantha. But for Samantha to have just found this woman, only to lose her so quickly? For the umpteenth time, Gloria wished she'd told Samantha the truth a very long time ago. It would have at least afforded her more time. 'What about this Linda? Your... your mother?'

Sam shrugged. 'I genuinely don't know what's happened, but I'm going to try and find out.' She smiled slightly. 'I think you'd like her.'

Gloria leant forward and clasped Sam's free hand. 'How could I not like someone who brought you into my life?'

The final traces of resentment and hurt from the past few weeks melted around Sam's heart as she pulled Gloria into a tight hug. She clung on for several minutes before gently pulling away. 'Which brings me onto the next thing,' she said carefully.

Gloria's eyes tracked to where Sam was looking. Through the large patio windows, she watched the stranger lounging in one of her wooden patio chairs, laughing as the two children tore around the garden. Poor little mites didn't look as if they'd ever seen grass before.

'Could you look after Tayquan and Shondra?' Sam asked.

'What, here?' Gloria exclaimed. 'Well, I...'

'I can't take them. I'm out all hours and I can't have them going into care. Vera hasn't got anywhere for th...'

'I'd love to have them,' Gloria interrupted. 'Of course they can stay with me. They can stay as long as they like. They're your half-brother and sister, Samantha – a part of you.'

Relief flooded from Sam like a sieve. 'Thank you.'

'It won't be a hardship. I love children.' Gloria smiled, the prospect of having a reason to get up in the morning having already been resolved by Samantha being back in her life now tripled with the joy of having youngsters around again. 'But what about your mother?'

Sam smiled, her eyes glittering with tears. '*You* are my mother. You always have been, but I want Linda in my life too.'

'Then I'll do everything I can to help you find her,' Gloria said, her eyes also filling with tears.

'As will I,' Seb added. 'But you've got to take on board that this might not be what it seems. I hate to say this, but it all adds up.'

Sam nodded sadly. She may not have voiced what was in her mind, but it was true the rest of what Vera had said earlier had set the alarm bells clanging. Seb's initial instinct could have been correct. Linda's enthusiasm at getting to know her could have been a setup.

But until she knew that for sure, Sam wouldn't stop hoping her suspicions were wrong.

47

TWO WEEKS LATER

'Are you sure I can't tempt you into coming back to bed?' Seb's lips trailed down Sam's throat.

Smiling, Sam wrapped her arms around Seb's neck, finding it almost impossible to keep her eyes from wandering over his naked torso. 'You could easily tempt me, but I must get going.' She planted a kiss on his lips and turned back to the scrambled eggs. 'We're getting a bit too used to lazing around in the mornings.'

Seb's eyes danced mischievously as he playfully slapped Sam's backside. 'Probably because I'm loving it!' He raised an eyebrow as he moved to sit at the table. 'Would you rather me not be here?'

Sam laughed. 'Hardly! You know how I feel about that. About you...' She looked down shyly, blushing. 'It's just...'

Seb pulled Sam onto his lap. 'I told you: they've accepted it. How many more times?'

Sam nodded reluctantly. Seb might have said his family had now accepted their relationship, but she didn't know that for definite, and things still felt fractured.

Getting up, she hid the smile slithering from her face. Seb's insistence on staying at her apartment in the aftermath of Liam's attack had allowed her to fall into a comfortable cocoon. How long would it be before he decided he'd have to return to his own place? Knowing this new normality couldn't continue was crucifying.

Plating up the scrambled eggs, she laid Seb's plate in front of him. 'We've ascertained Liam was acting alone and the jumps on the patches weren't connected. That's been dealt with, so I'm not in any danger. You don't have to stay.'

Seb frowned. No, he didn't, but he *wanted* to. 'It does look like it was just those bozos involved, but I want to be with you, Sam, you know that. But talking about that jump...' he said tentatively. 'You haven't said a lot about, well... what could have been behind it.'

Sam frowned. *No, she hadn't said much about it.* She'd told Seb about Vera's theory – thinking Linda's boyfriend had killed her – and she'd also told him that the man had been knocking Linda around. And then the *other* theory had been mentioned... The one that in some ways, was even worse than the alternatives...

Her forehead creased. The people behind the latest jump were no longer – that was a fact. But the more Sam thought about it, the more she became convinced that one of the men killed that night might have been called *Tom*...

The very same Tom that Linda had been shacked up with...

It added up – the timings were correct – and so Sam had realised she had to take on board that Linda could have been part of the whole thing.

Her real mother's wish to be part of her life might have been a smokescreen to make money and, when the jump was intercepted and she realised her boyfriend was gone, the sensible thing to do was to do a flit, knowing the truth would soon be out.

But leaving those kids?

Sam frowned. If only she had an ID on those men or if there had been enough left of them for Vera to see, then she'd know for definite.

Seb watched the expression on Sam's face with concern and reached for her hand. 'Thinking about Linda?'

Sam shrugged sadly. 'Aren't I always? I just wish I knew.'

Seb sighed. He'd put the feelers out and had scouts doing digging. He'd even paid another visit to the Hen and Chicks, but no one had heard of this 'Tom' bloke who lived with Linda, let alone knew what he'd looked like.

As much as he was loathe to acknowledge the concept, it was feasible that Linda and this man *had* been involved. They'd been after Sam's money and drugs. And yes, if Sam's theory was right, the bloke may well now be dead, but that still didn't reveal the answers as to where Linda was.

He squeezed Sam's hand. 'If Linda doesn't want to be found, there's not a lot we can do.'

'I know,' Sam said quietly. She breathed in deeply, needing to get off the uncomfortable subject. 'I really should go. I'm seeing Gloria and the kids this morning.'

And that was one happier outcome from all of this. Aside from a few wobbles, Tayquan and Shondra had settled into Gloria's amazingly well, even though their mother had disappeared into thin air.

'Don't forget we're going out for drinks tonight,' Seb added. 'It'll take your mind off things.' He may not yet know Linda's whereabouts, but he could put *other* parts right for Sam. And that he intended to do.

* * *

'I still don't get why you bother with these,' Amelia moaned, dumping a netted bag of lemons on the countertop. 'There was me thinking you were going to start offering the punters ice and a slice in a G&T instead of that foul cheapo lager you dish out at the bar.'

Tom's eyes swerved towards the boxed-off section of the back room. The tacked together sheets of hardboard hardly constituted a 'bar', but as his plans to regenerate the Aurora into something rivalling the Broad Street gaffs were now on an enforced hold, he wasn't wasting further energy. It was what it was.

It was all he could do for now. If he'd carried on in the state of mind he'd been in a couple of weeks ago, he'd have lost everything by now. Luckily, he'd seen sense.

Okay, so all of his hard work and well-laid plans had come to nothing, thanks to that pointless cow upstairs, but he still had the ability, the participants *and* the customers to make money with what remained of his empire. He also had the brains to capitalise on a niche in the market – one that would pay handsomely.

'Just cook more of that shit up, will you?' Tom muttered, refusing to give in to temptation and smash his knee into Amelia's nose for thinking she had enough clout to make condescending digs.

In all fairness, the fat old sow had turned out to be helpful. In his absence, Amelia had kept the women in line and now that was all that was left, along with his side-line of saddos gambling their money away, he was glad of her. Plus, she'd followed his instructions about Linda with minimal questioning, which meant he didn't have to set *his* eyes on the foul, treacherous slut.

Amelia didn't need to know the ins and outs of why and for how long Linda would be here. He didn't know that himself yet. Neither did she need to know why Linda wasn't permitted to leave her room. And Amelia had better not ask. Not if she, her daughters and her nephew wanted to remain in his employment.

Amelia was more than happy to take the extra wedge to keep Linda dosed up, so he'd put up with the occasional outspoken quip escaping from the gash across her face that constituted a mouth.

Ugly fucker she may be, but Amelia was useful. And he needed useful.

Talking of which...

'The woman upstairs is due another shot soon.' *The woman who would not be named.* Her name was off limits. Tom glanced at the clock. 'Keep an eye out for when her punter leaves.' He nodded at the safe. 'There's some top-up bags of brown in there.'

Amelia moved towards the corner of the room, reaching to open the small safe. 'I meant to say, cheers for giving Chas a break,' she grinned. 'My nephew's a canny one. He'll have some fresh girls here before you know it.'

Tom smiled thinly. It wasn't a case of giving anyone a break. He was light with hands on deck since Steve and Lee had got bumped off. It wasn't like he could show his face about too much over Luke Banner's neck of the woods for a while either, so he hadn't a lot of choice but to take Amelia's recommendations.

It was a shit binning the cookhouse off, but Tom was damned if Luke would continue supplying. If *he* couldn't benefit from the crack, then no fucker would.

Besides, there was enough left over for Linda's use and that was all that mattered.

For now, his priority was girls, girls, girls.

48

'Wow! that's amazing!' Sam gasped, pretending to be fascinated at the bizarre contraption Tayquan and Shondra had fashioned from material and wood in the back corner of Gloria's large garden.

'It's ace, isn't it?' Tayquan proudly clambered up to a horizontal plank of wood offering a perch above the ground. 'Auntie Gloria brings us sarnies out here too!'

'I made the decorations,' Shondra added, running her fingers over the draped material Sam recognised as curtains from one of the spare rooms.

Sam's heart swelled with the joy on the kids' faces. 'It looks brilliant,' she enthused. 'The perfect hideaway!' And very similar to one she'd made herself many years ago at the same age. Their happiness helped dilute the ever-present guilt and disappointment over her failure to find Linda. 'I'm going back in the house to talk to Gloria, so I'll see you in a bit, okay?' she said, hurrying back towards the house.

Entering the back lounge, she found Gloria watching from the window.

'They've settled in really well,' Gloria smiled. 'I love having them here.'

'I'm glad,' Sam said. Everyone seemed happy, so surely that was the main thing, wasn't it?

Even Gloria hadn't let the photograph telling the world Linda Matthews was Sam's real mother faze her. It was like the truth being out in the open had cleansed her. But Sam couldn't bring herself to look at the photograph that had made the front page of the *Mail*. It brought back too many reminders of the night it had all gone wrong.

'Vera popped by yesterday,' Gloria continued, handing Sam a cup of tea. 'She's still very worried about Linda.'

'Aren't we all?' Sam muttered.

'You're still adamant we shouldn't go to the police?' Gloria asked, the tremor in her voice audible.

Sam shook her head. 'Yes, and you know why.' The police would have no choice but to place the children in the care system. No one wanted that. On top of that, under the circumstances, it was likely the authorities would close the door to Linda being reunited with her children if she and Seb located her. No. *Once* they located her.

Gloria clutched Sam's hand. 'You'll find her, I'm sure of it. You mustn't give up.'

Sam smiled weakly. 'I've no intention of doing that.' But the longer time went on with no word or sign of Linda, the worse it got.

Aside from having to accept the theory that her mother and this Tom person had only been in it for the money, she also had to entertain the possibility that Linda was indeed back on what Vera referred to as 'devil shit'.

Even Vera now reluctantly agreed it was possible.

It was a thought that did not sit well. The whole thing was hurtful and uncomfortable, but feasible all the same.

Gloria saw the worries ticking silently in Sam's mind. 'How's Sebastian?' she asked brightly, wanting to steer the subject away.

'He's fine,' Sam smiled. 'Great, in fact. I just wish he didn't have to go back to his own apartment.'

Gloria grinned, desperate to tell Sam what was arranged, but she couldn't. *She'd promised.*

* * *

Linda didn't bother opening her eyes as the man grunted on top of her. She couldn't remember where he'd come from, let alone who he was.

It wasn't like it mattered. Nothing mattered, apart from getting relief from her own mind. And that she would earn once this fat bastard finished. She hoped he wouldn't be long because she was choking for a hit.

It was strange because every so often she had lucid moments, yet still couldn't work out how she'd got here – wherever *here* was. She had no idea, but, quite frankly, didn't care. It was better that way.

This setup was familiar and it was almost nice in a way. She knew it well. The dribs and drabs of what she *did* remember made her wonder why she'd bothered trying to change her life in the first place. Why change something which worked?

Linda knew she'd never been destined for anything else. Not really – even if others had occasionally succeeded in blagging her into believing there was a place for her elsewhere.

They'd lied. Everybody had lied.

With an almighty groan, the nameless man collapsed to one side, his slobbering mouth searching for Linda's. 'Fuck off,' she muttered. Opening one eye, she pushed the man's face in the opposite direction. 'No kissing.'

Back in the day, she'd never allowed kissing with punters, and it was even more important now to stick to those rules because, like most things lately, she wasn't sure what had happened to her mouth, apart from that it fucking hurt. There were a couple of teeth missing. She could feel the gaps with her tongue and the constant throbbing and rancid poisonous taste in her mouth. It was bloody agony and there was no way she could stand anyone's mouth on hers. She could barely eat, for fuck's sake.

Another reason why she needed a fix. At least it dulled the pain.

Linda ignored the man as he clambered off the bed and put his clothes on. She just wanted him to leave because then that woman would appear with the payment. That was all she was hanging onto right now.

* * *

Amelia stared at the figure on the bed, almost drooling for the mix she pulled into the syringe. Her eyes travelled over the ravaged face of the woman Tom had mysteriously brought here a couple of weeks ago. In a right state, she'd been. Smashed up to buggery.

Amelia frowned. She'd thought the poor cow was dead at first, but she wasn't. Beaten to within an inch of her life, yes, but not dead.

She should have gone to the hospital really, but when Amelia voiced that, Tom left her with no difficulty understanding that was not a viable option. Nor was it acceptable to ask questions, so she hadn't.

Tom said the woman had been mugged, but Amelia had her own thoughts. Thoughts she'd keep to herself.

She watched the mix of crack and heroin fill the syringe. Yes, she'd known the fresh bag of lemons meant another batch of this deadly mix. The question was, why?

Pulling the tourniquet tighter around the woman's thin bruised arm, Amelia wanted to offer a smidgen of solidarity to the poor bitch, but how could she, when she was the one administering this poison?

She almost laughed. It was fuck all to do with her. She was getting extra cash for this and had a cushy number here at the Aurora. She didn't have to spend time on her back these days either, as she was so busy organising the other girls.

No, she was onto a good thing, so she wasn't rocking the boat.

'Come on then, love.' Amelia grabbed Linda's arm. 'Let's get this into you.'

Linda's dead eyes stared at Amelia, the anticipation of much-needed relief from herself almost orgasmic. An unwanted image of Sam flashed into her mind and she blinked, desperate to remove it.

The life that she'd very nearly had, which included her daughter, had now gone.

Hadn't her friend once said that she'd put crack before her kids?

A lone tear escaped Linda's left eye and rolled down the grey skin of her cheek.

That was right, wasn't it? She'd had a friend once. She'd had children, too – including that beautiful first daughter of hers. And she'd failed them all.

Saliva drooled from the side of Linda's mouth. She deserved this.

And why? Because she wasn't fighting to get out of this place – this setup. She'd accepted it. Almost *happily* accepted it.

The powerful urge for the gear was stronger than anything. She'd had the cheek to lie to herself that she cared about those people, but how could she, if crack was more important?

And it was *very* important. Without it, she was nothing. Like she always had been.

Linda's broken mouth twitched into a half-smile, feeling the prick of the needle, then the hot rush as the drugs powered up her vein, bringing blissful oblivion.

* * *

'Oh no, Seb!' Sam cried. 'I thought we were going for a drink, not a fancy meal!'

She smiled self-consciously at the doorman at the entrance of the Burlington. She loved the champagne bar here, but she wasn't wearing anything suitable.

She'd spent far longer at Gloria's than planned. She'd only dashed back to the Orchid to have a word with Kevin, but even he was nowhere to be seen. She shouldn't have even left until she knew for certain he was back on site, but Seb had insisted.

'Relax!' With his arm around Sam's waist, Seb shepherded her through the lavish doorway into the wood-panelled bar.

Sam frowned as they continued to one of the private function rooms, the subdued lighting at least hiding the embarrassment on her cheeks. 'Why are we going through here?'

'Peace and quiet,' Seb grinned, nodding to a waiter who dutifully opened the door.

Sam's mouth flapped open as the group of people sitting around the table was revealed. Her eyes flitted from Mal and Judith to Andrew and Neil, then on to Kevin and Gloria. 'What the...?'

Standing up, Mal handed Sam a glass of champagne. 'We were starting to think you weren't coming!'

'W-what's this about?' Sam spluttered. She turned to Gloria. 'Where are the kids?'

'Vera's looking after them,' Gloria smiled. 'Now come and sit down.'

Sam's eyes flicked back to Seb as she hesitantly lowered herself onto the chair he'd pulled out for her.

'We all know how things have been of late.' Mal's booming voice resounded around the room. He looked at Sam pointedly. 'I, for one, took it upon myself to behave quite out of character... which I regret.'

Sam reddened, and inclined her head with acceptance at his clumsy apology.

'But,' Mal continued, 'the people you least expect are usually the ones to show you the error of your ways.' He smiled at Judith and Neil. 'Yes, a lot of things have happened over the course of the last couple of months and beyond. Many of which were out of our control.'

He took a long drink from his malt whisky. 'But there were things we could and *can* control, so from now on, I would like to officially close the longstanding rivalry between our two firms.'

Sam felt the tight squeeze of Seb's hand and looked up to see

Andrew smiling in her direction – a genuine smile. Gloria and Judith grinned like Cheshire cats and even Kevin looked happy-*ish* – as much as his face ever allowed.

A surge of relief washed over her. This didn't solve the issue with Linda, but it did take a huge weight off her mind. She'd never thought this day would come, but it was just what she needed.

'I can also now admit that these two make a very striking couple.' Mal smiled in Seb and Sam's direction. 'I wish you all the best.'

Getting up from the table, Neil opened the door and ushered the waiting photographer inside before taking his place back at the table.

'Smile for the camera!' Mal said as the flashbulb went off. 'This photo will show the city our rivalry is officially over. No one can play us off against each other now.'

Sam glowed with happiness as the photographer made his way back out of the room. So, as well as the business rivalry, this meant that her relationship with Seb was accepted. She beamed at him happily. 'Is this down to you?' she whispered, her eyes glittering.

'I might have had something to do with it, yes, but it was general consensus too.' Seb took Sam's hand. 'It's what you want, isn't it?'

'Definitely!' Sam cried. Getting to her feet, she smiled at the people around the table. 'You don't know how much this means to me. Now our businesses really can go from strength to strength.'

'I'm hoping it will mean something a little bit more personal than that. At least to a couple of us here.'

Sam turned in confusion, only to find Seb dropping to one knee. Her heart flew into her mouth. *He wasn't going to...?*

'I know it hasn't been long.' Seb's green eyes sparkled. 'But I know what I want. And that is you. I love you, Sam, and want you to be my wife. Will you marry me?'

Sam heard her own breathing, loud in the loaded silence of the room. Her mouth moved but nothing came out. She felt like she might pass out when Seb opened a velvet box containing a diamond ring with a central violet amethyst.

'Well?' Seb raised an eyebrow, a nerve in his neck twitching nervously.

'Yes!' Sam breathed. 'Of course I'll marry you!'

Rising from his knee, Seb placed the ring on Sam's finger and pulled her into his arms, his mouth on hers.

'Steady on!' Andrew laughed.

Reluctantly pulling away, Seb grinned. 'I think this calls for a second toast, does it not?' He looked down at Sam and winked, then leant close, his lips brushing her ear. 'And I promise you we'll find out what happened to your mother. Together.'

Tears of happiness rolled down Sam's cheeks as glasses clinked around her. They would find Linda. They *would*. And if what they found wasn't good, she'd have Seb Stoker at her side.

EPILOGUE

Deb Banner glared scornfully at her father slumped in the chair, his hand gripping a can of Special Brew, even in sleep.

Her face screwed into a scowl. *Pissed again*. Weeks he'd been in this state. That was when he wasn't locked away in that fucking shed, even though there was no need any more because his work had evaporated.

Her eyes tracked out of the window into the back garden – once nicely tended, now overgrown and scattered with rubbish.

So much for all the promises. His assurances that if she stuck out the final year of school, he'd pay for the kit required for that hair-dressing and beauty course at college she'd had her heart set on.

Her lips twisted. She'd reluctantly finished school, but he'd lied. He'd lied to get her out of his hair whilst he buggered about cooking crack. She realised that now.

It had been *him* who'd amassed those past debts, not her. Giving her all that old welly about how much he'd struggled when her mother left just didn't wash. What a load of bollocks. The truth was her father couldn't be arsed.

Him running a cookshop might have brought kudos at school to begin with, but it had fast turned into an embarrassment when that bloke who'd bought all that clobber – the one who was apparently going to make things right – had disappeared off the face of the earth and her stupid cowardly father hadn't the balls to confront the guy over why his promised work had dried up.

All he'd done during his new phase of regular drunken mumblings was cry and say he couldn't hack the threats.

Deb scowled harder, wishing she had the money to buy a jerry can of petrol to chuck over the useless prat. What sort of father was he?

She glanced at her holdall, her mouth setting determinedly. If he thought she would hang around, allowing her life to go down the pan like his, then he'd got another think coming.

Fuck that. If she couldn't go to college, then she'd do something better. *Much* better.

Besides, who wanted to slave away for a couple of years to end up standing like a servant cutting hair? She'd only have ended up doing blue rinses and must have had rocks in her head to want to go down that road.

She was destined for better things. Something to earn her not just decent money, but bloody *brilliant* money. And that wouldn't take two years, either – it would be *straight away*.

Deb rearranged her breasts in her skin-tight crop top, then admired her pert figure in her skinny jeans. Like Chas said, with her looks, she'd make a fortune, so why wait?

And why wait indeed?

She might have only been with Chas for a couple of months, but at least he appreciated her and always had money. Not only that, but he'd promised to get her a cool job at the place his aunt worked, and she believed he'd be true to his word.

Unlike *him*. She glanced at the sleeping figure in the chair one last time.

Without a backward glance, Deb walked out of the front door and pushed the key back through the letterbox. It wasn't like she needed it any more. She wouldn't be coming back. She was done with this dump. She was destined for great things, she could feel it.

Deb's spiky heels clacked on the pavement as she made her way down the road to the pub where she'd arranged to meet Chas.

Her new life began now.

ACKNOWLEDGMENTS

As ever, love to my husband and son, as well as to my parents and the rest of my family, who have always had unwavering belief in me.

A massive thanks to my lovely editor Emily Ruston and the whole team at Boldwood Books.

Also, special thanks to Jess, Sue and Caz – you're all fab!

And last, but by no means least, to all of the wonderful readers who have read and enjoyed my books. You give me the incentive to keep writing and I love you all!

MORE FROM EDIE BAYLIS

We hope you enjoyed reading *Fallout*. If you did, please leave a review.

If you'd like to gift a copy, this book is also available as an ebook, digital audio download and audiobook CD.

Sign up to Edie Baylis's mailing list for news, competitions and updates on future books.

https://bit.ly/EdieBaylisnews

Takeover, the first in the Allegiance series, is available now.

ABOUT THE AUTHOR

Edie Baylis is a successful self-published author of dark gritty thrillers with violent background settings. She lives in Worcestershire, has a history of owning daft cars and several motorbikes and is licensed to run a pub.

Visit Edie's website: http://www.ediebaylis.co.uk/

Follow Edie on social media:

twitter.com/ediebaylis
facebook.com/downfallseries
instagram.com/ediebaylis

Boldw😊😊d

Boldwood Books is an award-winning fiction publishing company seeking out the best stories from around the world.

Find out more at www.boldwoodbooks.com

Join our reader community for brilliant books, competitions and offers!

Follow us
@BoldwoodBooks
@BookandTonic

Sign up to our weekly deals newsletter

https://bit.ly/BookandTonicNews

Printed in Great Britain
by Amazon